THE SERPENT'S TONGUE

NOVA 02

THE SERPENT'S TONGUE

NOVA 02

C. T. EMERSON

Copyright © 2023 by Iguana Publishing, L.L.C.

All rights reserved. No part of this book may be reproduced in any form or by any electronic or mechanical means, including information storage and retrieval systems, without written permission from the author, except for the use of brief quotations in a book review permitted by copyright law.

Paperback ISBN-13: 979-8-9867134-2-7

ebook ISBN-13: 979-8-9867134-3-4

Cover and illustrations by Andie Eikenberg.

This book is a work of fiction. Any names, characters, companies, organizations, places, events, locales, and incidents are either used in a fictitious manner or are fictional. Any resemblance to actual persons, living or dead, actual companies or organizations, or actual events is purely coincidental.

CTEmerson.com

To you, my gracious reader.

Contents

Prologue: The Inexorability of Virtue	1
Chapter 1: A Long-anticipated Adventure	19
Chapter 2: Disciplined Imagination	31
Chapter 3: The Ruins of Snowgem	43
Chapter 4: Ghosts of Wisdom Past	55
Chapter 5: Interdimensional Travel	69
Chapter 6: Congressman Solomon	81
Chapter 7: The Griffith House	93
Interludes I – II	109
Chapter 8: Nova's Touch	115
Chapter 9: One Man's Potatoes	123
Chapter 10: A Hutchinsonian Masterpiece	137
Chapter 11: The Lord of the Squelchers	153
Chapter 12: A New Rule	165
Chapter 13: The Dance of Diplomacy	177
Interludes III – IV	189
Chapter 14: The Whigs	197
Chapter 15: Pockets and Elixirs	213
Chapter 16: Perks of the Family	227
Chapter 17: Fun and Games	243

Chapter 18: Seeking Truth	259
Chapter 19: The Mantle of a Genius	273
Interludes V – VI	283
Chapter 20: Roli	289
Chapter 21: Nova's Breath	301
Chapter 22: The Tlamacaz	319
Chapter 23: A Well-deserved Break	337
Chapter 24: News from Goodwin Forest	349
Chapter 25: Skeletons and Jack-O-Lanterns	361
Chapter 26: The Nightmare of Linlithgow	375
Interludes VII – VIII	393
Chapter 27: The Day of the Dead	397
Chapter 28: The EWoC Initiative	415
Chapter 30: Shameless Simulation	431
Chapter 31: Servants of the Void	445
Chapter 32: Project SMG	463
Chapter 33: The Cocktail Hour	485
Chapter 34: Counsel Worth Little	495
Chapter 35: The Case of Mr. Wyatt	509
Chapter 36: Of Kings, Pharaohs, and Warlords	521
Interludes IX – X	541
Chapter 37: The Original Sacred Beast	549
Chapter 38: Truth and Injustice	563
Chapter 39: Providence Foretold	577

Chapter 40: Draconic Demise   587

Chapter 41: Hazy Hot Fumes   599

Chapter 42: The Fire Drake's Cavern   619

Chapter 43: Judgment Delayed   633

Chapter 44: Arbitration   645

Chapter 45: The Cradler's Rocks   657

Bloopers

NOVA 02

Prologue: The Inexorability of Virtue

Desaixton, GA was a charming enough town on the Original Side of the Key. Every year since the 1850s, the locals put on a summer festival complete with rollercoasters, potato-sack races, and apple pickings. As far as they were concerned, no other town within a hundred miles could claim a better mid-year jubilee.

But what the Desaixtonites never realized—except for those in the *know*, of course—was that a much *better* festival occurred at the same time every year. In fact, it even occurred in the same place. All one had to do was find themselves on the right side of the key. The *Other* Side of the Key, where magic ran free and aplenty.

"Bless their hearts," little old ladies on the magical side often said about anyone suggesting a trip over to the Original Side. Why pop over to the Original Side when magic existed in this one? "Assuming you know which door to open, of course," they'd laugh over slices of caramel cake.

On the Other Side—the magical side—Desaixton had been founded much earlier than its nonmagical counterpart. Its roots traced all the way back to the early sixteenth century, and the locals prided themselves on that heritage, often bragging about different "bits and bobs" their ancestors

* Prologue: The Inexorability of Virtue *

played a role in throughout the years. That and their far superior summer festivals.

"We've got a legacy to represent in these parts," Bobo Daudgeril reminded Mayor Beckley as they walked over to the Alligator's Den for a stiff drink as fireworks whizzed around the air in all directions. Children of all ages were enjoying their last week of summer before school resumed, so it was their right to keep as much smoke in the air at any given moment. Especially when the mayor walked nearby.

"See right there," Daudgeril continued, gesticulating at a statue of a barrel-chested man with powerful, crossed arms. "We never needed a fancy mall or shopping district to serve the great, the honorable, the *magnificent* Cuahtemoc Ohtli Tamul and his brave soldiers when they fled Tenochtitlan in need of resuscitation—no sir!"

Lance Wyatt, who'd been listening from a nearby park bench, let out a short chuckle. Bless Mayor Beckley's heart. The new, ambitious man from Atlanta didn't know what he was getting into if he thought he was going to get folks like Bobo Daudgeril, an old southern lawyer, to greenlight the construction of a *shopping center*.

Lance shook his head, smiling wryly as Daudgeril pointed at the statue some more. For the most part, Lance agreed with the mustachioed lawyer. Every kid in town knew Cuahtemoc's story. The town of Desaixton had hosted the legendary Aztecan warrior and his soldiers back in 1527. To commemorate the event, the townsfolk had erected the statue without a fuss.

Lance loved the statue.

NOVA 02

Deciding it deserved a better look, he stood up from his bench and planted himself front and center. For a moment he basked in the glory of a fellow Powerhead, his hands on his hips. During his time, Cuahtemoc went on to co-found Tenochprima Academy, where Lance now went to school. He'd saved his people from the sacking of his home city of Tenochtitlan and re-located them far away from the conquering Spanish. All without ever wearing a shirt.

Lance took in a deep breath, wondering if he'd ever live up to the same lofty heights. Or if his pecs would ever look that good.

A peach pit pelted him on the head.

He'd tried swatting aside the projectile when seeing it out of the corner of his eye but missed it entirely. Oliver and Emma, his friends at school, would have pulled off the swat—their Gifts, Wisdom and Bravery, were much better suited for fluid movement than his Power.

A second later the pelter appeared from behind the statue laughing. It was his older sister, Stevie. She puffed out her chest in imitation of Cuahtemoc before giving up and laughing even more. Where Lance was broad like an ox, Stevie came thin, like a gazelle, and their faces weren't at all similar either. Lance's boyish, friendly demeanor held more in common with their brother, Elton. Still, Lance and Stevie did at least share their father's strong brow and crackling blue eyes.

Lance nursed the growing welt on his head and glared at his sister. "What was that for?"

* Prologue: The Inexorability of Virtue *

Stevie crossed her eyebrows, feigning deep confusion. "My entertainment, of course. Have you been hanging around Elton too much? His stupidity can be contagious, you know?"

"Settle down, you two," their father, Paul, answered from the bench Lance had vacated.

Lance nursed his welt some more and turned to look at a nearby bus stop. "I should have just said goodbye at home," he muttered.

"Now that's just being mean," Stevie chided, closing the gap between them and wrapping an arm around his shoulder.

Her arm quickly abandoned him, however, when a seahorse-drawn carriage clicked and clacked into view on a nearby cobblestone street. She guffawed with glee at the sight of it, raising her arms with dramatic delight.

Lance shook his head. "Seahorses?" he asked.

Behind them, their father, Paul, stood from the bench, leveraging his trusty cane. "Bleargh," he groaned as his bones cracked.

"Here," Lance said, "let me help—,"

Paul's cane appeared at eye level in a flash. "I don't need anybody's help, boy."

"Aren't they great?" Stevie interjected with a wave at the seahorses. Lance couldn't tell if she was expertly defusing the situation or was genuinely taken aback by the animals. Wisers like Stevie tended to be hard to read. Especially when they wore dreamy grins on their faces. Then again, horse sized seahorses floating in the air were a rare sight. Even on this side of the key.

NOVA 02

"Hopefully you get something faster over the Atlantic," Lance countered stiffly.

"I'll miss you, too, little bro," Stevie said, rejoining him to burrow her head into his neck.

He aimed a shove at her, but she dodged it as easily as a dog stepping away from the advance of a turtle, rolling over to his other side to nuzzle there instead.

"Bah!" Paul directed towards Lance. "Don't take my curmudgeoning personally. I'm proud of you, son! Both of you! Even if I get grouchy."

"I didn't do anything to be proud of," Lance muttered, looking away from his father. He knew what the old man was getting at.

Paul shook his cane in the air emphatically. "Didn't do anything? You stood by the Trinova when *The Damned* faced him not two months ago! That's more than anybody else from my generation can say!"

Lance couldn't help but glance at his father's prosthetic leg at the mention of *The Damned*. Some wounds, even in a world where magic existed, couldn't be healed. Especially those received during the time *The Damned* had been in power, fifteen years prior.

"Exactly!" Paul said, following Lance's stare and whacking his prosthetic with his cane. "Had there been more people like you when *The Damned* first came to be, I might still have my leg!"

"Awww," Stevie crooned. "Look at you two, bonding like humans." She came in for another hug, this time wrapping them both up in it. "You don't have to be gorillas all the time, you know?"

* Prologue: The Inexorability of Virtue *

"And you, too!" Paul grunted as they broke away. This time he directed his cane at Stevie. "You're going to research *The Damned* while you travel, correct? Be more like Cuahtemoc, here, and make the world a better place!" He gestured at the statue just like Bobo Daudgeril had. They all stared at it for several seconds, taking in the chiseled features of the man the statue captured in time. Cuahtemoc had seen the future with the help of his Tenochprima Academy co-founders. What they saw had frightened them enough to leave behind clues for Lance and Stevie's generation to find. Clues on how to stop *The Damned* from returning to his full power.

"Good, good," Paul breathed. Lance knew his old man was happy nobody ruined the serious moment with ill-timed humor. If Elton had been there…

Paul began to cough, eyeing the bench as his chest rose and fell.

"At least let me help you sit down!" Lance insisted.

The cane waggled in the air.

"Fine!" Lance growled. "Stevie?" he added, gesturing to the carriage.

Stevie followed him to the seahorses, giving her dad one last kiss on the cheek.

"Well," Stevie said when they reached the carriage. She leaned forward and back on her toes for a moment. "Guess I'll see you in a year."

Lance nodded, this time initiating a hug himself. "Stay groovy," he said, imitating her dreamy-sounding voice. "I'll have my notebook at school. Keep me and Elton posted on what you find out. I'm sure we're going to need your help."

NOVA 02

Stevie rolled away, nodding. "Don't worry, lil man. We'll figure this out. With me out there unearthing the skeletons in his closet, *The Damned* won't stand a chance against you, Oli, and Emma."

Lance found himself opening and closing his fists as the carriage flew away into the sky. All the talk about *The Damned* had put him in a sour mood. By the time he rejoined his father, he squeezed his hands harder and harder.

He stopped when he caught sight of the old man's missing leg.

Lance just stared. He didn't care how hard it was going to be, or how much work was going to be required to help Oliver and Emma defeat *The Damned*. A Wyatt never gave up. They were hard workers. A **diligent** bunch.

His father reminded him of that as he pushed himself up from the bench with his cane.

"Jack, you're being an ass! What makes you think you—,"

"IF I AM BEING AN ASS, IT'S BECAUSE WE WASTED ALL NIGHT TALKING TO THE WRONG PEOPLE!"

Emma Griffith slammed her bedroom door shut and put on her trusty old pair of black headphones. "Sweet child of mine" would do the trick. For the life of her, she couldn't understand why anybody thought classic rock wasn't relaxing.

* Prologue: The Inexorability of Virtue *

A second later, the music took over the sounds of her parents' shouting.

That's better, she thought, grabbing a mug of peppermint tea from her nightstand. She took a sip, wiggled her toes in bed, and listened to the sweet, calming sound of the rock n' roll.

Absentmindedly, she traced a finger up the black cord of her headphones. When she reached the earpieces, she gave them a thump with her finger. These headphones were the corded kind, and they'd been her constant companion since her tenth birthday.

Her parents had fought then, too.

They'd always been obsessed with maximizing the potential out of every social interaction. Could the governor's secretary make it? Was the mayor on his way yet? Of course not. Why would either of them show up to a ten-year-old's birthday party?

Emma shook her head as the song's chorus kicked in.

Why had it mattered to her parents? Why had the attendance list been more important than her birthday? And why was it important now if her mother hadn't kissed her father's colleagues' asses well enough at whatever gala they just got back from?

Her parents made her sick. Their focus wasn't right. It wasn't *fair*. It wasn't **just**.

The thought hummed in her skull, but it didn't comfort her knowing her parents were twisted. Reeling in frustration, she made to throw her phone against the wall.

NOVA 02

She stopped herself just as she was about to pull the trigger. Not for worry over breaking anything, but because she'd have to untangle the headphones from her red hair to get in a good throw.

"That and because somebody else would have to fix my mess," she told herself. *"That's not fair, either."*

Rolling her eyes, she went back to tracing the cord of her headphones down to her phone. She could have a fancy pair of wireless headphones just like everybody else with a snap of her fingers. Heck, she could ask Charles, the family butler, to go out and get her a pair that night.

But she didn't.

The knots in the cord and the frayed cushioning in the earpieces comforted her. They'd been with her all this time, through every screaming match, and every lonely bus ride to school.

A message vibrated on her phone just as the song changed.

It was from Oliver.

She smiled at the text, basking in the blue light of her phone's screen. She'd been gone all summer, forced to travel Europe with the same goblins still screaming down the stairs. They'd only gotten back the previous evening.

But now she could see her friend again. Her best friend, the Trinova. For a moment she wondered when they'd go on their next adventure together—rounding out last year at Tenochprima Academy with a terrifying battle against *The Damned* had been a rush.

* Prologue: The Inexorability of Virtue *

Then another message popped up on her phone. This one was from Professor Watkin, and she wasn't the only recipient. Both Oliver and Lance, her other best friend, were on the thread.

"Weird," she thought, opening the message.

"Pack your things. I'm picking you up on the way to school. Be ready for a scrap."

Emma jumped out of her bed and punched the air with glee. A second later, she'd wrenched open her closet door, darted inside, and planted her hands on either side of a small safe, using it as a counterbalance to halt her momentum.

Her green eyes sparkled with determination as she began fumbling with the combination dial. Before Charles had gotten her this safe over the summer, four very nice pairs of shoes used to occupy the same shelf. Now those same shoes sat stuffed in an out-of-sight basket she wouldn't mind losing during a move.

Click. The safe's hatch swung open.

Emma snatched the contents immediately. To anybody on This Side of the Key, where magic didn't exist, the fabric she pulled out of the safe might look like an innocuous piece of red-and-brown fabric.

She chuckled at the thought, pulling the cloth onto her arm.

As the red alder weave prickled at her skin, she grinned. Some girls at Tenochprima Academy might prefer something a bit more fashionable for their magical source and channel, but Emma couldn't care less. She was an adventurer. The kind of girl that could beat anybody in a duel. The kind of gal that could keep up with a Trinova.

Her grin widened just as the fabric synched tight over her forearm and lower upper arm, seemingly on the sleeve's own accord. She wouldn't be able to use magic on this side of the key of course, but right then, she knew she could knock out anybody.

Well… maybe not Oliver. But he didn't count. He was *the* Trinova after all.

Elodie Lalandra, Headmaster of Tenochprima Academy, stumbled onto her kitchen floor, alone. The cold stone tiles prickled against her bare feet, but she welcomed the sensation. It energized her. In all likelihood it would also coax out her genius.

All it took was a question to get her brain going like nobody else's—it just had to be the *right* question.

This time, a simple remark over dinner had proved to be the catalyst. A question about Cato Watkin, the Academy's History Professor.

"Watkin's turned things around, eh?" Dave had asked innocuously enough at dinner.

Normally Elodie would have replied with something banal and inspected the entrée at hand, but her husband's question had wormed its

* Prologue: The Inexorability of Virtue *

way into her brain where it still sparked wildly, thrashing like an eel against a barrier reef.

With a shudder in the kitchen, Elodie flagged mid-stride, placing a hand on a seven-foot porcelain chicken for support. When she steadied, pulling herself up, she and the statue were eye to eye. She patted it on the head with the affection of a loving mother. It guarded their home, keeping an ever-watchful eye open for intruders. How else could she have known the boy—Oliver García, the *Trinova*—had passed through her apartment just before the end of the previous school year?

At least some things were going to plan.

A squeaking noise followed; not from the chicken, but the tiles leading back to the dining room.

"There you are," Dave said, half-smiling. "I thought you might have gotten up for seconds..." His voice trailed off, and between the two curtains of his well-kept, white hair, Elodie saw his handsome cheekbones tighten.

"El," his voice barked, "are you having an episode?" He always went an octave deeper when things got serious.

Elodie looked from her husband to the porcelain chicken. When she spoke, her voice trembled against the thoughts in her head. "Sweetheart, do you ever worry we were *wrong*?"

Dave twitched his nose noncommittally. Then, he stepped past her towards the living room. "I'll get the lights."

He knew her so well.

🐚 NOVA 02 🐚

She closed her eyes, blocking out the morning sun trickling in from the open-faced terrace on the other side of the living room past the kitchen. Tenochprima Academy's grounds were bustling as the new extraman students arrived for orientation. Last year, one of those new extramen had been the Trinova. Sometimes she still couldn't believe the myth had come to life.

Dave would see to the distraction. By hand, of course. He'd never been blessed with magic. "Elodie," Dave said, polite but firm. "Tell me what's really bothering you." He'd lit a candle and made himself comfortable on their couch after closing the curtains to the terrace. He patted the couch, motioning for her to join him.

She didn't answer until she'd snuggled up onto his chest and felt its comforting rise and fall.

"Cato," she finally said.

"Ah," Dave murmured, stroking her dark-brown hair. "His mood swings getting to you? At least he's happier now, right?"

Elodie forced herself to shake her head.

"We've been through this," Dave continued. "More than once. He made his mess. We don't owe him a thing."

"I know," she croaked. "He was a *fool*, clinging to his principles like that."

Beneath Elodie's ear, Dave's thoughts hummed in his chest. Eventually, he'd understand what she'd left *unsaid*. Even if it took him a while to put it together. Everyone else, including her kind, loyal husband, couldn't hope to keep up with her brain. She'd grown patient over the years.

13

✴ Prologue: The Inexorability of Virtue ✴

"Cato Watkin," Dave said, deliberately slow, "bet *everything* on his principles and lost, remember? All *The Damned* left were their ashes. Don't tell me you're getting cold feet?" He gave her body a light shake as he asked the question, trying to jostle her thoughts out of her temples. "We can't beat *The Damned* with virtue, you hear me? Cato proved that beyond a shadow of a doubt when he took his stand."

She let him go on. He'd get there eventually.

"The only thing he was right about was the Trinova. Which only proves we were the wiser ones. We thought we'd be fighting this battle with just the Whigs, but this García boy could prove helpful in a pickle. It didn't make any sense to make a stand against *The Damned* back then."

Elodie shook her head. Dave was close to the truth, but he hadn't grasped it yet. "Cato," she rasped into her husband's shirt. "He's back!"

Dave frowned. "I-I'm not sure I catch your meaning. Where did Cato return from, exactly?"

"No!" Elodie croaked, her voice catching. "Something brought his *hope* back."

Dave chuckled but he didn't fool her. Nobody could. "Well of course something did! The Trinova's here, isn't he? Cato gambled on the fairytale being real, and that whoever the Trinova ended up being could help us stop *The Damned*. I'd be relieved for a partial victory, too, after betting the farm on it!"

Elodie shook her head and groaned into Dave's ribs, her thoughts jutting into her temples like sharpened blades.

"No!" she said, louder than before. "It's deeper than that! Oliver García brought the old Cato Watkin back! Don't you get it?"

Dave finally started sounding nervous. "Well," he said, coughing, "that's a good thing! I much preferred the Watkin of old over the brooding, depressed man we've watched over the last fourteen years."

Elodie shook her head even harder, and, at long last, the dam in her mind broke, releasing the full scope of her genius. It sparked into life, channeling golden strands of perfected thought, theory, and discipline. When she pulled herself up and out of her husband's shirt, it was with a straightened back.

"Yes, Cato Watkin bet everything and lost," she said, relishing the heightened state of her brain with a deep breath. Why couldn't thinking this well always be so easy? There wasn't anything she couldn't solve in this state, and not even memories of Cato's nightmarish demise could dampen the rush she felt.

Most days she made do with what she estimated to be half her brain. Other days, she'd be stuck inside with all the curtains pulled tight, unable to speak with anyone but Dave in uttermost darkness. Rarest of all was when she reached the height of her genius. Like she did now.

Exhaling, she turned to her husband, her expression pitying. "Understand this. Cato Watkin bet on his *principles*, not the Trinova's arriving. Worst of all, he bet on us backing him and his principles. When his gambit failed, you and I both saw what was left of the legend. Cato emerged from the Sage's Sanctum completely and utterly broken. Only one

* Prologue: The Inexorability of Virtue *

thing could have returned Watkin's faith. And it wasn't the Trinova, don't you see?"

She stood, channeling magic from her favorite ring—the diamond one with which her husband had proposed all those years ago—onto the curtains. They burst open, allowing sunlight back into the room. When she returned her eyes to her husband, they blazed with a level of determination she hadn't felt in years.

"Cato Watkin," she announced, "rekindled his faith because something made him believe in his principles again."

Dave buried his head in his hands and let out a long groan.

"Which means," Elodie went on, "the naïve man intends to pass on his flagrantly irresponsible teachings to the Trinova and risk our failure against *The Damned* for a second time in a row."

In the Sage's Sanctum, *The Damned* fled his tormentor. The monster that chased him in his purgatory had grown reckless in recent weeks, following him at a faster pace than ever before. At every tight corner the beast now slammed into walls, sending bits of flaking stone and disintegrated grout flying in every direction. At times, when *The Damned* looked over his shoulder, he even saw the abomination on all fours.

The sight of the monster made him shudder. *Him.* The most Powerful man on Earth.

NOVA 02

Every click, sniff, and screech that echoed around the corridors of his personal purgatory filled *The Damned* with a dread he never thought possible.

All those years ago, when he'd first listened to the creature's horrible sounds, the eerie, dissonant voices in his head had paralyzed him into complete inaction. That moment of weakness had cost him the lives of his most loyal supporters.

All thirty-nine of them.

Today, he fled his tormentor along a route he'd developed in the Western corridors of the Sage's Sanctum. He couldn't repeat his route too often, unless he wanted to risk getting cut off, but he also couldn't bear to face the Eastern corridors. The remains of his fallen supporters lay within those halls, serving as an accursed reminder of his failure. Not that he felt regret for their lost lives. No, they were a memento of his weakness. Of his inability to predict the moves of his enemies.

A crunching explosion signaled yet another near-capture from one of the monster's outstretched, clawed hands. Just in time, he flared his Power to counteract the immobilizing effect of the screech that would follow.

The horrible sound still made his skin crawl, no matter how many times he heard it.

But more recently, these narrow escapes had begun to bring a smug smile to his lips. *The Damned* had lagged ever so slightly a second before the swipe came, deeming it **Prudent** to lull his tormenter into a hasty lunge. It had worked, having been informed by a tickling sensation on the back of

* Prologue: The Inexorability of Virtue *

his neck. Over time, he'd come to recognize that was where his **Prudence** had manifested.

Cato Watkin, the fool, had been wrong about many things, but his crackpot theories on Virtue training had been more accurate than the idiot had ever realized. With fourteen years of practice under his belt, *The Damned* knew he had no equal waiting for him on the Other Side of the Key. Even if a real Trinova now prowled the grounds of Tenochprima Academy, nobody could stop him. It didn't matter how ungrateful or narrow-minded they could all be—this was his manifested destiny and he'd be truly damned before he ever gave up on it.

NOVA 02

Chapter 1: A Long-anticipated Adventure

FINALLY! The detection tool went off! I thought I was looking at another waste of time, but his magic seems to think otherwise. I can't wait to report back... maybe that'll calm him down. He wasn't exactly in a good mood when I shared my secret last week. It still hurts when I think about it.

4th *of June, the second year of the* 10th *Age*

You'd be hard pressed to find a stranger scene than the one in Santiago García's house on Saturday, August the twenty-eighth.

Oliver García, Santiago's nephew, sat at the kitchen counter, conversing with a talking dog named Archie. Nearby, Santiago loaded his favorite rifle while seated, leaning against the wall beside a door leading to the one-story-house's garage.

Sometimes Oliver still couldn't believe his luck. Last year he'd discovered he wasn't just a normal, skinny fifteen-year-old, but a magical superpower called the Trinova that only turned up once every thousand years. According to legend, there wouldn't be much he *couldn't* do once he reached his full potential. But he had a long way to go before then.

Oliver gauged his uncle as the man loaded his rifle. He'd always been good at reading people—at picking up on their social cues—and, for once, Santiago's normally sharp, steely eyes looked uncertain. The man kept looking at the window past the kitchen counter or to his left at the garage door. The uncertainty just looked wrong on a man so broad and muscular.

* Chapter 1: A Long-anticipated Adventure *

Oliver thought he knew why Santiago was uncomfortable. What could powder and flame do to anything on the Other Side of the Key where magic existed? The last time his uncle had been in the parallel dimension, he'd left on his own volition after getting spooked when hearing a story about *The Damned.*

"It'll be helpful," Oliver offered.

When Santiago answered by furrowing his eyebrows in confusion, Oliver pointed at the gun. Santiago tsked and put down his cleaning rag. "¿Dicieron a las siete, verdad?"[1]

Oliver almost laughed. His uncle preferred to speak in Spanish in front of the boxer-breed dog, no doubt hoping the animal wouldn't understand their native tongue.

Oliver understood right away, of course, but he wasn't sure if Archie did, so he threw the dog an apologetic look before scowling at Santiago. "English, please. You shouldn't insult a being as old as—how old are you, anyway, Archie?"

While Archie tilted his head, debating an answer, Oliver felt the urge to pinch himself. Archie would make the news if he ever revealed his true form on This Side of the Key. Normally, he weighed over four-hundred pounds and could fly. He was a sacred beast called a feathered serpent.

Archie blew smoke from his nostrils, betraying the illusion of his brown boxer dog form. With a voice like rolling boulders, he growled telepathically

---

[1] They said we're meeting at seven, right?

in their heads. *"I mastered Spanish the moment Cortes' accursed foot stepped into the Americas."*

Santiago let out a high, false laugh. "Guess we shouldn't be surprised about anything anymore. No wonder you talk funny, demon dog."

"Funny is in the eye of the beholder," Archie huffed, closing his eyes and settling down for a cat nap.

Oliver nodded along, but he also knew Santiago had a point.

Cato Watkin, Oliver's History Professor at Tenochprima Academy, said he'd pick them up at seven o'clock sharp for a special mission. The only problem was the sun was setting.

Oliver peered at the microwave, where a green light flashed 19:26.

There wouldn't be another time to perform the mission Professor Watkin had in mind. Oliver's second year at Tenochprima Academy began the following Monday.

Santiago followed Oliver's gaze towards the clock and scratched the stubble under his chin. "Did they go without us, or what?"

Oliver shrugged and looked at Archie. He still lay curled up, calm as ever. "Watkin can't get the artifact without me, so they're probably just late."

Santiago snorted. "You're not as humble as you used to be."

"You know that's not what I meant."

Santiago cracked a smile. "Just kidding, jefecito."

A knock came from the door to the garage, causing them to jump.

"That should be Professor Watkin," Archie rumbled.

* Chapter 1: A Long-anticipated Adventure *

Oliver nearly tripped over himself as he barreled towards the door and yanked it open. He didn't care if they were thirty minutes late because he'd already waited all summer. What was a few more minutes?

A lean man stepped inside, smiling at them in turn. It was Professor Watkin. As always, he was dressed sharply—this time wearing sky-blue pants, a white linen shirt, and a navy frock coat. The only constant in the man's garb was the frayed silk belt that hung around his waist. It looked out of place on his athletic frame, at least when compared to the rest of his colorful clothing, but then again, so did the long ponytail that trailed down his back. From his shoulder, Jaiba, the keel-billed toucan squawked.

Caw-caw!

"Good evening," Watkin said, mischievously cheery.

Santiago stood and lumbered towards the man. Despite being the same height as Cato, Oliver thought of his uncle as taller give that the man was just *that* much wider than everybody else—a gift of muscle leftover from his military days. Well, everybody except Broderick Blackwood, Tenochprima Academy's Dean of Discipline. That man was the size of a mountain and he, and Oliver did *not* see eye-to-eye.

"Good to meet you," Santiago's low voice rumbled. He offered Watkin his right hand. "Oliver's told me a lot about you." His left hand still held his rifle.

To most men, Santiago's presence might have proved intimidating, but Watkin wasn't like most men. Oliver half-expected his professor to say something witty and insulting. He'd grown accustomed to the handsome man walking circles around even the brightest brains at school. But Watkin surprised Oliver by taking and shaking Santiago's hand with a determined grimace. "And you, as well. Oliver's comportment and success at school say a lot about the man who raised him."

Oliver raised his eyebrows at that. Maybe Watkin had a rule to be extra polite with student families.

"Thank you," Watkin added, lingering on the handshake, clearly making Santiago uncomfortable in the process.

"Alright enough of this mushy stuff," said another voice from the garage that made Oliver's heart skip a beat.

It was Emma Griffith—Oliver's first friend from the Other Side of the Key. She'd been traveling all summer with her family and had a healthy tan to show for it. Not only that, but her red hair reached past her shoulders now. Had she always looked this confident? Though she tried not to smile as she walked inside from the garage, a quiver of one threatened to escape the corner of her mouth. She gave Santiago a nod, Archie a wave, and Oliver a light punch on his shoulder as she took a counter stool next to him.

"Nobody mind me," coughed a final voice. Where Emma's voice had barely any sign of a southern twang, this one came thick.

Oliver laughed out loud at the sight of his other best friend, Lance Wyatt. "You been working out, man?"

Lance flashed his teeth. Despite having gained close to what looked like ten pounds of muscle over the summer, he still looked endearing to Oliver's eyes. The mop of shaggy blonde hair and slightly crooked smile remained the same, capturing the heart and soul of the goofy boy Oliver had grown

* Chapter 1: A Long-anticipated Adventure *

to call his best friend. "Stevie had me adopt the Elton regimen this summer," Lance said, coughing politely. "Elton's excited to keep it up with *you* at school this year before he graduates. Lord knows you need a sandwich." He moved away from Oliver, dodging Oliver's swipe towards the back of his head—it landed anyway—and stepped towards Santiago, offering him a handshake with his eyebrows raised. "Now you're from proper stock, mister. Good to meet ya."

For the moment, Oliver felt giddy. "I didn't realize Emma and Lance would be joining us, Professor," he directed towards Watkin.

"Nonsense, Oliver," Watkin said, shutting the door to the garage. "Emma and Lance here require just as much training as you if we hope to stop *The Damned* from obliterating you on sight."

The room went silent.

Even Santiago, who didn't know much about the Other Side of the Key, knew about *The Damned*. In life, he'd been a man so evil that a higher power had erased his name from memory. At least that's what the stories said. For the time being, the evil man was stuck in a purgatory of sorts.

But just last year, the Iguana's Scroll they found had prophesized the evil man's escape. Reaching into his pocket, Oliver pulled out the scroll and re-read it out aloud for everyone to hear.

> *When the Gifts of the Three,*
> *are encompassed within thee,*
> *look to Tenoch's Temples*
> *to master your fundamentals.*

NOVA 02

Speed is of the essence,
to defeat an evil presence,
that has lusted for release,
since the dawn of divine peace.

When he finished, Oliver folded the ancient parchment and tucked it away, exchanging nods with Emma and Lance. They'd already interpreted the prophesy to mean he was the only person who could stop *The Damned*. But he'd need all three artifacts—or the *Gifts of the Three*—to do it. And even though they'd already recovered one at the end of their first year at school, two were still out there.

Santiago snapped his rifle-chamber shut. "What's our mission?"

The sound of deep river eddies filled the room which turned out to be the noise Archie made when laughing. *"Ever the man of action, Santiago."*

"Indeed," Watkin agreed. He tapped his staff against the kitchen floor. When a key popped into existence, he reached out a hand to catch it.

Oliver nodded his head appreciatively. "I guess we shouldn't be surprised that you can do magic on This Side of the Key—I thought it was impossible?"

"Yes, Oliver, it *is* impossible," Watkin replied, winking. "Remind me to teach you how to do it before… well, before the end of next year, I suppose." With a grunt, he twisted his staff in the air. The green jewel on its pommel left a blur of color wavering in the air. Seconds later, a door frame appeared in the middle of the kitchen.

* Chapter 1: A Long-anticipated Adventure *

Santiago looked unamused. "You'll get rid of that, right?"

Watkin waved away the question. "It will disappear after the last of us passes through it." A further twist of the man's staff later, a blue door materialized within the frame, complete with a toucan-shaped doorknob. Jaiba squawked in approval from Watkin's shoulder while the man gestured from the doorknob to the bird like a proud father.

Emma and Lance laughed out loud, but Oliver managed to restrict himself to a smile, scratching the back of his head shyly at the same time as his uncle.

"Where are we going, anyway?" Lance asked. "You never told us the mission. Something about a fight?"

Santiago nodded his head at the word fight. In addition to the rifle, he'd strapped a sheathed bowie knife the size of Oliver's forearm onto his left thigh.

Watkin turned away from the doorknob to survey them with his hands behind his back. Next to him, his staff stayed vertical, seemingly on its own accord. "Consider today a lesson," Watkin announced. "I've discovered the location of a second artifact."

Collectively, their jaws dropped; except for Archie's. He grinned at being in-the-know, sticking his tongue out doggishly.

It had taken Oliver, Emma, and Lance *six* months to find the first artifact the Tenochprima Founders had left behind for a Trinova to find—a necklace imbued with the Gift of Bravery. For ordinary wearers, the necklace blessed the user with the ability to tackle any obstacle without fear. For Oliver, a one-of-a-kind Trinova who could wield all three Gifts of

NOVA 02

Magic, it boosted his Bravery to unparalleled levels, granting him composure in conflict unavailable to most anyone else. Even now Oliver wore the necklace underneath his t-shirt, where it smoldered against his skin like a coal.

Emma beat Oliver to the question that burned at his lips. "Which artifact is it?"

"I can't be sure," Watkin replied, putting a hand to his chin. "But I've monitored this Temple location for two decades and believe it reasonable to assume it hides Augustus' Gift."

Oliver's heart rate picked up. Though he never told Emma or Lance, boosting his Gift of Wisdom was at the top of his list. He couldn't think of a better way to go toe-to-toe with *The Damned* than to best him at Wisdom. In life, Augustus' Wisdom had been unparalleled—and Oliver wanted his to be, too.

"But you've never entered the Temple?" asked Lance, his cheery face crestfallen.

Watkin raised an eyebrow. "As we discussed at the end of last year, I hypothesized safeguards exist to only allow a Trinova to take the Gift. Had I assisted you, I could have risked the artifact's destruction. You three,"— he added, pointing at Oliver, Emma, and Lance—"proved me wrong when you discovered the safeguard was much simpler and more brilliant. Only someone who already possess the Gift can take the artifact from the temple."

Oliver thought that curious. Watkin's magical manifestation was Wisdom which meant he'd been able to take Augustus' Gift all summer.

* Chapter 1: A Long-anticipated Adventure *

Unable to stop himself, he piped up. "Then, why didn't you go and get Augustus' Gift at the end of last year? You already have Wisdom, so you'd be able to take the artifact if you could get through the traps and beasts guarding it. Are there too many for someone to get through alone?"

Watkin gave Oliver a contemplative look. "Blessed with Wisdom, indeed. Simply understand that I know it's not for me to receive. The Gifts are for you. I deemed it prudent to wait for you."

Silence followed for a moment. Oliver saw the same pensive thoughts on Emma and Lance's faces. Why did Watkin always speak in riddles? Clear, definitive answers would be a nice change after the challenges they faced last year. At the same time, however… another Gift lay at their fingertips.

Emma stood. "You heard the man. We've got another artifact to grab, so let's get going!" Bounding across the room, she approached the door with a dark red key. "I'm assuming this door opens like any door to the Other Side, right?"

"Not quite," Watkin replied. He tapped the wood with the jewel on his staff and motioned for her to step back. Then he unlocked it with his own key.

A cracking noise sounded, and the door frame flashed green. A moment later, and a torrent of frigid air *blasted* through the kitchen. It billowed in great gusts as Santiago gave out a yelp, sending the pots and pans hanging above the sink to clatter against one another and the napkins on the counter to flutter across the room.

"Everything returns to normal after we leave, right?" Santiago shouted through the din.

NOVA 02

"Do we have to go in there, Professor?" Lance asked, peering through the shimmering surface the door had revealed. At first Oliver didn't understand Lance's hesitation, but then he looked through the doorway properly.

Whirling blankets of ice and snow awaited them.

Santiago groaned at the sight. "I ain't dressed for that."

Jaiba, who had been quiet until then, gave out a loud squawk.

"Right you are," Watkin muttered. "Trust me, everyone, I have... let's call them coats? Yes, coats waiting for you on the Other Side. And as I said, today is a lesson. Just try to keep up as I teach."

"Keep up?" Emma mouthed at Oliver with raised eyebrows.

Though Oliver was sure Watkin had a few tricks up the sleeve of his navy frock coat, the Forest Temple they'd explored last year had been riddled with traps, monsters, and even a shadow of *The Damned*. If this Temple proved similar, Watkin would likely need them to help. It would take a team effort.

"I'll go first," Emma volunteered. "Sometimes y'all make it obvious you're not Brave. You're good Oli—too much Wisdom holding you back." She winked at him, making his stomach twist for some reason, and walked through the door. "Cold! Cold! Cold!" they heard her squeak from the Other Side.

Watkin followed next, Archie right behind. "That feels much better," the sacred beast exhaled as he crossed the threshold. Instead of emerging as a dog, his true serpent form took to the skies. Watkin raised his staff in agreement, covering himself and Emma in shields of warmth.

* Chapter 1: A Long-anticipated Adventure *

Nodding his head, Lance followed, leaving just Oliver and Santiago behind.

Santiago scratched the back of his head for a moment. "Feels like I should be locking up the house, but Cato said this would disappear, so we're good to go right?"

"I'm glad you're coming with us," Oliver said, understanding the nervous babbling.

Santiago ruffled Oliver's hair and lumbered through the frame, stooping slightly to avoid hitting his head. "*Ala madre*, that's cold! Where's that coat, Mister Cato?"

Oliver followed, giving the kitchen a final warm look before crossing over into the world of wind and snow.

Chapter 2: Disciplined Imagination

He made a big show at this quarter's Free World Coalition summit. Credited me with finding the site in Crater Lake, Oregon and how it's gonna be "our lynchpin for success." Everyone stood to clap but something just feels different after all my time away. I can't put my finger on it.

12th of June, the second year of the 10th Age

No sooner had Oliver begun re-appreciating the improved color palette of the Other Side of the Key did he notice a warming presence trickle down his body from head to toe.

"*I missed you, magic,*" he thought as Watkin's 'coat' of warmth took effect. Around him, the snow, ice, and wind in the air all continued billowing as if he weren't there. A look behind his shoulder revealed a weathered blue door standing between two trees.

"Ready, everyone?" Watkin asked. Only then did Oliver realize the snowstorm had somehow also quieted around them.

"You're warming us up and muting the storm at the same time?" Emma asked. She pressed her lips together and flared her nostrils, looking around. "Impressive."

Watkin ignored the compliment as Archie's rumbling laughter took over their headspaces again. "Dear child, you have much to grow."

Watkin looked up the mountainside. "The lesson," he intoned, "begins... now!" For a moment longer, he surveyed the path ahead of

* Chapter 2: Disciplined Imagination *

them. To Oliver's eyes, they appeared to be at the base of a mountain. Did Watkin expect them to hike this in one day? It would take ages with all the snow on—

A wave of Earth, rubble, and snow exploded beneath them, shooting their party twenty feet into the air. For a desperate moment Oliver thought they were under attack, but then he looked at Professor Watkin and realization dawned on him.

Instead of falling, the Earth had stabilized around them, forming a platform that was hurtling up the mountainside at a breakneck speed. At the front of their mound, Watkin conducted the action with his staff, impartially lifting trees, bushes, sheets of ice, and even the occasional winter hare out of the way. Every time Oliver thought he'd be struck by a frightened animal or blanket of snow, they popped out of existence and reappeared behind them after they'd passed.

Oliver took a better look at Watkin. They weren't being attacked at all—their History Professor was just performing magic at a scale Oliver didn't know was possible.

Desperately, he chanced a look at Archie who swam through the air above them. *"How is this happening right now?"* he shot through their private mental connection.

Archie smiled as much as his mandibles would allow before replying. *"Magic shares a symbiotic relationship with imagination and discipline. To excel at the former requires devotion to the latter."*

Oliver gaped in reply. What was that supposed to mean? Just how much did he have left to learn? Giving up on Archie, Oliver focused on standing safely. To his surprise, the motion proved easier than anticipated so he ventured towards the front of the mound to join Watkin.

Jaiba hopped over to the shoulder closer to Oliver and peered down at him.

"Hello, Jaiba."

Jaiba cocked his head, switching from one eye to the other and trading glances between Watkin and Oliver.

Caw-caw!

"I thought so," Oliver mused, imitating Watkin.

"Simulareth," Watkin muttered. To Oliver's shock, the man let go of his staff. With a reflexive lurch of panic, Oliver made to catch the staff. But instead of falling and being left behind, the staff floated where Watkin had left it. Better yet, it continued to conduct in its owner's absence.

By Oliver's count, that meant Watkin was performing three pieces of magic at the same time without even breaking a sweat.

Jaiba took flight as Watkin stepped away, keeping an eye on the staff as he flapped in place. Only now did Watkin give Oliver his full attention. "What are you learning right now, Oliver? Emma, Lance, join us at the front. You, too, Santiago, should you be interested."

Oliver thought hard as the rest of their party lined up shoulder to shoulder at the front of the mound.

If he were being honest, he had no clue how the staff continued to perform magic without Watkin's direct input. That broke the rules of magic as far as he was aware. But the Earth? Oliver himself knew how to move

33

* Chapter 2: Disciplined Imagination *

great quantities of Earth. Up until a few moments ago, he'd foolishly thought he was good at it, too.

Not wanting to give up and say nothing, Oliver fluttered his lips and tried, "I think you've left your spell inside your staff so that the Earth will continue moving while you can focus on anything else."

Watkin clapped his hands and rubbed them together. "Excellent. And am I correct in thinking your Extraman studies neglected this concept?"

"Hey now," interrupted Emma. "Professor Belk taught us quite a bit of Earth fundamentals last year."

Oliver winced. It was difficult to focus on anyone talking with trees popping in and out of their sight every second. Santiago, who was less used to magic, went beyond wincing. Every few seconds or so he'd duck, unable to stop himself from reflexively dodging the looming trees.

Watkin shook his head. "I don't critique Professor Belk, rather the curriculum restricting her." Eyeing the haughty look on Emma's face he added, "but I also appreciate the loyalty to her. She may become an ally of ours in the future.

"But I digress. Oliver, you are correct. Magic, especially elemental magic, can be conducted without direct attention. The school hasn't bothered introducing non-direct magic yet because even the faculty struggle with it. I'd imagine they'll re-introduce it within a decade. We know the Founders taught the concept, but with magic being untenable for so long without the presence of Nova, the school curriculum began to neglect it in the nineteenth century."

NOVA 02

"Professor," Lance interrupted, "my parents could never give me a straight answer on this, but how did the Founders know what to teach if they couldn't perform magic? Wasn't magic impossible for like eight-hundred years while Nova was... out of sight?"

Oliver's jaw dropped. Now that Lance mentioned it, how *did* the Founders know about magic let alone practice it when they founded the school in the 16th century?

Watkin raised an eyebrow as he surveyed Lance. "That is quite the question, Lance. Nobody knows for certain. Most just assume they knew something we don't. Others have studied the subject extensively and come away frustrated."

A moment of silence followed. Could the Founders have been wielding magic during the Age of Darkness between the ninth and tenth Ages of Magical Proximity? As everyone thought over the puzzle, snow and earth continued to roll beneath them. All the while, they drew closer and closer to the summit.

Oliver looked at Watkin and saw no discernible emotion resting on his face. But now was the time to risk a few more questions. It would take a subtle approach.

Lance opened his mouth to speak but Oliver held up a hand and spoke first. "What about you, Professor? Did the subject frustrate you?" He mouthed sorry to Lance as Watkin closed his eyes.

"I've only ever been truly frustrated once in my life," Watkin mused before re-opening his eyes. "And while I appreciate the question, your training isn't quite complete enough for me to share my theories."

* Chapter 2: Disciplined Imagination *

This time it was Watkin's turn to hold up a hand, stopping Emma and Lance's protests.

"But I promise I will in due time. First, the Cradl—,"

Jaiba let out an ear-piercing squawk.

"Quite right, Jaiba," Watkin said, twitching his nose. "First, we focus on the remaining artifacts, agreed?"

Emma crossed her arms but nodded in unison with Oliver and Lance. Satisfied, Watkin grabbed his staff and returned his focus to the traveling Earth wave beneath them.

"Ah, we're nearly at the peak. Here, you may want to reload with these, Santiago." He tossed a bag the size of a kitchen cabinet over his shoulder. Oliver couldn't tell from where Watkin had pulled it.

Santiago opened it with a frown. The frown morphed into a grin just as his face began reflecting a deep blue glow emanating from the bag. Whatever Watkin kept in there shone brightly.

"Magic bullets?" Santiago asked, looking up.

"Indeed. Most enemies on This Side of the Key will find your bullets a mere nuisance. The bullets I just shared, however, ought to teleport them a mile away. But I'd recommend not shooting anything larger than Archie."

With a noise like a pig at a trough, Santiago dove further into the bag. Then he reloaded his rifle with unbridled glee.

Just as Oliver decided to ask what lay ahead, Watkin brought down his staff with a conductor's flourish.

With a resounding crunch, the Earth ceased rolling beneath them, and good thing too, because they found themselves at the lip of a crater taking up the entire top of the mountain. One more step and they may have tumbled down a steep, rocky surface that led into dark, icy water stretching for nearly five miles to the other side.

The wind howled louder than it had at the foot of the mountain, whipping snow and ice around mercilessly and making it clear as to why no trees grew this far up the slopes. Looking at the lake in the crater below, Oliver's eyes traced funnels of wind dancing on the water's surface until they buffeted against the ruins of a dark, blue temple standing at the lake's center.

His heart skipped a beat at the sight of the temple. Unless his eyes were being tricked, the building looked to be long destroyed. But it was hard to tell through the wind and snow.

Santiago deflated at the sight of the icy lake. "How are we supposed to get all the way over there?"

Watkin stepped up next to him and placed a consoling hand on his shoulder. "Welcome to the Ruins of Snowgem!"

"Professor," Emma said, squinting through the snow, "is there even a temple left?"

Oliver had to agree. Though he struggled to make out the finer details of the midnight-blue temple in the distance, he saw enough to guess one wave might cause what remained to collapse in on itself.

* Chapter 2: Disciplined Imagination *

Watkin waggled his eyebrows up and down. "It doesn't *look* like there's much left to explore. Let's check it out, just to be sure."

"Okay," Lance said. He unbuckled his war-hammer from his belt and Oliver was pleased to see it still crackled with ice from his freezing spell from late last year. "What's the play here, coach?"

At Lance's question, Watkin's eyebrows stopped waggling and his cheeks drew in with his lips. He glanced from the lake back to their party and then at the ruins.

"Well, Lance," he finally said. "We can't have any of you getting hurt before school. So, the play is simple." He tightened the frayed sash belt around his waist. "I'll get you to the final room and turn things over to Oliver when we see the artifact. Everyone ready?"

Oliver, Emma, and Lance exchanged looks. Even Santiago raised an eyebrow.

Then, dozens of questions exploded out of their mouths.

"What do you mean we can't get hurt?" Emma sneered.

"You're just gonna take out all the obstacles yourself?" Oliver asked, frowning.

"How are we getting across the water?" Lance asked with a scratch of his head.

Santiago just blinked.

Watkin waggled his eyebrows again.

"Follow closely."

Then, he leapt into the crater.

NOVA 02

Roaring, Archie chased after him, fire blazing from his maw. *"You do not want to miss this!"*

Oliver's necklace vibrated on his neck, beckoning him forward. One look at Emma told him she was ready to do the same. The others would follow.

With a crunch of his shoes against the snow, Oliver leapt after Watkin.

He immediately regretted it.

Wind slammed into him from every direction as he plummeted through snow, air, and what certainly felt like powerful ebbs of magic.

Below, he saw Watkin working his staff, his ponytail streaming behind him, while a quick peak over his shoulder showed Lance screaming past an extended tongue. Last of all, Emma was pulling Santiago down with her.

Bless her.

A flash of green pulled Oliver's vision downwards again.

Had he been doing anything but plummeting at terminal velocity, he might have gasped at what came next. He settled for an incredulous grin instead. At Watkin's direction, a channel of funneling water *rocketed* out of the lake. It twisted and rolled until it resembled a mile long snake perched on the surface of the lake.

A second flash of green followed, and though Oliver couldn't hear the spell past the din in his ears, he was willing to bet it was a derivation of the *estalla* spell he'd learned last year—a spell that expanded air to devastating effect. For a moment, time stood still as air billowed through the waterchannel. Then, the water exploded outward, hollowing out into an enormous tunnel headed all the way to the ruins.

* Chapter 2: Disciplined Imagination *

Oliver could have cast the next spell himself, but he thought Watkin might not appreciate his lesson being interrupted. And, if he were being honest, he didn't know if he could pull it off at this scale.

Sure enough, a third flash of green froze the tunnel of water just as Watkin entered it, whooping with glee.

Apprehension crawled across Oliver's skin as he entered next. Would he need to cast a spell to land on the ice safely? Instinct told him to trust Watkin as his frayed sneakers made contact.

He barely felt a thing. If anything, the tunnel's finish was so perfect it shot him forward faster than before. He whooped too, hearing Lance, Emma, and Santiago echo him further behind.

The tunnel twisted and turned in semi-circular motions, but no obstacles or imperfections threatened to stop them. A moment later, they popped out in turns, straight through the decrepit temple's main entrance and onto a magical cushion Watkin had already prepared.

"*Remasco*," Lance muttered with a sympathetic look towards Emma and Santiago. "That better?" he asked as the anti-motion-sickness spell kicked in. Blessed with Power, he was immune to motion sickness just like Oliver.

Santiago raised a hand in thanks while Emma puffed her hair out of her face and straightened herself up. "Now that's the way to travel, Professor," she said with a light burp.

Oliver took stock of their surroundings. They had landed in a cave just past the temple's front façade. Instead of sinking into water, however, the ice tunnel had landed them onto the smallest of dark-sand beaches blanketed in darkness.

NOVA 02

But Watkin already streamed ahead of them. With a few creaks and groans, they pressed forward after him, kicking up sand in the process. Archie zipped around them all, his head swiveling back and forth in every direction.

"You guys heard him," Santiago barked, keeping up quickest. "Stay close!"

* Chapter 2: Disciplined Imagination *

NOVA 02

Chapter 3: The Ruins of Snowgem

These meetings used to be about collaboration and planning. Now everyone's just saying what Tío wants to hear.

30th of June, the second year of the 10th Age

Keeping up with Watkin proved easier said than done. The man tore forward inside the Ruins of Snowgem like a chupacabra after its prey.

First, they descended a circular staircase, being careful not to slip on the icy moss covering the stone floors or cut their hands on the sharp barnacles suckered onto the walls. Soon thereafter they reached a foyer.

Like the Forest Temple from last year, the entryway hosted the husk of a long-deactivated sun dial. But Watkin didn't stop to inspect it. He zipped right past within a few seconds.

The following room opened up into thirty-foot ceilings just like the Forest Temple's second room. When they entered, Oliver half-expected the same wolf-giant to clatter its shield at them.

Instead, however, a bipedal monster with a snake's neck craned its head towards Watkin, stretching its neck. It stood ten feet tall and rolled a scimitar in its hands.

"Ah," the snake hissed, looking between Watkin and Oliver. *"He waits only for the Advent. Too many of you have come."*

Watkin flashed a brilliant and handsome smile. "I don't care anymore, my slithery friend."

* Chapter 3: The Ruins of Snowgem *

Oliver, Emma, and Lance gaped as Watkin engaged with the beast. Instead of striking first, which Oliver was certain Watkin *could* do, the man waited for the snake to make the first move. It scuttled towards him in a crisscrossing motion that mirrored the aquatic movements of a crocodile, striking as fast as a whip.

Before the beast's scimitar made contact, Oliver felt a pulse reverberate across the room. It had come from Watkin.

As if he were on a park stroll, Watkin dodged the monster's strike, ducking at his waist. The sword whooshed over where his head had just been.

Without an object to stop its blow, the snake lost its balance and careened past Watkin, hissing furiously. With a light push to the monster's lower back, Watkin knocked it over entirely. Then, without missing a beat, he slammed his staff-head down; not onto the snake, but the space into which it had rolled to try and dodge.

A resounding thud echoed across the large chamber.

Already, a door to the next room revealed itself with a scraping noise as stone slid across stone.

"Lance," Watkin said, turning to them with a jovial tone. "What did you observe."

All of them gaped as Watkin ignored his downed foe and the door continued scraping open behind them.

"Umm," Lance sputtered after Oliver elbowed him in the ribs, "well… you didn't even have to try, did you?"

"I did try. Better yet, I succeeded. Emma, how about you?"

NOVA 02

Emma straightened her back. "You predicted what that… snake-thing would do."

Watkin nodded at that. Then he looked at Oliver. "And how did I?"

Oliver thought hard, not wanting to sound stupid in front of a man who'd just taken down a considerable enemy in fewer than five seconds. Unless he was mistaken, Watkin had seen into the future before engaging with the snake—how else could he have known to duck at *exactly* the right moment, let alone follow it up with a strike that knocked the monster out cold? But seeing into the future wasn't possible, was it?

Just as he resigned himself to sputter a similar response to Emma, he remembered the scanning pulse from the beginning of the fight. It had felt like he, along with everything and everyone else in the room had been x-rayed. Could that have been a secret spell to help Watkin predict movement? He'd have to guess.

"I think you used some kind of magic to predict the snake's attacks before you even stepped up to fight it."

The corner of Watkin's mouth quivered. "You're closer to being *exactly* right than you realize. But I'll settle for partially correct answers from all of you. I did predict the sacred beast's movements, I did visualize them, and, as a result, I didn't have to try any harder than necessary."

Archie growled. *"This beast does not merit the title of sacred."*

"Right you are," Watkin said, turning to give Archie a bow. "My apologies. To the rest of you, I'll be doing much of the same throughout the rest of the Temple. I won't pause again until the final room. Pay attention to how I watch the cues my enemies make."

* Chapter 3: The Ruins of Snowgem *

"Yes sir," Oliver, Emma, Lance, and Santiago echoed. Oliver raised his eyebrows at Santiago who blushed but didn't meet his eyes.

From the ground the snake monster groaned, beginning to lift its head. Watkin stiffened.

But Santiago reacted quickest. The air erupted with a loud crack as he shot the beast with one of the magic bullets.

For a moment the snake monster looked down to where a long, shiny-blue needle stuck to its leg. Its shoulders sagged as it realized its fate. Before it could slither or hiss in protest, it popped out of existence with a noise like blowing bubbles.

Watkin's expression turned even more jovial. "I don't envy that swim back. Nice one, Santiago." Then, turning back to Oliver, Emma, and Lance he added, "remember, you three, take notes."

Without another word he bound through the door leading to the next room and beckoned for them to follow.

Over the next several rooms, Professor Cato Watkin demonstrated just how much Oliver, Emma, and Lance had left to learn. He didn't defeat his enemies. He *annihilated* them. And Lance had been right—not once, did Watkin look like he was doing anything other than going out on a casual stroll.

In the second room, pig-like creatures walking on two hooves, not four, brandished sickles at them the moment they stepped inside. To reach them, Watkin covered distances at speeds Oliver didn't think possible for a human being. At first, the creatures squealed with delight at the sight of their perceived prey, but it didn't take long for the squeals to turn into desperate

NOVA 02

screeches for help. Watkin moved from one to the next in blurs of blue, white, and bright green. Some of the pigs tried swiping at him with their sharp weapons, but they couldn't touch him. He always knew where to move next.

As they crossed into the third room, Santiago hissed into Oliver's ear. "You said this guy was your *history* teacher!"

Oliver tried shushing his uncle as they stepped inside. He didn't want Watkin to overhear.

"Just a nerdy professor!" Santiago continued, his eyes pressed wide.

In front of them, Watkin dodged between six baboons that foamed at the mouth. Every time they swiped with venomous claws, he stepped, slid, or bent out of the way before landing a knock-out blow.

"This… this guy could kill us all with no problems. Did you know?"

"Nope," Emma said, slipping in between them and answering on Oliver's behalf.

The back of Oliver's neck erupted into goosebumps as they watched. If Watkin was this strong, what did they have to worry about? They'd be able to take on anything.

But then Oliver's goosebumps receded.

Everyone spoke about *The Damned* as if he were the most Powerful human to ever exist. If Watkin wasn't regarded as the strongest, what did the strongest even look like? Even if he did find the two remaining Gifts from the Founders, would they be enough? Worse yet, he still had to pass his classes at Tenochprima this year. Abe and Brantley, his residential

* Chapter 3: The Ruins of Snowgem *

advisors last year, had told him his hardmore year would be far more challenging than his extraman one. How would he find the time to do both?

Gloom threatened to envelop him as Watkin slammed his staff into the last baboon's head, knocking it over unconscious. His eight attackers now surrounded him in a perfect circle. He, meanwhile, still hadn't broken a sweat.

Oliver shook his head at the sight. If he had to guess, he was getting a rare look at the capabilities of a master of Wisdom. If he wanted to reach the same heights, he'd have to work harder than anyone at school. And he'd have to do the same for Power and Bravery, too.

Emma nodded her head appreciatively at the crumpled remains of the baboons. "Nice one, Professor."

Oliver nearly jumped at her voice. When had she sidled up that close to him? Watkin ignored them all and dashed down the next set of stairs.

Lance took his turn to make Oliver jump, speaking from his other side. "Don't worry, brother. You'll be as good as Watkin in no time." He rolled his hammer in his hands and headed for the stairs. Before his head disappeared, he yelled back at them over his shoulder. "The Founders didn't sit around dreaming about you for nothing."

Emma placed her arm on his shoulder in agreement. *That* brought his goosebumps back. Santiago had enough sense to follow Lance.

"He's right, you know," she said, keeping her hand on him longer than ever before. "You're going to learn everything there is to learn, and it's gonna be brutal. But by the end of it, you'll be ready to take on anyone, got it?"

Then she too bounded down the stairs.

Oliver stood frozen in place. It took a roll of his shoulders and head before he could move. "*Pull yourself together, García.*"

"*Indeed,*" came Archie's voice in his head.

"Ah man. Could you hear all that?"

"*Worse. I felt it.*"

Oliver flushed at the neck as he took the stairs. He'd have to find a way to block out Archie's presence for private conversations.

Evidently everyone had been waiting for him at the bottom of the stairs. Lance grinned knowingly causing Oliver's face to also burst red.

Santiago winked at him. "You get lost going down the stairs, flaquito?[2]"

Watkin paid none of them any attention. "This temple," he breathed, running a hand down fifteen-foot-tall mahogany doors blocking the way forward, "greeted us with fewer challenges than the one in the Forgotten Wood. Most puzzling. Yes… puzzling." He didn't address any of them directly. Instead, he spoke out loud, mostly to himself, now surveying the door's twisted iron-ring handles.

Lance shook his head. His goofy grin didn't look all that goofy anymore now that he was covered in muscles. "Maybe it's got something to do with

---

[2] Flaco is an affectionate term for a family member or friend who is thin.

* Chapter 3: The Ruins of Snowgem *

the fact that normal people would have had to climb a mountain and swim across an icy lake before even entering this frozen tomb. Where are we anyway?"

Watkin stared at Lance, completely nonplussed. "You know, perhaps you're right. Which is altogether concerning. Perhaps the Founders didn't anticipate my magic? Or maybe they did but only from us? But they knew about ~~ ~~, didn't they? Then again, perhaps not. What if…"

Oliver's heart began to race as Watkin continued rambling and this time it had nothing to do with Emma's hand on his back. Had he just heard Watkin try and say *The Damned's* real name out loud? The world had muted around them when he'd said something a moment ago—had Watkin been able to utter the name out loud? Wouldn't that mean Watkin was privy to the erased memory?

Oliver's head felt fuzzy just trying to hold onto the conversation. If he didn't say something quickly the memory might slip from—

"Uh, Professor," Emma interrupted. "I think your brain needs to reboot."

Watkin ceased rambling and shifted his stare towards Emma.

Oliver felt his brain leak out an entire thought. What had he been thinking about? Why was his heart racing? Oh right, Emma. He blushed again as Archie shook his head next to him.

Watkin grinned at them all. "Forgive your old professor. For a moment there… well sometimes thoughts can be hard to wrangle, you understand?" He shot them all an apologetic look.

NOVA 02

Santiago chuckled at Watkin, giving Oliver a wry look. "I think you've got more thoughts in your head than the rest of us together, Cato."

Watkin shrugged. Then, he pointed his free hand at the iron door handles. "Oliver, would you do the honors? The lesson isn't over."

"Hang on, Professor," Lance interrupted. "What if *The Damned* shows up like he did at the Forest Temple? What's the gameplan?"

Watkin's eyes twinkled, which Oliver understood to be practiced patience. "All part of the lesson, Mr. Wyatt."

"See ya, Lance," Emma laughed. "You two are back to a last name basis."

Oliver ignored them both and shoved aside his unfocused thoughts. He needed the next artifact, and it was only a door away.

He turned the left handle.

Whoosh!

Wind swelled around them as the door creaked open, fluttering their hair back and forth. Oliver frowned as his dark bangs whipped around his eyes.

Accustomed to magical entrances by now, he went first, followed by Santiago. Oliver shot the man a funny look as he swept his rifle across the room. Though he appreciated Santiago sticking close to him, it would be safest for him to be furthest away from trouble. Before he could think on it much longer, Watkin followed, and Oliver thought he felt a pulse spread across the room again.

"You're gonna have to teach me that technique, sir," he said as Emma and Lance filed in last.

* Chapter 3: The Ruins of Snowgem *

Watkin's eyes whirled as he replied. "You may not ever require it if we find Augustus' gift in here."

Emma whistled as she stepped inside. Santiago gave her an aghast look. "Quiet!" he hissed.

But Watkin placed a hand on Santiago's shoulder. "No need, Santiago. The room is clear for the time being."

They all lowered their weapons, sighing in relief.

Unlike the Forest Temple, the trophy room here was narrow. But a familiar sight greeted them at the far side where a podium stood, flanked by torches.

Oliver stepped forward with long, slow steps, swiveling his head in every direction. Even though Watkin had scanned the room, the fallen sun dial in the temple's foyer likely meant *The Damned* had been before. Which meant… they could be stepping into a trap.

As he drew nearer, he began to make out what waited for him.

In a small, hinged box, a blue ring winked torchlight at him.

"A ring?" Lance asked. "Why didn't they leave you with real weapons?"

"Tut-tut," Watkin chided. "The best attack requires no physical contact."

"Hmm," Lance replied, twirling his hammer as though he'd won a key point in a debate.

Oliver shushed them with a finger to his lips. He'd reached the podium. "Everyone, ready?"

NOVA 02

Even though he couldn't see them, he knew Emma was readjusting her magical sleeve and Lance more than likely was rolling his hammer in his hands.

What did he have to lose? Even if *The Damned* tried to manifest again, they had Watkin with them this time.

He grabbed the ring and rammed it onto his left pinky.

As soon as he touched the ring, the air around the podium began churning in whirling masses of red and black smoke.

"*Oliver!*" Archie growled. *"Step back! Now!"*

Panicking, Oliver heeded Archie's words and clambered backwards. He would have tripped, too, if Santiago hadn't grabbed him by his shoulders and straightened him out.

Watkin yelled out over the noise. "Is this what happened at the Forest Temple?"

"Yes!" Emma shouted. "He'll be here soon!"

Despite his confidence in their abilities, apprehension crept up Oliver's chest at the sight unfolding in front of him. The wind came from a mass of red and black smoke aggregating near the double doors they'd just entered.

As the dark maelstrom solidified into a shape, apprehension turned to involuntary dread in Oliver's chest. *The Damned* was forming in front of him for a second time in three months.

* **Chapter 3: The Ruins of Snowgem** *

Chapter 4: Ghosts of Wisdom Past

I asked him why he hasn't checked out the Oregon temple yet—it's been over a month since I came back and reported my findings. He just smiled at me and said he'd already explored it years ago! I was FURIOUS! Why make me climb all the way up the mountain in the freezing snow if he'd already been there?! He's testing me for something, and I can't understand why. Does he think I'm getting cold feet?

14th of July, the second year of the 10th Age

When a fully formed man stumbled out of the maelstrom of red and black smoke, Oliver didn't cower. As Madeline's necklace burned hot on his chest, he raised his fists and felt for the pool of magic available to him through the ring on his right hand.

Ragged breaths escaped *The Damned* as he fell to his arms and knees after popping out of the air. Santiago immediately pointed his rifle at the man, but Watkin grabbed the barrel and shook his head.

"I thank you for my reprieve, boy," *The Damned* croaked. Although his breath sounded less haggard than last time, his voice still made anyone's skin crawl—this was the unnaturally exhausted voice of a man stepping out of purgatory. Slowly, *The Damned* straightened, taking a moment to flatten the edges of his tattered forest-green cloak. "I'm impressed. You've discovered a second artifact nearly as quickly as I did. I'll be free of my torment soon, and when I am, you'd do well to swear fealty to our cause.

* Chapter 4: Ghosts of Wisdom Past *

Your friends can, too. Everyone will have to before the end. I won't say that—,"

The Damned stopped speaking the second he looked up, stiffening his shoulders and narrowing his eyes to slits.

But he didn't glare at Oliver. Hesitantly, Oliver took his eyes off *The Damned* and followed the man's murderous expression.

It fell on Watkin.

"Was *I* your penance?" *The Damned* spat. "Or did you fool yourself into thinking you'd be mine? There isn't enough magic in the world to save you from my—,"

"Be silent," Watkin interrupted. "I didn't fear you then, and I don't fear you now. The Prophet's Advent has arrived. And you're out of time, *Solomon*."

Oliver gasped at hearing *The Damned's* true name. Clarity enveloped him as two memories flooded his brain.

He was back at school in the Research Lab reading over news clippings.

"Shocking scenes at Tenochprima Academy earlier today as reporters discovered the school in an uproar over one student's alleged disappearance during the Magical Five Tournament's Dueling Final.

"Look uhh, it was just a trick of the light, mid-duel," Headmaster Highbury told a group of the press restricted to the school's landing strip.

Reporters were hurried away when asked who cast the spell, but our sources can confirm the student in question is none other than Solomon Tupper of the heralded Tupper family. Headmaster Highbury all but confirmed this to be true when he banned the press from the grounds after being directly asked about the boy."

NOVA 02

Then Oliver saw Emma and Lance underneath the Golden Willow where they'd received the Iguana's Scroll during their first year at school. They stared at a section of wall Lance gestured towards. "*Tupper was here. Sorbelux.*"

When Oliver recovered, his head felt like it'd been split open with a pickaxe. He gasped in pain, holding his temples as he tried to remember where he was. Only when the splitting sensation faded did his consciousness return to his body where he'd left in the deepest corner of the Ruins of Snowgem.

He staggered in place, taking a step back and raising his fists for a battle as he recovered. But none had broken out yet.

To his left, however, Archie roared in pain, filling the room with noise and fire as he slammed against the roof and the walls around them. Oliver tried reaching out to comfort his friend through their mental bond, but a wall of frustration and anger blocked him.

The fire passed over them harmlessly as Watkin's protective coats held strong. Solomon Tupper—*The Damned*—waved a lazy arm at the flames, breaking them before they ever touched his skin.

"You release me from my curse?" the man growled.

Watkin laughed. "As the secretor, I'm entitled to select my secretees. And they stand in this room—as your enemies, they'll need to study your past unencumbered."

Then, without further warning, Watkin pulsed the room and rushed *The Damned*, crossing the distance to meet him in less than a second. The air around Watkin's staff crackled with green energy as he swung it, but Tupper

* Chapter 4: Ghosts of Wisdom Past *

twisted away from the blow. The man hadn't accounted for Jaiba, however, who descended upon him, squawking and scraping. Watkin, meanwhile, had already pivoted, slamming the butt of his staff towards Tupper. Oliver willed for the staff to make contact, but at the last moment Tupper twisted to catch it with an outstretched hand before wrenching it away. Then, the man twirled it, maintaining Watkin's momentum to strike at Jaiba.

From the sidelines Oliver readied to charge in, if anything to save Jaiba, but a flash of green puffed over the bird, teleporting it to where Lance stood.

Tupper hadn't stopped at attacking Jaiba either. He kept swinging Watkin's staff, bringing the weapon down on its owner in a flurry of jabs.

Watkin dodged, slid, or backed away from every strike. "Come now," he jibed, "have you been neglecting your training? Purgatory is hardly an excuse."

Dread dawned on Oliver when he saw an opening Tupper could take—right into Watkin's ribs. Throwing caution to the wind, he stepped forward to help.

But Watkin slipped away from Tupper's lunge, as though he knew it had been coming all along. With Tupper imbalanced, Watkin punched up at the extended staff, forcing *The Damned* to drop the weapon.

After Watkin regained control of his staff, Oliver let out an involuntary yell. Their professor turned and hurled the staff like a spear. Not at Tupper, but back at *Emma*.

NOVA 02

Yelping, Emma ducked, and just in time, too. Only then did Oliver understand Watkin's maneuver. Tupper had appeared behind Emma with a stained dagger in his hand.

The green jewel on the rotating staff connected with *The Damned's* head with a crash, shattering like glass.

And, just like that, Tupper fell, disappearing in a cloud of smoke. Watkin had defeated their foe before the man could fully manifest away from wherever he was trapped.

"WOO!" Lance cheered. "That was amazing, sir!"

Santiago pushed his lips together in agreement, his eyebrows raised.

Watkin gave them a short bow, grinning again, but then he hurried towards Archie, dodging the occasional thrash, before placing a hand on the serpent's feathered brow. Archie calmed immediately, falling into a deep sleep.

"And now," Watkin said, turning back to the podium, "for the greatest honor of my life. Oliver, get up here." He grabbed Oliver by one shoulder and wrenched him forward.

Oliver didn't immediately understand what Watkin meant, but then he remembered one of the Founders was likely to appear. After stopping *The Damned* from escaping just last year, Madeline's ghost had risen to warn him about his return.

At first, nothing happened. Then, the room turned cold. It condensed their breaths and cracked the walls, forming ice around them in quick bursts. Just when Oliver worried if the drop in temperature might extend

* Chapter 4: Ghosts of Wisdom Past *

past their protective coats, a light flickered above the podium and a man appeared. A man he'd only ever seen in his visions.

Down from the air, stepped Augustus Thomas Henderson, co-founder of Tenochprima Academy.

"Hello, Oliver," the ghost said in a voice that warmed Oliver's spirits in spite of the bitter cold in the air. Augustus wore tan breeches and a frock coat, not too dissimilar from Watkin's, and even appeared to be of similar age to their history professor. Where Madeline's voice had rattled when they'd spoken to her, Augustus' rang forth effortlessly, as if he stood next to them in the flesh. He beamed at them in turn, but then paused on Watkin with a frown. "And who are you? I'd expect the burly man is Oliver's father, and the rest his friends. But you are yet to feature in the Fate available to me."

Watkin didn't immediately respond. Though he wore his usual smile, his eyes moved back and forth quickly. "It is an honor to meet you, sir. You have no idea the scope of your influence."

"I can surmise," Augustus answered, beginning to smile.

He turned to Oliver, gearing up to speak again, but Watkin interrupted him. "Apologies, sir, but if you do not know me now, you *must* know me later in yours and earlier in mine. Do you understand?"

NOVA 02

Augustus paused at that. Then, he stepped away from Oliver and closer to Watkin, peering at him more closely. "I believe you'll find that I do understand. Fascinating—this conversation is not transpiring as expected. Watkin, you said?"

"Yes, sir," Watkin added, flourishing a bow. "Cato Watkin. And I must tell you. Any push you make, it mustn't be subtle."

Augustus observed Watkin for a few seconds, a curious expression on his face. Then, he nodded his head slowly, and Oliver got the impression the two men now shared a deeper understanding than he could ever hope to understand.

At that, Watkin stepped away, receding behind Oliver. "No further distractions from me, I am sorry."

"Indeed," Augustus said, "onto the Trinova! Oliver, the pleasure is mine! How very good to meet you."

Oliver chanced a look at Watkin but saw no immediate answers there. Later then. Thereafter, he gave Augustus his full attention.

"Good to meet you, too, sir," Oliver replied, emulating Watkin by giving a short bow—did people from the sixteenth century expect a bow? "I've appreciated the visions you've shared with me so far. With your help, we got the Iguana's Scroll and recovered Madeline's necklace. Now, we also have your ring." First, he pulled down his shirt at the neck to display the necklace. Then, he raised his left hand to display the blue ring wrapped around his pinky finger. Only now, as everyone stared at the ring, did he revel in his victory. Although he didn't feel any additional surges of Wisdom from the strange wooden artifact, he hardly expected his primary Gift to be

* Chapter 4: Ghosts of Wisdom Past *

boosted much further, artifacts aiding him or not. Secretly, he just hoped he'd be able to master Watkin's pulsing technique.

"Excellent," Augustus declared, placing his hands on Oliver's shoulders. They felt surprisingly real. When he spoke again, it was with a kindness Oliver didn't think he'd ever felt before. "And how was Madeline's visit?"

Oliver chuckled. "Very different, sir. I feel like you're here in the room with us. But she felt more like a ghost!"

Augustus smiled at that. "I'll be sure to tell her."

"Woah," Lance gasped. "You're really speaking to us from the past, aren't you?"

"Yes, it's the turn of the seventeenth century where I stand. I have a rare ability, and I call it *Nova's Sight*. To be clear with Oliver, however,"—and he let go of Oliver's shoulders to take a light step back—"you cannot expect any more conversations of this quality going forward. Though I've discovered a way to imprint one-time conversational channels into solid objects, they require a great deal of stored magic, and it is next to impossible to guarantee a conversation with the intended recipient."

If Oliver understood correctly, Augustus confirmed the Founders performed magic during the last Age of Darkness. That was how they'd founded the school on the Other Side of the Key. But they only had a limited supply while Nova was out of Sight until the twenty-first century.

"But you say," Augustus continued, "I also discover how to leave you visions ... most curious. And you, Cato, how did—,"

Watkin cut him off. "I beseech your subtlety."

NOVA 02

Augustus floated in place, shifting his gaze to each of them in turn. Finally, he cocked his head, settling back into Oliver's eyes. "How comforting to know I will continue to push the boundaries of magical law. But I digress, perhaps too much.

"Madeline told you *The Damned* will escape his purgatory. That is all we know for now. If anything, I regret leaving this artifact behind early in life. But then again, had I not, perhaps I'd never unearth what you've confirmed I'll eventually discover … Anyhow, my sight, which allows me to view the immeasurable possibilities before us, shows us the inevitability of *The Damned's* escape in almost every render of fate and … and …"

Augustus paused as a cloud of a thought hovered over his head. Then, he really began to smile. "Cato, I don't think I paid you enough attention … you're the reason he doesn't have a name, aren't you? Yes, it's all beginning to make sense. So much sense… Of course, he mustn't know … not if you're, well … how long has *The Damned* been in purgatory?" He looked at Oliver. "Fifteen years?"

Oliver, Emma, Lance, and Santiago exchanged bewildered glances as Watkin nodded. What on Earth was going on between these two?

"Be that as it may," continued Augustus, "Oliver, you'll require all three artifacts. Go, next, to the Fire Drake's cavern north-west of the Academy where Cuahtemoc's Gift and conversation wait for you. Regrettably, he's already spoken with you, at least from my time-period, and he wasn't able to hold onto the channel long."

Augustus' voice began to rattle like Madeline's had.

* Chapter 4: Ghosts of Wisdom Past *

Oliver gave him a confused but appreciative look. "Thank you for the help," he said, raising his left hand again.

"Right!" said Augustus. "I'd nearly forgotten!" He mirrored Oliver, raising his left hand back at him, displaying the ring only on its owner's hand, centuries prior. "I envy the heights you'll reach with all three Gifts available to you. But do not neglect the hard work. You do not come out ahead in many of the strands of fate available to me. If he escapes this year, the majority of your fateful successes come from your *immediate* engagement."

Oliver gulped at that. While he appreciated the honesty, it strained his Bravery not to react.

Augustus stared at him for a moment, calculating something. "Do you understand? Only a handful of strands show a delayed approach that ends successfully."

Slowly, Oliver nodded. He'd have to confirm with Watkin, but Augustus was telling him he'd have to duel Solomon Tupper the moment he escaped if they had any hope in stopping him.

Augustus raised his hands at Oliver's nod. "Alas, all good things must come to an end. Forgive me, all, but for my final moments, allow me to say hello to an old friend."

Oliver almost interrupted to ask what he was talking about, but then saw where Augustus was headed.

As the prophet began to fade, he bounded over to Archie and tapped the feathered serpent on the forehead.

NOVA 02

Growling, Archie woke. By the time he finished blinking into focus, Augustus was just a faint shadow.

"*Augustus?*" Archie managed. Tears welled into his eyes, falling in great, boiling drops onto the stone floors where they sizzled against the ice. "*I thought the children succumbed to hallucinations! You never told me? Why?*"

"My very old, friend," Augustus said, his voice catching. "As you just remembered, you developed a close relationship with the False Prophet. I could not risk confiding in you until that relationship ended." He paused to look over his shoulder at something they couldn't see. "Rasmus is hatching as we speak, and Madeline and Cuahtemoc ask that I share their love." Archie howled in pain, but Augustus held him tight. "We're so proud of you."

Archie's tears continued to fall as he nuzzled his head into the disappearing shoulder.

A moment later, Augustus was gone, and, from Archie, Oliver felt wave after wave of crushing sorrow he couldn't begin to comprehend.

When Augustus popped out of existence, hundreds of questions whirled around Oliver's head. What on Earth had Watkin and Augustus been talking about? Had Archie really been close to Solomon Tupper, *The Damned?* What had Watkin done to make Tupper hate him so much? It was almost too much to digest in one sitting and threatened to overwhelm him,

Chapter 4: Ghosts of Wisdom Past

but that didn't stop him from turning to Watkin to begin his interrogation. He warmed as he saw Emma, Lance, and Santiago about to do the same.

Archie, however, was not in any position for rational conversation.

Great gulfs of fire erupted across the room as he roared a guttural yell that made everyone's hair stand on end. No words Oliver could understand spilled from the serpent's maw, only shouts of Nahuatl tinged with misery. Before anyone could reach out with a single, comforting tendril of thought, Archie unfurled his wings and barreled back up the stairs. They could hear his destruction as he passed through each room above them like a condensed hurricane. Eventually, they heard nothing else but the pitter patter of dripping water.

Even Watkin looked at the stairs with concern. He shook his head, grimacing. "It will take time for Archie to clear his thoughts. I will speak with Lalandra about it. We may have to assign you another Guide in the meantime, Oliver."

"Hang on," Emma said, glowering with her arms crossed. "You can't just deflect our questions with that."

Lance nodded along. "Yeah, we deserve some answers!"

Watkin didn't respond but took a deep breath instead, his eyes flickering behind their lids. When he re-opened them, he looked as cheery as when he first entered Santiago's kitchen.

It prickled Oliver's patience. Now wasn't the time to be cheery.

"I," Watkin said, hesitating as he flourished his fingers in thin air, feeling for something. "I will answer as many questions … as I can."

NOVA 02

Emma scoffed. "No more riddles, Professor! Last year we only had *scraps* to go off and—you heard Tupper and Augustus—we're out of time!" Oliver, Lance, and even Santiago threatened to shout in agreement, but Watkin held up his hand.

"I won't withhold answers out of a need for secrecy, but a need to respect Oliver's training. And, quite frankly, even I don't know all the answers."

Lance crossed his arms and mirrored Watkin's grin sarcastically. "We'll settle for your best guesses because we all know they're probably right."

Watkin paused, glancing around the room, but then gave up at the sight of his shattered staff and the green jewel in a corner of the room. "Tell you what," he said. "Let's hold off on the inquisition momentarily. It just so happens I need to pay our favorite blacksmith a visit. So, I suggest we discuss your questions over drinks while he completes an order of mine. Does that sound fair?"

After exchanging quick glances, Oliver, Emma, and Lance nodded in unison.

A moment later, they shuffled out, following Watkin in a somber line. Chunks of displaced stone littered their path where they hadn't been before, evidencing Archie's pained escape from the bottom floor.

"Do you think he'll be okay?" Lance whispered.

"I don't know," Oliver whispered back. "We only had a couple Tupper memories come back to us. Based on what Augustus said, Archie had a whole friendship slam back into his head at once."

* Chapter 4: Ghosts of Wisdom Past *

By the time they reached the baboon-looking monsters, one or two of them groaned back into consciousness. For a moment they readied themselves to attack, but when they recognized Watkin, they began to squeal in terror, crawling over themselves to get as far away as possible.

Emma watched the retreating animals. "Funny," she said, with a grim smile on her face. "You don't need Power to be Powerful."

Santiago nodded along next to her, his lips pressed tight.

By the time they reached the icy shores of the sandy beach above the surface, moonlight winked at them through intermittent gaps in dark clouds above them. Curiously, Oliver realized the gusts of wind and snow had quieted to gentle flurries.

Watkin squinted at the skies, observing the same. "The safeguards protecting this place begin to fade. Wolves will arrive to scavenge for any remaining secrets."

Oliver shook his head, feeling the wood around his pinky finger. "We already have the real secret—don't we sir?"

"We have the prize," Watkin contested. "Our battle with *The Damned* will leave traces. I'll ask Elodie to delay Congress from investigating. She owes me quite a few favors."

"Great," Oliver thought. *"Something else to ask about."*

Chapter 5: Interdimensional Travel

I'm going to do some digging around. I don't know what changed while I was gone, but things feel different. It feels like Tio has evolved into something else. Something more.

23rd of July, the second year of the 10th Age

The journey back to the door at the bottom of the mountain allowed Oliver plenty of time to ruminate over what he'd heard in the Ruins of Snowgem. Two thoughts in particular crashed into his brain over and over again.

Instead of communicating with Augustus' ghost, they'd communicated with Augustus directly—through *time*. And that meant that Augustus had the rest of his life, back in the early seventeenth century, to leave any remaining breadcrumb trails for Oliver to follow. So, in a way, Oliver had just played a direct role in defining what Augustus would do with the remainder of his life.

Thinking about it too much stretched the limits of Oliver's brain, forcing him to shove it aside and worry himself sick over his second takeaway.

Tupper was going to escape soon—the man had said so himself—and, according to Augustus, Oliver needed to defeat him to save the world from destruction. Oliver had barely kept up with Watkin while he'd fought Tupper moments before—how was he supposed to do that to Tupper when the man escaped at full strength? Tupper had gone toe-to-toe with Watkin as just a shadow.

* Chapter 5: Interdimensional Travel *

Oliver began to sweat as his panic tested the resolve of his Bravery. He liked to think he'd gotten used to dealing with stress while sneaking around all last year looking for answers in decrepit temples guarded by ghostly specters. But knowing he'd have to fight the most powerful piece of filth known to man at any moment threatened to eat him alive.

Could he do it? What would happen if he couldn't? How had Tupper ended up in purgatory last time? All the questions in his head made him want to pull out his hair, so he shook himself and forced his brain to ignore them. Watkin wasn't going to answer his questions until they got back to Davidstown anyway, so what use was there in worrying?

First, they re-crossed the lake on an ice raft Watkin whipped up in a second. Then, they trudged up the side of the crater by foot—"more rock than Earth, here," Watkin told them apologetically. And, finally, they descended the mountainside on another rolling wave of Earth that Watkin conducted with ... well just his hands, which was different. Maybe he had on a magical sleeve under his coat as a back-up in case he lost his staff. Which was a good idea, Oliver realized. Maybe Miyada could give him another channel and source if he asked.

Then Oliver remembered he already had a backup. Two in fact. Madeline's necklace and Augustus' ring. Remembering that he had Augustus' artifact made his heart skip a beat. He felt for the metal on his pinky finger, feeling his anticipation grow, and frowned.

While Madeline's necklace clearly boosted his Bravery, Augustus' ring didn't seem to be doing too much for him. Oliver kept his eyes on the simple wooden band for a moment longer, thinking. Wisdom had always been his main Gift—maybe it couldn't be elevated any further.

He shook his head and switched to observing Santiago who occupied the middle of their platform. Santiago kept a low profile, not wanting to fly off as they bumped to-and-fro down the mountainside. In one hand he held his rifle, in the other he squeezed his bag of magical bullets with a vice grip. He kept tossing concerned looks at Watkin. Oliver would have laughed if he hadn't been so anxious about what lay ahead. When Santiago noticed him staring, he scuttled close like a crab.

"Everything good, jefecito?" he asked.

Oliver nodded his head but didn't speak, continuing to look around.

But it was no use, Emma had noticed, too, and decided to join their huddle.

"What did y'all think about Augustus?" she asked, pressing next to him. He did his best to ignore the fact that she smelled like summer flowers.

Lance joined the huddle last, fidgeting with his hammer. "Confusing," he said. Though his voice didn't tremble, it didn't sound confident either. "Watkin was talking in riddles, wasn't he? It sounded like an apprentice meeting his master back there."

Santiago grunted. "Agusto had never heard about Watkin before they started talking. The ghost only knew about you, Oliver. But by the end they sounded like best friends."

"Hmm," Oliver agreed. "I still can't get over the fact that Watkin was the secretor to Tupper's name. And I hope Archie's okay... wherever he

* Chapter 5: Interdimensional Travel *

went." He grimaced at the thought of his friend flying around aimlessly, screaming in pain at his returning memories.

Emma gave him a quick pat on the shoulder.

Oliver nodded appreciatively, but still worried.

Lance swallowed, clearly thinking about something else, too. He flicked his blue eyes at Oliver anxiously.

"What?"

"Well," Lance said, not meeting his eyes. "Did you think you'd have to battle *The Damned* right away?"

Oliver's insides lurched. He wanted to say "yes, of course," but he couldn't. Despite all his Bravery, the idea of needing to fight Solomon Tupper to save the world made him sick to his stomach.

"Eh," Emma interjected, "we won't learn more until we sit down for answers."

Oliver nodded at her gratefully before they all turned their heads to look at Watkin. Only a few hours ago he'd been a history professor who used to play professional Coatlball. Now, his whole past seemed a mystery. Who was this man and what did he know about Solomon Tupper?

"I can feel your stares," Watkin said, coughing politely. "Don't worry, I can reveal much. I am just debating the best way to begin."

Inwardly, Oliver thought he'd believe it when he heard it.

"We'll start," Watkin added, "with an explanation on how I travel around easier than most." Taking a deep breath, he brought his fists together, ending their descent only a few yards away from the door they'd taken from Santiago's kitchen.

NOVA 02

"Home!" Santiago shouted, motioning for the door.

"Not so fast," Watkin said, raising a finger. "Let me go first so I can modify our destination."

Collectively, Oliver, Emma, and Lance gasped.

"You can reroute doors?" Oliver asked, widening his eyes suspiciously. "I thought they were static."

Watkin grinned. "Long ago I discovered the rules around interdimensional travel are constrained mostly by the side of the key where magic exists. But there are no such rules on the side where magic does *not* exist." He walked up to the door and placed his hand on the doorknob. His face concentrated into a grimace. "So, when we want to go from the magical side to the original, we can really pick any door from which to exit. You just have to concentrate hard enough... ah, not that far, can't be barging into the White House uninvited... to find the right door. There it is!"

"No way," Emma breathed as Watkin activated the previously inanimate wood in front of them. It glowed at the edges now. "Is that how you got us so far away from North Carolina?"

"Exactly," Watkin said cheerily. "Earlier today, I'd permanently mapped this door to Santiago's kitchen so we could travel here, to Crater Lake, with ease. To avoid yetis or snake monsters traveling to Santiago's house, I'll be changing the mapping to Davidstown. That will also get us to Miyada quickest!"

Lance grinned. "How come nobody else has discovered this, sir?"

* Chapter 5: Interdimensional Travel *

"I'm sure they have," Watkin answered, smiling back. "But nobody is fool enough to admit it. You'd have to go through hoops in the Magical Senate."

He watched Lance pass through the shimmering doorway first and then looked back at Oliver. "Trusting fellow, isn't he? Could have sent him to Antarctica if I'd wanted to."

Santiago laughed nervously, stepping away from the door. Oliver shook his head. "With all due respect, sir, you don't get to crack jokes until we get some answers."

Watkin shrugged his shoulders and, for once, looked pained. "Fair enough."

Feeling awkward at reprimanding his professor, Oliver took the door next. On the Original Side of the Key, he found Lance leaning against a brick wall he recognized. They'd exited just behind the shop belonging to the Master of Keys in Davidstown. Cicadas chirped in a noisy chorus all around them, ringing with a familiarity that warmed Oliver's heart. But the subdued color palette here, noticeable even at night, would never satisfy him again after spending time on the Other Side. After the rest arrived, Watkin re-activated the door, and they stepped through once again to return to the Other Side.

The last time Oliver and Emma walked around the magical side of Davidstown, passersby had clogged the streets as students prepared for the upcoming school year and families enjoyed the sights and sounds. This time, however, it was already past midnight and although most of the shops were closed, some remained open, leaking warm candlelight onto the

NOVA 02

cobblestone streets like wavering, friendly ghosts of yellow. The streets themselves stretched wide, leaving plenty of room for a bustle of activity that felt notably absent during the late hour in which they'd arrived.

"So," Emma said as their shoes clicked and clacked on the stone beneath them, "you've pretty much discovered a way to travel anywhere in the world by just re-routing doors before you enter them."

"That's correct," said Watkin, not fully paying attention as he led them to the blacksmith's anvil.

Nearby, an enormous, cloaked man glared at their interruption. He'd been conversing with a one-eyed woman holding onto a large, polka-dotted egg.

Watkin tipped a finger to his forehead in respect as they walked past the suspicious couple, and soon enough they arrived outside of Miyada's armory.

Instead of brand-names, window-booths, or even advertisements, only a wooden sign shaped like an anvil demarcated the armory from the other shops on the street. It hung from a nail on the building's façade, immediately above an open doorframe. From inside, a faint amber light reached their eyes.

Oliver stared inside, appreciating the simplicity of Miyada's operation; it would not have looked out of place in medieval times. Inwardly, he reminisced over his own visit in the shop just twelve months prior. Miyada had proved to be a mysterious man, but also the first to recognize Oliver as a Trinova.

* Chapter 5: Interdimensional Travel *

Before he could think on the memory too much, Emma shook Oliver back into reality. "Hey," she breathed, "while we wait for Watkin, let's go ahead and get our books and supplies for this year, yeah?"

Santiago grumbled. "We didn't bring any ameys though."

"That's no problem," Emma said, shrugging. "I can cover Oli and he can pay me back during the year at some point."

"Hmmm," Santiago replied.

Oliver knew what he was thinking. Even though Emma was being generous, they didn't want her to think they needed any handouts. "Thanks," he said before Santiago had a chance to say something aggressive. "I'll pay you the second we get back home."

Emma led the way, bringing them to Monsieur Lafitte's bookstore a stone's throw away. Given the hour, a sleepy clerk greeted them when they entered instead of Lafitte himself.

"Hardmores?" the clerk asked from behind a desk. She looked only a few years older than them, likely a recent Tenochprima grad.

Oliver nearly jumped as he realized she was starting right at him, her eyes wide and fully awake.

"Hey," the clerk said, "you three look familiar. Have we met before?" Her eyes bounced between them, not pausing long on Emma or Lance. She ignored Santiago completely.

They exchanged confused looks, silently agreeing they'd never seen this girl in their lives.

"Nope," said Lance. "We're just here for our books."

NOVA 02

"Oh, I remember!" the girl exclaimed. "On the news!" She pointed at Oliver as if he were an animal in a zoo. "You're the Trinova!"

"Allllright, lady," Emma growled. "That's enough of that. We'll just head to the back and grab our books." She had to push Oliver forward to unroot him from where his legs had frozen.

"We were on the news?" he hissed. "What news? I had no clue." Emma kept pushing him to the rear of the room and away from the girl who kept ogling at him.

Lance's eyes expanded. "Sorry! I keep forgetting y'all don't watch any real news channels on your side of the key." He looked sheepish as Emma glared at him. "We've been on the news all summer—well, mainly Oli has been. But Lalandra doesn't let anybody take photos or videos on campus so all they have is the photo from your Tenochprima application. They tried to get me to do interviews this summer, but Dad threatened to beat them with his cane anytime they tried."

"Stay focused you two," Emma huffed. "Celebrity status or not, we still have Tupper, Cuahtemoc's gift, and probably Watkin to worry about."

"I'm focused!" said Oliver. "Just feel like my privacy's been invaded. I look like I'm eleven in that application photo."

Lance laughed. "Who cares what you look like—you're the Trinova! Nobody's gonna be making fun of you."

Oliver wasn't too sure about that. Being a Trinova hadn't stopped people like Beto Warren, Cristina Morris, and James Harrison from doing their best to bully him last year. And if the whole Other Side of the Key

* Chapter 5: Interdimensional Travel *

knew about him... well that couldn't be good. Hadn't Archie once warned him about others using him to further their own agenda?

Emma was right, of course. No use in worrying about something out of their control, but just as he began to focus on their new set of books, a voice behind them made them all jump. It was the clerk.

"Yep," she said. "You'll be needing the books in that pile over there!" She continued to stare at Oliver as she pointed towards the hardmore pile they'd already found.

Emma curled the sides of her mouth in disgust. "Look, if you already know what books we need, can you just ship three sets to the academy for us?"

"Okay!" Her reply had come early and high-pitched. "You sure you don't want them shipped to your *home* addresses instead?"

Lance shook his head. "Uh, just school thanks. Emma, would you mind taking care of the bill?" Without waiting for a reply, he grabbed Oliver by the arm and began dragging him outside. Confused, Oliver resisted for a moment, but he stopped when Santiago grabbed his other arm. In no time at all they'd pulled him out the door and a peek inside showed Emma paying the clerk with an angry scowl etched across her face.

"What was that about?" Oliver asked angrily. "I don't need protection from clerks."

Santiago sighed. "We know you don't, jefecito. But that girl was one second away from proposing to you, and you're so polite you might have said yes."

NOVA 02

Lance didn't stop laughing until they'd been seated at an outside table behind Jacque's Joint, the American-Aztecan fusion restaurant where they'd dined when shopping in Davidstown last year.

While they waited for Watkin to join them, Emma treated them all to milkshakes—the ones that came loaded with giggles.

"We're going to need a laugh after today," she said, handing Oliver a strawberry flavored one.

Within minutes, they howled with inappropriate mirth as they took turns revisiting the scenes inside the Ruins of Snowgem and poking fun at different terrified expressions they'd remembered on each other's faces. Santiago, for instance, swore Oliver looked like he'd seen a ghost when they first saw the venomous baboons, and that Lance backed away, clutching his chest, after seeing the snake-beast in the first room. Emma laughed hardest at their expense, but Oliver didn't mind.

Despite the tension he felt, it was good to be with his friends again.

* Chapter 5: Interdimensional Travel *

NOVA 02

Chapter 6: Congressman Solomon

*I know he's always been the face of the movement, but now it feels like he **is** the movement. I'm not sure if I'm even needed anymore.*

11th of August, the second year of the 10th Age

When Watkin finally reappeared, he carried a new staff, catching their collective attention immediately. Where the last had been a darker brown, this one stood out as pale grey, and instead of an emerald on the pommel, a band of small, red jewels formed an embedded band near the top. Jaiba had settled down for a nap on Watkin's shoulder, his beak tucked between his side and wing.

It was with a heavy heart that Oliver downed a laughing antidote, but he knew he'd want to have his wits about him for the next conversation.

"I take it," Watkin sighed, landing onto a chair, "now is not the time to tell you about my new staff?"

He looked at them each in turn, raising one eyebrow, then the other. "No? It's red beryl as the source and American chestnut as the channel. Source and channel theory is a fascinating subject—if you change your minds, take Professor Chavarría's senior-year elective."

Oliver was proud that none of them took the bait.

Watkin drooped his shoulders slightly. "To business then, I suppose. But first, a little privacy." He cupped the top of his staff with his left hand and muttered, "*stratum silentii*." A suffocating sensation spread among them,

* Chapter 6: Congressman Solomon *

as if an invisible blanket had been drawn overhead. Watkin nodded, satisfied. "That's better. Let's take turns shall we. Lance, why don't you kick us off."

Oliver gave Lance a supportive nod of his head. Though he himself had a dozen questions ready to go, it didn't matter who went first.

"Well, sir," Lance began, gathering speed and confidence, "I'd like to know more about the conversation you were having with Augustus. It sounded like, well, at least for a moment there, that you were asking him for help…"

Watkin took a moment to pass his hand over the red beryl band on his staff before replying. For someone who didn't know Watkin, the man's delayed reply might appear innocent enough, but Oliver was beginning to understand him more and more. Every word that came out of Watkin's mouth was deliberate.

"And why not begin with the best question," Watkin eventually replied. "When we spoke with Augustus, it became clear he did not recognize me. A most alarming proposition in my mind given that he left me some very sage Wisdom in my youth."

Santiago raised his eyebrows, but Oliver had already put this together and was impatient to hear more.

"So, as he and I conversed, we realized that only later in *his* life did he know about me. Do you follow?"

To his right, a gasp escaped Emma's lips, and Oliver could almost hear Lance's brain click into gear. Santiago, meanwhile, belted out a laugh. "This is some time-traveler sh—stuff!" Oliver thought back to their meal at

NOVA 02

Jacque's Joint last year and suppressed a smile. Back then, Santiago left to attend an early mass service after getting spooked during a conversation about *The Damned*. Now, he leaned forward in his chair eager to hear more.

Watkin smiled at the interruption, appearing thoughtful. He didn't comment, but based on the twinkle in his eye, Oliver was sure he wanted to.

"Augustus looked to be about my age when we spoke with him today," Watkin continued, twirling his staff from one hand to the other. "So, when he left me Wisdom in my thirties, he must have been older than we just saw, perhaps in his sixties. And, more curiously, it was I, in the end, that told him he'd need to find me earlier in my life, and later in his, to leave me with the Wisdom I needed. So, in a strange way, earlier this evening, I ensured my own success in my youth. And so did you, Oliver."

Santiago, Emma, and Lance marveled at the thought, shaking their heads in wonder, but Oliver had to resist the urge to click his tongue. He wasn't going to settle for half the answers.

"*What* did you need help with all those years ago? How are *you* the secretor to *The Damned's* scrubbing?"

Watkin took to passing his other hand over the red beryl band on his staff, leaving an awkward silence. Santiago almost added a follow-up question, but Oliver flashed his eyes, shooting his uncle the kind of look that had usually gone the other way when Oliver was growing up.

The corner of Watkin's mouth twitched. "Solomon Tupper," he finally said, "was supposed to have been the best of us. As it turned out… the movement he ushered was built on a bedrock of lies and manipulation."

* Chapter 6: Congressman Solomon *

Nobody dared interrupt. This was the most they'd ever heard anyone say about their enemy.

"At first, we had no idea the lengths to which he went to secure his vision—one where the magical community would facilitate the peace of both sides of the key to build a utopia. He always said there'd be no need for another Age of Darkness, and that he'd be able to connect the Ages of Magical Proximity together. As it turned out, his vision meant culling society. He pushed to remove non-contributors from our population. He claimed we'd only gather up robbers, murderers, criminals, but by the time we started paying attention, we realized his scope extended to the lazy, the sick, the suffering... anyone who didn't meet his standards for a perfect world. *Sinovas* his supporters began to call them. It started in Connecticut, the state he served as a senator, but by the end, his society 'enrichment' campaigns were in place across the country. Practically everyone bought into it for the good of the many. The number of lives lost were... immeasurable. Few of those requiring enrichment were ever released."

The longer Watkin spoke, the graver his expression became. When he finished speaking, he appeared lost in his memories entirely. Looking around the rest of the table, Oliver saw Lance's face had turned chalk-white and Emma's mouth had thinned to nothing more than a slit. Santiago, meanwhile, looked like he might get sick.

"But then," Watkin went on, his eyes taking on a distant shadow, "Solomon Tupper made a mistake. He overestimated his abilities and... well, at Augustus' tomb in the Sage's Sanctum, he attempted to open a

NOVA 02

direct line of communication with the Founders. He'd set it up as a grand ceremony, but at a certain point during the ritual, the situation turned grim.

"By the end of the catastrophe, many lives were lost, and Solomon Tupper was sealed away in purgatory. Ironically enough, Augustus showed us this evening that you *can* in fact speak with the Dead. But only on their terms, it would appear."

"Were you there?" Emma asked in a whisper. "For the ceremony?"

For a moment, Watkin gazed at Emma with the same level of anguish Archie had displayed within the Ruins of Snowgem. When he replied several seconds later, his voice sounded hollow.

"I was delayed," he confessed. "I couldn't save anyone but Tupper's own son—you'll remember him from school. I took the baby to his grandparents afterwards. He inherited his father's Power but none of his subtlety."

Nobody dared interrupt.

"And then," Watkin said, shaking his head as if remembering a nightmare, "for his crimes, I scrubbed Solomon Tupper's memory from existence. Since the Senate would have carried on with his plans, I started a rumor that a higher power had performed the scrubbing and that the… *thing* that appeared during his ceremony… the thing that haunts him to this day, is his curse from that higher power. Those who know of the event refer to it now as the Sanctum Disaster."

The back of Oliver's neck began to crawl at Watkin's description of *The Damned's* curse. It brought back a vision he'd experienced last year. Tupper had been speaking to Oliver. Complaining about something that followed

* Chapter 6: Congressman Solomon *

him. That's when Oliver had heard a noise echoing through the tunnels. A collection of screeching, clicking, and sniffing that made his skin crawl.

"What haunts him?" Lance asked, sounding confused. "I thought he was just in a special prison?"

Watkin grimaced before answering. "No prison could hold him. No, a pesadriya haunts him, keeping him there."

Lance tried laughing back, but his voice cracked. "Tho-ose are just fairy tales! You're saying Tupper's running around Augustus' tomb being chased by bigfoot?"

"No, Lance," Watkin replied, his voice almost silent. "All of Solomon's sins caught up to him that day. A pesadriya was in that tomb before I fled, and it remains with him today unless he's found a way to kill it."

"He hasn't," Oliver said, realizing he'd already had a taste of the monster. The clicking, screeching, and sniffing… he'd heard the pesadriya himself in his dreams.

Watkin's eyebrows tightened. "You've had visions?"

"I've only just remembered," Oliver said, tracking the change in Watkin's demeanor. The man looked fierce now, his eyes marked by his sharply-pressed-together brow, and Oliver could swear he felt a pressure emanating from him that hadn't been there before. It weighed on his brain, making him draw on sympathy for the monsters the man had faced in Snowgem.

"Last year, before the Coatlball final," Oliver went on, goosebumps bursting forth on his arm as he whispered, "I *spoke* with Tupper! And down the tunnel he was in—well, I couldn't see the thing, but I heard a horrible noise that sounded like sniffing and screeching. I... I just couldn't move when I heard the noise. It froze me in place."

Watkin nodded even as his face hardened. "It would appear the pesadriya has taken on enough evil to evolve into its final form. Not surprising given the number of souls that fell in the tomb that day. I do not say I pity Solomon Tupper, but I certainly do not envy his situation."

Then Watkin stood to leave, grabbing his staff.

Oliver's face fell. "Wait a second! What about the rest of our questions?"

"I've given you enough to chew on," Watkin countered. Jaiba, who'd remained quiet on the arm of Watkin's chair until then, gave a sleepy *caw-caw* in agreement. The toucan flapped its wings, landing on Watkin's shoulder as the professor continued speaking. "Which brings us to your homework assignment. Your priority this year will be to prepare for *The Damned's* imminent escape."

Oliver felt his mouth go completely dry, and out of the corners of his eyes, he felt the others' stares press in on him.

"Thankfully," Watkin said, checking a pocket watch from within a fold on his traveler's coat, "we'll get you there by ensuring you have as ordinary of a school year as possible. Given what we learned today, however, I'll be surprised if you do. Something is amiss. We must be grateful Tupper let slip he plans to escape soon. And you heard Augustus, when he does, you'll be there to defeat him."

Oliver, Emma, Lance, and Santiago all stood, shouting different complaints, but Watkin ignored them. "Given the circumstances, I cannot guarantee anything extraordinary won't happen, but in your free time,

* Chapter 6: Congressman Solomon *

research pesadriyas and anything on Tupper. As secretees you'll now be able to find quite a bit more information on him. Leave the Fire Drake's Cavern research to me—if we're lucky, I'll know where it is by Christmas, and we'll have completed the Iguana's Scroll's assignment."

He turned to leave but then stopped. From nowhere, he pulled out a bright orange key and a framed mirror the size of a piece of paper. "Santiago," he said, tossing the objects to him. "If you're interested in moving to This Side of the Key, Miyada needs an apprentice at the armory. He has some fascinating ideas regarding ranged weaponry. You might find it easier to check in on Oliver if you're in the same dimension. If not, use that key to enter Davidstown and Oliver can chat with you through that notebook there. I repurposed one from school for you."

Santiago cradled the key and notebook within his large hands. "Thank you, Cato," he said, blinking owlishly. "I'll think about it."

"Excellent," Watkin grunted. "Miyada works hard but the quality is unmatched. He doesn't take on just anybody."

Turning away from Santiago, Watkin focused on Oliver, Emma, and Lance. Oliver tried mirroring a pleasant look of his own, but quickly gave up. On top of being tired after the day's events, learning more about how Tupper had earned his title of *The Damned* made him sick to his stomach. That and the fact that he'd have to duel the madman at any second. He'd known it would happen eventually, but he'd always assumed their fight would be ages away.

Oliver was sure some of his thoughts were visible on his face because Watkin anchored his attention on him. "I apologize for the dreary nature of our conversations this evening," he said. "But now that you understand what you fight against, I hope you'll work harder than ever to improve your capabilities. When Tupper does escape, it won't be a murderous maniac that attacks you, but a calculated genius that tears down your every ally until you have no more will left to fight. That's why Augustus spoke about strands of fate. We'll need you to defeat *The Damned* the moment he escapes, Oliver. Otherwise, he'll resume his manifesto, and I'm not sure we'll be so lucky to delay him for a second time."

Emma chuckled bitterly. "Yeah, no problem, coach. You wouldn't happen to have a pesadriya hidden up your sleeve in case we're not ready in time? A little extra jailtime for Tupper wouldn't hurt anybody now, would it?"

Watkin's face brightened, and he even raised his staff in the air in a *hear-hear* motion. "Thank you, Emma," he said, smiling handsomely. "I find a good sense of humor helps keep the darkness at bay."

With a twinkle in his eye, Watkin stood and hefted his new staff. Oliver frowned at the sight. Watkin couldn't leave—he had more questions left to answer. Oliver opened his mouth to say as much, but Watkin snuck his words in quicker.

"I look forward to your lessons this year. Oh, and Oliver, we'll begin private tutoring sessions as well. You're going to need more than your traditional curriculum to take down *The Damned*."

Then he winked, deepening Oliver's frown, and left.

Irritated, Oliver opened his mouth to shout, but stopped short. If he were Watkin, he'd probably be doing the same thing. They'd all heard

* Chapter 6: Congressman Solomon *

Augustus back in the Ruins. As much as Oliver wanted to hear more about Tupper's rise to Power—especially the bits that overlapped with Watkin's past—he recognized Watkin had just made everyone left at the table a secretor to *The Damned's* name. Now, they could research Tupper's past as much as they wanted when they got back to school.

Even then, Oliver still felt irritated. Watkin promised, "no more secrets." And still he kept some.

Sighing, Oliver turned to address his friends and uncle instead.

Directly across from him, Lance still looked a bit green in the face. Maybe even worse than the last time Oliver had looked at him. His friend's eyes were downcast, and his curly blonde hair looked like it would sag off his head at any moment.

What could be making Lance look *that* down?

Judging by the way Watkin had described *The Damned's* rise to Power, most everybody on This Side of the Key had gotten their hands dirty. Did that include anyone Lance knew? What if he had a cousin-twice-removed or something that was a big Tupper supporter? Just thinking about the possibility made Oliver thank the heavens that he grew up on the Original Side of the Key, without magic. Nobody in his family could have been a part of the mass incarceration and murder Watkin had described. Then again, he didn't exactly know any of his relatives from Mexico. It had only ever been just him and Santiago in the US.

Which brought Oliver's attention to his uncle. The man continued to ogle at his new key and notebook, which softened the spike of frustration Oliver felt about Watkin. Santiago still cradled the key, treating it with the

NOVA 02

reverence he usually reserved for his antique video game consoles. It had been impossible for Oliver to stay in touch with Santiago last year while they lived in different dimensions. But now, if Santiago took Miyada's job… the thought made him grin from ear to ear.

But then he looked towards Emma and his smile fell in an instant.

She also stared at Santiago's new key and notebook. But instead of mirroring their joy, her eyes shone a dull jade instead of their normal fierce emeralds. Worse yet, her lip trembled.

Catching Oliver's stare, she quickly put on a smile. Then, she shook her head.

"What?" Oliver whispered.

Emma looked away and then back, sighing. "I still haven't told my parents about Tenochprima."

Oliver's jaw dropped.

"Don't worry," she added, her eyebrows growing sharp. "They wouldn't care. Our butler takes care of all the bills and stuff in the house anyway. I've made him swear not to tell. You remember him, right? Charles—he drove us to the airport last year."

* Chapter 6: Congressman Solomon *

NOVA 02

Chapter 7: The Griffith House

Tío pulled me aside last night to let me know he trusts me fully, and that I'm the only person who he shares all his plans with. I'm glad because I was starting to feel like some of the others—Blackwood mostly—were more up to speed than me with the plan. I think Tío must have seen me looking down. I have to be better about keeping my emotions hidden.

14th of August, the second year of the 10th Age

Oliver's experience with resolving family issues, let alone *parent* problems, ran about as deep as a spilled cup of water. So instead of saying anything helpful to Emma he sputtered for a full seven seconds, incapable of coming up with even a half-decent reply.

Eventually, when Emma squeezed her eyes shut, his babbling slowed to a halt. When she blinked and focused on him again, her pupils shone with determination, and all the pain had disappeared.

Oliver latched onto that—shoving pain aside was something he was *very* familiar with. "Look," he said softly, "you can't just push your problems away. They'll only come back worse."

Was it hypocritical of him to give out that advice? Absolutely. But she didn't need to know that he'd ignored his issues with Santiago for the better part of fourteen years. Not yet, at least.

Emma's expression hardened. "Can we talk about this later? Not in front of Lance."

* Chapter 7: The Griffith House *

A thrill shot up Oliver's back as he registered what she was saying. She only wanted to talk to *him* about it. But why? Her eyes still surveyed him sternly, but he knew her better now—she was measuring him for something. Even with his double-dose of bravery, Oliver found it difficult to return her fierce stare. Was she hinting at something he should find obvious?

His mind raced back to when she'd placed her hand on his back when they were in the Ruins of Snowgem. The thought caused butterflies to swoon up from his stomach and into his head where they settled into a comforting ether. It felt *good* to think about Emma.

Oliver blinked, looking away from her. What was the good of Wisdom if it wouldn't help him sort out his feelings? He glanced down at Augustus' ring and felt the temptation to hurl it away. Then, with a start, he realized he'd forgotten to reply.

"Yes, of course!" he whispered in an urgent hiss. Thankfully, she hadn't looked away yet. "Whenever you're ready to talk, just let me know."

Emma's shoulders relaxed as she slumped into her chair. "Thanks."

Oliver copied her, falling back into his own seat. For added measure, he even blew his dark bangs off his forehead with an upwards puff of his lungs.

"Talk about what?" Santiago interrupted. He'd turned his steely eyes away from his new notebook and key, settling his attention on Oliver.

Oliver didn't like the way his uncle was smirking—mischief was coming.

"No jokes, Santi," Oliver growled.

"Aww," Emma pouted a little too intently. Oliver could tell she wanted the conversation to change. "I liked your cow jokes last year!"

Santiago shrugged his shoulders and stood to leave. "Okay, no jokes. I'm going to the blacksmith."

Oliver stood up. "You're taking the job?!"

"Psh! Why not? Only got bills and misery waiting for me back at our old house. At least here I'll have magic and,"—he shook the notebook in his right hand—"now we'll be able to platicar[3] whenever." Santiago paused, suddenly struggling to meet Oliver's eye. "Only if you want to, you know?"

Oliver went over to hug his uncle but stopped short when he remembered the pain he'd seen in Emma's eyes.

Santiago held up a hand and stood to leave, shooting Oliver a knowing look, along with a not-so-subtle waggle of his eyebrows. Then, he lumbered away, whistling a merry tune.

Oliver couldn't help but smile, keeping his gaze on his uncle until the man reached Miyada's anvil down the cobblestone road. Just over a year ago Oliver had never seen this side of Santiago. Now, because of magic, he got to see it all the time.

Emma's voice quickly brought Oliver back to reality.

"Lance?" she asked, quiet and sincere. "You alright?"

Oliver's stomach dropped. How could he have forgotten to check in on Lance? Their friend had looked properly frightened when Watkin finished telling them about Tupper a few minutes prior, and Oliver began to suspect he knew why.

---

[3] Colloquial Spanish (where I'm from, at least) for "speaking," "talking," or "chatting."

* Chapter 7: The Griffith House *

Lance swallowed, slow to reply. "I... well," he began, his face oddly stiff, "I was just thinking about Tupper. And the campaigns Watkin talked about."

"Don't," Oliver interjected with a side-to-side wave of his hand. "Even if you have a second cousin's uncle or something that supported *The Damned*, it's not worth worrying about. Watkin said Tupper lied to everyone and—,"

Oliver stopped talking because Lance looked up at him. His determined blue eyes were piercing.

"It's not that!" Lance interrupted. He looked away before continuing. "I think my dad might have—,"

Oliver's heart fell. Had his best friend's dad been a supporter of mass incarceration and worse?

"—been in one of the rehabilitation camps," Lance finished.

For a second time that evening, Oliver's jaw dropped.

Emma leaned forward, horrorstruck. *"What?* You think your *dad* was in one of the prisons?"

Lance shifted in his seat uncomfortably. "Well, Stevie always mentioned dad got really sick when she was little. So sick that he lived with our grandparents for a couple years. But mom and dad never talked about what he'd been sick with or anything. Ever since I can remember he's been missing his leg, and I've just been thinking." He dropped his gaze as he went on. "What if that story was always a coverup? Watkin said they put non-contributors into the camps, and my dad's never been very good with his Gift, has he? We always joked half his Power must have been saved up extra for Elton. But what if that was a lie? What if he ended up in one of those *sinova* jails for being… weak?"

Oliver felt the necklace on his chest grow hot. Reflexively, he shook his head and took the seat Santiago had just vacated to place a hand on Lance's shoulder. "There's no use in worrying about what you don't know," he said, shaking his friend by the shoulder. "And we're *never* gonna let Solomon Tupper or anyone else bring back these campaigns, got it?"

For the briefest moment, Lance's eyes threatened to well up with tears, but then he squeezed them shut and exhaled. "I'll be fine," he mumbled.

Oliver tried layering on another comforting look, and he took a moment to makes sure it worked.

Eventually, Lance's tense lip relaxed, and Oliver no longer worried tears would break out.

"Okay," Lance said, nodding his head. Like Emma, he spoke a little too forcefully, also eager to change the subject. "It's getting late—where are we gonna crash tonight? No disrespect to you, Oli, but no chance you map a door correctly first try if Watkin didn't know how. I'd rather not end up in the Cambodian jungle by accident right before our hardmore year starts."

Oliver grinned. When Lance finished speaking, he mirrored Oliver's shoulder grab, placing a hand onto Oliver's opposite side and squeezed hard.

Emma tsked, crossing her arms. "Boys make it look so easy." As Oliver and Lance let go of one another, she stood up, puffing an annoyed breath. "I'll close us out," she added before storming towards their waitress.

* Chapter 7: The Griffith House *

Oliver watched Emma as she jostled their waitress, attempting to wake the old woman from her snoring against the cash register at the front of the shop.

"Psst," Lance hissed, distracting Oliver.

Oliver almost scooted his chair back at the manic he found on Lance's face. Between the ear-to-ear grin and exhausted eyes, he wasn't sure what to expect.

"What?" he whispered back, narrowing his eyes suspiciously. "This is serious stuff. If you think you can keep changing the conversation with a joke or something, don't."

Lance pushed together his lips and pondered for a moment. Then, in a sudden motion, he grabbed a handful of Oliver's shirt.

"I *am* worried about dad," Lance said, keeping Oliver close. No amount of squirming could get him out of the vice grip. "But now that Emma's gone, let's talk about *you* for a second. What's up with you two? Did you take her on the world's worst date this summer or something?"

Heat rushed up Oliver's cheeks. When he finally managed to slap Lance's hand away, he hissed indignantly. "What are you talking about?" As he spoke, he shot a desperate look in Emma's direction. Mercifully, she was still attempting to wake up the waitress with more and more aggressive jostles. "And keep your voice down!"

Lance smirked. "Still working things out, are we?"

"Working *what* out?" Oliver gritted through his teeth. "Here I am going about living my life normally, and you and Santiago keep smiling at me like cats at a coffee shop—,"

NOVA 02

Lance laughed. "It's not a crime to be in love!"

Oliver sputtered, his entire face went scarlet, and, to his horror, Lance didn't stop there.

"If she's digging your skinny chili now, just wait and see how she feels after we put you on the Elton regimen. Girls won't stop looking at me now." He ignored Oliver's continued protests to raise his arms and flex his biceps. Then, he leaned back in, this time grabbing two fistfuls of Oliver's clothes. "Girls love *me* now! Not that I know how to talk to them. Just think how many will be lining up to talk to *you* after you hit your growth spurt!"

Squirming, Oliver took his own turn at changing the conversation by latching onto the distraction with insane determination. "What *did* Elton do to you over the summer anyway? Looks like you've gained ten pounds at least!"

"Thirteen, actually," Lance corrected. "It's not rocket science. Oh! I'll tell you more later—Emma's coming back." Then, with a would-be-innocent, sing-song voice, he added, "thanks for closing us out, Emma!"

She narrowed her eyes. "Why are you holding Oliver like you're going to strangle him?"

Oliver looked down at Lance's hands, which still held onto a third of his shirt. They hastily spread away.

Emma held up a hand to stifle a yawn. "You know what? I don't want to know. Let's go pick up Santiago."

"Sounds good," Oliver said, shooting up from his chair. "How much do we owe you?"

* Chapter 7: The Griffith House *

Emma furrowed her eyebrows into a straight line. "My parents can cover it."

Lance scraped his chair loudly to stand. Then, he pulled Oliver up with an offered hand. "Good luck unpacking that," he whispered.

Thankfully, Emma didn't hear.

They found Santiago outside Miyada's armory with his shoulders stooped over as he worked on something. When Oliver shouted a "hey!" towards the burly man, his uncle turned around surprising them with twitchy eyes and hands that kept opening and closing.

"Got the job!" he yelled, loud enough to make Oliver look around the street, embarrassed. "Pretty night, isn't it?

Emma laughed. "Excited about the new gig, huh?"

"What?" Santiago shouted. "Oh, yeah! The job. YES." He spoke so quickly his syllables began to overlap.

"Started-work-tonight-Miyada-gave-me-elixir-helps-me-focus-¿ya-sabes?"[4]

Oliver shook his head slowly.

---

[4] Colloquial Spanish for "you know?" In other words, "the elixir helps me focus, you know?" Santiago is emphasizing just how much this elixir helps him. Almost illicitly so.

NOVA 02

Santiago went on while the twitching in his eyes turned hysterical. "And-now-I-can-*see*-noises-we're-going-to-make-my-guns-better-he-said-we-can-use-them-on-adventures-with-you-guys!-We're-going-to-be-frontier-blacksmiths!"

"Careful with that elixir, alright?" Lance said, eyeing Santiago as if he might explode.

Oliver shared the concern but was still thrilled to have Santiago on the same Side of the Key. As though he were reading Oliver's mind, Santiago reached out and clasped Oliver's hand, pulling him into an embrace—the jittering made Oliver's teeth chatter.

"We're going to get some sleep," Oliver said loudly, as though he were speaking to a toddler. "And then we'll head to the airport in the morning, okay? But call anytime with that notebook."

"Sounds-good-jefecito!" Santiago shouted. Then, after a salute, he barreled back into the armory, yelling, "Sensei!-what's-next?"

Emma snorted a laugh as Santiago disappeared from view. "He's settling in nicely, isn't he?"

Oliver nodded, staring after his uncle fondly.

"C'mon," Emma continued, "my house is in Davidstown, remember? Y'all can just stay with me. I wish I hadn't been traveling all summer—could have invited you over sooner, Oli..."

Oliver's attention immediately abandoned Santiago's retreating figure as butterflies returned to his stomach in a hurricane of motion. He'd have to meet Emma's parents tonight? What if he didn't make a good impression? He probably stank of sweat, lizard goo, and baboon venom. How was he

* Chapter 7: The Griffith House *

supposed to explain that to a set of parents who didn't even know about Tenochprima Academy?

But Emma had never been one to second-guess her decisions. She was already making her way back to the doorway behind the Master of Keys' shop before Oliver could even think of a protest.

Hesitantly, he looked to Lance for advice.

Lance waggled his eyebrows. Then, he pushed Oliver hard in the back, forcing him to walk up next to Emma.

Oliver yelped as he came in step with her. She gazed at him questioningly but kept walking.

"Eh, don't worry about the time," she said, misunderstanding his yelp. "Sometimes I'll play cards with Charles all the way til sunrise."

Lance raised an eyebrow. "Your *butler*, right? You guys have a butler…"

"Ugh," Emma snarled. She shot Lance a nasty look. "Yes, I have a butler. Just one of the many perks offered to children who never get to see their parents."

When Emma looked back at Oliver, he racked his brain, desperately searching for something, anything to say. It was a lot harder talking to her now that he knew he liked her.

"He didn't mean anything by it," he finally whispered.

Emma waved a hand dismissively. "Ah, don't bother. Got picked on plenty in middle school after being dropped off by Charles in the sixth grade. Started taking the bus after that. Nice thing about Tenochprima is nobody seems to care where you come from or how much money you got. Magic makes none of it matter."

NOVA 02

Lance scoffed. "Tell that to Beto and his calf-leather boots."

Oliver scowled at the mention of Beto, his arch-nemesis at school. From the moment they'd met each other, Oliver and Beto had hated one another. Beto, who grew up on the Other Side of the Key, had clearly grown up with wealth, but unlike Emma, he chose to flaunt it any way he could. Nothing highlighted this more than the fact that he channeled his magic with a gilded scimitar instead of something normal like a magical sleeve, piece of jewelry, or a normal sword. Worse yet, for Coatlball, the premier sporting event at Tenochprima, Beto wore obnoxious pieces of expensive leather. He also pushed aside anyone he thought weak… calling them sinovas…

Oliver stopped in his tracks just as they arrived at the door behind the key shop.

"Y'all!" he shouted. "Beto!"

Emma exchanged a look with Lance. "What about him?"

"He called us sinovas last year! I didn't think about it until now, but he must be a supporter of *The Damned!*"

"Of course he is," Lance growled, his eyes darkening. "He's cousins with John *Tupper,* isn't he?"

Oliver could almost hear the glass shattering in his head. How had he skipped over that nugget of information? All last year he'd gone to school with Tupper's *son,* John, and he'd already made enemies with Tupper's nephew, Beto. Thinking about it made his stomach hollow out. He'd always pictured *The Damned* as a menacing presence lurking in the shadows, but now his enemy felt real, dangerous, and right in front of him. Who else in

* Chapter 7: The Griffith House *

his life might support Tupper's return? Or the re-introduction of Tupper's society enrichment campaigns?

After they returned to the Original Side, Emma led them down a handful of streets towards her family's home. They were a quiet troop as they walked, and with every step, Oliver felt his anxiety shift more and more from Tupper to Emma's parents. He still wanted to leave a good impression no matter what was going on, and being covered in dirt and what looked like snake-monster blood wouldn't be the best way to do it.

Just when he felt tempted to suggest they go back and crash at Santi's instead, Emma turned onto a long gravel driveway. After a gradual hill rise into a small forest, they approached a house that made Santi's one-story home look like a studio apartment.

Emma's family lived in a mansion, complete with a four-car garage to their left, cozy gardens to their right, and what appeared to be a large pool and deck behind the main, three-story building. At the front-door, stood Charles, the family butler. He wore black slacks, a black coat, white gloves, and no expression whatsoever.

"Miss Griffith," he said, hits tone flat but polite. "I trust you had a pleasant evening with your friends."

Emma grinned. "That's his trouble-making face, y'all. Don't be fooled."

Oliver and Lance exchanged confused looks. Charles' face hadn't even twitched.

"Yes," Emma went on, "we had a *very* fun night, Charles. You remember Oli?"

"How could I forget, Miss Griffith? The Prophet's Advent, was it?"

Oliver frowned. The fewer people that knew about him on the Original Side of the Key, the better. But here was Emma's butler, already aware of Oliver's status in another dimension. Then he remembered Emma's relationship with her parents—or lack-thereof. Charles was more than likely her closest family member. She probably told him everything.

"And Mr. Wyatt, a pleasure to meet you as well."

Lance's good manners threatened to wake up the entire neighborhood. "Howdy, Mr. Charles. The pleasure's all mine. You been working here long?"

"Pipe down," Emma jeered. "Charles has been helping us since before I was born." Oliver noticed her peer towards one of the rooms on the second floor. "Are *they* still awake?"

A smile creased the corners of Charles' mouth. "Mr. and Mrs. Griffith settled down for the evening five hours ago. Might I suggest the guest house for your friends?" Though he kept his hands near his abdomen, he pointed towards a stand-alone building nestled within the gardens on the right side of the estate.

"Good idea," Emma replied. Without another word, she turned towards the guest house, motioning for Oliver and Lance to follow.

* Chapter 7: The Griffith House *

"We appreciate you, sir," Lance said, tipping his warhammer towards Charles. "A real treat."

"Very good, sir," Charles intoned.

The gravel crunched noisily underfoot as Emma led them away from the main house and across garden pathways to the front door of a guest house. Had Oliver been less tired, he might have marveled at the Spanish-Colonial architecture, or the flowers and plants in the gardens, but he could barely keep his eyelids open.

Underneath a nearby pot, Emma retrieved a key, opened the door, and flicked on a light switch, bringing them inside to where a small, courtyard welcomed them. Further inside, starlight shone through the open ceiling of the courtyard, reflecting into several cozy rooms on two different floors. Each had a porch or balcony of wrought iron, completing the Spanish-Colonial look.

Oliver gazed around, resisting the temptation to let out a long whistle. The guest house alone was larger than Santiago's entire lot.

"Ok," Emma breathed, "bedrooms are upstairs. I'll be going back to the main house, but we'll wake you up with breakfast in the morning. Got it?"

They both nodded.

Emma gave them a look over and wrinkled her nose. "I'll see if Charles has any spare clothes for you. Are those fish guts, Oli?"

Oliver looked down at his clothes, mortified. Did he really look that bad?

"Who knows, really?" Lance answered. He sidled up close to ladle off some goo with his finger.

NOVA 02

He smelled it and grimaced. Then, he rubbed it back onto the only clean bit of cloth left on Oliver's shirt. "Could also be baboon venom."

Emma continued wrinkling her nose at Oliver as Lance took the stairs. "Hmm. Maybe take showers before getting into bed, then. I know there are spare pajamas in the drawers, so use those before Charles brings you more clothes in the morning, okay?"

An awkward pause followed for a moment as Lance disappeared up the stairs.

"Well, unless you need anything else," Emma muttered, half-turning to leave, "see y'all in the morning?"

Suddenly, Oliver didn't feel so tired anymore. "Hey," he said, his heart hammering as he stopped her with a light touch to her shoulder. "Thanks for letting us crash. I know it's not easy with your parents."

Bringing up Emma's parents had been a risk, and she accentuated that by narrowing her eyes and tightening her lips. She looked like she might storm out, or maybe even yell at him.

Oliver's mouth dried up, but he kept looking at her. After a tense stare-down, her face mercifully broke into a forced smile. "That's," she sniffed, "nice of you to say." Then she punched him lightly on the shoulder. "But really, take a shower. You stink."

Upstairs, Oliver heard Lance laugh as a showerhead turned on.

* Chapter 7: The Griffith House *

NOVA 02

Interludes I – II

Ms. Joan *loved* serving as Tenochprima Academy's Dean of Culinary Endeavors. As far as she was concerned, it was the best job in the world.

Every month, a handful of Michelin star restaurants did try and woo her away from her precious students, but she'd never come close to accepting any of them. Which one of those fancy restaurants, she wondered, would ever allow for a silly title like *Dean of Culinary Endeavors?*

Elodie Lalandra, the academy's headmaster, on the other hand? That delightful woman hadn't even blinked when Ms. Joan pushed for a different title during her Head Chef interview eight years ago.

"I want to be a Dean," she'd asked, squinting at the Headmaster suspiciously.

Elodie had grinned in reply with her eyes *and* her lips. "It's done," she'd offered, waving a dismissive hand. "I quite like the idea of a Dean of Culinary Endeavors, don't you?"

Ms. Joan smiled at the memory. She'd mainly been testing Elodie of course—nobody wanted to work for someone stuffy like a manager at a Michelin star restaurant—but Ms. Joan wasn't going to turn down a free win.

A snapping noise brought her out of her memories. It had come from Broderick Blackwood's impertinent fingers.

* Interludes I – II *

Was he *snapping* at her? In *her* kitchen?

"Are you even listening to me?" Blackwood asked, his upper lip curling beneath the rest of his big, bald head.

Ms. Joan's frown turned ugly. This was one of the rare times she hated being Tenochprima's anything, let alone Dean of Culinary Endeavors.

"Nah-uh," she said, snapping her fingers back at the monster-sized man. "Out of my kitchen." As the words left her mouth, the sliding, stone door leading to the Dining Hall and out of her kitchen began to scrape open.

Blackwood leered at the exit before turning back to her, standing as tall as an oak. "You can't kick me out," he sneered. "I'm ordering you to employ more *instructive* methods during your detentions. García got away with everything last year, and I saw more than one smile on his face whenever he spoke to you. As the Dean of Discipline, it is my right to—,"

"OUT!" Ms. Joan interrupted. She enforced her wrists with Power and began pushing at the giant man's chest. If he wasn't going to leave on his own terms, then he'd leave on hers.

At first Blackwood didn't budge, but when her pots and pans began to take turns wailing on his forehead, her pushing became easy. "Nobody snaps their fingers at me in MY kitchen and gets away with it! I said OUT!"

Blackwood tried growling something horrible, but a cast-iron skillet took the opportunity to whack him straight on the nose.

Bong!

Within a few more seconds, the Dean of Discipline collapsed into a heap of dust outside of her kitchen.

NOVA 02

"And don't come back until you learn some manners!" she shouted, waving her fist as the sliding door shut.

Sighing, Ms. Joan turned away from the muffled sounds of Blackwood's protestations and took to sitting at her desk. A cursory glance revealed a stack of letters that turned her sigh into a groan.

She forced herself to grab the topmost letter anyway. She'd been neglecting the letters all month. They came from people who had more in common with Blackwood than Lalandra—and they all wanted her to leave the academy behind. Opening up the first one, she rolled her eyes. Even the man's name was stuffy. Jim Beauregard.

She leaned back in her chair, debating whether to even write a reply, when a blast of hot air buffeted her face.

"Aaargh," she growled, shaking a fist at a short set of nearby stairs. When she'd first moved in all those years ago, the only available space to cram her desk had been the alcove next to the stairs. Only after she'd set the thing up had she realized why.

She peered down the stairs and wrinkled her nose. It wasn't that she wasn't *allowed* down those stairs, she just tended to forget what she was doing whenever she got too close to them. It likely had something to do with the heat. Waves of dry, hot air just like the one that had slammed into her were always billowing up from those stairs.

She shrugged, returning her attention to the stack of letters.

"Dear Mr. Beauregard..." she wrote.

111

* Interludes I – II *

Cristina Morris checked her watch from where she sat waiting in the Arrivals section of Boston Logan International Airport. It was already a quarter 'til eleven in the morning.

"Where is he?" she hissed to a boy sitting to her left.

Squat with dirty blonde hair, the boy completed his presentation of a total imbecile by crossing his eyebrows together in confusion. "Huh?" he asked stupidly.

Cristina waved a hand in annoyance. "Oh, James!" she said, giving up on her friend. "Just forget about it!" It would take a full two minutes to communicate with the dullard and she didn't want to waste time talking to him if the leader of their gang, Beto Warren, might walk around the corner any second.

She began chewing on her fingernails. They'd been waiting on Beto for thirty minutes already, and he hadn't messaged them with a change of plans or anything. *"Could he be traveling to school a different way?"* she thought. *"Maybe a personal charter?"*

She glanced at James again. *"Is he really going to leave me to travel alone with James?"*

"No," she told herself. He probably just had some important family matters to attend to. He did come from a *great* family after all. And he wasn't the kind of guy to waste her time willingly.

NOVA 02

She was still chewing on her nails when she realized Beto was only a dozen yards away, looking right at her.

Her heart skipped a full beat when their eyes met. He was in the middle of a throng of twenty or so other travelers stepping inside the airport.

"Good lord," she breathed out loud, unable to stop herself from tugging on her hair like a nervous little girl. Beto's handsome, lazy smile spread across his face the closer he got.

"Huh?" James repeated gruffly.

Cristina stopped pulling on her hair to stand up. "Don't be an idiot," she snapped. "And get up! Beto's here."

James' eyebrows raised as he joined her on his feet. He even straightened his back and gave Beto an awkward salute.

"Hi!" Cristina peeped with a little wave.

Beto's dreamy grin stayed on his face, highlighting his perfect teeth. "Sorry I was late," he said, exchanging a brief half-hug with James. His moves were so certain, so fluid, he even made James look cool. "How were your guys' summers?" he added, letting go of James and turning to Cristina.

Cristina let out a short prayer of thanks for being a Wiser when she went in for a hug next. Had she been a Brave or Powerhead, she might have missed the way Beto's shoulder and chest opened up invitingly, and her nerves would have gotten the better of her, leaving her hug-less.

As it was… she breathed in Beto's cologne for as long as she dared. When they spread apart Beto turned to look confidently at James.

"Summer was good," James reported to the taller boy. "Me and my dad visited Maine for a bit."

* Interludes I – II *

"Exciting," Beto said, shooting Cristina a quick wink. Before going on, he took a moment to run his hands through his hair and re-do the bun on the back of his head—he'd grown out his dark, curly locks even longer over the summer. "And your family?" he directed, still at James. "How are the Harrisons doing?"

Cristina knew she was staring at Beto while he and James continued catching up, but she didn't care.

Beto was unlike any of the other boys at school. The way he walked and talked—she'd never met another guy like him. Tall, handsome, athletic, he was the full package. He even had leadership skills she couldn't hold a candle to.

But he did have one flaw.

"You ready for Hardmore year?" James guffawed.

Beto's silky expression soured, making him look like an ordinary boy again to Cristina's eyes. One with insecurities and obsessions.

"It'll be good to get back and crush the Trinova," Beto said, miming the word "Trinova" with air quotes as a heat came into his eyes.

Cristina let out an impatient breath. She'd have to work on Beto a little bit. He couldn't be snarling at any mention of Oliver García if he wanted to become the guy to lead Champayan, their dormitory at school.

Still, Cristina thought to herself as Beto's smile turned handsome again, Beto had all the right ingredients. All he'd need was her Wisdom to keep up with the Trinova. And here she was, by his side to give it to him, whether he knew it or not.

NOVA 02

Chapter 8: Nova's Touch

The Whig leader I saw in Cambodia said hello this morning. I was headed out the door at Federal Hall—the one in the city—when he held the door and looked at me with a ridiculous smile. Then he asked if I'd visited one of our rehabilitation camps yet. I was stunned! He said it out loud for everyone to hear and nobody challenged him. Of course I haven't—they're not my job to supervise, are they? But maybe Tío should start inviting this guy to our Free World Coalition meetings—he's got charisma.

18th of August, the second year of the 10th Age

When Oliver woke the next morning, he found a pair of boxers, light-khaki shorts, and a navy button-down shirt waiting for him on a bedside table. He didn't know how Charles had been able to guess his clothing sizes but wasn't about to start complaining either. A quick look into the other bedrooms on the second floor later, and Oliver found Lance still sleeping. While he waited for the snoring to die down, Oliver took another shower, determined to never smell like fish guts or baboon venom ever again.

When he exited, wafts of bacon, eggs, and toast coaxed him to the bottom floor where Charles had left breakfast waiting underneath serving platters. As soon as Oliver started pouring coffee, Lance appeared, wearing darker shorts and a light-yellow shirt.

"Morning," he said, his voice still recovering from the late night. "Charles has us looking sharp, doesn't he?"

* Chapter 8: Nova's Touch *

Oliver resisted the urge to laugh at Lance's untidy hair, instead, giving him a mock salute and a plate of bacon.

"Bless you," Lance breathed, digging into the food with reverence.

Oliver stared around the kitchen while they ate, admiring the level of polish. Parts of the room reminded him of fancy department stores, including the refrigerator which took a while to find because it had been built directly into the cabinetry. On the whole, however, the kitchen never strayed too far away from its colonial architecture, always feeling cozy, in spite of its size and undoubtedly expensive appliances.

When Oliver attempted to rinse off his plate at the sink and instead flipped on an exhaust hood, he yelped, scaring himself half to death while Lance laughed.

Just when Oliver felt intrigued enough to explore the rest of the villa—a place like this had to have an in-home movie theater—Emma knocked on the front door and joined them, taking a seat at the kitchen counter. She wore athletic gear and had her hair up in a ponytail while she drummed her fingers on the white marble countertop.

"Okay, you two. I just checked my notebook and Watkin's left us some instructions. They're about as clear as mud." She handed Oliver her notebook—which was really more of a magical mirror than a traditional notebook—and pointed at the message for him to read aloud.

Oliver, Emma, and Lance—congratulations on yesterday's success. You should be proud of the way you handled the lesson. As a

NOVA 02

reminder, do not neglect the homework I assigned you for the year—your survival will depend on it.

Yesterday, the three of you may have noticed I pulled objects from seemingly thin air for Santiago's use—think back to the sack of ammo, his key, and notebook. Long ago, I invented a useful trick, and I'm passing it along to you now as you pack up for school.

Though the spell itself requires no energy of your own, it can be difficult to comprehend. In essence, you'll be creating a pocket of space nearby. If you succeed with the magical working, you can use that pocket of space as your personal, private, and mobile storage unit. I'd recommend closing it whenever you're finished loading and unloading.

I also recommend you develop a habit of pretending you're pulling items out of your shirt or coat pocket. Best not to share secrets with your enemies... Instructions below.

Regards,
Professor Watkin

Lance yanked the notebook away from Oliver. "No way," he muttered, re-reading the message for himself. "Is he seriously telling us he's got a storage container following him around at all times?" He went on to read the instructions, clearing his throat.

1. *Visualize your place in the universe, recognizing the three dimensions available to your senses.*

* Chapter 8: Nova's Touch *

2. *Feel Nova's push and pull on the space and matter around you (this can be performed on either Side of the Key).*
3. *Using Nova's energy directly, open as big a space of nothingness as you dare near your chest (I wouldn't try inside your body as that may kill you. This should feel like your Earth elementals from your Extraman year at school).*
4. *Place whatever you want into your dimensional pocket (such as your clothes, books, and supplies for school).*
5. *Using Nova's energy again, close the space of nothingness when you're done. This should conceptually feel like drawing a blanket over the new space you've created. Don't close it entirely as you'll pulverize all your belongings to dust. Rest in peace... sweet grandfather clock from my first apartment).*
6. *Delete these instructions after you've succeeded or given up. I call it a dimensional pocket but it's a working title! No doubt the three of you will come up with something much more clever.*

Emma grinned mischievously as Lance lowered the notebook with his mouth agape. "Think of all the possibilities!" she said. "You could hide a whole arsenal of weapons in there." At the look Oliver gave her, she rolled her eyes. "What? Watkin had a sack of magic bullets in his pocket dimension, not an extra set of clothing!"

Oliver raised his hands for peace. "You're right—I was just thinking about my trunk at home for starters. But also..." He stood up suddenly, another thought imploring him into action. "If we used that same logic of

NOVA 02

pushing and pulling through Nova, couldn't we just push and pull *anything* around us?"

Lance looked puzzled. "What do you mean?"

"Well," Oliver said, thinking out loud. "What if I wanted to open the refrigerator door from here. Couldn't I just use Nova's Touch to grab the handle?"

"That sounds too good to be true," said Emma. "Wouldn't somebody else—heck, wouldn't Watkin already be doing that if it was possible? There wouldn't be a point for verbal spells, elementals, or even sources of magic at that point."

Lance tossed the notebook back down on the counter with a sigh. "This is gibberish—pull open a space of nothingness? What does that even mean?"

Oliver took in a deep breath and concentrated. Within a few seconds, he felt himself reaching out with his mind, probing the room around them for Nova's presence. For a moment he didn't feel anything but Emma's attention, but after a few more breaths he felt... something.

A foreign presence moved softly through the world around them, like waves ebbing from an enormous metronome. Though he couldn't see a source for the pulsating movement, he was sure it could only be Nova's presence. In and out it went, pushing and pulling at the air around him, the blood in his body, and even the thoughts in his head. What if he just repurposed some of that motion to do his own bidding instead of Nova's?

Oliver shifted his attention back to the refrigerator's handle. If he could *just* pull it open with one strand of Nova's power, then his options would

* Chapter 8: Nova's Touch *

be limitless. Try as he might, however, nothing happened. Every time he felt Nova's energy begin to bend to his will, he only managed to feel himself touch the door's handle from a distance. Sighing, he switched back to Watkin's instructions.

Using Nova's energy, open as big a space of nothingness as you dare near your chest ... this should feel like your earth elementals.

Well, that sounded downright confusing. But he knew where to start after touching the refrigerator a moment earlier. Concentrating again on Nova, he motioned for a space in front of his chest to expand open. To his astonishment, a void roughly the size of the refrigerator he'd been focusing on appeared in front of him.

"Woah!" Emma shouted, stepping away from him.

Oliver quickly redirected the energy to collapse the void. "Sorry! Didn't mean to make one so big!" He patted down the counter where he sat, convinced he'd destroyed something.

"Does it matter?" Lance asked, his eyebrows raised. "I don't think it pushes anything out of the way or anything." He picked up the notebook Oliver had left on the counter and re-read Watkin's instructions. "No warnings about destroying anything but yourself or anything inside it. I say go for it!"

Oliver allowed himself a cautious grin. "Still... I don't need one the size of a refrigerator."

Emma shrugged and yanked the instructions away from Lance. "And why not? Check if you can get the space to copy the shelving and then you'll be able to organize and everything."

NOVA 02

"That's..." Oliver began. He'd wanted to say 'silly,' but what wasn't in magic?

It took nearly a minute of meditation to feel *Nova's Touch* again, but when he felt it twist and grab across the room, he latched onto it and asked it once more to bend to his will. This time, his pocket dimension opened into an exact rectangle with shelving resembling that of a refrigerator but with an enormous space at the bottom to fit a couple large suitcases or trunks.

"Ho-ho!" Lance shouted, slapping Oliver on the back. "You can start,"—he paused to dash up and down the stairs, returning with something in his hands—"by carrying around our dirty laundry!" Chortling, he tossed their clothing, still drenched in venom, blood, and fish guts, into the top compartment. To Oliver's horror, they reeked even more than before.

Emma wrinkled her nose. "May just be easier to throw them away at this point."

Oliver obliged, hastily chucking them into the waste bin. Then, he felt for Nova's energy and pulled the pocket dimension shut.

Satisfied, he nodded at Emma and then Lance. "Well, aren't y'all gonna try?"

Emma pressed her lips together, clearly unamused. "I'd rather not kill myself by accident."

"Yeah," Lance tagged on, "that's gonna be a 'no thanks' for me, too. Maybe once you get used to it, you can teach us. But for now, I don't feel like putting something important away and then needing to meditate for an hour to try and get it out."

* Chapter 8: Nova's Touch *

Oliver spluttered. "What are you talking about? An hour? Only takes a bit of concentrating."

Emma and Lance exchanged a look.

"Oli," Emma sighed, sitting down on the counter stool next to him. "It took *you* just a bit of concentration. You didn't notice, but we were also trying to feel for Nova out there, but we may as well have tried feeling for gravity's push and pull."

Oliver's face turned bright red as she began to grin.

Lance ruffled his hair. "You might be the dumbest genius in the world."

"I'm *not* a genius," Oliver growled, straightening up out of his chair.

Emma's eyes lingered on Oliver's, but before he could think on it too much, the front door behind them swung open and Charles stepped inside.

"Ms. Griffith, the car is ready."

NOVA 02

Chapter 9: One Man's Potatoes

I did some digging, and while I was gone, Tío convinced congressmembers Eliza, Bruce, and Devon to roll out our Systems of Freedom in New York, Vermont, and Delaware. That's four states now! It shouldn't have been a surprise—he does have several caucuses reporting directly to him.

21st of August, the second year of the 10th Age

A half an hour later, Oliver stepped out of the Griffith SUV and let out a sigh of relief.

For all intents and purposes, he ought to have been more stressed than ever. Augustus had as good as told them Tupper's escape was right around the corner. But Oliver had gotten used to feeling stressed last year. And most of that stress had been brought about by him, Emma, and Lance having absolutely no clue what they were doing.

Now, he at least felt confident. They had a *plan*. And they had Watkin to help them see it through. While Watkin looked for the location of Cuahtemoc's artifact, all Oliver, Emma, and Lance needed to do was research Tupper's past, train up for a fight, and learn as much as possible about pesadriyas—the breed of monster keeping Tupper in his purgatory.

"Oliver," Emma shouted, snapping her fingers in front of Oliver's head. "You there? Keep moving, will ya?"

He hopped to it, mumbling an apology.

* Chapter 9: One Man's Potatoes *

"You two sure there's a skydraft here?" Lance grumbled. He looked around with a hand over his forehead, squinting his eyes.

Oliver chuckled. "It's on the Other Side, remember?"

Lance flattened his lips, looking sheepish. "Right."

Emma's lips twitched, no doubt readying a cruel reply. Before she could share it, Oliver pushed them forward.

Finding the skydraft proved easier than last year since he and Emma knew where to go, but it still took longer than expected with Lance stopping them every few steps to marvel at everyday things. When they first entered the airport, he raised his fists at the automatic doors as they slid open, ready for a fight. He also made sure to maintain a wide berth from any escalator they walked past. As he watched him, Oliver made a mental note to not react stupidly in front of anything on the Other Side of the Key.

Eventually, they made their way down a short corridor separated from the normal airport terminals. Lance tried marveling at how nobody else in the airport even glanced in the corridor's direction, but Emma pulled him forward with a hand on his sleeve until they reached an outdoor area surrounded by concrete walls. A grubby door and gnome statue waited for them there.

"How d'you do, Mr. Gnome," Lance asked, stooping down to pat the gnome fondly on the head. Oliver briefly expected the statue to snarl or hiss at the affection, but then he remembered which Side of the Key he was still on.

NOVA 02

A rush of air interrupted his thoughts before they could stray too far, however. Emma had unlocked the door, and one peak inside the now oscillating doorframe revealed the same Skydraft from last year.

Oliver squinted at the billowing tornado hesitantly. Even though he knew he'd be fine jumping into it, there was something *wrong* about willingly stepping into a force of nature that destructive.

Emma on the other hand was already running into it, holding onto a hand glider Charles had fashioned up before they left. Within a second, the tornado yanked her skyward in great circular motions. Exchanging shrugs, Oliver and Lance followed.

They circled around each other when they reached the top, laughing in a world of fluffy-white clouds and barely visible gray pathways. Everywhere around them, enormous cumulus clouds manifested in different shapes and sizes. Though most stuck close to the gray pathways they now pulled themselves up onto, a larger concentration loomed ahead where Oliver knew the Northern and Southern Lines waited for them.

As they navigated towards the Southern Line in a single file, Oliver never leaned too far in one direction. He didn't feel like testing whether invisible safety barriers were in place or not.

"These platforms have been around for a lot longer than Tenochprima has," Lance muttered. "Some of the transports, like the Khufu ships go all the way back to the Fifth Age when a guy called Narmer united Egypt. Not saying this platform is *that* old but we could definitely be standing on Mayan or Aztec stone right now."

* Chapter 9: One Man's Potatoes *

Oliver nodded, impressed, thinking about Cuahtemoc as they arrived at the Southern Line. On the opposite side of the station, a few other travelers waited to take the Northern Line. "You sound like Abe," Oliver said to Lance. Abe had been their residential advisor, or RA, during their first year at school. He'd also been obsessed with the world above the clouds when Oliver and Emma first met him.

Lance grimaced at the comparison. Instead of immediately replying, he sat on a nearby bench and stared at the empty space between the two sides of the station with hollow eyes. "My father told me," he grunted. "He does a lot of reading since he can't get out of the house much."

Emma and Oliver exchanged a look. The less time Lance had to brood on his father's potential past incarceration, the better. Especially if they didn't even know if Lance's guess was accurate. There'd come a time to support him through that nightmare of a headache, but it wasn't now.

"Cool, cool," Emma said awkwardly. "I wonder if we'll get a Khufu Ship this time, too?"

Lance's attention snapped to Emma, and his eyes no longer looked hollow. "YOU ACTUALLY GOT A KHUFU SHIP LAST YEAR?!"

Emma backed away slightly as Power crackled around Lance's headspace.

"AN ACTUAL KHUFU SHIP?!" Lance shouted. He walked up to the gap where the ship would arrive and squatted down low, squinting his eyes to peer as far North as possible. "SOMETHING'S APPROACHING!"

NOVA 02

Oliver looked at the incoming ship and even though he could barely make out its outline, he knew it wasn't a Khufu Ship. There were no overlapping oars over a cabin, and it looked more like a ball than a ship.

He placed a hand on Lance's shoulder. "Tough luck."

"No," Lance said, grimacing. He used Oliver's hand to pull himself up, nearly knocking them both down into the gap. "It's normal luck. There's only a couple of 'em left in circulation anyway."

As the shape drew nearer, Oliver was surprised to see an animal pulling the vessel forward. The Khufu Ship had barreled through the skies on magic alone. This new transport, however, came tied to an enormous horse. At least, Oliver thought it was a horse. Instead of sinew and flesh, however, the animal was made of shaded winds and essences of ether. Oliver looked to Lance for an explanation, but Lance only shrugged.

"I don't know man," he said, still disappointed, "it's just a wind spirit."

The ship itself wasn't so much a boat, but more of a floating sphere painted yellow, orange, and red. When it slowed to a halt, an entryway popped into existence and a ramp shot out, clattering against the grey platform unceremoniously.

Emma curled her lip at the bulbous ship in front of them, entirely unconvinced. "What the heck is this one called, then?"

It looked so rickety Oliver almost suggested they wait for the next transport, but when he opened his mouth, the wind spirit at the front neighed and flicked its head towards the entrance. Its neigh carried in an eerie tenor, arriving in separate intervals as if carried by individual strands of wind.

* Chapter 9: One Man's Potatoes *

"I think it's a Trundholm," Lance offered. He looked at the horse more than the ship. "It's not *as* old as a Khufu Ship, but it should be a lot faster."

The horse's tail, which was also made of shifting winds, swished at Lance's words.

Not wanting to insult the beast by delaying any further, Oliver scrambled inside.

He regretted it almost immediately.

Dozens of passengers filled the Trundholm like fish caught in a net. Only a few benches occupied the middle of the spherical dome that formed the inside, but the seats looked to have been long occupied. Surrounding the benches, dozens of other passengers stood atop ancient wooden floorboards. With nothing to hold onto as the ship lurched forward, they wavered in place, awkwardly bumping into one another.

As Oliver, Emma, and Lance squeezed inside, Oliver tried scanning every face visible through the crowd. It was a habit he'd picked up after clearing the Forest Temple last year, but it proved nearly useless here. There were simply too many faces to register. It wasn't until Lance nudged and pointed towards the far side of the Trundholm that Oliver recognized anyone at all.

And he quickly wished he hadn't. Beto Warren, his arch-nemesis from school, stood on the other side of the ship.

NOVA 02

Oliver tensed at the sight of Solomon Tupper's nephew. Like Oliver, Beto also surveyed the other passengers on the Trundholm. But where Oliver looked on the world with curiosity, Beto did so with open disdain.

When he eventually locked eyes with Oliver, Beto's frown unfastened and his eyes brightened, morphing his handsome face into something that resembled a wolf more than a boy. A wolf that had just spotted a wounded caribou at the rear of its herd.

Oliver's blood boiled hotter and hotter the longer he looked.

Beto stood an inch or two taller than he had last year, matching Oliver's growth spurt over the summer. His smile was as dashing as ever—when he wasn't looking like a demented wolf—and he'd started tying his long curly locks into a knot on the back of his head.

It took every measure of Oliver's Wisdom to let the anger seep out of his pores. He had every reason to rage at the sight of Solomon Tupper's nephew. That arrogant face across the room represented everything wrong with the Other Side of the Key.

But the Wisdom in the back of Oliver's head helped him recognize a hard truth. He wouldn't be able to stop people from developing into Betos or Solomons by fighting their evil with his own anger. No, he'd have to take a different approach if he wanted evil to never develop in the first place.

As he relaxed, he realized Emma and Lance were having a much harder time reaching the same conclusion. They exchanged murderous glares with Cristina and James, who flanked Beto, occasionally cracking their knuckles or rolling their shoulders.

* Chapter 9: One Man's Potatoes *

"When we get off at the Charleston stop," Emma hissed, "I'm not taking any trash from those three. Somebody's gonna get hurt, and it isn't gonna be me."

Lance nodded his head vigorously.

"Listen, you two," Oliver began.

Emma's red-misted eyes shifted from Cristina's to his, almost causing him to jump back in fright.

"I am *not* listening to anything but a plan of attack right now. See how they're looking at everybody else as if they're better than them? Like everyone's a *sinova*? UGH IT MAKES ME WANT TO—,"

Others were beginning to stare, pointing and whispering at Oliver's ring, Emma's sleeve, and Lance's hammer. Oliver could see the lights behind each set of staring eyes dawn with apprehension as the passersby recognized the boy from the news—the first confirmed Trinova in recorded history.

Not wanting to be known for starting a fight on a Trundholm before the school year even started, Oliver shot a desperate glance towards Lance for help. But Lance somehow looked even angrier than Emma did. His arms bulged and his fingers twitched while he made a ripping motion with his hands. Oliver stared at the hands aghast, wondering who or what Lance intended to rip.

Throwing caution to the wind, he moved to step in front to stop them from rushing Beto, Cristina, and James.

Before he could, however, the floorboards of the Trundholm creaked behind them, groaning from the weight of an unknown presence.

NOVA 02

Anticipating a trap from Beto, Oliver turned sharply, feeling a pulse of magic from the necklace on his chest.

An enormous figure stepped closer, looming taller and wider than the three of them standing side-by-side. As it moved towards them, sunlight filtered through a hole at the top of the Trundholm and revealed a man Oliver barely recognized. But he *did* recognize him. And judging by the gasp that escaped Emma's lips, she did too.

In front of them stood a seven-foot-tall man wearing nothing more than a burlap produce sack over his mid-section. His eyebrows were beyond unkempt, growing far past the sides of his head, and he appeared to be branded on his arms. In each hand, he held onto a glowing potato the size of Emma's torso.

Oliver opened his mouth, tempted to compliment the man's potatoes, but stopped himself when he realized that would sound ridiculous.

The man furrowed his eyebrows as he surveyed them. "Saw you three in the news," he huffed, pointing at them in turn with his potato-laden hand.

Lance looked at Oliver, desperate for an explanation.

Tense as a board, Emma spoke first while gesturing at the potatoes. "See you found that potato that fell out of the Khufu Ship last year."

* Chapter 9: One Man's Potatoes *

The giant man's eyes crinkled as he broke out a warm smile. When he shifted his gaze towards Beto, however, the crinkling stopped.

Oliver followed the stare and was delighted to see just how uncomfortable Beto looked while the giant potato man pointed an arm at Cristina.

"Those kids over there? Are they as unpleasant at they look?"

Emma's entire frame relaxed at the question. "Like you wouldn't believe." Right on cue, Beto raised his head to scowl at them past a tilted chin.

"Thought so," the man grunted. Then, he handed Oliver one of the glowing potatoes. "Boil that in equal parts water for three months and use it as a base for an elixir."

After exchanging glances with Lance, Oliver took the potato so he wouldn't appear rude. It felt surprisingly warm to the touch.

"An elixir for what?" Emma asked, reading Oliver's thoughts.

The man looked them over for a few seconds before responding gruffly. "Temporary boost to your abilities. For our Trinova, here, that ought to be exciting enough."

Oliver paid the potato more attention now. Could this vegetable really boost his Gifts? Looking back up, he asked, "who are you?"

The man grunted and then looked past their shoulders with unfocused eyes before replying. "Nobody, really," he finally breathed out, shaking his head into focus. "Some used to call me Jim. But it doesn't matter. If you like the potato, just let me know, and I'll get you some more at the City

NOVA 02

Market in Charleston. You bring a lot of us nobodies hope, Oliver García. We'd rather not go through rehabilitation again."

Oliver's jaw dropped. *This man survived one of Solomon's rehabilitation centers.*

"Hang on!" Lance shouted. His lips grew taut, and whether he meant to do it or not, his Power began warping the air around his head. "Which camp were you in?"

Oliver's stomach fell as the question crossed Lance's lips. Sure enough, murmuring broke out all across the Trundholm, and from the other side of the carriage, Beto began to simper. Fury erupted inside Oliver's soul at the sight. *How dare he gloat in front of a man imprisoned by the Tupper family?*

Before he even knew what he was doing, Oliver felt for the strands of magic he knew hung in the air. They were invisible, malleable, and prepared to do his bidding, like bolts of lightning in a quiver. The murmuring turned to shouting as passengers scrambled to distance themselves from the crackling ebbs of energy now emanating from Oliver's frame.

But then a touch on Oliver's shoulder stopped him.

Oliver snapped his neck towards the touch and widened his eyes. He expected to see Emma's hand laying on his shoulder, but it wasn't hers. The hand on his shoulder belonged to Jim, the man who'd given him the potato.

He shook his head at Oliver with his long, twirling eyebrows furrowing into inquisitive disappointment. Stunned, Oliver allowed his grip on magic to fall. He almost didn't hear the collective sigh of relief reverberating across the room as he tried to understand the man's expression.

"That scum," Oliver hissed, pointing at Beto, "makes a habit of calling other people *sinovas*. You expect us to just put up with it?"

* Chapter 9: One Man's Potatoes *

Jim shook his head ruefully at Oliver as the Trundholm began to slow down. "That pup with the curly hair wasn't born evil—he was taught it. Does your Wisdom demand you attack him, unprovoked?"

Oliver wilted at the question, feeling his anger fade away into red embarrassment on his ears.

Emma, however, huffed and shook her head. Lance, meanwhile, was clamping his hands into fists that shook.

"Unprovoked?" Emma snarled. "You wouldn't say that if you knew what he was like at school."

Jim's eyebrows furrowed further, this time into an outright glare. "Trust me, when I say *you* have no idea what his parents were like."

Emma doubled down on her frustration, crossing her arms and glaring right back at the giant.

Oliver let go of the energy around him. "Peace, Jim. You're right."

Lance let out a tsk in frustration.

"C'mon, guys," Oliver added as the Trundholm's gangplank popped into existence and clattered down on the Charleston platform. "Once we're back at school chatting with Elton and Joel, Beto's stupid face will be just something to laugh about."

With mutinous glares, and one last look of fury towards Beto, Cristina, and James, Emma and Lance allowed Oliver to usher them off the Trundholm and towards the carriages.

Oliver paused at the foot of the gangplank and turned back towards Jim. "Thank you for the Wisdom."

NOVA 02

Jim's face softened, which raised his long, curling eyebrows. Then, he rose a fist and tapped it against his chest, muttering, "more than the greater good."

Oliver paused, unsure of how to reply. That had sounded an awful lot like what Madeline Desmoulins said last year.

You must demand good for all, not just the greater.

Unable to stop himself, Oliver emulated Jim, forming a fist with his right hand. When he tapped it against his chest, several passengers jeered and sneered, Beto chief amongst them.

But Oliver barely noticed them.

Because just as many other passengers had copied him, tapping clamped hands and fingers against their chests. "More than the greater good," they muttered.

* **Chapter 9: One Man's Potatoes** *

NOVA 02

Chapter 10: A Hutchinsonian Masterpiece

More red tape! We've also launched three more rehabilitation centers. How Tío got the other congressmembers to see the world the way we do this quickly I'll never understand, but our vision for the future is beginning to take shape.

25th of August, the second year of the 10th Age

When Oliver caught up to Emma and Lance on the Charleston platform above the clouds, he motioned for them to follow as he blazed past a sign that read "This Way to Tenochprima Academy." He was *not* keen to get into a public fight with Beto before the school year even started.

As they moved, fluffy white clouds whisked in and around them, revealing hidden pathways of grey stone. By now, Oliver was convinced he could step anywhere when up in the sky, but he'd have to test that theory more fully if Beto were to catch up to them.

When they reached an open platform peppered with giant eagles tethered to carriages of gold and purple, Emma looked over her shoulder and huffed.

"I know you're trying to avoid a fight," she shot through gritted teeth from just behind, "but if we want to bring Beto to justice, *don't* get in our way."

Oliver opened his mouth to agree, but then he saw James pointing right at him from only twenty yards away, Beto and Cristina close behind.

⁂ Chapter 10: A Hutchinsonian Masterpiece ⁂

Lance raised a muscular arm, gesturing at their enemies with Power sparkling around his torso. "Especially if they're looking at us like that!" he said, raising his voice.

Oliver knew what Lance meant. From across the way, Beto's eyes had lit up, ready for action.

Desperate to calm Lance down, Oliver placed his hands on Lance's ears and kissed his friend right on the forehead.

"I understand why you're upset," he snuck in while Lance recoiled away from him with wide eyes. "But fighting school bullies in public spaces isn't the way we take down *The Damned.*"

"Alright, alright!" Lance muttered as he went red in the face. "Next time you need me to calm down, promise not to kiss me, will ya?"

Oliver half-laughed, but then remembered who was barreling towards them. "Let's keep moving," he said grabbing Emma by the arm.

To Oliver's surprise, she avoided his eyes as she entered the nearest carriage that was already half full. Confused, Oliver raised an inquisitive eyebrow towards Lance.

Lance put up a wry smile, looking less embarrassed than before. "She's probably just jealous you didn't kiss her instead."

It was Oliver's turn to blush as he clambered into the open-top carriage after Emma. Behind him, Lance closed the door and cupped his hands around his mouth so he could yell at the giant eagles in front.

"Time to go, honored sacred beasts!" he shouted.

Oliver slapped the side of the carriage twice as he sat down next to Emma, emphasizing Lance's point. If anything, it helped him ignore how much Emma's touch seemed to burn his insides, especially after Lance's comment. For her part, Emma took turns focusing on either the plush, purple pillow in her lap, or the eagles at the front of the carriage.

The larger of the two opened its beak to address Lance. *"Scrawww!"* it said to Lance. *"We shan't move until you've paid us a compliment, tiny blonde boy!"*

The smaller eagle flapped its seven-foot wings, punctuating its co-captain's words.

Lance opened his mouth to speak again, but then his shoulders slumped. He looked down at Oliver hesitantly.

Oliver shot a glance over his shoulder and saw Beto was only yards away, pushing a gaggle of girls aside to get to them.

"My, my," Emma interjected, breaking her silence in a loud, flat voice. "What wonderful plumage you have, Mr. Eagle."

The eagles began to scratch their talons on the platform, leaving great grooves in the stone. *"Though you mean to belittle us with sarcasm, little girl, the joke is on you. Hear now, for you speak the truth—our plumage knows no equal."*

Oliver tried saying, "good thinking," in Emma's ear, but a bell tolled, interrupting him.

Gong!

Lance sat down in a hurry, pushing Oliver even closer to Emma. "Budge up!" he said as he took his seat, winking at Oliver.

"Ouch!" Emma managed. "Oli, that's my hand you're sitting on."

"Sorry!" Oliver tried replying, but again, he was interrupted—this time by the giant eagles. Without warning, they'd leapt into open air and turned into a dive. For a moment the world stood still, Beto's scowling face just

* Chapter 10: A Hutchinsonian Masterpiece *

outside the carriage, but then the reins tightened, and the carriage followed the eagles with a *lurch* that tugged the wind straight out of Oliver's lungs.

Even though he'd already taken the ride down once before and *should* have known what to expect, Oliver still felt every fiber in his body wishing he were anywhere else. Despite all his Power stubbornly fighting against motion sickness, and all his Wisdom telling him he'd come out alive without issue, there was something entirely unnatural about descending five thousand feet in a matter of seconds. The eagles reveled in it, however, tucking in their wings to increase their speed and screeching loud enough for the world to hear.

Only when they crashed onto the Tenochprima landing strip did Oliver, Emma, and Lance stop screaming. Oliver and Lance first exchanged relieved laughs, and when Emma emerged from beneath a pile of pillows, Oliver felt a thrill as she joined in.

A moment later, however, Oliver frowned. At the end of the runway, Rasmus and Merri, Emma's and Lance's respective feathered serpent Guides, waited for them among a throng of giant eagles and osori. Glaringly absent, was Archie.

A pang of guilt kicked Oliver in the stomach as he watched Rasmus and Merri levitate in place with incessant flaps of their long, narrow wings. The feathers on their faces were blue, like Archie's, but Oliver could only notice the differences now that his friend was gone. Where Rasmus' and Merri's mandibles were silver, Archie's were gold, marking his age.

NOVA 02

Remorse spiked in Oliver's stomach. He hadn't given Archie much thought since he'd disappeared from the Ruins of Snowgem in a rampage of sorrow. *"Where are you, Archie?"*

When they exited their carriage, Emma wasted no time to scratch Rasmus' lower mandible. "Missed you," she said.

"And I you," Rasmus replied, nuzzling into her shoulder and neck.

Hearing Rasmus' voice deepened the pang Oliver felt in his stomach. Archie's tenor was similar, but also more foreign, like that of a Spaniard—an Aztecan, Oliver corrected himself—speaking in a posh English accent. Shoving the pain aside, Oliver sighed and pressed towards the staircase leading down to Tenochprima's main campus.

The landing strip they had just crashed into was situated at the top of a very large hill descending towards a series of coastal lagoons. The campus had been built into the hillside centuries ago, by none other than Augustus, Madeline, and Cuahtemoc. Though they'd constructed most of the buildings within the mix of tropical and deciduous trees with brick, the school's crown jewel was certainly the enormous, thirty-layered stone temple situated at the foot of the hill, just before the lagoons. Aptly named Founders, the temple towered over everything else, and at its peak, a statue of a great feathered serpent clucked its mandibles disapprovingly at anyone who dared stare at it for too long. At the temple's base, a snarling statue of

* Chapter 10: A Hutchinsonian Masterpiece *

a large bear—an osorius—guarded the west while a flapping eagle statue surveyed the east. Four mossy, wooden bridges provided passage over a circular river surrounding Founders, linking the main temple to the other dormitories on campus, along with the academic building further up the hill.

Oliver looked at each of the buildings with a fond smile on his face. Up until Emma prodded him in the back.

"C'mon," she said, starting down the hill. "No use in waiting around for Beto. I'm sure he'd love an opportunity to kick us all the way down."

Oliver grunted in agreement, taking two steps at a time until he caught up with her. "Technically," he said, grinning at her side, "I never said I was against fighting Beto while at *school*. Just that we shouldn't fight him in public."

Behind them, Lance chuckled, but Oliver only had eyes for the smallest of smiles that had formed on Emma's lips.

Oliver only got to revel in his victory for a second.

From further below, a sound like a roaring gorilla echoed across the stone stairs, crashing against their ears in a wave.

"Hmm," Merri mused from above Lance's shoulder.

"Indeed," Rasmus agreed, pausing to levitate next to Emma. *"A boisterous boy approaches us through the jungle—your brother, by the looks of it."*

"My brother?" Oliver asked, scrunching his face together in confusion.

A hand appeared on his shoulder, making him jump.

"Mine," Lance said, shaking his head in resignation.

NOVA 02

Before Oliver could think to ask, "so what?", Lance shuffled his feet to bury them slightly into the stone beneath him.

Then, from just off the main staircase, Emma tugged on his shirt and motioned for him to join her. "Might not want to be next to Lance right now."

Oliver pushed his lips together appreciatively and side-stepped to join her just as a blur of pink, yellow, and green charged through a rustling bush to collide with Lance.

It was a good thing Lance had bent his knees and lowered his chest to intercept Elton, otherwise the much larger Wyatt brother would have tackled Lance into the hillside.

"LANCE-A-LOT," Elton shouted as he crushed Lance in a hug. Last year, Oliver remembered Elton's hug nearly popping Lance's eyes out of his head. This time, however, Lance mirrored his brother's energy, manic grin and all, as his entire frame crackled with Power.

"Did Elton teach you more than just how to lift weights this summer?" Emma asked with a raised eyebrow.

"AND YOU TWO!" Elton yelled, ignoring the question.

Emma took a step back and raised her sleeved hand. "Ehh, I'd rather keep my ribs where they are, thank you very much."

Elton raised his shoulders and dropped them, shifting gears quickly to face Oliver. Waggling his eyebrows, he offered Oliver a huge, knotted hand.

Without hesitating, Oliver clasped it and went to pull in Elton for a hug. Elton pulled back harder. *Much* harder.

* Chapter 10: A Hutchinsonian Masterpiece *

"Yes," Elton muttered as he crushed Oliver until his bones cracked. "This is nice. Very nice."

Desperate for oxygen, Oliver searched for the same crackling energy he'd seen Lance employ since the day before. He found it waiting for him in his chest.

Elton released him with his brow raised. "How did you learn my trick so quickly, huh? LANCE?!"

"I didn't say a thing," Lance peeped.

Oliver raised his hands for peace. "I just pick things up quickly, okay?"

"I'll say," Elton chuckled, taking a step back. "Look at you! If you had any more energy on you, you'd be a lightning bolt."

Oliver looked down at his arms and legs. A sheen of red energy positively glowed off his frame. Yelping, Oliver released the sense of Power he'd latched onto, dropping the glowing red energy in an instant.

"What did I just do?" he asked, opening and closing his fists. Though his heart now beat as fast as if he'd just run a race, he felt otherwise fine.

Elton resumed smiling and slapped his hand down on Oliver's shoulder. The force of the motion made his knees buckle. "You just flared your Power, my man. How'd it feel?"

Oliver took a moment to think before replying. "Powerful," he muttered stupidly. "It felt a lot like when I tap into Wisdom. But I didn't realize I could do the same for Power."

Elton shrugged, looking bored all of a sudden. "It's no secret, really," he said, turning to lead them all down the stairs. "It's called 'flaring' and Belk

NOVA 02

will teach you about it this year. I only got Lance started on it early to help with his weight training."

He kept talking about training, going into detail about Lance's improved bench press and deadlift numbers, so Oliver ignored him, and whispered to Emma instead.

"Have you ever flared Bravery before?"

Emma furrowed her eyebrows to think. "Not sure to be honest."

Oliver blinked at her, unamused and unimpressed with the answer.

Emma blinked back, taking the hint, but even then, she hesitated. After a moment, she even began pulling at her hair. Then, she lowered her voice, forcing Oliver to step closer so that he could hear.

"Don't laugh, okay?" she finally whispered. "But I'm not sure I've ever *needed* to flare Bravery."

Oliver pulled his head away and gave her an appraising, side-eyed look.

Emma let go of her hair to cross her arms and roll her eyes. "Oh, stop it! I knew I shouldn't have said anything!"

It was Oliver's turn to be honest. "I wasn't making fun! I told Beto the same thing once last year!"

Emma's frown transitioned into a barely suppressed a grin. "And what did he have to say to that?"

"You know what? I think it *genuinely* surprised him. For once, he didn't have anything jerky to say. Doesn't sound like he has any Braves in his life."

"Wait?" Emma interjected. "Are you telling me James isn't a Brave? What is he then?"

✶ Chapter 10: A Hutchinsonian Masterpiece ✶

Oliver hesitated, trying his best not to laugh. "I thought he was a Powerhead?"

"More like a *butt*-head, amirite?" Lance interrupted.

Emma snorted with laughter.

"Oli," Elton asked, crestfallen. "Are you not even listening to your workout regimen right now?"

Merri and Rasmus exchanged unamused flitters of their tongues.

"Now, really, Lance?" Rasmus grumbled. *"Must you be so crass?"*

Oliver was tempted to join Emma in her fit of snorting laughter, but hearing Rasmus' voice made his stomach twist with pain again. He distracted himself by bounding down the last several steps necessary to arrive at Hutch, where several familiar faces were tossing around a pigskin ball.

Oliver grinned at the sight. Though he'd had fun with Santiago over the summer, nothing quite beat the joy of playing sports, breaking rules, and making fun of stuffy professors with fellow teenagers. And though he *would* miss Founders Hall—where he, Emma, and Lance had lived during their extraman year—he was excited to be in Hutch, where practically everyone was someone Oliver could confidently call a *friend*.

He hurriedly wiped away a tear let out for his younger self. He'd never quite fit in at Hunterton High, his old school on the Original Side of the Key. But at Tenochprima Academy it didn't matter if he looked a bit different or acted a bit strange, because *everyone* acted a bit different and a bit strange.

NOVA 02

"Oli!" a voice shouted from the group of boys and girls passing around the ball in front of Hutch.

Oliver didn't waste time darting down the last few steps to give the voice's owner a hug.

"Appreciate you embracing like a normal person," Abe muttered. When they separated, he sneered at Elton and Lance, adding, "unlike these brutes."

When Abe continued, he was forced to ignore several pokes to the ribs from Elton. "Rumor has it you got up to some real Trinova stuff at the end of last year… and maybe some more this summer?"

Oliver maintained his grin despite wanting to frown as Abe looked over him. "Possibly…"

"If it isn't THE Trinova?" another voice grunted. This one was deeper and belonged to Joel, Elton's best friend. He hugged a lot more like Elton than Abe, forcing Oliver to tap into a spark of Power to keep his organs from being crushed. "Glad to have you in Hutch this year. The other dorms won't stand a chance!"

"Yesss," Elton agreed, eyeing Oliver as if he were a choice cut of meat. "A blank tapestry, ready to be turned into our very own Hutchinsonian masterpiece."

Oliver chuckled, shook his head, lowered his shoulder, and barged past.

* Chapter 10: A Hutchinsonian Masterpiece *

"Won't even give us a hint of what you were up to?" Abe asked, raising his voice hopefully as Oliver stepped away.

"Nope," Emma replied on his behalf.

"Not yet, at least," Oliver added with a shout over his shoulder. Behind him, he saw Lance patting Abe on the shoulder consolingly.

Abe recoiled at the pat. "Geez, you Wyatt boys keep getting bigger and bigger." Where Lance and Elton were barrel-chested and thick-legged, Abe was narrow and skinny, like Oliver, but stretched slightly taller and narrower. That and he wore glasses for some strange reason.

Still grinning, Oliver pressed forward to say hello to the rest of the group. Se'Vaughn Kirk and Trey Kemper were there. They gave him mock bows, proclaiming, "long live the King of Wisdom," to poke fun at one of the many ways Beto had tried insulting Oliver during their extraman year. Other familiar faces included Valerie Adams—Emma's short, blonde roommate— and a tall, confident girl whom Oliver recognized as one of Emma's old residential advisors, or RAs, Lizzie Korzelius. Last but not least—

"Brantley!" Oliver shouted when he saw Abe's roommate.

Brantley was just as heavy as Elton, only without any of the muscle. He snuck Oliver a side-eyed, aloof swing of the eyes and even continued tossing the pigskin back and forth with another legacy Founders RA, Clay Kim.

"You owe me, García," he finally said.

If Oliver hadn't seen the corner of Brantley's mouth twitch, he might have worried his old RA was angry. "Blackwood chewed me and Abe out something fierce after you did whatever it was you did at the end of last year. I better get a damn good explanation, otherwise you better believe I'll be throwing your skinny a—,"

"Arms into detention," Abe finished.

Oliver scowled. His bright mood had come crashing down at the mention of Blackwood.

"He's still teaching, then?" Emma snarled, reading Oliver's mind.

Abe tilted his head to raise an eyebrow at Oliver. "Shouldn't he be?"

"You have *no* idea," Lance interrupted, his eyes downcast.

With his palms open-faced for answers, Brantley looked from Lance to Emma, who crossed her arms defiantly, and then Oliver.

When Oliver shook his head, Brantley clicked his tongue. Then, he glowered at Elton and Joel. "Y'all better tell us what's going on, and quick."

"Nah, uh," Elton replied. He straightened his back and crossed an imaginary X over his enormous left peck. "I don't know a thing!"

Joel shook his head, looking disgusted. "Bro, I've just seen the boy. How 'my supposed to know a thing?"

"What's there to know?" Se'Vaughn interrupted. He, Trey, Valerie, Lizzie, and Clay had drawn closer.

Beginning to feel frustrated, Oliver raised his hands high for silence.

To his great surprise, the move worked. Within half-a-second, everyone stopped speaking and looked right at him. He felt his ears redden at the attention, but went on anyway, doing his best to keep his voice steady.

"Look everyone. I can't exactly tell you what happened after the Coatlball final last year—,"

149

* Chapter 10: A Hutchinsonian Masterpiece *

"Or what we did this summer!" Emma added.

"Or this summer," Oliver agreed. "Because if I do, we'll be putting your lives in danger."

For a moment, Oliver's friends looked towards one another, exchanging curious expressions.

Then, sheer pandemonium erupted.

"Who died and made you King?" Joel growled.

"You'd better hope I don't put *you* in danger!" Brantley shouted, shaking an enormous fist.

Next to them, Abe frowned with disgust, departing from his normally reserved demeanor. "This crap again? You spent all last year sneaking around looking for a freaking *painting* when all you had to do was ask Stevie about it?!"

"Yeah!" Elton grumbled, patting Abe on the back in agreement—the pat sent the thin boy flying into the nearby grass. "We'd have marched you straight to Lalandra's apartment ourselves if you'd just talked to us sooner!"

The commotion didn't stop until Oliver felt his frustration reach a boiling point. "ALRIGHT!" he shouted over the din.

Again, everyone stopped to listen.

"Listen," he said imploringly. While he spoke, he did his best to ignore the way they looked at him with reverent, wide eyes. "We don't even know everything yet. Just give us a couple weeks until we've got a firm strategy in place and then we'll bring you up to speed on how we'll get ready for *The D—*,"

Next to him, Emma slapped her hand onto Oliver's mouth.

NOVA 02

"Uh oh," Oliver thought.

For several moments, nobody spoke. They just stared, fearful and shocked. It made Oliver's skin crawl, reminding him of how the faculty had looked at him after he'd been revealed as the Trinova during the prior year's Ceremony of the Gifts. Back then, only the faculty had truly understood the heritage associated with Oliver's inherited title as a Trinova. While the students had gone off to celebrate and revel in the fact that a myth had come to life, the professors had stayed behind to interrogate Oliver. And for good reason. The last man who'd been rumored to possess Oliver's confirmed talents had ended up becoming *The Damned*.

* Chapter 10: A Hutchinsonian Masterpiece *

NOVA 02

Chapter 11: The Lord of the Squelchers

I'm not sure why it took me so long to meet him, but I've officially met the guy causing all this trouble. His name is Cato Watkin.

28th of August, the second year of the 10th Age

Elton broke the silence first, his expression grim. "If this is a joke,"—he struggled to find the right words—"well, it's not funny. I thought you three were just playing pretend, chasing down old legends and myths!"

"Oli," Abe interrupted, "are you saying what we think you're saying?" He paused to swallow air and adjust his glasses. "Should we be prepping for *The Damned* right now?"

Next to him, Joel tried laughing. "Don't be stupid. *The Damned* is dead!" But nobody laughed along. They all just stared at Oliver, pleading for more answers.

Desperate to pull back time and stop himself from speaking, Oliver closed his eyes to think. *"This is a mistake."* If rumors were to spread at school about *The Damned* being alive and escaping his purgatory, families were likely to hear, and then the press would get involved. Thinking of the press made Oliver's stomach feel hollow. With just his application photo, which made him look like an eleven-year-old, they'd managed to turn Monsieur Lafitte's shop clerk into a drooling fanatic. What could they do—better yet, what *would* they do—if they caught wind that *The Damned* was

* Chapter 11: The Lord of the Squelchers *

liable to escape at any moment? And that the newly revealed Trinova was the one spreading the rumor?

"That can't happen," Oliver told himself.

With his eyes still closed, Oliver's mind raced through the options available to him. He could lie and tell his friends there was nothing to worry about, or he could share more details and swear them to secrecy. Maybe Watkin could teach him how to become a secretor? That way nobody could betray—

"Alright everybody!" Emma shouted. When Oliver flickered his eyes open again, he saw that Emma had stepped in front of him to address the crowd with her chin held high. "Listen up! We don't know anything about *The Damned* and the last thing Oli needs is for any of you to slink off and tell people that we do." She paused to leer at everyone in turn, even pointing at Abe to shake an angry finger. "If you do that—well, Oliver will track you down and all your loved ones, and wipe your miserable lives off the face of the—,"

"Woah!" Lance interrupted, taking his own turn at addressing the crowd. "What Emma is trying to say is that... we'll... umm... we'll just... won't we?"

Thankful for his friends' loyalty, Oliver couldn't stop himself from smiling as he took over with his mind finally made up. "Look, everyone," he said, feeling his confidence surge, "we'll be happy to share what we were up to at the end of last year *and* this summer. But you'll need to give us a bit of time to get settled in at school and figure out what's next. We just learned some new information and we're not even sure what our path forward is yet." Oliver flicked his eyes over Brantley and Abe in particular as he spoke, because he'd caught mutinous scowls developing on their lips. "All I can say is that right now I'm *not* focused on *The Damned,* but on something the Founders asked me to do instead."

The tension in front of Hutch loosened considerably.

"Well, that's a relief," Se'Vaughn muttered.

But his voice was immediately drowned out by Abe, who seemed to have grown taller. "The scroll!" he shouted with glee on his face. "It was REAL, wasn't it?"

Oliver grinned back and waggled his eyebrows. Abe had been the one to tell him about the legend of the scroll last year. In a way, the nerdy boy was partially responsible for kick-starting Oliver's Trinova journey.

As Abe's glee turned fervent, Oliver inwardly rejoiced at the fact that his bait had worked. If his friends thought he was *just* looking for artifacts left by the Founders, all the better. It wasn't a direct lie—he was just keeping the details regarding *The Damned* to himself. The wisdom on his neck itched. Was that a sign he was doing the right thing? Or the wrong thing?

"YES!" Abe began to shout.

Brantley's eyes went wide as saucers as Abe turned to him with what looked like froth building up at the corners of his mouth. "Oh no," he breathed.

"PAY UP BRANT-MAN!" Abe shrieked. "FINALLY! ALL THESE YEARS YOU TOLD ME I WAS CRAZY! HAH! BUT I WAS RIGHT! THE TRINOVA SAYS HE FOUND A SCROLL AND—,"

* Chapter 11: The Lord of the Squelchers *

Brantley flared his Power and growled, silencing Abe immediately. "Alright then, Abraham," he drawled in a deep voice. He fished into his pockets and began pulling out coins that shone purple and light blue. "How much did we agree on?"

"Twenty-five," Abe answered smugly.

Brantley winced as Elton bent over to howl with laughter. Oliver's eyes, meanwhile, popped at the amount of money. Archie had procured just *four* coins for his first visit to the Other Side. That had bought them his textbooks and a full lunch.

Brantley kept pulling more and more Ameys from his pockets with a frown that deepened by the second. When he ran out, Trey and Se'Vaughn's laughter joined Elton's, and Joel had to sprint away to howl the loudest.

"Brantley," Emma said, grinning roguishly as Brantley turned his pockets inside and out, completely empty, "do yourself a favor next time and *never* bet against our Trinova."

After the laughter died down, Oliver followed Abe and Brantley to get settled into his new room in Hutch. As they walked, Oliver felt the weight from their summer adventure with Watkin begin to lighten. It was hard to think about Tupper's eventual escape, or the evil that might accompany it, when stereo systems playing the latest and greatest from Atlanta's rap scene flooded his ears.

Or when watching Joel rile up a crowd for bets on the outcome of something he called the *Lord of the Squelchers* tournament. What the event was, Oliver didn't have a clue—the only hint was the box Joel held in his hands. From it, an occasional burst of fire seared.

Oliver grinned. Gone were the days of his rule-bound extraman year. This year, he'd be one of the "older" students, and that came with a significant number of tantalizing freedoms.

Abe and Brantley dropped Emma off on the first floor before pointing Oliver and Lance towards their room on Hutch's third floor. Oliver smiled some more when he entered his new room, finding it almost identical to their room last year, complete with two full size beds, walk-in closets, wooden desks, nightstands, and even a set of tufted leather armchairs that took up the space on the rear wall between the nightstands and beds.

Elton joined a moment later with Lance's trunk in hand. "Need some help unpacking?" he asked.

"Yes please!" Lance said from the ceiling. He was hanging a thin yellow cloth beneath the room's main light source: a long, narrow section of glowing quartz. "Ah, that's better," he added after jumping down—he'd been standing on his bed—to observe his handiwork with his hands on his hips. Oliver thought it worked well. Instead of the blinding, white light, they now had a softer yellow sheen to their room.

"Yeah, real nice, Michaelangelo," Elton replied flatly as he dumped the contents of Lance's trunk into the middle of the room unceremoniously.

* Chapter 11: The Lord of the Squelchers *

Lance pushed an arm out, which should have sent Elton flying into the wall, but Elton flared Power, so the hit didn't move him an inch.

Grinning mischievously as his crackling energy subsided, Elton dropped the trunk and sat on Oliver's chair before catching an apple from Joel who walked in with his cardboard box under one hand.

"What's Stevie up to?" Oliver asked, wondering about the third Wyatt sibling. Elton and Lance's dynamic was fun enough, but when Stevie was in the room, too? Oliver wasn't sure there was a more entertaining bunch in the world.

"Stevie's gonna be traveling for a bit," Lance grunted.

Elton chewed on his apple loudly. "Wants to *discover* herself," he said in between bites.

Joel shook his box. Slithering noises followed. "Any bets?"

Elton looked Joel up and down. "Which one did Brant-man bet on?"

"The red one. Careful though. I'm giving better odds on Old Blueboo since everyone has the same idea—bet against Brant's first instinct."

"Who said my name?" a voice boomed. Brantley walked in, barely fitting through the door.

Elton took a bite from his apple. "You know, Ms. Joan *does* make salads."

Brantley shrugged. "Don't need muscles to beat your little—."

"Where is Stevie traveling?" Oliver interrupted. "I'm pretty sure Ms. Joan did something similar after graduation, too."

Elton tossed his apple aside and began picking at his ear. "She told Dad she'll be visiting all the places *The Damned* traveled to when he was young, but we'll see." Done with his ear, he flung a glob of wax towards Joel, who raised his box to intercept it.

Joel wrinkled his nose at the earwax that now stuck to his box. "We doing this or not?" he asked.

Elton scrunched his eyebrows together. "Doing what?"

Joel rolled his eyes. *"Lord of the Squelchers,* duh!"

Oliver's ears perked up. Out of the corner of his eye, he saw Lance stand on his tiptoes to try and get a better look at Joel's box.

Elton shot up and smacked his hands, rubbing them together. "Alright, I'll put an amey down on Blueboo."

While Brantley and Elton exchanged exuberant fist bumps followed-up by stoic head-nods, Joel flashed a dazzling smile. "How 'bout you, Oli? What does your Trinova Wisdom tell you?"

"To ask you what's in the box," Oliver thought to himself. *"And not bet."*

Lance looked at a clock situated above Brantley and the doorframe. "Don't we have to be in the Dining Hall in fifteen minutes for the Start of Year Feast?"

"Fifteen minutes, he says," Elton jibed, elbowing Joel in the ribs.

Joel wrinkled his eyes to laugh but went stern as a mourner just as quickly. "Don't be an idiot, Lance. This'll be over in five. Elton!"

"Yes, cap'n?"

"Sound the horn!"

This time Brantley did move out of the way when Elton dashed out of the room flaring Power.

"The horn?" Oliver mouthed at Lance.

* Chapter 11: The Lord of the Squelchers *

Lance shrugged.

A moment later, Elton dashed back inside for a second time, carrying a long, twisting horn. It caught Oliver's eye immediately, reminding him of…

"That's a feathered serpent's horn," he breathed as Lance's jaw dropped. "How'd you get it?"

Elton looked insulted. "Stole it, naturally."

It was Oliver's turn to let his jaw fall.

"You took it from the Bald-Cypress Havens?" Lance hissed. "You *have* to put that back."

Elton shrugged Lance off and began wetting his lips with loud slurps of his tongue.

"That's not even the right sacred beast hideout," Brantley said on Elton's behalf. "Eagles live in Bald-Cypress Havens, remember? The quetzal don't mess with it. They do their rituals and stuff in the Swampy Fortress."

Before Oliver could ask where the Swampy Fortress was, Elton blew into the hollowed-out quetzal horn, letting out a sound like a soft flute. Even though Oliver had expected the noise to be deeper, it had no trouble forcing its way into the deepest recesses of his mind. The sound urged him to do something reckless, resonating with the necklace pendant hanging around his neck. Oliver resisted the temptation, but he had to tap into the Wisdom at the nape of his neck to do so.

As cheers sounded across the dorm, Oliver glanced at Lance who had stepped towards Elton with five ameys in his hand and a fire in his eyes.

"I'll put this much on Blueboo, too!"

NOVA 02

Joel looked at the purple-blue coins with a longing expression, but then shook his head, disappointed. "As much as I'd like to accept your bet, do you even know who Blueboo is?"

"All bets are off now that the horn been sounded!" Elton announced as the room filled with people.

"Tends to make people—," Brantley continued. But then he paused, pushing together his lips to think hard.

"Reckless," another voice growled. It belonged to Abe, who had filed in with the batch of students that now filled Oliver's room.

Elton traced an imaginary X over his heart looking stern, but Oliver didn't miss the way his eyes shifted. Guilt was easy to spot. "We didn't take any bets after the horn!" he insisted.

"Uh-huh," Abe muttered as he sidled next to Oliver. "Stevie had to get Watkin to intervene after kids started losing too much money on this *tournament*."

"What is the tournament, anyway?" Oliver asked as Joel began announcing what "Old Blueboo" and "Big Red" had been up to over the summer.

"A wrestling match," Abe sighed.

"Between what?" a voice to their right asked. Oliver jumped at the sound, turning his head to lock eyes with Emma.

"When'd you get in here?" he managed to spit out, a little more shrilly than he would have liked.

* Chapter 11: The Lord of the Squelchers *

Emma smirked. "Shouldn't a Trinova be better at keeping tabs on everyone in his room?" Oliver blushed as she continued speaking. "I filed in with everyone else, dumb-dumb."

Oliver nodded, but stepped away towards Elton so Emma couldn't see him turn further red. "You've actually been to the Swampy Fortress?" he asked the burly, blonde boy, distracting himself.

"A wizard doesn't reveal his tricks, does he?" Elton replied, tapping a finger against the side of his nose.

Oliver stared back, unblinking and unamused.

Elton's grin weakened before he threw up his hands. "Okay, fine. No, of course we didn't steal it from the freaking quetzal sacred grounds. You'd get killed the second you showed up."

"Then how'd you get it?"

Elton resumed smiling, even wider than before. "Borrowed it from old Bald and Brash, of course."

This time Oliver couldn't help but grin back. *Borrowing* from Professor Blackwood, a man who openly supported Solomon Tupper, was fine by him.

"LADIES AND GENTLEMEN!" Elton announced. "THE MOMENT YOU'VE ALL BEEN WAITING FOR! LET THE LORD OF THE SQUELCHERS TOURNAMENT BEGIN!"

Giddy with boyish delight, Joel rubbed his hands together and pointed at his box. From his finger, he shot out a thin whisp of fire, igniting the box into flames.

NOVA 02

A noise came from inside the box as the flames licked higher and higher until they touched the ceiling.

Skreee!

Oliver backed away, concerned. Judging by the movement in the room, so had all the other rising hardmores.

"You can't just burn those poor animals alive!" Emma shouted angrily.

Oliver looked at Abe who waved a bored hand. "They're *magma snails*, Emma. They're literally hotter than lava."

"What's a magma snail?" Oliver whispered to Lance. "Are they going to melt through the floor?"

Lance shrugged with wide eyes while the cheering from the older students grew loud enough to bounce off the walls. And then, the cardboard collapsed to ash, revealing two snails.

Their shells were on fire.

But that wasn't the only strange thing about them. From the center of the crowd, the creatures wriggled free of their shells, revealing long legs that they already stretched against the side of their respective abandoned homes.

Old Blueboo, Oliver immediately realized, was both old and blue. His skin was dark and cracked, whereas Big Red's looked younger and lighter. But if Oliver were to bet on either of them, he'd be taking Blueboo every day of the week, just based on how nimble he looked.

The snails reveled in the attention.

As Oliver watched with his mouth hanging wide open, Big Red sprouted small rivulets of hair out of her head. She licked her nub-like hands and ran

* **Chapter 11: The Lord of the Squelchers** *

them through her new, shoulder-length locks with a dramatic twist of her head before turning her head dramatically toward her enemy.

Blueboo, didn't bother with changing his appearance, but he did wave at each of the manic juniors and seniors cheering for him. By the time he charged on his long, skinny legs, Elton frothed at the mouth, his stance wide and knees bent, shouting incoherent obscenities with his hands opening and closing. Eventually his excitement locked in on Lance, whom he picked him up, and tossed across the room onto Oliver's bed.

In less than five minutes, Old Blueboo secured Big Red in a headlock with one arm, still gesturing for cheers from the crowd with the other. Only after Joel slapped the stone floor ten times did Blueboo relent, spreading away with his little arms raised past his eye stalks.

With the fight over, Joel corralled the magma snails into a new box, regarding them with all the affection of an overindulgent grandparent. He flicked a crackling red stone towards Old Blueboo before shutting the lid, and Oliver would later swear he saw the snail eat the rock in one bite. The noise levels increased as Abe and Brantley coordinated settling everyone's bets. Eventually, however, the noise did die down, and before Oliver knew it, Abe had muttered *"remasco"* to remove the soot stains and snail goo from the floor and Elton began leading the entire group out the door and towards the Dining Hall for the Start of Year Feast.

NOVA 02

Chapter 12: A New Rule

I can't decide if this Watkin guy is somebody worth pursuing as an ally or better off getting out of our way. One thing's for sure—Watkin drives Tío crazy. Tío won't ever admit it of course, but I can tell. I've always been good at reading people.

2nd of September, the second year of the 10th Age

As soon as Oliver crossed the open-faced, forty-foot entryway into the Dining Hall, Tolteca, the school's public announcer, appeared before him. Not a man, or a beast, Tolteca was a sentient, floating sun dial painted turquoise and red. At times he'd attach himself to a crevice made to fit his six-foot diameter in the middle of the double-sided, curved staircase leading up past the foyer to the Dining Hall. More often than not, however, he chose to levitate across the foyer, or even other parts of campus, spinning in circles to grimace or blow raspberries at students who got too close to him. Despite the sundial's shenanigans, Oliver knew Tolteca was as old, if not older, than the feathered serpents that called Tenochprima home. If you were ever to catch Tolteca in the right mood, he'd likely prove to be full of Wisdom.

Emma giggled when Oliver pointed that observation out to her. "Yeah?" she said, sardonically. "I bet Xihuacota would be just as helpful down at her lagoon house."

* Chapter 12: A New Rule *

Right on cue, Tolteca stuck out his steel tongue. It flittered unnaturally between his teeth, which were made of opals, jade, and amethysts, to blow a raspberry.

"AT LAST!" Tolteca shouted. Oliver grinned at the sound of Tolteca's voice. There wasn't anything else quite like it. When the sundial spoke, it sounded somewhat like Archie's, but more robust, as if it were weighed down by a level of history and authority no living thing could ever hope to muster.

"THE HUTCH CONTINGENCY BLESSES US WITH ITS PRESENCE."

Oliver took a step back lest the steel tongue permanently re-arrange his face.

"Tolteca!" Elton yelled as though he were addressing an old friend. He even tried grimacing like the sundial, but it proved a cheap imitation. Tolteca evidently agreed, because he ignored Elton entirely, turning back to Oliver.

"YOU CHILDREN WERE ALMOST LATE. HAD YOU DISRESPECTED ME SO, YOUR PUNISHMENT WOULD HAVE EARNED A PLACE IN OUR HISTORY BOOKS!"

As Emma and Lance laughed nervously, Oliver winked at Tolteca. "Rest assured, we'd never be late, Tolteca, sir."

"JUST LIKE YOU'D NEVER OVERSEE A WRESTLING MATCH BETWEEN MEMBERS OF AN ENDANGERED SPECIES, AM I CORRECT?"

NOVA 02

Oliver's smile dropped faster than Lance gasped. Nearby, he saw Elton, Joel, Brantley, and even Abe looking down at their feet or up at corners in the ceiling.

"Technically," Emma interjected as Oliver stammered, "the Trinova never *oversaw* anything, he just watched—,"

"JUST KIDDING!" Tolteca interrupted loudly enough for a batch of students on the upper landing to glance their way and pause their conversations. "UP YOU GO! BEST NOT KEEP THE HEADMASTER WAITING!"

"Sir, yes, sir!" Elton shouted back with a mock salute. Then, before Tolteca could change his mind, they darted up the stairs and into the Dining Hall.

"Remind me to tell Elton not to try any crazy stunts in our room this year," Oliver whispered towards Lance as they walked into the Dining Hall.

Lance chuckled and fiddled with the clasp that kept his warhammer attached to his belt. "Good luck," he answered dryly.

"Did we really look *that* stupid?" Emma breathed, taking Oliver's attention away from Lance. He followed her outright stare which lay on several faces he didn't recognize.

Extramen.

"Even stupider," Elton answered, nodding sagely. "C'mon. We usually sit over here."

Oliver kept his attention on the fresh faces for a moment longer while Emma, Lance, Elton, and Joel moved towards Se'Vaughn, Trey, and Valerie, who'd sat down at the Hutch table. Though there was technically

* Chapter 12: A New Rule *

no assigned seating, Elton was known to lift anybody out of his chair and throw them two tables down.

Before joining them, Oliver remained in place to peer around at all the new faces. After a moment, he realized he stood by himself, but he didn't mind. Before Tenochprima he'd almost always stood by himself. And besides, Emma was right. These new extramen looked *young*. At best, most of them looked like new-born foals, curiously regarding the room with wide eyes and open mouths. At worst, some stared, clearly frightened about something—

"They're staring right at me. They're frightened of me."

Feeling a gush of blood rushing to his ears, Oliver scampered to the Hutch-dominated table, trying to keep as low a profile as possible. Fortunately, Headmaster Lalandra stood up from the faculty table at the same time as he moved towards the open seat between Emma and Lance.

The Dining Hall hadn't been altered much since Oliver's first year. Every twenty or so yards, thick stone columns lined with torches stretched from floor to ceiling, and in between them, dozens of oak and mahogany tables were arranged. The faculty always sat closest to the western wall while the older students sat furthest away, around the eastern and southern perimeters. This left the extramen to take the more central tables in the room, which were situated just past a ten-yard gap between the faculty tables and the student-body ones. As Oliver sat down, his eyes lingered on a thirty-foot-wide staircase on the opposite side of the foyer entrance, which he now knew led to the Temple's twenty-eight other floors. He grinned to himself as he remembered the times he, Emma, and Lance had ventured up those stairs to investigate for clues hinted at by the Iguana's Scroll.

Only when he blinked to focus his eyes did he realize he'd been accidentally staring at an extraman girl with shoulder-length, black hair. Panicking, he blinked several times to accentuate that he'd not been focused on her. Thankfully the girl took the hint, blinking and then looking away awkwardly until her eyes settled on Lalandra.

Oliver still cringed. He was *the* Trinova. He couldn't stare around at people, even if accidentally.

"If I have some extraman start spreading rumors about me..." he thought to himself. Cautiously, he ventured a flick of his eyes back at the girl.

She was *very* pretty.

Feeling like an idiot, he shifted his gaze away again, this time to focus on the Headmaster. Like the Dining Hall, Elodie Lalandra didn't look all that different from last year. Athletically built, if not a little thin, Lalandra exuded a presence that could silence debate halls. As always, she wore a slim pantsuit—this time navy—and a white blouse along with a purple hair bow that matched the frames of her circular glasses. Around her neck, a chain with jewels of azure blue cascaded over her blouse.

She hopped on top of the Guides' table—a stone and quartz block that took up the northern quadrant of the room—and raised her hands.

For a moment Oliver wondered how she commanded so much respect. Everyone in the hall had already stopped speaking several seconds before she'd even opened her mouth. Was it out of fear? Respect? Or something else?

* Chapter 12: A New Rule *

"Good evening and welcome!" Lalandra announced in a voice that nestled into Oliver's head like soothing water. Only twelve months prior, as an inexperienced extraman, Oliver had taken Lalandra's warming presence as a good sign. Now that he knew how manipulative Solomon Tupper had been, however, he scrunched his nose instead.

Curious, he flared Wisdom from the back of his neck. Within a second, everything but his focus drifted away, leaving his headspace clearer than before. When he resumed staring at Lalandra, though her voice still sounded comforting, he no longer felt the same calming sensation as before. Had Lalandra been directly influencing his will? The thought disturbed him.

Lalandra went on. "Yes, welcome! Especially to our older students. Your extraman counterparts have been busy these last few days during their orientation. Dare I say it, they've settled in quicker than any other class in living memory."

"That's interesting," Abe muttered from across the table. Next to him, Lizzie and Brantley nodded.

Oliver chanced a whisper back. "Why's that?"

Abe scratched his neck before replying. "Well, usually she just says the new kids survived orientation. Why's she focused on them settling in so well?"

"Hmm," Oliver answered, thinking to himself.

"Maybe," Lalandra continued, "they'll put up an even better fight than last year's extramen. Could we see the Emerald Trophy stay at Founders Hall for two years running?"

NOVA 02

Dozens of older students jeered from their tables as Lalandra cupped a hand to her ear, encouraging the noise.

"Or perhaps Champayan will reclaim their throne!"

This time, the jeering was deafening, coming loudest from Joel and then Elton after Joel elbowed him in the ribs.

"Then again," Lalandra went on with a raised eyebrow at Elton in particular, "will Hutch look to retain their first title in over a decade now that they've recruited several of last year's winners?"

This time, nobody jeered. Instead, conversations broke out at nearly every table. Oliver didn't need to bet on what—or *whom*—the conversations were about. If he hadn't just tapped into his Wisdom, he suspected he would have felt a flare of frustration. *"Why'd she have to mention me?"*

"Only time will tell," Lalandra finished, shrugging her shoulders cryptically. Then, she winked. "What we do know, however, is that *everybody* will be following our school rules this year, which includes a *new* one worth calling out!"

"That's also a first," Abe muttered again from across the table, just loud enough for Oliver to catch it.

Abe hadn't been the only student to notice the abnormality of the announcement. "Yes, yes," Lalandra mused while waving a finger at the older students who'd taken up conversation at the Preston table. "This is the first new rule of my tenure. But fret not, for the rule is simple and should not interfere with your lives much, if at all."

Oliver drummed his fingers on the table as Lalandra breathed in during a dramatic pause.

171

* Chapter 12: A New Rule *

"Until otherwise advised, all interviews with non-school entities, in-person or indirect, are banned."

Oliver wasn't the only one to look around with a confused brow. He quickly wished he hadn't, however, after locking eyes with the pretty extraman again. To have called her cute would have been an understatement. Cringing at himself, Oliver automatically shifted his eyes to Emma. When she settled her own gaze on him, clearly confused, he looked away again.

Lalandra continued waving her finger, this time at every section of the room in turn. "A zero-tolerance policy accompanies our new rule. Should you elect to break the rule, you will be expelled on the spot, *without exception.*"

"What on Earth?" Lance hissed in Oliver's left ear.

From Oliver's right, Emma recovered from her confusion. Grinning mischievously, she whispered, "are there any other zero-tolerance policies we should know about? Did we break any last year?"

Lance chuckled as Lalandra recounted the more familiar rules listed within Tenochprima's 256 page rulebook. "No chance we didn't between the lagoons and *sorbelux*. Surprised Lalandra didn't even talk to us about it last year."

Oliver started smiling, too, but then he noticed the number of unbridled stares coming from their Hutch-mates. Elton looked the least subtle, nodding at each of their words with an insane combination of twisting blonde eyebrows and flashing teeth.

NOVA 02

Oliver coughed in his throat, motioning his head towards the would-be-overhearers.

Lance looked up—a little too slowly for Oliver's tastes—and furrowed his brow. When he finally caught on, his cheeks turned pink, and he had enough sense to pretend to focus on Lalandra's retelling of the school rules. Emma, however, looked Oliver directly in the eyes—no doubt so he couldn't miss her green ones rolling all the way back into her head. With her face so close to his own, however, she got a different reaction out of him than she no doubt intended. Being so close to her freckled face made his insides squirm, and he was convinced a seasoned wiser might pick up on just how much his heartrate increased. To avoid risking a facial expression that might betray him, he closed his eyes and took in a deep breath.

He nearly buckled at the aroma of lilac and coconut that Emma's mere passing presence left behind.

"Eyy," a couple voices across the table crooned as Oliver opened his eyes. Se'Vaughn and Trey were smirking at him with raised fists close to their chests. Se'Vaughn even winked.

Oliver ignored them, flicking his attention towards Lalandra again.

Only he tried to. Instead, he crossed stares with the pretty extraman for a third time.

He almost cursed out loud, but recovered just in time, flaring Wisdom so acutely that his chair shook. It didn't matter that Se'Vaughn and Trey were exchanging whispers with Joel and Abe, or that he could still smell

* Chapter 12: A New Rule *

Emma, or that the pretty extraman's eyes lingered on him for a half second longer. With Wisdom, he could focus on what mattered.

"And what is that exactly?" he asked himself.

With Watkin personally looking into the location of the Fire Drake's Cavern, that left Oliver, Emma, and Lance to prepare for Solomon Tupper. Watkin had suggested they begin with a thorough investigation into Tupper's past. But why? Why couldn't Watkin just tell them about Tupper?

"What does he want me to discover for myself?"

And then there was the small matter of the nightmarish fiend that haunted *The Damned*. How was he supposed to figure out what a pesadriya looked like? He hadn't exactly heard of anybody keeping a "how-to" pamphlet on defeating a boogieman nobody knew anything about. Watkin seemed to think it had reached its "final form," but Oliver wasn't even sure what that meant.

Somebody nudged him in the ribs, bringing his attention back to the Dining Hall. It had come from his right.

"What?" he whispered towards Emma.

"Are you listening to this?" she asked, her eyes wide. Then she pointed to Lalandra, who seemingly had everyone's complete attention but Oliver's. Her voice echoed around the Dining Hall, unencumbered by any of the usual whispers, coughs, or laughs coming from the students.

"Yes, most frightening news," Lalandra said, shaking her head gravely. Oliver's ears perked up. "But it's not the first time we've heard tales of ghost, specters, or ghouls, is it? Take for instance *Xihuacota*. Though she haunts our shores, what is her underlying goal?"

NOVA 02

"To find someone to knit with," Abe answered in a voice that dripped in sarcasm. "Oh no," he added as every eye in the room locked onto him. Oliver looked past his old RA's blushing cheeks, focusing on the skepticism he'd seen in the eyes behind the glasses.

"Exactly," Lalandra continued. Shuffling noises ensued as everyone turned to face her again. "It is likely that the events in Goodwin Forest, Tennessee are no more than a sensationalized distraction from the media." She raised a pointed finger and shook it. "Let that be a lesson to each of you on power and influence—will you allow the thoughts and opinions of others to govern your mind this year?"

As several dozen students replied, "no, Headmaster Lalandra," Oliver leaned towards Emma and whispered as quietly as possible.

"What's Goodwin Forest?"

Emma closed her eyes for a second, tightening her lips. When her eyelids blinked open again, she looked irritated. "Honestly, Oli, you gotta be better about paying attention." When she finished speaking, she gestured with her head towards the other Hutchites students watching them brazenly.

Oliver grunted in frustration but conceded the point. No sense in running through their theories on anything suspicious in public. His station was too important for that now. Frustrated, he looked around the Dining Hall as Lalandra finished her speech and sat down.

Right next to Broderick Blackwood.

* Chapter 12: A New Rule *

Chapter 13: The Dance of Diplomacy

Tío and Blackwood were old schoolmates. Explains why they get on so well.

10th of September, the second year of the 10th Age

Whatever calm Oliver had managed to force over himself evaporated at the sight of Dean Blackwood. In no time at all a boiling inferno began in his stomach. It rose all the way to his chest until it nestled into his heart, demanding he take action against the evil man sitting only a dozen yards away.

Hearing about Blackwood retaining his position at school was one thing. But seeing him in the flesh, insufferable bald head and all, was another issue altogether. Tall as a tree and strong like an ox, Blackwood had always reminded Oliver of photographs of Santiago's old army instructors. He was a man of Power, with large, hairy forearms, and a deep voice that Oliver could hear even now, through the ruckus in the Dining Hall, as the unbearable man exchanged jokes with Headmaster Lalandra and Professor Desmoulins. For half a moment, Oliver relished the boil he felt in his blood—he could use that emotion—tap into it to drive his magic. But then he flared Wisdom, and felt the inferno reduce to a simper.

Blackwood had orchestrated an attempt to free *The Damned* at the end of last year, so how had Lalandra not fired him? Shouldn't he have been incarcerated? But there Lalandra was, talking with Blackwood as if he were an old friend, even laughing at something Desmoulins just said.

* Chapter 13: The Dance of Diplomacy *

"How," Lance's voice hissed through gritted teeth, "is Blackwood still teaching at this school?"

Across the table, Abe ordered his food nonchalantly, appearing entirely disinterested. But Oliver recognized just how stiff the older Wiser had become—he'd be listening to their every word.

"Forget it," Oliver whispered back to Lance, tilting his head towards Abe.

"Listen, Oli," Abe said, readjusting his glasses. "We get it. You've got to figure a few things out before you can bring us in. But it's like Stevie said last year. You're gonna have to *trust* us at some point."

Elton and Brantley opened their mouths to add more, but Oliver ignored them, allowing Lance to do the replying for him. While Abe spoke over Lance, insisting Oliver, Emma, and Lance trust them sooner, Oliver shifted his focus back to Lalandra, Blackwood, Desmoulins, and... Professor Watkin.

At the faculty table, Watkin had joined the conversation, and the four professors now spoke as if they were best of friends, catching up over their respective summers with too-cheery grins and overly high-pitched laughs.

Before Oliver knew what he was doing, his stare turned into an open leer.

How could they be so cheery together? Watkin definitely worked *against* Blackwood and Desmoulins—Oliver knew that for a fact—and he'd even heard Watkin once refer to them as "useless excuses for human beings." Hadn't they almost broken out into a fight at the edge of the lake last year, too?

NOVA 02

But here they were, smiling and laughing as if nothing had happened.

"It's just pretend," he realized.

Oliver's leer tightened as comprehension, sharp and cold, forced its way into his mind. There was a greater game being played by the adults—one where dishonesty and manipulation governed over everything else. It was a symptom leftover from Solomon Tupper's rise to Power, and Oliver knew he'd need to unravel it before he could begin trusting anyone.

His Wisdom vibrated on the nape of his neck in agreement. He took that as a good sign, but just before turning back, he settled his leer on Lalandra for a moment longer. He knew he could trust Watkin. But what about Lalandra? Did they share a trust? Were they playing the same game? Even if they were, did they want the same outcomes?

"Didn't Watkin say Lalandra owed him a favor?"

"How 'bout you, Oli?" a voice said, crashing into Oliver's thoughts.

Oliver nearly launched himself from his chair as he dropped his leer at Watkin—that wouldn't be good for optics—and faced Brantley with a smile, pretending he'd been paying attention all along.

Brantley shared an unconvinced frown with Abe before speaking again. "Real subtle, there, brother."

"You really do need to work on your facial expressions," Abe agreed, grimacing.

"I said," Brantley barked, "you worried about Goodwin Forest or not?"

Oliver looked to Emma and Lance for help, wishing he'd heard the preceding conversation, but Emma was in deep conversation with Lizzie, whom she hero-worshipped, so no help would come there. Lance,

* Chapter 13: The Dance of Diplomacy *

meanwhile, was going over a spreadsheet on Elton's notebook, saying, "absolutely not. His legs can't handle that many squats yet."

Sighing, Oliver settled for a slow shake of his head. "I'm the Trinova," he hedged. "Bravery, remember?"

Brantley pressed his lips together and nodded appreciatively, exchanging mirrored expressions with Joel. He tried to do the same with Abe, but the bespeckled boy tsked loudly, garnering the table's attention. "You're not *really* incapable of being afraid." But when Emma and Lizzie, who were both Braves, crossed their arms, Abe blanched. "Y'all really are fearless?! Like nothing at all when you duel people?"

Oliver grinned, welcoming the distraction. "Of course, we can feel fear." Then, with a wink, he added, "but not much."

For once the Powerheads at the table laughed normally. No boisterous echoing, or dramatic run-offs, just real laughs. Inwardly, Oliver wondered whether that was because they were a bit out of their comfort zone talking about Bravery. Either that or it simply came down to the fact that none of them had cracked the joke.

Oliver nearly jumped in his seat for a second time. This time because of Emma. She'd leaned in during all the laughter and put a hand on his shoulder as she crinkled her nose, chuckling, with the rest of them.

Oliver closed his eyes and flared Wisdom. Was he really going to have to do that every time she touched him? Or every time he smelled her? Or every time she visited his thoughts?

"Hmm. Most troubling. Great, now I sound like Archie. Oh, Archie. Hope you're okay."

NOVA 02

"Alright, Ms. Joan," Lance said as if he were announcing a game of Coatlball. Oliver's eyes snapped open.

Dramatically, Lance stood, waving aside heckles from Elton and Joel and then table-pounding from Valerie and Lizzie. Continuing with his theatrics, he rolled his muscled shoulders, cracked his knuckles, and unclipped his warhammer from his belt, reminding Oliver more of Stevie, not the quiet, little boy with wild blonde hair he'd met at the start of last year.

"MS. JOAN!" Lance shouted with a tap of his hammer on the Dining Table. "IT'S MY CHEAT DAY, AND I'D LIKE SOME BEEF BRISKET SERVED WITH ALLLLL THE FIXINGS!

I'M TALKING HUSH PUPPIES!"

"MM!" Elton shouted.

"FRIED OKRA!"

"OO!" Joel exclaimed.

"SOME MAC AND CHEESE!"

"Yeah, yeah," Brantley agreed, nodding his head as though Lance were delivering a sermon. Pushing his lips in and out, he stuffed a napkin under the collar of his shirt in preparation.

"AND FRESH COLLARED GREENS!" Lance finished.

A second later, the Hutchites cheered as a feast popped into existence, followed by a piece of floating parchment paper. As the boys celebrated—Elton even tried flipping the table with a flare of Power—Emma snagged the parchment before it fluttered more than an inch and flicked her eyes over the text.

* Chapter 13: The Dance of Diplomacy *

When she finished reading, she rose a triumphant fist. "MS. JOAN SENDS HER APPROVAL!"

More cheering followed, and Oliver noticed several heads from nearby tables turn to witness the commotion. By then, however, the Dining Hall had become a raucous affair, so Oliver did his best to not overthink the extra attention.

He knew from experience that most of the extramen would keep their attention on the Guides' quartz table. Even he couldn't stop himself from watching as a continuous stream of choice cuts spawned over the table, allowing the sacred beasts a rare opportunity to gnaw, break, hack, squelch, and gulp without restraint or limit. The giant eagles proved particularly disgusting, often times eyeing up a colleague to offer a polite sharing of regurgitated matter.

As Oliver stared around the room, he chanced a glimpse at the Champayan table. It didn't take him long to locate Beto's dark, curly hair. The slightly older boy looked to be approaching his older cousin's height, at around six-foot-three-inches, and commanded whatever current conversation the Champayan table was having. Though Oliver couldn't hear, he tried not to retch as he watched Cristina nod along with every word that came out of Beto's mouth.

Oliver's stare lingered a while longer. Beto was commanding more than just Cristina's eyelashes and James' ever-presently blank stare this time. *Everyone* at that table listened to his every syllable.

"Hmmm."

NOVA 02

Then Oliver noticed his fellow Hutch mates had reduced their conversation to whispers.

"What?" he asked, nudging Lance.

Lance tried masking a full-on head tilt by popping a slice of pizza into his mouth at the same time. Though it made him look like he was struggling to eat, Oliver caught on, turning his own head to follow.

None other than Headmaster Lalandra approached their table.

Alarm bells tolled in Oliver's mind as Lalandra's high heels clicked on the stone floors, louder and louder, until she arrived, standing behind Elton with a joyful expression on her face.

"Great to see you all in such good spirits this start of year!" she said.

Unsure of how to reply to something so open-ended, Oliver nodded his head with a polite smile.

Abe replied first. "You, too, Headmaster. Good summer, I hope?"

"The best!" Lalandra replied. Her expression wrinkled into a deeper smile that seeped into her eyes. "Ventured as far as South America this time!"

Abe beamed, sitting taller in his chair. "More research then, I take it?"

"More so leisure this time," she replied. Oliver noticed the smile retreat to just her lips as she spoke. "I do worry the artifacts I seek were either long ago destroyed or, at least, taken and moved elsewhere."

* Chapter 13: The Dance of Diplomacy *

The bells in Oliver's mind shifted to full on foghorns. *"Did she say artifacts? Was Lalandra also looking for artifacts like the Founders' gifts? Did Watkin know?"*

Oliver tried seeing if Watkin was monitoring the conversation or not but couldn't risk taking his eyes away from Lalandra for too long, lest she notice.

"But Professor Chavarría can tell you more during your elective class this year," Lalandra continued, nodding a finger at Abe and then Brantley. "You have *much* theory left to explore."

Then, rather abruptly, Lalandra turned to Oliver, still cheery. "Now I must request a bit of time from our Trinova. Oliver, may I speak with you?"

Hating himself for it, Oliver jumped into the dance he'd watched the faculty play. "Of course," he replied in an overly exuberant tone. "Do you mind if Emma and Lance join us?"

"Of course not," Lalandra answered, impressing Oliver—she didn't miss a trick. "We can't separate life-long friends such as yourselves, now can we?"

When Oliver made to stand, Lalandra rose her hand. "No need." Then she whispered, *"stratum silentii,"* and Oliver felt a dense, cool blanket trickling over his skin.

"Neat trick," Emma said, coolly. "Professor Watkin's already showed it to us though."

Ignoring Emma, Lalandra raised her hands and gestured around them. "Isn't it delightful?"

"It is," Oliver admitted. "How can we help you, Headmaster?"

NOVA 02

"Let's see what you want," he thought to himself. *"No lies. No secrets."*

Lalandra lowered her arms, but otherwise didn't budge from what Oliver assumed was a fake cheery disposition. "Don't you want to know about my summer research?"

"I'd rather know why Professors Blackwood and Desmoulins are still teaching at this school," Emma countered, frowning openly.

"People are watching us, Ms. Griffith," Lalandra said, still smiling. "You would do well to train yourself to not reveal your emotions."

Oliver bit back a retort. But just barely, and only because he knew Lalandra was right.

"Very well," he said, butting in before Emma could say something she might regret. He channeled a smile that could rival one of Beto's best simpers, and widened his eyes at Emma and Lance, beckoning for them to imitate him. "But we'd like to know all the same. Didn't Professor Watkin let you know what Professors Blackwood and Desmoulins tried to do last year?"

"No," Lalandra replied, still smiling. "He did not. Which raises another question. Did you find what you were looking for this summer?"

Oliver's grin fell. He was out of his element here, and judging by Emma's dilating pupils and Lance's thinned lips, so were they. He'd assumed Watkin would have informed the school of Blackwood's and Desmoulins' attempt to recover the artifact and free *The Damned*—why hadn't he?

"Two out of three, eh?" Lalandra continued, making Oliver's stomach drop even further. "That's comforting."

185

* Chapter 13: The Dance of Diplomacy *

"How does she know what we're up to? How does she know I have the necklace and the ring?"

"Headmaster," Oliver finally replied, doing his best to exude confidence. He pushed on, despite knowing in his heart that Lalandra, a seasoned Wiser, wouldn't fall for a raised chest or fake smile. "With all due respect, if Professor Watkin isn't sharing any information with you about... well, what we've been up to recently... then I won't either."

Oliver felt the necklace on his chest hum as he maintained eye contact with Lalandra.

Ever-grinning, the headmaster nodded and clapped, as if the conversation they shared were a delightful re-counting of a play. "I've not re-earned Cato's trust yet, but I will in time. Congratulations on securing the second artifact, and welcome back to school." Then, she turned to leave.

Just as Oliver allowed himself to deflate into his chair, Lalandra turned back, shooting him right back up. "I forgot to mention," she added, for once dropping her smile. "We'll be having one-on-one lessons this year, you and I. Your diplomacy needs training."

"My diplomacy?" Oliver replied, unable to keep the doubt out of his voice.

Lalandra shook her head dolefully as he stared at her aghast at the idea of diplomacy lessons. "Yes, Oliver. Your mantle threatens to consume you. I've denied anyone but students, professors, and staff from access to campus grounds this year, and I'm sure you noticed the absurdity of our new rule. I must warn you, however, I cannot protect you should you ever wander off campus."

As Lalandra's heels clicked away one step at a time, the noise in the room returned in deafening fashion. Oliver winced at the pandemonium in his ears, which featured plenty of angry questions from the older Hutchites. And even though he put on a stoic face while he told them Lalandra had simply asked for him to take one-on-one diplomacy lessons, inwardly, Oliver's heart beat faster than it had since he'd watched Watkin annihilate their foes in the Ruins of Snowgem.

"What did she mean about diplomacy lessons?" Emma whispered in his ear as they walked back to Hutch after the feast.

Lance glowered, asking his own questions, too. "Why the hell didn't Watkin tell her about Blackwood and Desmoulins? An-and if he didn't, how come she knows so much about what we were up to this summer?"

Oliver shook his head at both questions, just as in the dark. "What I want to know, is why she said she hasn't 're-earned' Watkin's trust yet."

Lance's glower turned to a confused furrowing of his eyebrows. "You think they don't trust each other? Why?"

"Oh, don't bother," Emma retorted with a dismissive wave of her sleeved hand as they entered Oliver and Lance's room in Hutch. Oliver ensured the door was shut as Emma continued speaking—he didn't know how to perform the *stratum silentii* spell yet. "If you're starting to think that Lalandra is some kind of secret supporter of *The Damned*, forget about it. She knew we were invisible with *sorbelux* the second half of last year and could have punished us whenever she wanted."

* Chapter 13: The Dance of Diplomacy *

"True," Oliver replied, thinking fast. "But that's not what's got me freaked out." He made sure nobody was hiding on the other side of the door before he added, "I just want to know how she lost Watkin's trust to begin with. There's a history between those two, and whatever happened between them is bad news. They're on the same side, against Tupper, but aren't working together? What's that about?"

When neither Emma nor Lance had a reply, Oliver knew he was onto something.

NOVA 02

Interludes III – IV

It had only been a few days since Santiago first learned to wield a hammer in Miyada's armory. Since then, he'd already forged a few throwaway rings, a dagger, and was even well on his way to crafting his first sword. He knew the blade wasn't going to be anything to brag about whenever he finished shaping it, but that didn't stop him from paying attention to every little detail. Forging was rewarding, fun work, and he didn't need a fortune-teller to tell him he wouldn't find a better job for the rest of his life.

Santiago reveled in that truth by swinging his hammer even harder.

Clink! Clank! Clonk!

With every swing, he felt his strength return—strength he hadn't felt in *years*. It gushed through his body as he worked, feeling like energy borrowed from a younger man.

Clink! Clank! Clonk!

Sure, it was tough work, by all definitions of the word. Between the smelting, casting, and hammering, he ended every day feeling sore and covered with at least one new cut or burn. But life wasn't supposed to be easy. Escaping the Sinaloa cartel hadn't been a walk in the park. And neither had been crossing the border with his sister. A little manual labor wasn't about to wear him down.

* Interludes III – IV *

Clink! Clank! Clonk!

Thinking of his sister made did make him frown, however. She'd changed his life when she died fifteen years ago, leaving Oliver in his care. After all the trouble he went through to get her a better life, she went and wasted it.

Santiago's hammer stopped at the bitter thought, shaking his head. That wasn't the right way to think. It wasn't her fault she died, and it wasn't Oliver's fault either.

And yet, Santiago still sighed as he kept beating the metal in front of him.

Clink! Clank! Clonk!

He was never meant to be a father. He'd always been a man of solitude. A man of the military. A man who sailed boats where the coast guard told him he shouldn't. A man who started the days with cigars and ended them with whiskey. Oliver knew it as much as he did, and, though they'd made the father-son dynamic work over the years, Santiago had never been able to shake off an underlying sense of guilt. Whenever he thought negatively of his sister, or got steely-eyed with his nephew, it wasn't because he was actually mad or resentful. It was because he felt ashamed.

Ashamed that he'd never found a better way to raise the boy.

Clink! Clank! Clonk!

Santiago growled at himself as he kept swinging. In the end, Oliver hadn't needed a better father anyway. The boy was pretty much a demigod on This Side of the Key and was likely the only reason Santiago got this job in the first place. A job that made him an apprentice of the best blacksmith in the country. And here Santiago was, feeling bitter about his sister.

Santiago let his frustration go and breathed in the energy the hammer swings gave him instead. He knew this job would eventually help him become his own man again. He'd break through the years of guilt and shame, but it would take time.

"You want to make a club or a sword?" Miyada barked, interrupting Santiago's thoughts.

Santiago didn't even flinch. He'd gotten used to the ornery blacksmith's constant spying by now.

"I'm forging you a sword, Mister Miyada," Santiago grunted.

Miyada cackled, still out of sight. "You keep that troglodyte hammering up and you'll be presenting me a flat sheet of metal."

Santiago's hammer stopped a foot above his head, allowing sweat to drip down his outstretched arm. "Don't you have, este,[5] a customer to deal with today, mister?"

The blacksmith's cackling redoubled, echoing across the cavernous dark room. "Hah! Now don't you get any ideas," he warned. "I don't need a bright-eyed apprentice interrupting a business transaction with their latest and greatest creation."

Santiago allowed a low chuckle. He *had* been thinking about presenting a bright idea, but not in front of a customer.

---

[5] 'Este' is a filler word in México. You'd use "uhm" for English instead.

* Interludes III – IV *

Then, Miyada stepped into view. The man always wore a strange apparatus on his head. Santiago still hadn't figured out what the contraption did, but he knew it had to be for forging.

"Do you have to x-ray me with that thing?" Santiago asked, leering at the lenses protruding from Miyada's head.

Miyada frowned from behind the mask. "I meant that, Santi. If you interrupt me, I will fire you."

"I know," Santiago grunted, shooing the man away using his hammer. "I have work to do, Mister."

Miyada lingered for a moment. "I like you, Santiago. No nonsense. Straight and to the point."

Santiago resumed his hammering. "I'll go easier with the hammer," he promised.

"Good man," the blacksmith replied as he waltzed away and back out of sight.

Santiago kept up his hammering until the sweat on his arm compromised his grip. When he started to worry the hammer in his hand would go flying over his shoulder on an errant swing, he paused to wipe himself off with a towel.

That was when he recognized Cato Watkin's voice.

"Did your little birds find anything in Venezuela?" the professor asked, his voice echoing across the armory as Miyada spoke with a shadowed man at the entrance.

NOVA 02

A pause followed. "Excuse me one moment, Cato," Miyada answered. Then, in a much louder tone he bellowed, "DID I TELL YOU TO STOP HAMMERING?"

Santiago waved a hand over his head apologetically. "Just taking a break, Mister!"

"IT'S MASTER! NOT MISTER!"

"SORRY, MISTER!"

"AND NO BREAKS! DRINK YOUR POTION!"

Santiago resumed striking the metal, but this time he didn't give it all of his attention. Some of it, he left on the echoing whispers.

Watkin seemed interested in something called "Crazylers Rocks?" No, that couldn't be right. "Craybears Blocks?" Santiago shook his head. Whatever they were, Miyada was helping Watkin find them. So, what was that about? He'd have to tell Oliver once he learned more.

After Watkin left, Santiago lifted his completed sword. He chuckled to himself as he looked for any blemishes or bends. Finding a light curve where it shouldn't be, he put the sword back on the anvil.

Clink! Clank! Clonk!

Maybe there was still time to be a decent father figure after all, Santiago realized.

At least, one for a Trinova—Oliver could use a spy watching the comings-and-goings inside the best armory in the country, right?

Grinning self-satisfactorily, Santiago took a moment to readjust the vice holding down the sword. Before resuming his swinging, he took a peek at a nearby cabinet where his rifle and bowie knife winked torchlight at him.

* Interludes III – IV *

Being a spy wasn't the only way he'd help his nephew. All he had to do was convince Miyada to try something new. Something besides swords, axes, hammers, and jewelry.

Something with a little more fire power.

Inside the Teacher's Lounge, Professor Bellona Belk collapsed into her favorite chair groaning louder than the leather. She didn't bother stopping her wrists from slamming into the table in front of her either.

Giggling met her from across the table. If she hadn't known who'd made the school-girl noise, she'd have rolled her eyes all the way back into her head.

"The table be damned," Belk muttered without yet opening her eyes.

Professor Irelda Zapien giggled some more, her silver curls bobbling alongside her. "Shame on you, denting one of Tolteca's tables like that, Bellona. I've seen him throw students into detention for less. What do you think he'll do to you?"

"Tolteca be damned, too," Belk grunted, clicking her eyelids open.

Zapien stared at her from across the table, the picture of cheery mischief. Her square face and button nose always got a wry grin out of Belk, she had to admit. No matter how grumpy she got.

"So what's this about, anyway, Irelda?" Belk went on, getting to the point. Earlier that evening, at the Start of Year Feast, Zapien had whispered in her ear to join her in the Teacher's Lounge for a nightcap, so here she was. "I've got a whole bunch of miscreants in Tancol this year. That Makayla Grant has probably destroyed the common room by now without me there to yell some sense at her."

Zapien laughed some more, somehow looking kinder as her eyes crinkled. Some women really did have it lucky. For as long as she could remember, Bellona Belk had the opposite effect. She made other people frown, not smile. Too intense, or so her husband told her.

"I wanted to see what you were thinking?" Zapien put in mysteriously.

Belk flinched, re-assessing Zapien's innocent expression. Before she could stop herself, she leaned forward in her chair.

"What about?" she asked, pretending like she didn't know.

"Well," Zapien said, having enough self-respect to look uncomfortable. "What did you think about Lalandra's proposition? About re-forming the Whigs?"

Belk drummed her fingers on the dent she'd made in the table. "Ah," she said, feeling a sense of aloofness come over her. She didn't need to give an answer on something like this over a nightcap. Not to Irelda Zapien, that was for sure.

"If Elodie wants me to stick my neck out," Belk answered, looking Zapien directly in the eyes, "she can ask me herself, eh?"

Zapien tried holding onto her kind smile, but it looked forced when she spoke again. "I," she began, stammering slightly, "I assumed you'd be against,"—she paused to look around the room, making sure nobody else was there—"*his* return."

* Interludes III – IV *

Belk stood to leave. "I am," she said, shrugging as she stepped towards the exit. "But I'm not sticking my neck out just yet, thank you very much. If my options are support Lalandra and a fifteen-year-old kid or the guy who took over the world last time he wasn't in purgatory…" She tilted her head from side to side with a melancholic grin on her face. "Well, I ain't picking the kid just yet."

All the way up the stairs to her apartment, Belk tried telling herself she didn't hate the way Zapien's face had fallen when she'd turned her down.

But eventually she gave up. Zapien was right. Belk didn't want to support *The Damned* again. Not after last time.

Chapter 14: The Whigs

Evidently Tío had Blackwood working at that school—at Tenochprima—to keep an eye on some woman for the last couple years. Her name's Lalandra or something like that.

12th of September, the second year of the 10th Age

Oliver didn't immediately rise the morning after the Start of Year Feast. Instead, he took a moment to enjoy the fluffy comforter weighing him down onto his bed.

Santiago had always warned Oliver that too much comfort made people lazy, and while Oliver saw *some* wisdom in his uncle's words, he had to admit it was a lot harder to stress about Solomon Tupper, pesadriyas, Blackwood, Lalandra, and what was sure to be a difficult school year when sandwiched between a plushy mattress and a blanket stuffed with duck feathers—were there extra fluffy ducks on This Side of the Key?

A hulking figure sitting in the tufted armchair next to his bed cut Oliver's thoughts short.

"Elton!" Oliver shouted. "What are you doing in here?"

Early-morning light trickled through the window, barely illuminating Lance's older brother. At the question, Elton turned his attention away from a notebook in his hands to glare at Oliver with disgust.

Then, he raised a finger and made a shushing noise.

* Chapter 14: The Whigs *

Bewildered, Oliver made to speak again. What was Elton doing in his chair? But Elton shushed him again, pointing at Lance who still snored softly in his own bed.

Oliver blinked several times, incredulous at having been silenced twice in his own room. Then, he shrugged. *"I guess,"* he thought to himself, *"this is what living near Elton will be like."*

As Oliver put on dark leather boots, tan breeches, and a blue collared shirt—the school's uniform he'd found in his closet—Elton continued staring at his notebook, occasionally commanding mental edits with an accentuated tap of a finger to his right temple.

Moments later, Joel entered, mouthing apologies for Elton's transgressions, promising many brandings and whippings, while Elton grunted goodbye.

Chuckling, Oliver woke Lance and waited for him to get ready before they met Emma in the Hutch lobby and made their way to the Dining Hall for a breakfast of pepper-and-onion frittata—"for the protein," Lance had insisted with a sage nod of his head—along with croissants and cappuccinos, which Emma insisted they'd enjoy just as much as she had when traveling abroad over the summer.

Despite Ms. Joan's excellent cooking, Oliver's incredulous mood soured significantly when Emma and Lance decided to revisit the previous evening's conversation with Lalandra.

"Why are they so obsessed with politics and diplomacy?" Lance hissed at Emma, slamming his hammer onto the dining table.

NOVA 02

Emma adopted a regal posture and imitated Lalandra. "You would do well to train yourself to not reveal your emotions."

Oliver smiled along politely but didn't commit to a real reply. Between knowing that Lalandra had been at least somewhat right and feeling a swoon in his chest when Emma briefly improved her posture, responding directly would have been a bad idea.

"We're hitched to Watkin's wagon at this point," he finally said. "Lalandra might seem helpful, but if she were trustworthy, Watkin would have told us."

Lance shrugged. Then, between bites of eggs and peppers, he countered, "but Watkin didn't exactly warn us about her though, did he?"

Oliver opened his mouth to reply, but Emma rapped her knuckles on the table loudly.

"Watch out," she said, tilting her head towards the older Hutchites joining them for breakfast.

Lance grunted in frustration. "We'll need Lalandra's private conversation spell if we want to keep this up."

Oliver ignored Lance to pay attention to Brantley and Abe instead.

"I thought," Brantley grunted in his deep drawl as he sat down, "we'd be guaranteed the trophy this year, but Lizzie said that Beto gave a speech to the Champayans last night."

Oliver's attention sharpened at the mention of Beto.

Abe nodded his head, looking over a roster of names on his notebook. "Yeah, she told me that, too. Apparently, he got the whole dorm to start full on cheering by the end of it."

* Chapter 14: The Whigs *

"That's interesting," Oliver thought.

Brantley scowled. "Beto can strut all he wants, but they don't have a Trinova on their team."

Anticipating their stares, Oliver pulled his notebook from his bookbag and pretended to give it his full attention. One look at his weekly schedule really did catch his eye, however. What he saw on it brightened his mood immediately.

"What's got you smiling like that?" Emma chided from over his shoulder.

Lance chuckled, pulling Oliver up. "You look like Elton when he's got a steak on his plate. C'mon, we've only got fifteen minutes to get up the ridge."

Oliver began to splutter as they slapped their bookbags over their shoulders. "We don't have Shielding class! And… and that means—,"

"No Blackwood on Mondays!" Emma chortled, patting him on the back consolingly.

Oliver deflated as he looked down at his notebook again. On his first read-through, he'd somehow missed seeing *Shielding for Intermediates* slotted beneath Tuesdays and Thursdays, and for one, glorious moment he thought he'd somehow gotten out of his least favorite teacher's class.

Emma started laughing. "We saw Blackwood last night! Did you really think he'd just refuse to keep teaching you?"

"Well," Oliver countered, pressing his lips together and raising his eyebrows, "maybe I should offer it up to him? Out of the two of us, I'm not sure who'd be happier if we never saw each other again."

NOVA 02

Emma didn't stop laughing until they entered the Founders foyer.

There they dodged Tolteca's spinning frame—"ENJOY YOUR CLASSES, CHILDREN,"—as they discussed what Professor Zapien might have waiting for them for their first ever hardmore year lesson in *Channeling 201*. Oliver made sure to turn and wave cheerily back at the sundial when they reached the osorius statue outside, and though he couldn't quite make out Tolteca's face at that point, he bet it more likely than not that the sundial had winked at him with a stone lid over one of his emerald eyes.

The air felt palpably muggy when they crossed the southern bridge and began the climb up the hill to the Academic Building. The Founders had built the building's four visible floors and basement high up into the campus' ridge, and though Oliver wanted to think he'd spend a majority of his time down on flatter ground in the dormitories or playing Coatlball, he knew he'd spend just as many hours, if not more, "on the ridge," when attending lessons in the academic building, dodging skeleton monsters in the Simulation Room, or studying in the Research Lab.

Within a quarter of an hour, they took the final set of stairs up to the second floor of the Academic Building without having broken a sweat despite the heat and humidity.

"D'you think it's the oxygen from all the plants?" Lance asked out loud, pointing at the mix of oak, ash, palm, and ceiba trees that covered every available foot of hillside behind them.

"No chance," Emma retorted. "Plenty of leaves on the Original Side of the Key, and we'd be sweating a river over there."

201

* Chapter 14: The Whigs *

Oliver took one last look at the trees and temples behind them before commenting. Between squawking toucans, the occasional feathered serpent flying overhead, or piles of snoring osori, there was always something extraordinary to look at on Tenochprima's grounds. "I'd guess," Oliver finally added, "we're just getting stronger and stronger with magic."

Emma gasped as they entered room 110. Since they were the first to arrive, Oliver turned on the lights with a whisp of energy sent from his ring. "Hold up," she said dropping her book bag unceremoniously on the table nearest to the giant, rectangular mirror hanging at the front of the classroom. "Are you saying magic is,"—she struggled to find the right words for a moment, motioning with her hands—"improving our freaking cardiovascular health?"

Oliver shrugged again. "Why not? I was sweating after that climb last year."

Lance flexed his biceps and waggled his eyebrows. "And here I was thinking all my weight training was the difference."

Professor Zapien burst through the door.

She paused at the doorframe, letting the careening door smack against the interior wall and back into her stout frame. She had been smiling, but she dropped her expression when her eyes locked on Lance's raised and flexed arms. Only when Emma flicked Lance on the forehead did Zapien recover, shaking herself as though she were a dog exiting water.

"If it isn't you three," she said beaming endearingly past her helmet of curly, silver hair.

NOVA 02

Oliver appreciated that she directed her beam at Lance and Emma, too, because ever since he'd become the Trinova, most people didn't even give his friends much of a once-over anymore. Zapien's kindness, however, had always felt genuine, and she reminded Oliver of aunties from his early childhood birthday parties.

"You're in for a treat this year," Zapien said, chuckling as she stepped towards her lectern at the front of the room. With a wave of her hand, the mirror flickered to display the year's curriculum in white text on a black backdrop. Oliver grimaced as he read through the columns of words. There were far more areas of study on this list than their extraman year equivalent.

"Hardmore year!" Zapien continued—more loudly because Se'Vaughn, Trey, Valerie, and several other hardmores had entered. "Yes, as poor, gaping Lance here has just realized, we'll have far more material to cover this year than you did last!"

Whatever cheery conversation Se'Vaughn and Trey had been having ended at the sight of the board. Trey's round face went from handsomely stoic beneath his light-brown hair to openly disgusted.

"Is every professor going to be this mean to us this year?" Se'Vaughn asked, grumbling as he sat down behind Oliver.

"Some more than others," Zapien replied, winking cheerily. Then, as more and more students filed in, she whispered towards Oliver, "make sure you speak with Chavarría after your regeneration class."

Surprised at having been snuck a secret message, Oliver couldn't help but check to see if anyone had overheard. Looking over each shoulder confirmed even Emma and Lance had missed Zapien's subtle injection.

* Chapter 14: The Whigs *

Emma had been busy chatting over the curriculum with Valerie, and Lance had been too busy arguing with Se'Vaughn over who'd gained the most muscle over the summer.

Just as Oliver was about to give Zapien a thumbs-up to indicate he'd received the message, he noticed none of Beto, Cristina, nor James were in their classroom.

A whiff of lilac and coconut froze him in place as Emma leaned close to follow his gaze across the classroom. "Block schedule starting this year, remember?" she whispered. "We won't have Beto in every class anymore."

"Your hardmore year is going to be a *lot* tougher than your extraman one," Zapien announced, bringing all conversations to a close. Despite the dreary proclamation, she paused to smile at each desk. "As far as our curriculum goes, I'll go ahead and tell you now that you'll see a pattern across your teacher's lesson-planning this year." She raised her eyebrows to emphasize her words, pulling her curly bangs up in the process. "Last year, we introduced you to either an application or focus-area of magic. Here in this room, for instance, we learned about channeling, a focus-area of study on our source of magic, Nova, and how to channel its energy in the broadest of senses. In other rooms, you learned about the applications of destruction, shielding and regeneration, along with the other focus areas of biomes, mathematics, history, and political science."

Oliver felt a sliver of impatience needle his brain. They didn't need a rehashing of their prior year lessons. Well, at least he didn't. Instead, he wanted to know what was going to be so different for their hardmore year—wouldn't it just be a continuation?

"For anyone keeping count," Zapien continued, looking stern, "last year you took *five* classes on focus-areas and only *three* dedicated to applications of magic: destruction, shielding, and regeneration."

Appreciative head nods and muttering spread across the room. Oliver even raised his eyebrows. *Does that mean there are more applications?*

Valerie lifted one hand and tugged at her blonde ponytail with the other. "Is channeling not an application, Professor?"

"Excellent question, Ms. Adams," Zapien replied, taking a step away from her lectern to gesture at the mirror. It whirled for a moment before displaying two new lists. "There are five applications of magic, actually, and they are Destruction, Shielding, Regeneration, Conjuration, and Possession!"

"Possession?" Emma whispered into Oliver's ear. "That sounds evil, doesn't it?" Oliver flared Wisdom to stop himself from blushing at the sound of Emma's hushed voice in his ear and fixated on Zapien, nodding along determinedly as she continued to speak.

"Five applications and five focus areas," Zapien continued, swelling with a deep breath as she stared at the lists on the mirror. "And hardly enough time to get through it all. So, we better get started, eh?"

Groans sounded out across the room. Unlike the prior year, when most teachers took the first day of lessons as an opportunity to leisurely introduce the concepts for the year, or even let the students out early, Zapien jumped straight into their new materials. The mirror at the front whirled into motion, returning to its display of the year's curriculum.

* Chapter 14: The Whigs *

"We'll continue to refine your channeling of both Nova's energy and your own, personal stores, but by the Day of the Dead we'll also have you *conjuring* your first supporting spirits. D'you ever wonder how your older opponents on the Coatlball Trench could attack you with a brick wall, a net, or even a flock of birds? What? No, Trey, that's a rhetorical question—put, yes, just put your hand down. They conjured spiritual support to their side! Now you might be thinking that sounds sinister but really you're just giving bored old spirits the opportunity to do anything but watch us…"

An hour later, Oliver felt his brain beating against his forehead.

"She didn't even stop to answer questions!" Lance growled after they exited the classroom. The door banged off the brick wall having been pushed open a little too forcefully. "Does she really expect us to take on twice the reading, essays, and tests just so we can channel *and* conjure? Who needs conjuring anyway?"

Oliver rolled the question over in his head. "Well," he admitted with a sigh, "we did get pretty far with just elementals last year."

Emma brushed away a toucan that came close for a nuzzle on the open-faced stairway leading up to the fourth floor of the Academic Building. "Not now, bird!" It flew away after a haughty snap of its beak. "Why didn't anybody warn us! I just assumed we'd have the same amount of work, but Zapien said,"—she began counting with her fingers until she'd covered both hands—"it's like we're adding *two* new classes! How do they expect us to play sports when—,"

"Oh no," Oliver interrupted. They'd just cleared the fourth-floor landing and a head of curly hair tied into a bun waited for them down the hallway. "Look who's joining us for regen."

Lance closed his eyes and scowled. "Don't say it."

"García!" Beto taunted from outside classroom 440. He held a copy of *Intermediate Regeneration Techniques* in his right hand, which he waved towards them in a beckoning motion.

Oliver flicked his eyes around the hallway as they approached, expecting a trap. But Beto simply stood by himself, his shoulders relaxed, and his hand hadn't even twitched towards the hilt of his scimitar.

Emma scowled when they were only a few yards away. "What do you want?"

"Don't remember saying *your* name, Griffith," Beto replied, a smug expression on his face.

Lance stepped close to Beto, flaring Power so that the world around him warped. "Go on," he said, rolling his shoulders, "say something stupid."

Beto matched Lance's step forward, closing the gap between their noses to an inch. "I won't waste my time talking to a *Wyatt*."

Oliver didn't like the way Beto emphasized Lance's last name.

Neither had Lance, apparently, because his face turned sour, and he twitched both his hands towards the handle of his warhammer.

In the back of his head, Oliver felt a buzzing sensation guide him to place a hand on Lance's right shoulder, so he acted on it.

* Chapter 14: The Whigs *

The second Oliver's hand landed, Lance flinched and stopped, even if his fingers did still twitch.

"Are you just here to start a fight, Beto?" Oliver growled. "You already know how that'll go."

Beto took an insufferable moment to swipe away the crackling, warped energy around Lance's head with his own enforced fingers before replying sardonically. "I'd like to see you try and fight me again this year. But not in a hallway, over… well, nothing. The stakes are too low, don't you think?"

Oliver's mind reeled in surprise. When had Beto become so even keeled? Last year, he would have already started a fight.

Simpering with satisfaction, Beto patted Lance on the cheek twice. "Chat more later?" Before any of them could reply, he slipped into Chavarría's classroom.

With caution, Oliver pulled Lance around from the shoulder. "Class is about to start. You good to head inside?"

Lance shook with fury, staring into empty space. "He said my last name funny on purpose, didn't he?"

Emma, for once, didn't look fierce. The corners of her eyes drooped. Oliver recognized her expression as pity.

"He was talking about my dad," Lance croaked. "Wasn't he?"

Emma placed her hand on Lance's other shoulder in consolation. "Hey, he's just trying to get us in trouble, remember? That was his number one play last year."

NOVA 02

"I need to talk to my parents about this," Lance breathed. "I can't have Beto knowing something I don't. If my dad really was in one of those... what did Jim call them?"

Oliver felt anger bubble up in his chest as he remembered what Jim, the potato farmer, had said when they exited the Trundholm a few days prior. *"You bring a lot of us nobodies hope, Oliver García. We'd rather not go through rehabilitation again."* Then he remembered seeing Beto's cruel grin after Lance asked Jim which center he'd been in.

"Rehabilitation centers," Oliver said out loud, unable to keep the fury out of his voice.

"He's just baiting you two!" Emma implored as Oliver's vision threatened to turn red. "Ugh," she snapped, dropping her consoling hand from Lance's shoulder, "this is why I never go for the affectionate route—it just doesn't work! You two need to forget about Beto and focus on—,"

Emma had enough sense to stop speaking when a fourth presence joined their huddle. "There you are," Professor Chavarría said, looming over them. He stared past square glasses and eyelids that had just begun to wrinkle, which, by Oliver's estimate, placed the professor in his mid-forties. The rest of Chavarría looked well taken care of, however, giving him the overall appearance of a very nerdy, but also bulky professor—a cross between Professors Watkin and Blackwood, but less well-dressed.

"Elodie warned me," Chavarría said in the slightest of accents, reminding Oliver of Santiago, "that you guys might be distracted this year, but I never thought you'd be late to your *first* class!"

"Sorry, professor," Oliver and Emma muttered.

* Chapter 14: The Whigs *

Chavarría grunted, but otherwise maintained a neutral expression. "Don't worry about it." Then, he scratched his chin and added, "what's wrong with Lance?"

"Uh," Oliver blustered. He couldn't exactly spell it out for Chavarría, a relative stranger, could he?

Emma sighed. "Beto happened, Professor."

"Hmm," Chavarría mused. "I've got more experience with his older cousin, but I think I get the gist of it."

Oliver brightened at that, but only internally. If Lalandra and Watkin were anything to go by, he should wait longer to make an opinion on Chavarría before deciding to like him.

Emma, however, grinned from ear to ear. "Was John the same way, sir?"

"I don't really know Beto that well yet but if he makes you want to get an exorcism every other Sunday, then yeah."

Maybe Chavarría could be somebody to trust after all.

With Lance still immobilized by shock and fury, Oliver pulled his friend forward, only to be stopped by Chavarría's outstretched arm. Puzzled, Oliver looked up.

Why was the man avoiding his eye?

"Take this," Chavarría said, keeping his gaze low. "You should… well, you should read that."

Puzzled, Oliver took the crumpled-up piece of paper that fell out Chavarría's hand. But he didn't open it until he, Emma, and Lance were settled in at the back of the class.

Only after they were settled, did Oliver bring out the piece of paper.

NOVA 02

"Go on," Lance whispered. Though his lips were still tight with anger, he'd at least stopped crushing the handle of his warhammer. "Open it."

After a quick look over his shoulders to make sure nobody had snuck behind them to snoop, Oliver unfurled the crumpled piece of paper.

"Elodie's reforming the Whigs. You are not alone."

Chapter 14: The Whigs

Chapter 15: Pockets and Elixirs

Lalandra looks crazier than a bag of cats but she's sharper than anybody I've ever met. She doesn't have any formal caucuses reporting up to her like we do, but my spies tell me she's got a group of loyal followers that meet with her every Tuesday night. Hard to tell if we'll make an ally out of her or not. She's likely to run for office.

17th of September, the second year of the 10th Age

As soon as Oliver finished reading Chavarría's message, the letters began fading into illegible blotches of ink.

"The Whigs?" Lance asked. This time his anger had completely receded, replaced by curiosity that he punctuated by narrowing his eyes.

Emma looked curious, too, perhaps even more so. A strand of red hair fell from her ear, forgotten, as she wrinkled her brow. "Oli," she asked quietly, ignoring that Chavarría had kicked off the lesson at the front of the class. "Maybe Watkin wasn't the only one fighting against *The Damned* last time around. Maybe we *can* trust Lalandra."

A familiar feeling of warm, fuzzy assurance spread through the back of Oliver's head as the idea wrestled against his own logic. On the one hand, perhaps there *were* more allies on This Side of the Key than just Professor Watkin. On the other hand...

"But then why isn't Watkin working with her openly?" Oliver countered. "We went over this yesterday. She must have broken Watkin's trust back in the day, and we need to find out how before we can start—,"

* Chapter 15: Pockets and Elixirs *

Underneath the table, Lance punched him on the thigh. Above the table, he shushed Oliver and tilted his head to the right. Oliver followed the tilt, seeing confused stares on Valerie and Trey. Se'Vaughn even shook his head at him, wide-eyed, gesturing towards Beto's table.

"After class, then," Lance grunted conclusively.

Oliver nodded, wishing he'd been quieter, and tried focusing on Chavarría's lesson.

But paying attention to the upcoming curriculum felt entirely hopeless after enduring Beto's taunt and reading Chavarría's secret message. For better or worse, Oliver's responsibilities were now greater than simple schoolwork. Then again, hadn't Watkin specifically told him the best way to prepare for *The Damned* was by focusing on school? To learn as much as about magic as possible before facing the greatest evil ever known to man?

Reluctantly, Oliver redoubled his efforts, jotting down as many thoughts in his notebook as possible.

"Elixirs," Chavarría announced, "are the bedrock for regeneration theory." Oliver implored his notebook to record the words. More than once, he had to delete a nasty thought or two about Beto that slipped into his stream of consciousness.

"Nova offers its energy to us willingly, but it can only do so much for you *directly*. Through the application of regeneration, and the methods of elixir-making or imbuements, we can reformat Nova's energy into semi-permanent states of storage that not only store magic, but also create more refined solutions and efficient applications—only after combining them with organic materials from our own planet, of course."

NOVA 02

For a moment, Oliver felt the urge to daydream like he used to on the Original Side of the Key. But then he realized what Chavarría had just said and straightened in his chair. That nugget of information practically screamed for his attention. He'd always thought of elixirs and imbuements as *imitations* of Nova's actual magic, not improved applications of it.

And if magic could become even stronger when mixed with leaves, mushrooms, quetzal eggshells, or any other regular "organic" materials they could get their hands on, just how powerful of an elixir could he create with something special? Something like a magical potato handed to him by a strange, giant farmer dressed in burlap sacks…

Inwardly, Oliver's consciousness bucked. Where had he put that potato Jim had given him? How could he have taken the gift so flippantly? Was a crown jewel sitting on his desk back in Hutch, unprotected? What had Jim told him? *"Should give anyone a temporary boost to your abilities. For our Trinova, here, that ought to be exciting enough…"*

"That could be useful in a pinch," Oliver muttered out loud.

Even Beto turned around to give Oliver a funny look. Chavarría, however, ignored Oliver's outburst and carried on lecturing.

"What?" Emma asked in a hushed undertone. Everyone else had resumed staring at the front of the class where Chavarría's mirror now displayed the ingredients and timings required to imbue their channels with lightning.

Oliver waved a silent hand at Emma, mouthing "I'll tell you later." Then, he focused on every word that came out of Chavarría's mouth, taking the most notes he'd ever jotted down in his life.

215

* Chapter 15: Pockets and Elixirs *

Maybe, Watkin had been right to tell them to focus on their studies after all.

By the time they reached the safety of the Dining Hall for dinner, Professor Chavarría wasn't the only teacher who'd given Oliver something to think about.

Just after lunch—during which Oliver sprinted back to Hutch to store the magical potato, Iguana's Scroll, and iguana skeleton they'd recovered from the temple beneath the willow last year into his pocket dimension for safe keeping—Professor Belk had surprised him.

After separating everyone into groups of three to practice advanced fireball techniques, she waved him over to the front of her stadium-sized classroom. When he jogged over to her, her usual, oversized gold bracelets clicked and clacked against her stumpy wrists as she clapped her hands together.

"Two down, right?" she said, barely moving her lips. "That was fast! Do you know where the third one is yet?"

It had taken Oliver a flare of Wisdom not to stammer out something stupid. Eventually, he managed to reply, "I'm not sure I know what you're talking about, Professor."

"Hah!" she'd replied. "You're even starting to *talk* like Watkin, are ya? Good. Excellent. That'll prep you well."

NOVA 02

Oliver had wanted to reply, "perhaps," but stopped himself because that would have only proven her correct.

Then, after he'd awkwardly excused himself and spent an hour avoiding eye contact with her, even Professor McCall, who never did much other than drone on about math, said something odd. Just as Oliver was about to enter classroom B10 for their first lesson on *Geometry's Role in Magic,* McCall took a moment to whisper into his ear.

"My wife and I support you!" the dusty, old man chirped gleefully.

Oliver had been so surprised, he barely managed to give dusty, old McCall an awkward thumbs-up. That had come from a man who only ever looked stoic in brown or grey breeches and jackets.

"Nice one," Lance said, providing Oliver with a sarcastically ridiculous thumbs-up of his own.

Emma, meanwhile, had been too grumpy to play along. "I still can't believe they teach *math* over here," she muttered all too loudly. "What's the point?"

The way McCall had narrowed his eyes and twitched his mustache at her made Oliver worry for her eventual test scores.

Between the cryptic messages from Lalandra, Chavarría, Belk, and McCall, Oliver didn't know what to think by the time he twirled bucatini pasta onto his fork in the Dining Hall for dinner.

It all came down to *trust.* In a world where Oliver needed to trust people, there came a question. And a decision really. Could he trust others where Watkin didn't?

* Chapter 15: Pockets and Elixirs *

"What do you suppose," a voice said loudly, interrupting Oliver's thoughts, "the Trinova thinks about at dinner?"

Joel had asked the question.

Elton leaned back in his chair and began stroking an imaginary beard between puffs from a make-believe tobacco pipe. "Do you think he'd deign to tell us if we asked, good chap?"

Oliver sighed but couldn't resist a light smile either.

"Oh!" Joel squawked, tilting forward slightly as though he were staring at Oliver from over a garden fence. "I do think he heard us."

Elton feigned hurt in his eyes and dramatically held an up-turned hand to his brow. "And yet, we still have no answer."

"Geez," Emma interrupted. "He's thinking about everything he's got to do this year, alright?"

Oliver tried not to frown, but Abe, who'd been quiet until then, widened his eyes as he caught onto Oliver's wince. "Aaand," Abe said, nearly hopping up and down in his seat as he scooched closer, "he still doesn't want us to know *what* he's worrying about!"

"He can't be worried about his grades?" Elton asked, forgetting his fake pipe to appear genuinely puzzled. "Cuz Lord knows those don't matter."

Joel replied quickest, flashing a smile between his strong cheekbones. "Maybe he's worried about just how easily we're going to win the Emerald Trophy this year?"

Oliver couldn't stop himself from chiming in. "About that."

☙ NOVA 02 ❧

He cringed as nearby conversations came to a screeching halt. Valerie had even paused her fork halfway to her mouth, completely unaware that her long, blonde braid now lay in Dijon mustard.

"I," Oliver stammered, feeling a lump welling up in his throat. "Well, I don't have Archie back yet. So, just don't expect me to be a one-man army or anything."

After a brief silence, Emma put a hand on Oliver's shoulder. When he looked at her, he expected to see the same pitying expression she'd given Lance inside Chavarría's classroom.

But her face didn't look sympathetic at all.

"Oli," she said, a smile forming on the corner of her mouth, "even if we put you on a horse out there, you'd still be more useful to us than any other player."

Despite her touch, Oliver frowned. "You're expecting way too much from me," he whispered, laying his insecurities out for everyone to hear. "I'm just a hardmore."

Abe shook his head some more. "You think too little of yourself, Oli. Don't you remember what you did to John Tupper with *estalla* and *abrilla* last year?"

Oliver almost growled back, "thanks for piling on even more pressure," but stopped himself, thinking back to the laughs Watkin and Lalandra had exchanged with Desmoulins and Blackwood.

"This is why the adults play their dance," he thought as realization dawned on him. *"Appearances can be just as strong as the truth. I should just put on a smile and say we'll cruise our way to victory."*

* Chapter 15: Pockets and Elixirs *

But as he deliberated within himself, a different thought snuck into his head. He remembered something Archie had said to him last year. *"Remedying the sins of your forefathers requires that you employ greater principles. To create a better future, you must understand the scope of their sins, remaining agnostic of their mistakes. Do not stoop to their pettiness."*

Shame flooded into Oliver's throat. It shoved the knot of self-pity he'd been feeling back down into his stomach. He'd just about taken the easier path—one of manipulation and scheming. His friends deserved better than that. They deserved the truth. As Oliver reached his decision, he felt his Wisdom hum on his neck again. The sensation was becoming more and more familiar by the day.

"To be honest with you guys," he finally replied. "I'm starting to feel the pressure a bit. I'm not any different from any of you. Imagine if you had to worry about more than just your grades or Coatlball stats."

The whole table fell silent as they all addressed him. For a moment, Oliver worried they'd break out into shouting like they had when they all caught up outside Hutch during the previous afternoon.

Abe broke the silence first, his eyes sharp. "We hear ya, Oli. We'll lay off the pressure."

Oliver pressed his lips together and nodded his head in thanks. It took a bit of effort to stop his eyes from watering. Had he really been feeling that much stress?

"Even if," Abe added, his cheeks drawing back into a roguish expression, "you won't tell us what you're up to… for—how long did we agree on, Elton?"

Elton scraped his chair to within inches of Oliver's, bringing their faces uncomfortably close.

"Two weeks," he said, flashing a wide smile.

Oliver met Elton's eyes. Though he wanted to backtrack, and say he may need more time, he'd already given his word. Even if he wanted to, they'd never let him hear the end of it.

The humming sensation he'd felt on his neck returned, this time buzzing as though a bug we're crawling underneath his collar. *"Maybe,"* he thought to himself as he slapped the back of his neck, *"I need to stop flaring Wisdom every five minutes."*

Then, feeling confident about his decision, he exhaled and nodded. "Two weeks."

"Two weeks to figure out why Watkin doesn't trust anyone else. And whether I need to do the same."

Cornering Watkin, however, proved more difficult than Oliver, Emma, or Lance anticipated. After exploring the Ruins of Snowgem, they assumed the man would treat them like old pals and answer all their questions over a cup of coffee—even if it came at the expense of interrupting his research.

"But, professor," Oliver pleaded at the end of their first lesson of *Carthage through the Ninth Age*. They'd tried waiting for the rest of the class

* Chapter 15: Pockets and Elixirs *

to leave before asking their questions, but Watkin made to follow the others outside the classroom as soon as the bell rang.

"We just had a few questions about Headmaster Lalandra," Oliver went on, doing his best to keep any tone of accusation out of his voice. "She's offered me one-on-one lessons just like you did, and we were just wondering if you'd think it'd be a good idea or…"

At the mention of Lalandra, Watkin stopped in his stride and turned back. Oliver's words trailed off, dying in his mouth at the look Watkin gave him.

Usually Watkin wore a cheery smile, or an appraising, analytical twinkle in his eye.

Now he just looked stern and irritated.

Oliver looked to Emma and Lance for support, not sure how to handle Watkin in an uncooperative mood. He'd always had time for their questions before.

"Oliver," Watkin said, removing a watch from the front pocket of the same traveler's coat he'd worn to Snowgem. "Take the Headmaster's lessons. There's no harm in them." Then, after the last of the other students had left, he shook his head at all three of them. "If I am curt, I apologize."

For once, Oliver found it hard to look someone in the eyes.

"But do not ever approach me again as if we are team-members on a heist." Only then did Watkin at least try and smile, but it only came across as a disapproving one. "We are short on time. I spend every moment outside of my history lessons searching for the Fire Drake's Cavern, and this conversation is *wasting* that time." He tightened his sash belt as Oliver,

NOVA 02

Emma, and Lance looked at one another, nothing but sheepish. "How goes your research on *The Damned* and pesadriyas?"

"Umm," Oliver began.

"We're getting started this afternoon in the Research Center!" Emma snuck in. "Um, sir," she added hastily as Watkin's disapproving smile twitched.

Caw-caw!

"Sorry, sir," Oliver snuck in. "Should I save my questions for our one-on-one lessons, then?"

"Yes," Watkin acknowledged. "Until such time, good luck with your studies and your *research*."

Then, with a polite tilt of his head, Watkin departed, exiting the room with irregular clunks sounding from his new and improved staff hitting every other stone tile on the floor.

"You should have led with 'where's Archie?'," Lance mumbled as they left the classroom last. "Why'd you start with, 'hey, do you and Lalandra hate each other for some reason?"

"I didn't say that!" Oliver snapped back. He pressed on towards classroom 415 where Professor Desmoulins taught *Fauna of the Magically Inclined*. "I just asked if I should take Lalandra's lessons or not. I never said anything about how we think it's funny they don't work together."

Lance turned his head, locking eyes with Oliver before rolling his own back into his head as slowly as possible. "Really?" he shot back. "You think the Wisest guy since Augustus won't see through that in half a second?"

223

* Chapter 15: Pockets and Elixirs *

"Knock it off," Emma growled. Oliver and Lance stopped to stare at her, completely nonplussed.

"Since when do you play peacemaker?" Lance asked, offering Oliver a bewildered look.

Oliver knew he was supposed to take that as an apology from Lance, so he mirrored the look, and even added a grin, which was easy given that Lance's confused blonde eyebrows were reminding him of Elton.

"No use in arguing," Emma went on untroubled. She walked ahead without them. "Let's just get on with it. If we want to stop *The Damned*, we're gonna have to know everything we can about him. Watkin's right—we need to get going with our research. You can ask him all about Lalandra during your private lessons."

Lance shrugged as Emma disappeared up the staircase leading to the fourth floor. "I guess she's right?" he asked Oliver. "Between us, I'm happy Watkin's on artifact duty. I'll take sifting through old newspapers clippings instead of a wild goose chase any day of the week."

They debated the best way to go about their research all the way up to classroom 415. Lance seemed content going back to the Research Lab like Emma had suggested. Oliver, however, argued it'd be easier to be spied on there, and that'd it be better to access the World Magical Database remotely using the mods Stevie had installed on their notebooks last year.

Those thoughts came to a screeching halt when they entered classroom 415 and came face-to-face with Professor Desmoulins.

It was their first time being so close to Madeline Desmoulins's descendant since… Oliver suppressed a smile at the memory. Desmoulins and Blackwood had attempted to recover Madeline's necklace the same night Oliver, Emma, and Lance were in the Forest Temple at the end of their extraman year. Naturally, Lance had dinged the two professors' heads in with his hammer—it was the least they deserved given that they supported *The Damned*.

"There you three are," Desmoulins said in an aloof, airy voice. He always tried too hard to sound cool—an impossible task with his thin, heart-shaped, and chinless face. And was there a faint scar above the man's eyebrow where one hadn't been before?

Of course, Desmoulins didn't strictly know that Oliver, Emma, and Lance were the reason why he'd collapsed in the temple last June, or that they'd been in the temple at all for that matter—Oliver had been keeping them invisible through *sorbelux* after all. And yet, when Desmoulins ushered them inside, Oliver was glad he kept Madeline's necklace hidden beneath his collared shirt. He didn't want to give Desmoulins any reason to suspect he now possessed a priceless Desmoulins family heirloom.

Hurrying inside, he made for the two empty tables at the rear of the room. They were almost always the last to be taken, and it wasn't hard to understand why.

Desmoulins kept a red and green plant on top of the rear-most windowsill; one that had a *mouth*. It reminded Oliver of a Venus flytrap, only seven-feet tall and covered in venomous veins that were visible to the naked eye whenever directly lit by sunlight. While most of the red, green, or yellow specimens that littered the classroom innocently bobbed up and down to a rhythm Oliver wasn't privy to, the giant flytrap leered at anybody

* Chapter 15: Pockets and Elixirs *

who came too close, sometimes licking the rim of its mouth as its digestive sack gurgled.

When Oliver neared the open two tables, however, he forgot all about the plant. Emma had taken one of the rear tables for herself, but she looked unsure of herself. And it wasn't hard to understand why.

Behind her, Beto Warren sat at the last open table. He leaned back in his chair with his arms behind his head and stared right at Oliver.

NOVA 02

Chapter 16: Perks of the Family

No clue what they talk about during these meetings—they've got this spell that Lalandra uses every time they meet. It's annoying, really. Most of the time everybody ignores someone like me. It's obvious I can't do magic, so there's no need to worry about me listening, right? It's normally why I make such a great spy.

19th of September, the second year of the 10th Age

Oliver narrowed his eyes at Beto.

Beto grinned lazily and even patted the open chair beside him invitingly.

"What's the play?" Lance hissed. "We can't just stand here all day."

Growling, but never taking his eyes off Beto, Oliver took the seat next to the Champayan boy, leaving Lance to sit next to Emma. He couldn't let Beto taunt Lance about his father.

"Was worried you'd be late, García," Beto said smoothly.

Oliver ignored him, cursing the fact that he'd arrived later than usual. *"He's just going to bait you,"* he intoned to himself repeatedly. *"He's just going to bait you. He's just going to bait you."*

"I hope you don't mind," Beto went on, taking a moment to run his hands through his curly hair so he could fix the bun on the back of his head. "But I asked Desmoulins to pair us up this year."

Oliver had just been about to ask whether Beto's stupid hair compelled him to order custom, heavy-duty products, but he was too shocked to say anything snide at all. "What do you mean, *pair* us up?" he hissed.

* Chapter 16: Perks of the Family *

Beto didn't even bother keeping his voice down and Desmoulins didn't seem to notice either.

"Well," Beto breathed, adjusting his hair with one last shuffle at the roots, "as far as the professors are concerned, you and I got off to a bad start last year."

As Oliver stared at Beto, aghast, the Champayan boy put on an exaggerated, puppy-dog frown before sliding back into his sleezy grin. "Couldn't have them thinking we were mortal *enemies* or anything, so I had Professor Desmoulins—he's a *dear*, family friend, by the way—adjust his curriculum for us."

Despite knowing he needed to work on keeping emotions off his face, Oliver began to stare at Beto with disgust. "What is the matter with you?" he growled. "Are you getting some kind of sick pleasure out of this?"

Beto raised a hand to his chest and put on a shocked face. "Sick pleasure? See? This is what I'm talking about. We don't *need* to be enemies."

Oliver snorted.

"Well," Beto went on with a thoughtful expression. "You do make it hard not to be enemies, what with the whole sinovas as friends habit you've got going on. I'm willing to look past it, but you'll have to work on that for me. All vices in moderation, am I right?"

Oliver flared his Wisdom so fast that the air at their desk compressed and expanded, fluttering the leaves of several nearby plants, along with Emma's red hair. *"He's just baiting you. He's just baiting you. He's just baiting you."*

NOVA 02

But with every insufferable noise coming from Beto's side of the desk—a clearing of the throat, a scooch of his chair, a drum of his fingers on the desk—Oliver felt more and more anger accumulate in his stomach, and then his chest, and then his head. Beto could literally do anything, and it would drive Oliver insane with hatred. Beto, for some stupid, classist reason, thought he was better than everyone else. There were novas and sinovas in the world, and anybody who wasn't the former could drop dead.

"Disgusting."

Oliver managed to stop himself from flipping the table and flat-out attacking Beto by latching onto a single, comforting thought. Beto wasn't born to be classist; someone had taught him to be. He tried holding on to the comforting thought, but it barely helped.

When Beto yawned loudly a moment later, drawing a bitter leer from Emma, Oliver realized his only hope was to ignore the boy and listen to Desmoulins' lecture.

Desmoulins had kept teaching his class, as if it were normal to have a heated discussion and frequent interruptions go on at the same time as a lecture. Evidently, he was introducing griffins, at least that's what the mirror at the front of the class displayed. Oliver could barely read the words. Not because he was in the back of the classroom, but because his vision shook from anger.

He enforced himself with Wisdom again, allowing the raging inferno in his head to dissipate.

* Chapter 16: Perks of the Family *

"The Vikings," Desmoulins said airily from the front lectern, "were the first to formally record a griffin encounter when they landed in Canada during the Ninth Age, around 1000 CE."

Desmoulins paused with another lazy grin. The sight of him trying to act cool, despite likely being willing to toss any of them into a rehabilitation center for poor grades, did nothing to lessen Oliver's towering mood.

"It mustn't have gone well, however, because the Vikings were sent packing, weren't they? Outside of the occasional Mayan artifact depicting a griffin surrounded by chupacabras, we don't know much about the noble creatures at all."

Desmoulins paused again. Expecting another aloof display, Oliver prepared to tap into his Wisdom to stifle his anger again. But then he noticed something in Desmoulins' demeanor change. The thin man's knuckles turned white from where they gripped onto his podium, and instead of laughing at a self-delivered joke, or smiling cheaply around the room, he began to teeter back and forth behind the lectern, his eyes wide as dinner-plates.

"But!" he said, raising a finger. "Not too long ago, we did get the quetzal to share a *bit* of their knowledge about griffins."

Oliver suddenly found it very easy to pay attention. What had Desmoulins meant by *getting* the feathered serpents to share their knowledge? Had humans tricked the quetzal into sharing something they didn't want to? For the first time Oliver could remember, Desmoulins' class was enthralled, hanging on to every word.

"The griffin, as it turns out, is the *original* sacred beast."

A few whispers broke out, and even a few scoffs.

"Professor?" Cristina asked, raising her hand from the front of the class. Oliver twitched at the sight of her. He hadn't seen her when he walked in. He needed to keep a better eye on his enemies.

While Desmoulins motioned for Cristina to ask her questions, Oliver shot Beto a quick, poisonous look. "Why couldn't you sit next to *her?*"

Beto shrugged, winking at him for a second time.

"What do you mean by the *original* sacred beast?" Cristina asked Desmoulins.

"A great question!" Desmoulins cheered, grinning as he grew over his lectern—he'd risen to the tips of his toes. "I wish I could tell you, but we don't have a clue! The quetzal, osori, and giant eagles get awfully buttoned up the second you start talking to them about sacred beasts and their origins. It took a *great* man to get even that information out of them!"

Emma looked over her shoulder at Oliver, briefly shifting her wide eyes from him to Beto before returning her attention to the front of the room. Oliver didn't need to hear her thoughts to understand what she was thinking. Desmoulins had just been talking about Solomon Tupper. What information had he weaseled out of the quetzal?

Then a darker thought crept into his mind. Had Archie, who they knew had been Tupper's guide while at school, been the one to spill the information?

By then, Desmoulins shifted his lecture to cover the quetzal in more detail, making it almost impossible for Oliver to get thoughts about Archie

231

* Chapter 16: Perks of the Family *

out of his head. He still had no clue where his friend was, or if he were even remotely close to recovering from his pain.

Frustrated, Oliver slammed a fist on his table.

Beto grinned. "Oh, that's right."

Oliver removed his fist from the dent he'd left in the mahogany wood.

"Your guide?" Beto asked, pretending as if he cared. "He's *missing*, isn't he?"

"He's on quetzal business," Oliver snapped.

"Is that right?" Beto replied, dropping his smile. He placed his hands on the table and leaned close, softening his eyes and lowering his eyebrows. "It must be hard knowing your Guide quit on you."

Oliver exhaled for a full five seconds, feeling relief barrel past his frustration and anger.

"He doesn't know a damn thing. He's just baiting me. And I almost fell for it."

"Or," Beto went on, "do you think he's fallen victim at Goodwin Forest?"

Oliver almost let out a breath.

Could Beto actually know something after all? Oliver hadn't paid much attention to the Goodwin Forest news when Lalandra first brought it up, or even when Brantley mentioned it the next day. But were the reported stories in the forest actually worth looking into? Better yet, Oliver asked himself as Beto continued looking smug, were the disappearances at Goodwin Forest connected to *The Damned* somehow? There was little chance someone like Beto would be privy to such information, but Oliver wasn't about to turn down a willingly provided hint, ill-informed or not.

NOVA 02

With his mind made up, Oliver clenched his fists on the table and reopened them slowly. He didn't think for a second that his fake anger would work on somebody like Lalandra, but it just might on Beto.

"There's nothing," he sneered at Beto, "going on at Goodwin Forest!"

Beto's evil smile returned, more manic than before, reminding Oliver of the boy's twisted cousin. "The media isn't reporting the *truth* because they don't want to accept it themselves. I, of course, know exactly what's going on—perks of the family, you know?"

Oliver leaned closer still, curling his lip in as exaggerated fashion as he could muster. He could feel a secret in the air—one he imagined Beto wasn't supposed to share.

"You don't know what you're talking about," he said, swallowing. He hoped Beto would take it as a nervous accusation.

"All the victims, García."

Here it comes.

"Didn't you put it together?"

For a moment Oliver felt smug, but then Beto's continuing confidence seeped the smugness from him. Beto didn't look like a bully anymore. The manic look on his face had more in common with the twisted son of a cartel leader. And anything that had Beto looking that pleased could only be bad news.

"The victims, don't you know?" Beto repeated.

Oliver's apprehension doubled.

233

Chapter 16: Perks of the Family

"They're the people you pretend to care about. They're all *sinovas*. Bums, vagrants, thieves, underachievers. I even heard one was just a kid who wasn't doing well at the local elementary school."

When Oliver clenched his fists again, he no longer had to *fake* being angry at all. He looked at Beto with murderous daggers in his eyes, wanting to shout something horrible, to stand up, to flare his Power, to pummel Beto with punch after punch, never letting the boy's wretched feet touch the ground again.

But then the bell rang, and Emma locked eyes with him.

His anger withered at her look, giving way to self-loathing. Recovering, he turned back to face Beto.

"I don't *pretend* to care about anything," he hissed as he packed his things. "I'm... I'm ..." He struggled to find the word he was looking for and even felt his neck itch for the umpteenth time in the last couple of days. "I'm confident about what's right," he eventually managed. Then, he poked Beto firmly in the chest.

Beto snarled in response, smacking Oliver's hand away. *"And,"* Oliver went on, taking his own turn to sneer, "if you had any sense, you'd agree with me. Killing off underachievers isn't right."

He felt slightly stupid when he turned away, partly because Beto began to laugh, but also because he could tell he hadn't *quite* said the right thing. But what was he supposed to have said? It felt like the Wisdom at the base of his skull had wanted him to say something else. *"I am... **what** exactly?"*

He shook the thought aside. In the grand scheme of things, Beto was just a nuisance. A mosquito on his shoulder. He, Emma, and Lance had to focus on preparing for the real enemy, not a bully. If Goodwin Forest had something to do with Solomon Tupper's escape from his purgatory in the Soothsayer's Temple, then Beto may have just provided them with some important information. But at the end of the day, how Tupper escaped hardly mattered. Oliver just needed to be ready for it.

"What did he say?" Lance tried asking while they made their way to their next lesson. He clearly hadn't overheard because he spoke with innocent curiosity instead of the hammer-wringing anger he'd shown the last time they were in the hallway. Emma, for her part, looked suspicious more than curious. She'd drawn her eyebrows together, cowling her face with a fierce expression she usually reserved for exploring tricky dungeons.

For once, however, Oliver didn't even bother catching them up.

Despite their continued questions, he barreled down the stairs towards classroom 310, nearly bowling over a group of terrified extramen along the way. He almost stopped to apologize, but he couldn't risk it. They had *Shielding for Intermediates* next. And that meant dealing with Broderick Blackwood for an hour. Oliver felt the color in his face fade slightly as he thought about what lay ahead. He could barely stay calm when it was just Beto needling him. But throw Blackwood into the mix, too? No, he needed to get to Blackwood's classroom first and entrench himself behind as many friendly Hutchites as possible.

* Chapter 16: Perks of the Family *

"C'monnn," Lance tried again, this time when they crossed the threshold into Blackwood's classroom. The room looked the same as it had last year, neat as a military barracks with two columns of desks facing a dark, foreboding lectern. An open space left a gap between the desks and the lectern, allowing Blackwood ample room to demonstrate shielding applications before having the students try them out on themselves. Other than the desks, lectern, and a borderless mirror at the front of the class, the only other objects in the room were the bricks in the walls and the glass on the windows facing the hallway.

Oliver raised his hands to dismiss Lance's question. "Later," he muttered. Then, he tensed as he entered, bracing himself for the Dean.

"Huh," Emma said, scratching her head. She tossed her notebook onto one of the two desks in the rear of the classroom. "No Blackwood in sight? That's a puzzle."

"He may not even be that bad today!" Lance said in an unconvincingly cheery tone.

Emma let out a mirthless laugh. "Yeah, and I'll start putting on mascara every day. Get your head out of your a—,"

"Bald and brash entering," Oliver interjected.

Blackwood's presence nearly took up the whole entryway. He paused on the step, blocking out most of the sunlight behind him, and took a deep breath, letting his chest rise and fall like a barrel bobbing in the ocean. "If it isn't the *Trinova*," the man growled in his glacier-deep voice. He made straight for their table, ignoring the front lectern entirely.

NOVA 02

"*Maybe getting here early was a mistake,*" Oliver thought as Blackwood drew closer. The giant man's enormous boots thudded audibly with every step he stook.

Thud. Thud. Thud.

As Blackwood walked, loose bits of stone and grout rose and fell, scattering in different directions. As if that weren't enough, when he reached their table, he grabbed a nearby chair and flipped it around so he could wring his mammoth hands on its back while facing them. He hadn't said a word yet, and Oliver wasn't foolish enough to go first. Instead, he met the man's glare, even if it felt like staring down an osorius.

Blackwood snorted. Then, with his neck muscles bulging, he turned his head towards easier prey.

First, he tried Emma, but she glared back without flinching. Oliver felt a surge of pride for her as Blackwood snorted again. When the evil man turned to look at Lance, however, the blonde boy hesitated under the pressure, shifting his eyes to Oliver for support.

"Twitch your eyes at me again, Wyatt," Blackwood grunted, "and I'll recommend you for weekly etiquette training."

As Lance recoiled and blushed, Blackwood returned his eyes to Oliver's. He rolled a thought from one jaw to the other, flexing his cheek muscles before speaking.

"García," he finally barked. "How was your *summer?*"

* Chapter 16: Perks of the Family *

When Lalandra had asked Oliver about his summer, alarm bells had tolled in his head. Now, with Blackwood asking too, an entire discordant orchestra sounded off a warmup. *"Just how many people know about Snowgem?!"* Oliver thought, reeling internally.

He barely managed to keep his face stoic when he answered. "Summer was good… sir. Played soccer back on the Original Side of the Key, but otherwise kept things quiet."

Blackwood's glare turned into a contemptuous smile. "Soccer?" he mouthed. His gunmetal-blue eyes didn't mirror his supposed humor. "Gifted thrice and you spend your time playing children's games? What a waste."

"Yes, sir," Oliver replied. Beto had already goaded him into enough rash action for one day. He wouldn't let Blackwood do the same.

"Just have to be polite," he instructed himself. *"For one hour. That's it."*

Blackwood rolled his jaw around again, his piercing gaze never faltering. Seconds trickled by, but Oliver stared right back, refusing to yield by maintaining as pleasant and neutral a smile as possible. Eventually, a bead of sweat formed on his temple. It hung there for an agonizing moment, threatening to drip down the side of his face.

Then the classroom door banged open.

First Se'Vaughn entered—he flashed a smile at Oliver—and then Trey followed, looking at Blackwood. When Trey saw Blackwood glaring at Oliver, he drew his lip back, looking either disgusted or confused. Probably both.

NOVA 02

Realizing he'd looked away at the distraction, Oliver flicked his eyes back to Blackwood.

Slowly, the Dean turned his stoic expression into a satisfied grin. He lingered there for a moment, ensuring nobody could miss his victory, before finally retreating to his podium.

Thud. Thud. Thud.

"What a little man," Emma hissed while the rest of the class filed in—their scuffling feet and scraping chairs masked her voice. "He really thinks he just dominated you, doesn't he?"

"Yep," Oliver grunted. Even though he knew it was stupid to care about losing a stare-down, the fact that Blackwood *did* drove him crazy.

"One hour. Polite. For ... one ... hour."

Up front, Blackwood pounded a fist the size of a small basketball against the mirror, bringing up the upcoming year's curriculum. From then on, Beto—who'd settled in towards the front of the class with Cristina and James—turned his head every few minutes to give Oliver an evil waggle of his eyebrows or flash of his teeth.

Oliver ignored him.

Instead, he daydreamed about fighting Blackwood and Beto in a duel. That could be decent preparation for *The Damned,* couldn't it? Could he take them both on at the same time? He'd beat Beto, of that he was sure, but Blackwood? He chanced a direct look at the barrel-chested man's six-foot-seven-inch frame.

Well, he wouldn't be winning a wrestling match, that was for sure.

* Chapter 16: Perks of the Family *

An hour of make-believe duels later, the bell rang, and Oliver's brain snapped into focus. Knowing Blackwood, he'd only have a few precious seconds to escape more snide remarks.

He stood. Then, before Blackwood could even think to say, "you are only dismissed when I say so," Oliver thought to do something he'd never done before.

In a moment of pure instinct, he flared Power. But instead of ushering the surge of energy across his whole body in an uncontrolled burst like Elton had taught him, he concentrated the flare into his legs. If he was thinking about it the right way, and he'd like to think his Trinova instincts would have his back, this type of flare should concentrate the Power to only where he needed it. Just in his legs. That way he could get over to the door as quickly as possible.

He made it to the door in half a second. And he didn't stop there.

A great crash ensued as his knee burst through the heavy mahogany, shattering it as if it were nothing more than a thin plane of glass. By the time he realized what happened, he was on the floor, halfway down the third-floor hallway.

When he came to, his knee *screamed* at him, and his forehead didn't feel any better, throbbing like a stressed heartbeat. After spending several moments in agony, his focus began to trickle back.

In the time he'd spent wallowing in agony on the floor, Blackwood's classroom had emptied. Only after the sound of scuffing shoes subsided did Oliver notice his cheek was pressed against the stone floor. Without getting up, he groaned, spitting out sharp bits of wood and blood. When he raised himself to a semi-seated position, he saw Emma and Lance waiting for him at the top of the main staircase leading back down the ridge towards the Dining Hall. He didn't like the looks on their faces. Was he that much of a mess? Why did they look fearful?

When a shadow moved closer, Oliver understood.

Blackwood loomed over him with his hands on his hips, blocking out the sun. Though the Dean's face was barely visible with the light behind him, Oliver didn't miss the man's lips tighten into a smirk. "Let's see," he snarled. "One detention for damaging school property and a second for leaving my classroom without permission." He tsked before going on, never once offering Oliver a hand up. "We'll schedule both detentions before the Coatlball tryouts I think. Tut-tut. Two years in a row you risk spoiling your tryouts. What a disappointment you're turning out to be."

If Oliver hadn't been so shocked, he might have hurled an insult, or at least, "that's not fair!" But he *was* shocked. What on Earth had he just done? How had he gotten to the door so fast? And why was the door—he looked around at the splintered wreckage surrounding him—*in pieces?* Wordlessly, he stared at the splinters forming a perimeter around him. He barely registered it when Blackwood took out a small, black-framed mirror and announced, "Mr. García to serve double detention on September 25th, 7:00 A.M, at the Swampy Fortress."

Only after Blackwood left did Oliver notice Emma and Lance scrambling over to help him up.

* Chapter 16: Perks of the Family *

NOVA 02

Chapter 17: Fun and Games

You'll never believe who showed up at the last night's Whigs meeting—Cato Watkin! I'm still shivering about it. The moment I saw him I nearly spat out my drink and left. I don't think my cover is blown, but I'm pretty sure I've just confirmed Lalandra is the brains behind the Whigs.

20th of September, the second year of the 10th Age

"He said they're all *what?*" Abe sputtered.

"Sinovas," Emma repeated in a hushed tone.

Abe looked to Oliver for confirmation, his glasses askew. Oliver didn't know what else to do other than nod his head and look as grim as possible.

Abe clicked his tongue, sounding more like Brantley who also lumbered next to them. So far, the larger, older boy hadn't reacted to the news, but Oliver didn't rush him for a reply. It had taken himself over a week to wrap his head around what Beto had let slip, and he had the luxury of knowing about *The Damned's* past—even if it wasn't all of it. *"Maybe,"* he realized, *"that's why Watkin wants me to keep researching Tupper so bad. The context will help land on ... what? ... how to beat him?"*

According to Beto, the people disappearing in Goodwin Forest, Tennessee were the same kinds of individuals Tupper had identified for rehabilitation when he'd been in Power. And most were never seen again.

At first Oliver had wanted to take Beto's story to Watkin. But then he remembered how angry their History Professor had been the last time

* Chapter 17: Fun and Games *

they'd approached him. So, after two weeks of marinating, along with several heated discussions with Emma and Lance, Oliver decided he could wait to update Watkin. In the meantime, he'd honor his promise to the older Hutchites and bring them up to speed.

Or at least start to.

That morning, they'd met up in the Hutch common room and pretended to get a head-start on Desmoulins' essay assignment on griffins. In reality, they were hoping to isolate Abe and Brantley without drumming up any attention in the process. Eventually, they'd get the rest of the Hutchites looped in, but he, Emma, and Lance had agreed to start with their old RAs first. They'd proven their trustworthiness last year by not ratting out Oliver and Lance for sneaking around the campus grounds at night or asking too many suspicious questions.

When Abe and Brantley finally entered, Lance spoke first, nonchalantly asking Abe his rehearsed question on Desmoulins' preferred writing style for essay submissions. Then, after they nodded their heads at Abe's words, Emma casually suggested they take a break to spy on the Founders Coatlball team.

"Don't mind if I do," Brantley crooned with a troublemaker's grin. "Last session before their tryouts, right? They'll be peeing their pants if they know the Trinova's watching."

Once they were safe outside of Hutch and away from prying ears, Oliver cut off Abe's observations about the campus' relatively mild weather and relayed his conversation with Beto.

NOVA 02

At first, Abe maintained a neutral expression while they walked down the adobe brick path that led to the Coatlball trench. By the time Oliver revealed sinovas were the victims at Goodwin Forest, however, the older boy's normally kind face grew taut with disgust. He punctuated his emotions by kicking out at a loose stone on the pathway, sending it careening into the thicket surrounding them. A creature that looked like a mix between an anteater and a racoon emerged from the brush with the rock in its hand. For a moment, Oliver thought the creature might throw the rock back at Abe, but it only placed the rock back on the path and offered Abe a solemn thumbs up before padding back into the thicket to rejoin its chattering compatriots. Abe grumbled a "thank you" before carrying on kicking.

Brantley still hadn't said a word, so Oliver looked at him directly. People usually spoke if he looked at them quietly for long enough.

"Hmm," Brantley eventually muttered, "didn't Beto call you a sinova last year, too?"

Oliver saw where Brantley was going with his line of thinking, so he opened his mouth to steer the conversation back in the right direction.

At least he tried to.

"Let's skip a step," Emma said, clasping her hands behind her head and turning to walk down the pathway backwards. She kept her eyes on Brantley the whole time, which was a good thing, as far as Oliver was concerned, because her confidence was making his head spin.

245

* Chapter 17: Fun and Games *

"Even if it was just an empty threat," she went on, oblivious to Oliver's blushing, "it's too dangerous to do anything but take it seriously. You're in the inner circle of the Trinova now, gents. It's not just fun and games."

Abe crossed his arms and furrowed his eyebrows, though not nearly as much as Brantley, who's brow now resembled an angle from one of McCall's geometry lessons. "A sinova could mean anything to a boy like Beto," he countered. "His cousin was the exact same kind of pig. Why should we give a da—?"

A ripping sound drew everyone's attention to Lance. He'd been trailing behind them, keeping quiet, but there was no ignoring him now. Lightning bolts of Power crackled from his frame, and, evidently, he'd wrung the handle on his hammer one time too many. For a moment, he stared at the undone leather in his hands with an empty expression beneath his curly, blonde hair. Then, he lifted his chin and leered at Brantley.

"We should care," he said, his voice hollow, "because people like my dad were sinovas in the eyes of *The Damned* and his supporters."

"Vulna recuperet," Oliver intoned as Brantley scratched the back of his head, unable to look Lance in the eyes. Over a few seconds, Lance's handle mended itself, popping back together with one stitch at a time. Oliver couldn't help but admire his handiwork while Brantley bumbled through an apology. Professor Chavarría had taught him the spell last year as a way heal wounds from a nasty chupacabra bite, and though he'd used it to heal his knee after he'd shattered Blackwood's classroom door, he'd not expected it to fix a broken hammer handle. He tucked the thought away for future repairs.

NOVA 02

"Thanks," Lance muttered.

Brantley had shifted his skepticism into a shamefaced expression, softening his eyes quite significantly in the process. Abe's face, however, had grown so tight he now came close to resembling Tolteca. "Are you being serious about 'inner circle' stuff right now? This isn't just some schoolboy issue with Beto?"

Oliver and Emma exchanged a look. Beto wasn't exactly just a schoolboy issue, was he? Then again, how were Abe and Brantley supposed to know about the Tupper connection? At least Brantley had appeared to know about Lance's dad potentially being in a rehabilitation center.

Brantley raised an eyebrow. "You telling us Beto has something to do with *The Damned?*"

Abe's jaw fell this time. In a second, he recomposed himself. "That would explain why he feels okay saying sinova all the time. Most kids would get suspended for saying a slur."

"No," Oliver interjected. He swept his hand domineeringly from left to right to emphasize his point. "We told you a couple weeks ago we'd bring you up to speed, and that's what we're doing. Beto doesn't matter in the grand scheme of things. But anything having to do with disappearing sinovas does—it could be *very* bad news."

"That's pretty definitive," Abe replied, chuckling dryly. "What do you need us to do?"

"You can start by swearing yourself to secrecy," Lance grunted.

"Done," Abe promised, crossing an imaginary X over his heart.

* Chapter 17: Fun and Games *

Brantley, on the other hand, went back to glowering suspiciously. "I figured we already trusted one another," he drawled accusingly. "Guessing I was wrong?"

Oliver nearly faltered under Brantley's gaze—the older boy knew they weren't telling them everything they knew, and he was calling them out on it.

"You said you weren't working on *The Damned,*" Brantley went on. "That you were just looking for something from the Founders. But this sounds like more than that. You telling us the truth or not?"

Emma sighed audibly, turning to walk forward, but this time Oliver made sure to speak before her.

"We trust you, Brantley," he insisted in a warm tone, "which is why we're telling you about this before anybody else."

Abe's stone continued bouncing down the pathway—he'd kept it going during their entire conversation. With one last punt he launched the rock into the clearing ahead of them. Each of them followed, exiting the thicket towards the eastern bleachers that overlooked the Coatlball trench. Shouts, yells, and roars now echoed all around them, indicating the Founders practice session had already begun. The noises stabbed Oliver in the gut, reminding him of Archie's absence. He shoved the pain aside just as his eyes began to water—he really missed Archie— and re-addressed Brantley.

"You always had my back last year," he said, blinking, "and it's time we return the favor. We're trusting you with the truth."

Brantley's shoulders relaxed mid-stride, which was easy to spot given his hulking frame. Less visibly, Abe's face twitched into the briefest of smiles.

"Fair enough," Brantley grunted.

"That doesn't sound like an oath to me," Emma piped in.

Brantley tsked, giving Emma a dry look. "I swear to keep this secret, but you better give me the whole truth as a thank you some time soon." Then, he turned back to Oliver. "Okay, Oliver. What do you need us to do?"

Oliver opened his mouth to outlay the plan, but then he noticed Lance still sulked at the rear of their group. "Lance," he offered, "you good to catch these two up to speed?"

Lance looked at Oliver, dumbfounded. For a terrible moment, Oliver worried his friend would shrug off the request and continue to brood. But then, mercifully, Lance's eyes sparked to life. "Yeah," he said, darting forward to join Emma at the front of their troop. "Definitely." His brow furrowed as he thought hard.

Brantley chortled. "You really are just like your brother."

"Bless him," Abe agreed, "doing the best with the mental hardware he's got."

"Shut up," Lance barked, pointing a strong finger at Abe. The cloud hanging over his head shifted as he stepped up, and within seconds he'd replaced it with a resolutely tight jaw. It suited his bulky frame. "The plan is simple. We're,"—he pointed to himself, Oliver, and Emma—"going to focus on what the Founders asked Oliver to do."

"Which we still don't know anything about," Abe interrupted.

"And you're never gonna," Emma retorted from up front over her shoulder.

* Chapter 17: Fun and Games *

Lance carried on as if neither of them had ever said anything. "We'd like y'all's help investigating the Goodwin Forest nonsense."

"Meaning?" Brantley prompted. They'd almost arrived at the eastern bleachers, so Oliver rolled his hands at Lance in a *hurry-up* motion. They couldn't risk anyone over-hearing. Not for the first time, Oliver reminded himself to learn Lalandra's privacy spell.

Lance shook his head. "Isn't it obvious? We need to know who's been disappearing, when and how each disappearance has gone down, and what the locals at Goodwin are saying!"

"And how on Earth are we supposed to learn all that?" Abe asked, sneering. He looked at Brantley, but the larger boy just shrugged his shoulders at him.

"Look up news articles!" Oliver interjected hurriedly. "Contact local reporters. Mobilize the rest of Hutch if you have to! Play it off as if you're doing it for an essay or something! You're just researching what *The Damned* did for an essay for Lalandra or something—you're in a class with her this year, right?"

Abe's expression faltered more and more with every word that came out of Oliver's mouth. "That doesn't sound very fun," he said, looking sour past his glasses.

"No, it doesn't, does it?" Oliver laughed. He couldn't stop himself from smiling at Abe in an *I-told-you-so* sort of way. "You heard Emma. You're in the inner circle now. None of this is fun and games."

In front, Emma had paused at the stairs leading up to the seating area of the bleachers. "If it makes you feel any better," she said as Abe and

Brantley stepped past her, "we'll be researching just as hard at the same time—only for the other stuff."

"The Founders stuff, right?" Abe asked. "And what is that, again?" He paused halfway up the stairs, peering at Emma over his glasses. But then Brantley ran into him and kept walking up.

"You heard 'em," Brantley grunted as he pushed Abe further and further up the stairs with his belly. "We've got our to-do list and they've got theirs. Now before I start freaking out about the length of our to-do-list, let's go watch some extramen blow bubbles at Coatlball!"

A roar from a nearby osorius shook the bleachers as Oliver, Emma, and Lance emerged from the stairs shortly after their ex-RAs. *"Tuxtairis,"* they chorused to blink away the harsh sunlight beaming down onto the Coatlball bleachers.

Only a couple dozen yards away, Elton, Joel, and Lizzie sat in the middle of the second row of the bleachers. Abe and Brantley had just joined them and begun exchanging fist-bumps and handshakes.

"That went better than expected," Emma hissed quiet enough for only Oliver and Lance to hear as they walked forward. "Just one less thing on the list, right?

Oliver scratched his chin and hedged, "ehh, Brantley got a bit feisty about it."

* Chapter 17: Fun and Games *

"Can you blame him?" she countered. "Must be tough wanting to help and being told 'no, we don't trust you,' for a year."

Lance laughed while Oliver winced with guilt.

"Oof," Lance said, chuckling, "twist that knife more, will ya, Emma?"

Emma turned around and stuck out her tongue.

Oliver knew she was joking but she'd been right—he needed to do a better job trusting others. Maybe Watkin had a good enough reason not to trust Lalandra, but that didn't mean Oliver had to keep his friends like Abe and Brantley in the dark. When Oliver sat down, the nape of his neck purred. Evidently his Wisdom agreed with him. He took it as a good omen, especially when he began to feel as though a cork had loosened in his brain, releasing a tremendous amount of bottled-up anxiety.

Trusting Abe and Brantley felt… liberating. For so long he'd gotten used to sneaking around, holding onto secrets, and, though he hadn't realized it, the nature of the investigating and manipulating had drained him. He wasn't just relieved to share his burden with somebody else. At a more fundamental level, he was simply thankful to have friends that backed him. Ones that he *could* trust.

He took a moment to stare around, smiling buffoonishly as he appreciated each of his friends in turn.

Up until his eyes landed on Elton's.

Elton's eyebrows bobbed up and down at a frightening pace as they traded stares, thoroughly managing to undo Oliver's short-lived peace-of-mind. "What?" he asked, glaring with suspicion.

NOVA 02

Elton kept waggling his brow as he stood up and squeezed Emma out of the way so that he could sit next to Oliver. Joel followed suit a moment later, pushing Lance out of the way on Oliver's other side.

Oliver sighed.

"What's good, Oli?" Joel asked, picking at a tooth with his fingernail.

Oliver made to reply, but Elton cut him off with a burp that he blew into Oliver's face. "So glad you could join us," he said gregariously.

Oliver wrinkled his nose and waved the burp's fumes away.

"You're gonna be joining the Hutch Coatlball team, right?" Joel asked casually.

"Yeah..."

"Hah!" Elton shouted with glee. "I told you he wouldn't get cold feet on us!" Then, he slapped Oliver on the back.

Just to be safe, Oliver enforced himself with Power. Good thing, too, because when Elton's trashcan-lid-sized hands connected with his back, jettisons of wind buffeted all around them.

"Yes," Joel grumbled back as his dreads flopped around in the gusting maelstrom. "You did." He flipped Elton a purple coin, looking disappointed.

Elton caught the amey and pocketed it with one swift motion. "Some of us thought after your little speech in the Dining Hall that you'd be backing out."

"Well," Oliver thought. *"I almost did."* But he didn't feel like telling Elton that when the older boy held onto his shoulder with the strength of an elephant's trunk.

253

* Chapter 17: Fun and Games *

"I never doubted you," Elton added, quieter than before.

"Get off him, will ya?" Emma snuck in.

Elton shoved her away with a hand to her face. "Shush, chatty donkey."

"Onto business?" Joel asked, ignoring Emma's bright red face and protestations. Lizzie grabbed Emma's arm and began whispering to her with a shake of her head. "You can't make stupid people stop being stupid."

"To business," Elton went on. "Now. Oliver. I'm sure you noticed my lump of a brother,"—he gestured towards Lance who grimaced at Oliver apologetically—"went from looking like a pudgy schoolboy to a movie villain's incredibly handsome and misunderstood son?"

"Uhh," Oliver managed.

"Yes," Elton said, nodding sagely. "It can be hard to appreciate the handiwork of a master. My little brother came to me, nothing more than a blank canvas of baby fat. But now we could hang him up at the Met." Elton's voice caught in his throat. During the pause, he lifted an overturned hand to his forehead. "You'll have to excuse me," he went on, his voice catching. "My own brother, you see? Look at him now."

As Elton wiped away fake tears, Joel pressed on. "And now you come to us, Oliver, a wee lad, expecting to bear the weight of the world on a pair of shoulders that..." He paused to flourish his fingers at Oliver, the disappointment on his face palpable.

Elton took over, sounding grimmer than ever before while he re-draped his arm over Oliver's shoulders. "I'm just gonna say it, Oli. You've got the physique of a footlong hotdog."

NOVA 02

A scoff from Abe saved Oliver from having to figure out a reply. "Imagine trying to tell the Trinova he's too weak."

Brantley boomed out a laugh in agreement. "Elton, Oliver could throw you over the bleachers like a pigskin if he wanted to. Whatcha worrying about his physique for?"

"Don't listen to them," Elton murmured into Oliver's ear defiantly. For good measure, he used his hand to rotate Oliver's head back until they were eye-to-eye. "Just ask Lance."

Everyone turned to look at Lance. He faltered under the collective attention, blushing red. "Well," he managed, "I do feel better than ever before."

Joel slapped the back of his hand against Lance's shoulder as if he and Elton had made an excellent point. Oliver had no idea what that point was, however, so he turned to Elton for clarification.

Elton sighed in response, placing two fingers on the bridge of his nose. "Oli. The man said he feels good. Don't *you* want to feel good?"

Emma laughed on Oliver's behalf. "He's gonna need a better reason than *it'll make him feel good* for it to make sense. He's got enough on his plate as is." In his own head, Oliver agreed completely. He already had too much to do with their research, essays, and homework. And Coatlball hadn't even started yet, let alone dungeon simulations or dueling, the school's two other main extracurriculars.

"Fine," Elton griped. "I'll give you a real reason. What if you do all this Trinova prep—,"

* Chapter 17: Fun and Games *

"Which you still haven't told us about," Joel interrupted. Brantley and Abe shifted in their seats, suddenly very interested in a hot-potato passing maneuver between two extramen in the trench.

"Just to find out," Elton continued, unphased, "you need more than just magic to beat *The Damned*."

This time Lizzie laughed, and Oliver could see why Emma had idolized her since their first day at school. He hadn't spent much time around the older girl last year, but he was getting to know her better now that they were all in Hutch together. Even now, when sitting down watching a Coatlball practice session, she held her shoulders back with the discipline of a sage. "You think they're going to settle things over a wrestling match?" she chortled at Elton.

"I'm just saying," Elton grumbled with his hands raised, "I'd sleep better knowing Oli could beat *The Damned* in a good old-fashioned bout of fisticuffs if it came down to it."

"Can you grow a handle-bar mustache?" Joel asked, his tone utterly serious.

Lance leaned forward so that Oliver could see him past Joel. "They're going to keep asking you until you say yes," he warned.

Oliver shook his head as the others laughed. "Fine," he allowed. Anything to get them to stop talking about his physique in public. "I'll do it."

"Eyyyyy," Elton and Joel serenaded, jostling Oliver from side-to-side with brotherly affection.

"You won't regret it," Joel assured him.

Elton leaned in close, barely moving his lips to whisper, "and I daresay it'll help with the ladies, too."

Oliver hated his ears for betraying him—they'd gone as red as Archie's tailfeathers. But at least Emma hadn't noticed. Unpacking how he felt about her could derail his entire semester.

He shot Elton a sardonic grin before elbowing the blonde boy in the ribs.

It felt like connecting with a wall of stone.

Elton cackled as Oliver rubbed his sore elbow. "It'll take more than that to crack these obliques," he snickered.

Oliver frowned, wishing he'd enforced his elbow with Power. But what if he'd sent Elton flying off the bleachers by accident? He needed to practice his enforcement techniques. And find time to do Desmoulins' essay on griffins. And research *The Damned*. And look into pesadriyas. And…

The list made him feel sick to his stomach. Now he also had to train with Elton?

* **Chapter 17: Fun and Games** *

NOVA 02

Chapter 18: Seeking Truth

Watkin and Lalandra are definitely allies. Conveniently, they've just launched nearly identical campaigns for senate in Virginia and Illinois. They want to convince the South and the mid-west to reject Tio's greater good policy-making.

Let them try. We've got the backing of the people. Not them. The people know we're turning the world into a better place.

22nd of September, the second year of the 10th Age

While the Hutchites continued watching the new batch of extramen play miserably, Oliver winced. Not too long ago he wore their shoes, and he distinctly remembered committing a cardinal sin that had earned him the most dramatic verbal smackdown he'd ever heard in his life.

Though he now recognized the event as a rite of passage, he also thought the older students enjoyed the ensuing ridicule a little too much. Tradition mandated that any extraman misfortunate enough to call the Coatlball trench anything but a trench—such as a "field" or "pitch"— be ridiculed in public for all to hear.

Some honored that tradition more exuberantly than the rest. Some like Stevie and Elton.

"Oliver García," Stevie had shouted, swelling with mock outrage. "Do you really think the glorious, the worrrrld-famous—no, the *timeless*—game of Coatlball could ever be played over a common field?"

* Chapter 18: Seeking Truth *

"Don't be ridiculous, lad" Elton piled on. "Fields are to trenches as peasants are to aristocrats. The noble sport of Coatlball could never be played in anything other than a proper trench."

Though he'd never admit to it, lest he receive another verbal chastening, Oliver still thought the word trench wasn't appropriate enough to capture the scope of where Coatlball was played. Though the trench ran the length of a soccer field at the depth of a house or two, most of the game took place in the air above the trench, where two-thirds of the students rode their feathered serpents or giant eagles to pass the ball around. Only the students with osori for guides remained within the trench itself.

"Hey, that girl looks pretty good out there!" Abe shouted, interrupting Oliver's distracted thoughts.

Shaking his head, Oliver followed Abe's outstretched hand and finger. The boy pointed at an extraman student leading the makeshift Founders team. From the middle of the trench the girl barreled forward on a roaring osorius before checking back to make herself available for a pass.

Brantley let off a deep chuckle. "Real subtle, brother."

"What?" Abe retorted in an innocent voice. "She's making all the right plays."

"And *why* were you looking at her?" Elton jeered.

This time Joel laughed. "Your Wisdom helping you figure that one out or do you need us Powerheads to spell it out for you?"

Only then did Oliver recognize the girl. It was the pretty extraman he'd locked eyes with during the Start of Year Feast. To say she looked cute in

NOVA 02

Coatlball boots and athletic gear would have been an understatement. Somehow, she managed to make the Founders' dorm practice jersey, which wasn't much more than a tattered rag over her long-sleeve compression shirt, look like a fashion statement.

"Well, once you *boys* are done staring," Lizzie chided, "join me in spying on the rest of the team, will ya?"

Oliver snapped to attention, blushing and coughing awkwardly as Lizzie went on to tut-tut loudly. The rest of the boys followed his lead, and Elton even shook his head as though he were clearing it from water.

Abe recovered quickest, following Lizzie's gaze towards the trench to size up the rest of the new students. "They're uh… well, they're not great, are they?" On cue, a pudgy boy dropped an open pass from the cute girl, waving an apology.

Brantley grimaced, hissing air over his teeth.

"They're awful," Emma agreed. She leered at the younger students within the trench and even began to curl her upper lip when a girl giggled after throwing a pass a good seven yards wide of her teammate.

"That's a little harsh," Oliver thought, staring at Emma while she continued to leer. Then again, Emma didn't ever settle for anything less than her best—she just expected the same level of commitment from everyone else. It was something he admired about her. He stared at her for a moment longer, relishing the opportunity to get an extended look. Had her freckles always complemented her red hair so well?

* Chapter 18: Seeking Truth *

Then Emma narrowed her eyes and pushed together her lips, clearly debating something. "I gotta admit. That one chick is pretty good." When she finished speaking, she casually turned her head toward Oliver's.

Panicking, Oliver looked away, worried she might read his thoughts. He wanted to be sure Emma felt the same way before… well, he wasn't sure what he'd do, exactly, but he wasn't about to rush into anything without a plan.

He shook his body clear of the thought—*"for later"*—and forced himself to think about *The Damned* instead. When he realized he found it more comforting to stress about his enemy than his feelings for Emma, he suppressed an ill-humored laugh.

But then another thought occurred to him, and his stomach somersaulted around his guts. What if Emma thought he'd looked away because he'd been caught staring at the cute extraman girl? With his stomach spinning, he snapped his gaze back to Emma, desperate to meet her green eyes.

Oliver's somersaulting stomach dropped. Emma kept her eyes fixed intently on the practice session. Worse yet, she focused in on the extraman girl again. "Well," she muttered, "we know *she's* not going to struggle to make any friends."

"Nope," Elton and Joel agreed, leaning forward in their seats. They, along with Brantley and Abe, latched onto the opportunity to resume ogling.

"Get a grip, you baboons," Lizzie barked. "She's a human being not a block of cheese."

NOVA 02

The sound of a sharply blown whistle drew Oliver's attention to Professor Zapien. The stout professor motioned with her hands to signal the end of the practice session, and Oliver's poor mood improved at the sight. Even with the new crop of students being terrible, Zapien still clapped her hands and distributed thumbs ups as the extramen dismounted their osori looking pitifully timid. The world could use more Zapiens.

Then, Emma sat a bit straighter in her seat on the bleachers, re-drawing Oliver's attention like a beacon.

"What?" he asked, trying to meet her eyes for a second time.

"I just can't see a team of osori winning anything," she said, still keeping her focus on the trench. "Hope their RAs this year are on eagles and serpents otherwise they're going to get flattened every game."

"Easy there," Abe pipped. "We got third place my extraman year with our osori. Remember that, Brant—yoooh my word!" Abe's voice had gone an octave higher. "She's—I think she's coming this way!"

Elton shot straight up from his seat. "Who?"

"The—the," Brantley sputtered. He pointed brazenly at a trio approaching their bleachers. A girl, flanked by two boys.

"It's her," Joel hissed. He began smoothing out his jeans and t-shirt.

"Good," Emma grumbled, crossing her arms. "She's probably here to give you animals a piece of her mind. Staring her down like a pack of wolves—shame on you."

A light clicked in Oliver's head as Elton argued with Emma over whether they should feel ashamed or not. She wasn't jealous that he'd ogled

* Chapter 18: Seeking Truth *

at the girl. No, she was disappointed in them. They'd been pigs in her eyes, letting her down by treating this poor new girl like an object.

Relief stormed through Oliver, wiping away his concern. All it came down to was Emma's high standards. He could just explain to her he hadn't ogled at the girl... and that he'd just been following the conversation. Which was entirely true.

Excited, Oliver sought out Emma's eyes for a third time as she and Elton finished arguing.

But she ignored him again, this time deciding to exchange whispers with Lizzie just when the new extraman trio popped up from the bleachers' staircase, waving hello.

Elton looked to Oliver as the trio approached.

"What are you looking at me for," Oliver snapped. "This is *your* mess!"

"Yeah, why don't you tell her why your staring is appropriate?" Emma said smugly.

"I don't know!" Elton yowled with panic in his eyes. "You're like a living God man—do something!"

"She's not going to turn you into stone, is she!" Oliver growled, crossing his arms. "Talk to her!"

"Isn't anybody going to wave back?" Lance hissed. The trio had waved hello and, so far, none of the Hutchites had done anything but exchange internal, awkward glances and hushed conversations.

"Hello!" the girl said in a high, cheery voice as they finished bridging the gap. "I'm Sara, and these two,"—she pointed to a tall, skinny boy to her

264

NOVA 02

left and then a short, pudgy boy to her right—"are my friends Ethan and Drew!"

Oliver couldn't help but brighten when the girl spoke. She carried a slight accent that he recognized as belonging to a second-generation Latina. It likely meant she'd grown up in the US with at least one parent thoughtful enough to pass on her family's language, customs, and traditions—something he could relate to.

"How's it going?" the boy named Ethan sighed, waving half-heartedly. He stood taller than Elton and Lance, though leaner, and had light-brown hair that he kept short on the sides and longer on the top. His grey, tired eyes assessed each of the Hutchites, but only once, surveying them for… threats? Oliver wasn't sure whether he liked the boy, but, if the Other Side of the Key had taught him anything, making assumptions about anybody or anything was a waste of time. He'd start everyone off as a ten-out-of-ten in his mind and give them the opportunity to lower their score. Emma's high standards could probably agree with that.

Unlike Ethan, Drew stood shorter than everyone else, and if Brantley hadn't been there, he would have also been the widest. He wore glasses like Abe along with a necklace featuring a symbol Oliver recognized from one of Santiago's old video games. Over his shoulders, he carried an overstuffed backpack that hadn't been closed properly—a sheet of paper stuck out of the zipper—which contrasted against his meticulously maintained short, black hair. He never shifted his gaze away as Oliver sized him up.

Last of all, Sara didn't require any faith to start off in anyone's list as a ten-out-of-ten. She no longer wore the frayed Founders pinnie over her

265

* Chapter 18: Seeking Truth *

athletic gear and her dark hair shone in the sunlight as she surveyed them with a kind, round face.

"We're all from Hutch," Emma said, breaking the silence curtly. "And you'll have to forgive these troglodytes," she added with a lazy, dismissive twist of her wrist towards Elton and Joel, both of whom still gaped. "They're not worth your time."

Lizzie nodded with her arms crossed in agreement as the boys gasped, collectively horrorstruck. Oliver recovered quickest, resisting the urge to smile. He could appreciate Emma getting straight to the point, even if she had been a bit too blunt.

"Ah," Sara said, raising one of her eyebrows as she looked from Emma to the boys. Her milk chocolate eyes lingered on Elton and Joel, quivering with disappointment, but only for a moment before she looked cheery again. Smiling, she offered a hand to Emma. "You must be, Emma?" she stated more than asked. "We've heard a lot about you!"

Emma took the hand, shaking it hard. "That's, umm, nice," she said, pressing her lips together in bemused confusion. "Do we know each other?"

Sara shook her head, keeping her eyes bright. "Oh, we don't *know* you. At least not yet. Professor Zapien told us we should though, and we started by looking you up in the news and the reports on last season's Coatlball games!"

"Don't forget the dueling reports, too," Drew interrupted. Oliver had to double take at the sound—Drew's voice came surprisingly deep. When the boy finished speaking, he pushed his glasses back up the bridge of his nose.

NOVA 02

A smile tugged at the corner of Emma's lips. "Uh-huh," she said, letting go of Sara's hand. "That's sweet. But, um, also creepy."

Next to Sara, Ethan sighed, turning to leave. In the process, he revealed a broadsword that ran down from the side of his head to the opposite side of his lower thighs. All the Hutch boys gaped at it—who could wield something that heavy effectively? "I told you this wasn't a good idea," Ethan mumbled, sounding exhausted. Oliver didn't know how to gauge the boy. Was he really that bored by them? Why was his Nova source and channel the size of most extraman?

"Nonsense!" Sara chimed. She tugged on Ethan's shoulder, rotating him back into place without expending much energy. Ethan didn't complain. But he did sigh again.

Sara went on, unphased, sticking out a hand to Lance. "And you're Lance, right?"

Lance took Sara's hand in his own saucer sized mitten but let go of it quickly. "Yep!" he said in a high voice. "Sorry for all the staring earlier. You're, uh—well, you were the only half-decent player out there."

"Thanks!" Sara said, rocking back and forth in place for a moment awkwardly. Then, she clapped her hands and turned to Oliver. "That makes you, Oliver!"

"The Trinova," Drew breathed.

Ethan shook his head, wincing.

Oliver nodded, otherwise ignoring the two new boys, before offering a hand to Sara. "Good to meet you," he said in as friendly and normal tone

* Chapter 18: Seeking Truth *

as possible. She shook his hand with surprising strength, making him wonder if she was a Powerhead.

"Good to meet *us?*" she asked, smiling incredulously. "The honor is ours. You three are our inspiration!"

Oliver smiled back but wasn't sure how to reply. If he hadn't been interested in Emma, Sara's smile alone would have given him something to daydream about. And though she hadn't sounded breathy when she spoke, he didn't have a response ready for a compliment from a girl *that* cute. He glanced at Emma quickly, looking for support, but blanched at the level of intensity coming from her green irises. *"Geez,"* he thought letting go of Sara's hand. *"I'm just shaking her hand."*

"Well!" Sara went on, still cheery, "hope to see you around! Let us know if you ever need help with anything!"

"Like battle plans for a duel!" Drew suggested earnestly. He re-adjusted his glasses again when he finished speaking, his eyes glittering with excitement.

Since Emma wasn't helping, Oliver looked to Lance for support instead. But Lance seemed just as bewildered, if not more.

"Okay," Ethan said flatly. He turned again, beckoning for Sara and Drew to join him with a tilt of his head. "Time to go. You guys are weirding them out just like I said you would." This time Sara followed Ethan, but she did wave goodbye, smiling at Oliver, Emma, and Lance in turn.

Drew lingered for a moment, opening and closing his mouth as if he were desperate to say something else. Oliver thought he heard the words

NOVA 02

"Coatlball tactics" cross the boy's lips, but before he said anything, Sara beckoned for him.

"C'mon, Drew," she intoned over her shoulder in a sing-song voice. Elton and Joel buckled at the sound, and Oliver couldn't blame them. He wouldn't have been surprised to see songbirds land on Sara's shoulders.

Drew clicked his tongue in frustration but followed anyway. "We're gonna help you take down *The Damned!*" he declared as he waddled away.

After the trio was out of earshot, Oliver's lips twitched into a smile just as Elton and Joel burst out laughing. Lance joined the laughter, too, but Oliver looked to Emma for her reaction.

"What do you think that was about?" he asked.

Emma shrugged, avoiding his gaze. "They're just a bit awkward."

"A bit," Lance said, his laughs dying down. "That Drew kid would do Oliver's homework if he asked him to!"

Oliver ignored the comment, drawn to the scowl on Abe's face instead. Abe had sharpened his eyes and made for the stairs so he could peer after the extramen.

Oliver thought he knew what the older boy was thinking, so he joined him as he began walking down the stairs.

"A little *too* eager to help," Abe said quietly. "Don't you think?"

Oliver debated for a moment but then shook his head. "They're not exactly experienced enough to mess with my emotions, are they? Even if they could, I'd feel them doing it."

* Chapter 18: Seeking Truth *

Oliver kept walking but then he realized Abe had frozen in place on the final stair behind him. "People can do that?" he asked, blanching. He began probing his head as if investigating for invading thoughts.

Emma stormed past them, narrowly avoiding Abe on the stairs. "It's not them you should be worried about!" she snarled.

Abe's hands fell from his head, and his eyes looked hurt. "What's up with her?"

"She's just got high standards," Oliver exhaled while Emma continued storming off without them towards Hutch. "For all of us," he added.

A thud returned Oliver's attention to the bottom of the stairs. There, Elton had landed next to Abe with his chest puffed out. He gestured at Emma's disappearing figure within the crowd before crossing his arms and tapping his foot sharply. "Look at you, Oli, fawning over a girl for her *standards*. Disgusting behavior, really."

"Oliver," a muffled voice added, rich with disdain. It belonged to Joel, who appeared behind Elton with his hands clasped behind his back and his chin held high. "It's unbecoming to be attracted to a girl for her morals. What would your uncle say? Be better, like the rest of us. Didn't you see Sara's—"

A hand appeared, taking a hold of Joel's ear. "Finish that sentence and I'll cut off your hair," Lizzie snarled. She came down the stairs last alongside Lance but didn't stay long enough to hear Joel's protests. With a contemptuous pinch of her lips, she released the ear and dashed off to join Emma, her movements graceful as always.

NOVA 02

Abe sighed while Elton helped Joel nurse his ear. "It'll take weeks to get them to talk to us again," he said, slumping his shoulders. Then, he made to chase after the girls, apologizing loudly as he went.

"We don't have weeks," Lance whispered into Oliver's ear as they made the journey back to Hutch. "We're supposed to meet up early tomorrow to look up pesadriyas, aren't we?"

Oliver's posture tensed at the reminder. "We can apologize to her first thing," he promised, sounding much more confident than he felt.

* **Chapter 18: Seeking Truth** *

NOVA 02

Chapter 19: The Mantle of a Genius

Tío didn't take my report well. Says I should've alerted him of the Whigs' dealings sooner. How was I supposed to know? Watkin never showed up to any of their meetings before. Tracking him is like trying to track smoke—we'd assumed he was meeting with the Whigs elsewhere, not that Lalandra was leading them in his absence.

Still, we've got profiles on every single one of the attendees now. They won't be able to sneeze without us knowing it.

30th of September, the second year of the 10th Age

As the days in September trickled by, late summer winds gave way to cooler breezes, affording many a student the opportunity of a pleasant weekend.

For most, it was the best time of year to be a Tenochprima Academy student. With homework piles still low, and final exams only visible as a barely tangible threat on the distant horizon, most found themselves enjoying a spot of unsupervised free time away from their parents *and* professors either on the shores of the lagoons, in the lagoons—wherever allowed, of course— or on a hike around the most remote sections of the campus grounds.

Oliver, Emma, and Lance, on the other hand, barely had enough free time to maintain proper hygiene.

* Chapter 19: The Mantle of a Genius *

More than once they were forced to endure retellings of amazing visits to the Swampy Fortress or Bald Cypress Havens by Valerie, Trey, and Se'Vaughn. Trey swore that he and Se'Vaughn witnessed the birth of a quetzal when they passed through the Bald Cypress Havens, up until Se'Vaughn broke down to admit they in fact hadn't even seen a single feathered serpent given the species' undying need for secrecy.

All Oliver could do was smile and nod along as he heard their stories, all the while screaming internally over whatever was next on his nightmarish to-do list.

It didn't help that Emma had decided to minimize all communications with him after the incident at the Coatlball trench—or the "false accusation," as Lance called it. Neither of them heard much from Emma as the days passed by. Even whenever they sat at the same table.

At first, Oliver tried telling himself he was okay with the cold shoulder given just how little free time they now enjoyed. But deep down, Emma's new, icy persona stung him hard.

If only she knew how he really felt about *her*, and not Sara.

Over the course of the month, they'd reduced their sleep schedules to six hours a night. It was the only way, they agreed, to complete their schoolwork, squeeze in rainy practices for Coatlball, cram into mock Dungeon Simulator sessions, workout with Elton, *and* research *The Damned* every week. Abe and Brantley had always warned Oliver that his hardmore year would make his first year feel "like a cakewalk," but Oliver had never paid the warning any serious attention because the older boys had never known he'd also been searching the grounds most evenings for Trinova clues all last year. Naturally, he'd assumed his hardmore year would be more of the same.

Only now, with his eyes bloodshot and the Coatlball and Dungeon Sim tryouts scheduled for that very afternoon after his double detention, did Oliver appreciate Abe and Brantley's warning. This year, the tests came quick and the essays quicker, leaving them little time to relax… let alone any time whatsoever to chase a potential romance with Emma.

Lance had taken the change to their sleep schedule poorest. He arrived to their first early morning session in a foul mood, kicking indiscriminately at table legs, chairs, and cushions on his way to sitting down. When he finally settled down onto a chair, he let out a groan and massaged his thighs. Oliver didn't blame him. Elton's workouts had his own legs feeling like sacks of useless jelly.

Emma had no patience for any foul moods. "Tupper's going to bust out of purgatory *any* second," she growled with an intent leer, "and you're complaining about your beauty sleep? Buck up, man. You signed up for this, and you'll see it through, so help me!"

Despite the snarl in her tone, just hearing Emma's voice again brought Oliver a level of comfort he hadn't known he'd been missing. It had been days since she'd said anything that wasn't a reply to a direct question.

Lance didn't seem to share Oliver's opinion, however. He glared back at Emma, snarling for several seconds before raising his voice. "I need sleep! Sleep I tell you! How long can we keep this up for?"

Emma retaliated by tapping Lance on the head with her knuckles. "Is this as hollow as it looks?" Oliver started laughing while Lance swatted her

* Chapter 19: The Mantle of a Genius *

hand away. "Tupper's gonna come straight for us, *you hear me?* We're the ones who stopped his escape from purga—what did Watkin call it? It doesn't matter. From hell or whatever!"

Oliver's laughter died in his mouth like ashes in a smoldering hearth.

Emma didn't stop there. "So, who do you think the madman's been thinking about murdering while getting chased around by that... that nightmare!"

A few huffs and puffs from Lance later and they'd hunkered down, ready to work. One quick reminder of Tupper's impending escape had hardened Lance's eyes and it wasn't hard for Oliver to guess why. If his own father—or Santiago, rather—had been a survivor of Tupper's rehabilitation centers like Paul Wyatt had been, Oliver would likely be out with Watkin every night searching for the Fire Drake's Cavern. He knew Lance felt the same way, especially after having seen his reaction to Beto's taunts at the start of the semester. Lance would be all-in given what they suspected about his father.

Emma, meanwhile, had only nodded when Oliver asked if she'd be willing to join them in the Hutch common rooms every morning at five o'clock sharp. "It's for our research on Tupper," he'd added, nodding slowly with his eyebrows up, hoping for a more fulsome reaction.

Emma had only deigned to nod again, but, to her credit, she hadn't missed an early morning since. And though she'd begun bringing Valerie as a buffer during their *normal* studies and practices, she at least had enough sense to not invite her roommate to the "Tupper Sessions," as Lance started calling them. Those were the sessions where they whispered in secret, under

NOVA 02

Lalandra's privacy spell, *"stratum silentii."* It had taken Oliver a few attempts to master the new magic, with Lance doing the testing from the other side of the common room—"I can still hear you!"—but eventually Oliver mastered the flow. It came down to feeling for, and directly influencing, the air around them. He tucked away the methodology in his back pocket, impressed by the uniqueness of the technique. Lalandra deserved more of his attention. With a spell like that, who knew what else she had under her sleeve.

More pressing, however, was *Tupper*. Emma was right—they had no clue when Tupper might burst down the door and reduce them to three piles of neatly stacked dust.

It had been with elevated heart rates and stony expressions that they began their research on the enemy. As newly minted secretees to *The Damned's* real name, the sheer volume of information available to them was overwhelming. But what they found on Tupper surprised them. Based on Watkin's retellings of the man's rise to Power, they'd expected to find reports describing somebody close to *The Damned's* son, John, the psychotic boy who'd nearly burned Beto's leg off during a duel late last year.

But there weren't any articles describing a murderous man, or any disturbing school presentations from a clearly unbalanced boy. What they found were thousands of articles, dozens of archived essays and presentations, several documentaries, and even a series of recorded speeches about a man that the entire Other Side of the Key collectively regarded as…

* Chapter 19: The Mantle of a Genius *

"The Prophet's Advent," Oliver announced in a hollow voice. He read the words aloud, his shocked face illuminated by the backlight of his notebook. The words had come from an article published shortly after Tupper's graduation from Tenochprima Academy. It went on to say, "he will undoubtedly become the next great leader in the great American pantheon."

Over the next several weeks, in between classes, practices, workouts, and studies, they discovered Tupper had been a busy boy at school, an even busier man shortly after graduating, and then the busiest man Oliver had ever heard of after launching a political career at just twenty years of age.

A cursory review of an entire *series* of books written about the man's political career indicated Tupper had been a senator for fourteen years before succumbing to the accident at the Sage's Sanctum. Before then, he'd been regarded as the greatest American politician since George Washington or Abraham Lincoln, depending on which article he, Emma, or Lance unearthed.

After blanching at the fourteen years' worth of political policies, maneuvers, and campaigns to sift through, Oliver, Emma, and Lance collectively raised their eyebrows and decided to start with Tupper's four years at school instead. "Best to go from the beginning, eh?" Lance had grumbled.

NOVA 02

It had been an excuse to put off the bulk of their work, but Oliver never felt the need to challenge it.

To their dismay, however, even Tupper's time at school proved to be thoroughly, and annoyingly, well-documented. Based on the newspaper articles written about Tupper the teenager, *The Damned* had been omnipresent during his four years at Tenochprima.

Before he'd even graduated, reports, interviews, and news outlets all regarded Tupper as a genius. Oddly enough, the only other individual Oliver, Emma, or Lance came across as being heralded in the same light was a certain Elodie Lalandra. She'd graduated school just one year before Tupper showed up.

Emma had been the one to connect the dots during their current *Tupper Session*. "Listen to this, you two," she said, too shocked to be stiff or cold. When she opened her mouth to go on, she spoke between bites of a to-go order of Ms. Joan's waffles—she'd been thoughtful enough to send over one of her waddling cauldrons to deliver breakfast every morning at Hutch. "Loofs ike Landra din't ju wri abut ight refation wen she wa at sool!"

Oliver reached for the notebook in Emma's hand, giving up on understanding her past the bits of waffle in her mouth.

Tenochprima Hardmore Primed to Become the Next Lalandra

Just when we thought we'd gotten over the heartbreak of Elodie Lalandra's return to the Original Side of the Key, Headmaster Highbury delighted reporters this morning with a shocking revelation.

* Chapter 19: The Mantle of a Genius *

Solomon Tupper—yes you read that right, of the Tupper family—appears ready to take on Elodie Lalandra's gilded mantle in only his second year.

"Look, uhh," Headmaster Highbury told the Jamestown Press, "just when we were resigned to accept Elodie's refusal of Senator Keith's unprecedented offer of apprenticeship, I daresay we've got another crown jewel on our hands. Augustus would be delighted at our recent crop of student leaders. To think we're so close to achieving his dream... Well, let's just say it's a point of immense pride for all of us."

Earlier that morning reporters had flocked to Tenochprima grounds after the school's long tenured, and highly respected, professor of political science, Peter Baker, resigned just two weeks into the Fall Semester. He did so without prior warning, leaving Headmaster Highbury little choice but to take on the classes himself until the position can be filled. Highbury refused to comment on the reasons behind Baker's sudden departure, but our sources caught up with the political science expert on his way out.

"In my thirty years of teaching," Baker said from the back of the eagle-drawn carriage preparing for his departure, "I've only been dumbstruck twice. First, when Elodie Lalandra dropped 'The Siren Call of Totalitarianism' on my desk, and then again earlier this morning, when Solomon Tupper dismantled Elodie's magnum opus from the ground-up in only his second political science class. I am unfit to teach this quality of student."

NOVA 02

Who could forget Lalandra's award-winning thesis on the potential rise of totalitarianism? Shockwaves spread across the entire nation two years ago when Baker convinced Lalandra to publish her warning against Augustus' teachings, and how they could pave the way for a totalitarian regime despite their noble intentions. With newer students like Solomon Tupper, however, perhaps Lalandra's masterpiece will soon be chalked up to simple fearmongering.

"The timing of Tupper's genius?" Headmaster Highbury later commented. "Serendipitous. Nova's return to orbit is anticipated within the next decade. With leaders like Solomon Tupper rising ahead of schedule, at long last we can draw comfort in Augustus' vision unfolding properly. Perhaps this next Age of Magical Proximity can be the one to bridge the rest to come."

For more, be sure to read our exclusive deep-dive into Lalandra's maligned decision to return to the Original Side of the Key—'Investment Banking; Why Tenochprima's Genius Traded Manifest Destiny for Mergers & Acquisitions.'

Oliver had wanted to dive straight into the next article on Lalandra, but Emma gave him a stern shake of her head. "Do we have time to look into Watkin and Lalandra right now, too? Or just Tupper?" Oliver could only grumble a half-excuse before agreeing to press on with just Tupper.

Just thinking about the volume of information available to them stressed out Oliver so much he felt his shoulders grow tight. At their current rate,

* Chapter 19: The Mantle of a Genius *

they wouldn't get through their nemesis' time at school until after Christmas.

Letting out a breath of air, he rubbed his eyes and leaned back in his chair in the Hutch common room. His notebook lay momentarily forgotten, displaying a Tupper-authored essay titled, *'Faction-based policymaking; a critique of Federalist No. 51.'*

"Just five minutes of rest," he thought to himself, feeling drowsy.

NOVA 02

Interludes V – VI

"I thought they were great!" Sara Reyes chirped as she walked towards classroom 310, positively bouncing with joy. Nothing was going to sour her mood. Not after she'd finally met Emma, Lance, and the Trinova.

Had her first meeting with the Trinova and his friends gone perfectly? Probably not. But she was a glass-half-full kinda gal, and, in her heart, she knew they'd all be good friends in no time.

Drew cackled alongside her after she spoke, taking one-and-a-half steps to match every one of her more confident, lengthier strides.

"They're gonna love our help," he snickered as he readjusted the straps of his over-stuffed backpack. "So much data they're just leaving on the table," he went on, shaking his head with grim consternation. "But don't worry. I'll have battle strategies and Coatlball plans ready for them soon."

Sara smiled at him, doing her best to ignore the dozen or so faces shamelessly staring at her as she walked closer and closer to classroom 310. Eventually, Drew grinned back. Cautiously at first. But then more and more confident by the second. It made her bubbly mood soar even higher.

All the way up until she heard a sigh to her right.

Ethan, the third member of their troop, was always sighing.

* Interludes V – VI *

It was one of the reasons why she liked him. He kept up with her strides just fine with his long, powerful legs. Curious, she tilted her head to get a better look at him, raising one of her perfect eyebrows.

Ever since absorbing Ethan into her two-person gang, she'd noticed the boy was more than content to slow his pace down so that he never outstripped her—always supporting, never commanding. Which was strange, given how tall and strong he was. His sword alone, a giant, two-handed claymore strapped to his back, encouraged most to label him as a Goliath-type brute, likely obsessed with owning every room he stepped into.

But Sara could tell Ethan wasn't like that at all. In fact, the only brutish thing about Ethan's character was the way he walked in a straight, unwavering line. At all times, he knew where he was going. It was up to everybody else to get out of his way.

Ethan let out some more air when he realized she'd never stopped staring at him.

"Go on," she encouraged in a sing song voice. A boy walking past them buckled at the sound.

Drew shrugged. "I think you guys weirded them out too much," he said dully.

When Sara stared for another moment longer, her eyes twinkling merrily, he shrugged again, remaining entirely unaffected.

That was another reason why she liked him. She could be herself around him—and Drew for that matter—and not worry about them reducing themselves to enamored piles of useless masculine immaturity. Even some

NOVA 02

of the Trinova's friends had struggled with that. Maybe even the Trinova himself… she was still getting a read on him.

"Maybe we did weird them out," Sara said, laughing. This time a nearby girl buckled. "But I'd like to think we put on a good impression wherever we go."

She genuinely believed that, too, even when a hardmore boy lowered his shoulder to barge past Ethan. No doubt to teach an extraman a lesson about ego or something silly.

"How dare the extraman walk in a straight line?" she mimed to herself, giving the curly haired boy a deep voice insider her head.

Boys were so petty.

Whatever the older boy's motivations were, she didn't care to find out. So before his and Ethan's shoulders met like converging tectonic plates, Sara slipped to Ethan's left flank in quicksilver motions until they'd swapped places.

The older stranger didn't have time to get out of the way, given just how much he'd committed to his shoulder barge, but Sara still had plenty of seconds. With a twist of her flexible torso, she dodged the petty attack effortlessly, even finding a half-second to place her hand on the boy's shoulder—*ooo, he smells nice*—and whisper, "that's no way to make friends."

The boy turned around to stare at her, his jaw agape, causing a minor commotion within the posse that dotted over him. He was undoubtedly *not* used to being outclassed.

Sara gave him a breathy smile and wiggled her fingers at him tauntingly as the distance between them grew.

* Interludes V – VI *

"C'mon, Beto," a thin, sallow-faced girl said from boy's side. She had to tug on his arm to get his attention away from Sara.

Sara and Drew laughed all the way until they ducked into classroom 310. In between them, Ethan just sighed. "They're not gonna like us after that."

Georgina McCall's hand froze, only halfway finished dolloping creamy mashed potatoes onto her husband's plate.

"Elodie asked *you*?" she repeated, shock and bewilderment plastered across her round, soft face.

Fred McCall twitched his silver-white mustache. Then he rustled a finger through it. Georgina needed to know he was *not* amused.

"And why shouldn't she?" Fred asked, trying his hardest to leer. He quickly gave up, however, after his wife brandished a mischievous smile to counter him. She even resumed ladling his potatoes.

"Bless your heart," she said, still looking like trouble. "How about an extra serving of potatoes for the *scary* little man."

Unamused, Fred twitched his mustache again. Intimidating anyone—let alone his firecracker of a petite wife—came difficult when he had a square face, button nose, and pudgy chin. Doubly so given that he could only deliver his anger from a frame spanning five-feet-and-four-inches. The last inch wasn't even real either. Unless he counted the extra height from his abundant, fluffy white hair.

NOVA 02

Which he did.

"You think I shouldn't join them, then?" Fred poked back. "That I should stay on the fringes like we did last time?"

Georgina dropped the bowl of potatoes down on the dining table, hard. Then she leered at him. "We, is it? *I* don't recall cowering from the sidelines myself, thank you very much."

Fred's cheeks swirled rouge almost at once. "Now don't you play the hero," he said trying to sound gruff. "Where were you when center 13 fell? When Watkin made his stand?"

Georgina sat down huffing.

"Fine," she said, throwing up her hands.

It was Fred's turn to smile mischievously.

"We were both cowards," Georgina finished.

Fred raised a glass of red wine. "To us, then," he said, clearing his throat. "The long-living, cowardly McCalls."

If Georgina had had a mustache, he knew she would have twitched it.

She compensated by sniffing indignantly. "I may just join Elodie to spite you if you're not careful."

McCall raised his eyebrows in mock surprise. "Subsequent to which you would be most sorely missed, I'm sure."

* Interludes V – VI *

NOVA 02

Chapter 20: Roli

Watkin's rising in the Virginia polls somehow. Apparently, there really is a vocal minority supporting him. It's beyond annoying.

23rd of July, the second year of the 10th Age

Oliver's eyes snapped open inside the Hutch common room. When he realized where he was and that he'd been dozing off, he let out a long groan, looking around the room for a distraction before diving back into his Tupper research alongside Emma and Lance.

Last year they'd spent countless hours studying with a different view at the bottom of Founders Hall. Back then, their go-to study spot had been inside one of the glass viewing domes underneath the waters of the lagoons. They'd likely spent over half their year inside that beautiful glass room, complete with leather chairs and ottomans, after discovering it to be the perfect place for comfortable, private, and efficient studying.

Looking around their current environment, Oliver couldn't help but pine for the polish they'd once had.

Though perfectly comfortable, Hutch's common room came with more simple fireplaces, mundane wooden mirrors, and beat-up blue couches with cloth upholstery. When Oliver realized he was acting like a spoiled kid, he shook himself further awake.

Nearby, Elton practiced giving an oral presentation on *Calculus-based Possession* to a sleeping Joel. A bit further away, Abe screeched at his dagger

* Chapter 20: Roli *

in frustration for not conjuring a friendly spirit quickly enough for his self-imposed ten-second time frame.

"It's gotta be that pulsing technique," Lance suddenly growled from his chair. Oliver winced in frustration, immediately regretting taking his mind off Tupper. Lance must have taken his peering around as an excuse for another break.

He looked Lance over before replying. His friend's eyes were underscored by dark, purple bags. Their pauses didn't come often given their workload, but when they did, they always talked about the same thing: Oliver's upcoming one-on-one lesson with Watkin. It was only a week away, just on the other side of tryouts, and a couple of early graded tests for Belk and McCall.

"Hmmm," Oliver mused noncommittally. Checking his watch, he decided a break wouldn't hurt. Then, he tossed his notebook onto the table in front of them and leaned back.

"Sometimes," he thought to himself as his mirror clattered to a halt, *"breaks are good."* Next to him and across from Lance, Emma slapped her own notebook down.

"I was getting tired, too," she muttered, tucking her hair behind her ears. Her eyes looked hooded, too.

Seeing her exhausted expression, along with Lance's, made Oliver wince. Maybe they could stand for more breaks.

A poke to his arm directed his attention towards Lance's wide eyes. "I'd kill to be able to do Watkin's pulse thing." His pleading stare was relentless. "Remember Snowgem?"

NOVA 02

Oliver breathed in. He *did* want to learn how to pulse like Watkin. And why wouldn't he? With it, their professor had annihilated an entire roomful of foaming, venomous baboons.

But something told Oliver that Watkin wouldn't just teach him combat techniques. "That pulse probably took Watkin a lifetime to master," he countered, rubbing his eyes some more.

Emma opened her mouth to speak but hesitated.

Oliver tsked his tongue, finding himself too tired to care if he irritated Emma. He didn't know how long she was going to keep up her icy, angry persona, and it was at that moment that he realized he didn't care to find out. He needed them all to be on good terms if they were going to have any hope of getting through the year. So, after briefly asking himself, *"what would Emma do?"* Oliver threw his hands into the air and spoke with exasperation thick on his voice.

"Look, Emma, I'm sorry we ogled Sara a few weeks back. We didn't mean anything by it."

Lance's eyes expanded wider than the coasters on the table as they waited for Emma's response. A year ago, and even weeks ago, Oliver wouldn't have risked seeing the flared nostrils and outraged leering eyes on Emma's face, but they didn't have the luxury of being normal kids anymore.

Before Emma could put together the thoughts behind her tightened jaw, Oliver kept going. "And," he added, raising a finger, "you were right to be disappointed in us. But it does feel a bit unfair that you've given us the cold shoulder for over *three* weeks. We," he said pointing between himself and Lance, "didn't say any of the crap Elton and Joel did. We just happened to

* Chapter 20: Roli *

glance at a cute girl. We're not being creepy, and it feels like you're assuming the worst of us."

By the time Oliver finished speaking he couldn't believe everything that had tumbled out of his mouth. He wasn't surprised by the message itself—he'd agonized over Emma every hour since he'd betrayed her "principles"—but he hadn't exactly planned to say it out loud; especially the part about her being unfair.

As he realized what he'd done, his cheeks flushed, and he even felt Madeline's necklace vibrate on his chest. Had a simple apology required him to subconsciously tap into his enhanced Gift of Bravery?

Cringing, he checked on Emma.

She'd re-doubled her leer, reducing her eyes to slits of green. "That's *not*," she hissed, surprisingly quiet and even toned, "what I was thinking about."

Oliver's insides crumpled.

"Oh."

"I'm just gonna," Lance said, popping up from his chair awkwardly, "go away, then." He darted to Elton's couch like a dog with a tail between its legs, shoving Joel's sleeping body out of the way as he sat.

Oliver, meanwhile, kept his attention on Emma. Though her cheeks and lips had tightened, she didn't look angry. Or, at least, her nostrils weren't flaring anymore. He took that as a good sign.

"Apology accepted," she said, her tone stiff. Then she began scratching her arm, not meeting his eyes. "For what it's worth. I'm also sorry for laying it on too hard. I thought you, of all people,"—her eyes flicked onto his for a second—"would understand you shouldn't treat people like a piece of candy." Oliver nodded, thinking back to the girl at the Davidstown bookstore that had ogled at him. "But you're right. You guys weren't the ones being creeps." She gestured towards Elton and Joel with her thumb. "Those two were."

Then, the familiar mischievous crinkle on her lips returned.

Oliver smiled back—admittedly halfheartedly given how tired he felt and nodded again.

Emma moved her hand from her arm onto his, which he'd kept on the table.

"Lance," she shouted over her shoulder, while Oliver's insides squirmed at her touch, "you can stop being weird now." With a squeeze, she released her grip.

Lance shuffled back into his chair without delay. "Good," he said, scratching the back of his head. "Because Oli's silencing spell was still on—Elton and Joel couldn't hear a thing I was saying."

On cue, the older boys punctuated their annoyance at Lance's silent distraction with rude hand gestures.

An awkward silence followed while Elton continued remonstrating behind Emma. Oliver hadn't appreciated her being cold for so long, but he still admired her for her principles. And, at least they'd now moved on… And she'd… touched him?

"What I really wanted to ask," Emma said, interrupting Oliver's thoughts, "was if you'd given the pocket dimension theory any more thought?"

* Chapter 20: Roli *

Oliver's face fell and, in his stomach, he felt his relief turn to raucous guilt. "I knew I was forgetting something," he grumbled.

"Wait?" Lance asked, shoving his eyebrows close together. "Was there something we had to work on there, too? I thought you already figured out the pocket dimension!"

"I did," Oliver said, gulping past his knot of shame—it had crawled up into his throat. "But remember when I told you I could feel more than just the pocket dimension? I think there's something more to the thought process that even Watkin doesn't understand."

Emma nodded vigorously, semi-undoing the already askew bun of hair on top of her head. "Exactly! I bet if you and Watkin sat down to think about it, you might figure something else out. What if there was more to it than just opening up a secret closet?"

"Ehh," Lance argued, "I doubt Watkin hasn't already thought about it to death."

Oliver pressed his lips together while they continued having the conversation without him. Back at Emma's house, he'd opened up a pocket dimension on the Original Side of the Key. As far as he was aware, that broke the rules of magic, and he'd only been able to do it after concentrating for several minutes on the elusive, vibrating touch of... what? Nova's influence in the air?

Next to him, Emma's and Lance's voices rose, their argument over Watkin's secrets getting heated, but Oliver continued ignoring them. He hadn't opened up his pocket dimension since chucking Jim's potato and the

Iguana's Scroll inside for safekeeping. Maybe it made sense to practice the form ahead of Watkin's lesson.

Absentmindedly, he reached for Nova's influence in the air, and commanded it to open his pocket dimension. As always, it was easier on This Side of the Key.

As soon as the closet zipped into existence, a green blur shot out.

"*FREEDOMMMMM!*" a tiny voice squeaked.

Oliver stood up so fast that he sent the table in front of them flying. It rocketed up and over Emma, narrowly avoiding her chin, and didn't stop until crashing into a splintery halt against the wall opposite them. The debris only avoided Brantley and Joel because Abe had enough sense, and the quickest reflexes, to re-direct the shrapnel.

Brantley, who had just walked into the room with a cinnamon roll in hand, dropped both his jaw and his breakfast.

In the uproar, Oliver had lost track of the green blur. Fearing the worst, he dropped his *stratum silentii* spell so that the others in the room could listen. If this were a remote attack from *The Damned,* he'd need everybody alert to the danger.

To Oliver's horror, Emma and Lance didn't look nearly as scared as they should be.

"GUYS!" he shouted. "FOCUS!"

* Chapter 20: Roli *

They blinked, focusing, not on combat… but on Oliver's left shoulder.

"At long last my isolation is ended!" the hidden voice decreed from nowhere Oliver could see—it had to be telepathic. He turned his head, primed for a battle, only to lock eyes with the small, beady-eyed face of a green lizard.

"Well, hello," the creature squeaked. *"I must thank you for the potato. Haven't had a meal like that in,"*—the creature flicked its tongue out, sticking it onto Oliver's nose momentarily—*"well, it must be centuries!"*

Oliver nearly screamed. He managed not to, just barely, before swatting at the lizard, desperate for it to be anywhere but on his shoulder. The creature dodged his swipe with a playful peep, scampering across his back to re-appear on his other shoulder. There it creased its little face into an undeniable smile.

"A playful joust! I don't suppose you have any more root vegetables? I ate the last morsel several days ago—quite scrumptious, thank you."

This time Oliver shot his hand towards the lizard with an enforced bout of Power. He'd expected his fingers to latch around the creature's scaly torso, but, to his astonishment, the lizard dodged again before clambering onto the top of his head.

Determined to get rid of the creature once and for all, Oliver readied himself to flare both Power and Wisdom.

"Oli!" Lance shouted. "Stop!"

Oliver's hands ceased moving around his head.

"I," Lance stammered quickly, "I think that's *Roli!* The iguana skeleton that had held onto the scroll, remember?"

NOVA 02

Oliver glared at Lance mutinously and then Emma, too, because she was staring at the sticky, slimy creature on his head with no short amount of glee on her face. Muttering, Oliver looked up, even as he remembered the message on the back of the Iguana's Scroll.

Take Roli with you—he's the last of his kind.

From atop Oliver's head, *Roli's* outstretched face stared down into Oliver's eyes. He flit his tongue in and out again, licking his chops playfully, and then raised a pudgy foot to wiggle his toes in what could only have been a friendly gesture. His scales were almost entirely shades of green, except for on a flap of skin extending from his neck where they shone orange amidst the torchlight in the Hutch common room.

"*Ah, yes,*" Roli crowed. "*You're admiring my dewlap, aren't you?*"

"Dewlap?" Oliver asked, leering suspiciously. The iguana felt heavy on his head, stressing against his neck muscles.

Roli pointed to his neck flap with his longest claw, inflating his throat with a breath. "*Some refer to it as a beard. But it's called a dewlap.*" He waggled the scales above his eyes.

Oliver squinted at the dewlap, feeling entirely skeptical.

"*Go on. Touch it.*"

Oliver hesitated, looking to Emma for support. But she only burst into a fit of giggles.

"I," Oliver managed, "I don't want to touch it."

* Chapter 20: Roli *

"WELL, I DO!" somebody else boomed. A breath later, Elton barreled over, followed by a wide-eyed Joel, a timid Abe, and a stunned Brantley. During all the ruckus, Oliver had missed Valerie and Lizzie also walk into the room. Them, and Professor Watkin, of all people, who surveyed the scene with a curious tilt of his head. He wore black gloves and his now-familiar traveler's coat, and his eyes were bloodshot. Had he been searching for the Fire Drake's Cavern all night?

"Oliver," Brantley sputtered while Elton stroked Roli's dewlap with awe. "Where? How did—,"

"You get a talking iguana?" Abe finished.

Joel joined Elton for a turn of admiration, but this time Oliver backed away. *"Yes,"* Roli hummed, as Oliver stumbled. *"Bathe in my majesty."*

"Okayyyy," Oliver blurted out as Emma and Lance caught his shoulders. "That's enough Roli for today!" Then he directed his attention to Watkin, who'd stayed on the perimeter of the action so far, opting to remain closest to the stairs leading back down to the lower levels.

"Sorry about the table, sir," Oliver added with a hasty gesture towards the remains of the splintery mess. "I was just," he hesitated, looking up at Roli again. "Surprised."

Watkin waved his hand, allowing his curious stare to turn into an open smile. The table, meanwhile, re-constructed itself in seconds. Watkin's eyes twinkled as it did, complementing the man's face. He looked so much more amenable when he grinned than when he told them off for wasting his time.

"Not a concern," he said, eyeing Roli with an outright sparkling expression. "As charming as your new friend might be, however, I require a moment of your time." He motioned with his staff towards the staircase below. "Alone, if you don't mind."

Oliver's thoughts raced in his head. On the one hand there was no chance he'd miss out on a private conversation with Watkin. Especially if the man were coming back from a night out searching for clues. On the other hand…

"But sir," Oliver said, shuffling his feet. "I have double detention in the kitchens with Ms. Joan in a few minutes. Can we wait until after tryouts this afternoon? Bla—Professor Blackwood thought the detention should come before tryouts today."

Watkin sniffed once and checked a pocket watch hidden in his coat. When he looked back up to speak, he reminded Oliver more of the stern Professor Watkin than the smiling one.

"I'll accompany you there."

Not ready to get chewed out again, Oliver apologized to Roli before taking him off his head—this time the iguana acquiesced to his grab. Then, Oliver handed the iguana to Lance.

"I'll be back soon," he said, patting Roli on the side.

Roli squeaked indifferently, shifting his head to Lance. *Tell me, blonde boy. Do you carry any root-vegetables on your person? I would suggest something else, but over the centuries I've forgotten what anything else tastes like.*

Oliver gave Lance a pointed look as he left. "Lock him up in the room until I'm back, okay?"

"What about tryouts?" Lance hissed. He held Roli's wriggling form as far away from his own body as possible— *I'll settle for celery if I must! Ah yes,*

* Chapter 20: Roli *

I remember now. My previous master provided me with a host of different vegetables at my bidding—and not just of the root genus. In fact, I also commonly enjoyed solanum, morning glories, and daisies as large as fists!"

"I guess I'll have to meet you there," Oliver said, shrugging at Lance. Then, he followed Watkin outside Hutch.

NOVA 02

Chapter 21: Nova's Breath

He calls his voter base a silent majority, but he doesn't realize just how vocal our majority can get about supporting what's right—our rehabilitation centers have reduced crime in New York by thirty-six percent.

Still, as a precaution, we've installed Blackwood's right-hand-man Eldrick Tramby to run against Watkin in support of Tio and our vision for the future. Never thought I'd meet a man more sinister than Broderick, but here we are.

29th of September, the second year of the 10th Age

When Oliver and Watkin exited Hutch, Oliver took the straighter path towards Founders Hall where his detention would be in Ms. Joan's hidden kitchen on the first floor.

He stopped, however, when he realized Watkin had taken the path leading left, up the ridge to the Academic Building. The man didn't offer any explanation as he continued walking, and only gave Oliver a wry half-smile and a pointed nod of his head. He expected Oliver to join him.

Oliver obliged without much hesitation.

Strictly speaking, he didn't know how Watkin would get him out of missing his double detention with Ms. Joan, but he also didn't care either. Just as long as Blackwood couldn't punish him for it.

"If I can't even get you out of double detention," Watkin began, managing a mischievous raise of his eyebrow despite his bloodshot eyes,

* Chapter 21: Nova's Breath *

"then how pathetically unhelpful do you think I'll be when *The Damned* escapes."

Oliver caught up with Watkin's lengthy strides in an instant, energized by the idea of flouting *Dean* Blackwood's rules. "Thank you, sir," he said breathlessly.

"Don't thank me yet," Watkin replied, looking tired again. "We'll have your first lesson now instead."

"Any luck with the Fire Drake's Cavern, sir?" Oliver asked as they walked.

Watkin's staff clunked against the stone and brick walkway for a few moments before he answered.

"It's in Goodwin Forest."

Oliver's jaw slackened, but only as far as his eyebrows rose—less than half an inch. He'd practiced limiting his emotional reactions as much as possible ever since Lalandra had scolded them—*"your diplomacy needs training,"*—but it was hard going. By definition, surprises were surprising.

Oliver shoved his self-pity aside and stood, working his brain and jaw. If Watkin had found the location of Cuahtemoc's Gift, then they were *wasting* time. What did Coatlball and Dungeon Simulation tryouts matter if the final artifact was in front of them? They had to go and retrieve it immediately if Oliver had understood Augustus properly.

"Did you want to go over something before we head out?" Oliver asked, pausing in his stride. "Otherwise, I'll go get Emma and Lance."

Watkin held up his hands, turning to stop with him. "Come," he said. "I have much to share with you and not much time to do it."

NOVA 02

A short walk later, they resumed the lesson inside Watkin's office, where Watkin sat in a winged leather chair and removed his gloves, placing them on a leather-bound book on his desk.

Oliver thought to ask, *"why are we waiting around?"* but opted to keep his mouth shut instead. They'd leave soon enough if Watkin wanted them to.

Watkin sighed in his chair, keeping his eyes closed for a full three seconds. Then, he pulled out a small vial containing a clear-blue liquid from seemingly thin air—giving Oliver a pointed look in the process—and took a swig.

"I told you," he said, shuddering as the drink went down his throat. "The Fire Drake's Cavern is in Goodwin Forest." He paused to smack his lips and place the empty vial down on his desk. "But that doesn't mean I can actually find the accursed place."

Oliver slumped down into one of the two chairs across Watkin's desk. "Why didn't you lead with that?" he asked sullenly. "You made it sound like we were about to wrap up the prophecy of the Iguana's Scroll."

Watkin's tired face took the time to put together a smile. "If anything in life ever presents itself to you as simple or straightforward, run the other way. Nothing good ever came to anyone easily."

"That's something Archie would say," Oliver grunted, not bothering to keep his frustration out of his tone. Then, realizing he wasn't talking to Emma or Lance, he sat up in his chair and nodded respectfully.

"Bah!" Watkin barked. "Worrying about giving me the proper reaction is an exercise in futility. Even if you did put up a convincing lie, I'd see right through it."

* Chapter 21: Nova's Breath *

It was Oliver's turn to smile. "You don't think a Trinova could trip even *you* up?"

Watkin surprised Oliver by lifting his right eyebrow. They studied each other for a moment, with Watkin even swapping out one raised eyebrow for the other.

"Excellent segue," Watkin finally said, his eyes merrier than before. "You asked me earlier on what topics we would focus our lessons. Unless I'm mistaken, your preference, along with that of Emma and Lance, would be for me to train you in the art of *Nova's Breath*, or what you so miserably call my 'pulsing technique.'"

This time, Oliver did manage to keep his expression stoic. He didn't even twitch as Watkin described *exactly* what he wanted.

But then Watkin took a pause, and Oliver's neck betrayed him into a guilty swallow.

"My preference, however," Watkin went on with an impish flourish of his fingers, "is to teach you Virtue Theory."

Oliver's disappointment spread across his entire face, culminating into a petulant frown.

Watkin's grin didn't waver. "If only," he cried out, "your diligent, prudent, and maybe even a little conceited history professor had a way to teach you both!"

Oliver blinked, nonplussed.

Watkin cleared his throat excessively. Then, he raised one of his hands to the heavens. "I said, 'if only your diligent, prudent—,"

"If only," Oliver interrupted, his expression flat, "my conceited history professor had a way to teach me both."

Watkin snapped his fingers, looking jubilant. "It just so happens that my teachings on Virtue Theory will lead you to the *Nova's Breath* ability you so desperately covet!" Then, he leaned forward in his chair, furrowing his eyebrows with an intensity Oliver could feel from the other side of the desk. "So then, Oliver. Let us begin our first lesson with…"

Oliver waited.

"Yes, sir?"

"A question!"

"For me?"

Watkin faltered. But only for a second. "I can't engage with that level of stupidity, so we'll move past it."

Oliver wondered if he should have been the one to drink the liquid in Watkin's vial.

"Why," Watkin asked, "since man discovered fire, have we wrestled with the applications of virtue?"

Oliver clicked his tongue. "Professor, do we have the time for this? Shouldn't we be out searching Goodwin Forest?"

Watkin's intensity re-doubled, revealing the face of the man Oliver had seen take down the slew of monsters within the Ruins of Snowgem.

"Have I ever given you a reason not to trust me?"

Normally Oliver would have said "no," but he'd made a promise he'd start being more honest to others and he wasn't going to break it, even for

* Chapter 21: Nova's Breath *

Watkin. That had been the game *The Damned* played, and Oliver wasn't going to be a party to it.

"Yes," Oliver replied curtly.

Silence followed, swelling between them until it gnawed at Oliver's insides. He'd expected Watkin to wave his answer away, or maybe offer up a sarcastic chuckle, before pressing onward.

What he hadn't anticipated was for Watkin's face to fall into a sad, little frown. Or for the man's eyes to crest down at the corners.

"Ah," Oliver blurted out apologetically, "I just mean that last year you didn't ever really help us until... I mean? I get that you couldn't. Or at least why you thought you couldn't... And this year, I'm only saying, you haven't told me everything you know... like what's going on with you and Lalandra... and... how you know *The Damned*... and..."

Eventually, Oliver had enough sense to stop talking. Even though he meant what he said, he was only making things worse. At some point, the hurt in Watkin's eyes gave way to a steely resolve that reminded Oliver of Santiago before his uncle had been exposed to magic.

Watkin punctuated the change with a glib wave of his hand. "You've made your point and I concede to it. One party keeping the other in the dark cannot lead to trust. Very well, by the end of our lessons, I promise to answer any and every question you have."

Oliver's eyebrows raised. "Even stuff about Headmaster Lalandra?"

"Yes," Watkin said nodding his head impatiently.

The change in the man's tone made Oliver wish he'd just said, "of course I trust you, Professor," but Oliver had drawn a line in the sand with his principles. He wasn't going to manipulate anyone with lies, even if it meant losing out on a convenient tool. Besides, he'd gotten Watkin to promise him answers, which was a significant win. He, Emma, and Lance would have a lot less trepidation about going into a conflict with Tupper if they understood what had gone on between him, Watkin, and Lalandra before the accident at the Sooth… sayer's… temple…

The line of thinking brought Oliver's brainwaves to a screeching halt after realizing something so obvious he couldn't believe he'd ever missed it.

After Snowgem, Watkin had assigned them the task of researching *The Damned's* past as much as possible. And after starting the assignment earlier that month as a freshly-minted secretee to *The Damned's* true name, Oliver could now appreciate just how much information on Tupper's past—along with Watkin's and Lalandra's—was available to him.

Watkin had *already* provided him, Emma, and Lance a way to have their questions answered, and Oliver had been too slow to realize what that meant.

Tentatively, he looked back into Watkin's eyes. "I'm sorry, sir," he croaked. "I've only just put together why you asked us to research Tupper by ourselves. You wanted us to understand what happened last time around in as unbiased a way as possible. I should have realized that I could ask you follow-up questions if we had any after putting things together on my own."

Watkin's only reaction so far had been to roll his jaw, but Oliver wasn't finished. "I'm sorry," he finished as earnestly as possible, "for not

* Chapter 21: Nova's Breath *

understanding your instructions sooner…" Then, without looking Watkin in the eyes, he added, "that would have changed my answer about trust."

Watkin chewed on his jaw some more.

Then, just when Oliver was worried Watkin would take a leaf from Emma's book and turn to an icy persona for several weeks, the man's face re-brightened.

"I appreciate your saying that, Oliver. The next time you feel any doubts about my motivations or methods, I only ask that you lay them aside."

"Of course," Oliver grunted. He finally felt comfortable enough to return his eyes to Watkin's. So he did.

They were twinkling again.

A flutter of wings announced Jaiba's entry into the room. The toucan landed on Watkin's shoulder just as the man went on speaking. "Good!" he decreed with a playful flourish of his hands. "You've just experienced my favorite form of teaching. It's called benign neglect."

From Watkin's shoulder, Jaiba nodded his large beak up and down. *Caw-caw!*

Oliver shot Watkin a confused look, but no helpful explanation came—at least any that Oliver could understand.

"It's not for everybody," Watkin went on, "but I inherited the teaching style from my late parents. I spent my twenties wishing they'd played a more active role in my upbringing, but like any good training method, the benefits only began to manifest, and I daresay exponentially build on themselves, the older I turned. Much more powerful to learn from your own mistakes than be given a solution, eh?"

"Hmm," Oliver offered.

Watkin nodded, leaning forward again. "You're right. We're wasting time."

Oliver didn't think saying, "technically you're the one wasting time," would help, so he kept the thought to himself.

"Onto the lesson: Virtue Theory. I repeat my earlier question, why do humans grapple with virtue?"

Oliver stalled for time by leaning back in his chair and clasping his hands behind his neck. They felt clammy, so he let go quickly.

Engaging in a philosophical discussion with Watkin could only end up going one way. Oliver knew it. And he'd be willing to bet Watkin felt the same way. But he also knew that Watkin would have a reason for asking the question, so there was no use in delaying the inevitable.

"Because morals are important?" Oliver offered up, feeling incredibly stupid.

Watkin nodded, raising his eyebrows as if Oliver had said something brilliant. "And why are morals important?"

Oliver let out a breath. He was out of his element. For a moment, he even felt a sliver of sympathy for James, Beto's head crony. To him, every conversation probably felt like this.

"Because they make us do the right thing?"

Watkin pondered the half answer thoughtfully. "And what defines right and wrong?"

* Chapter 21: Nova's Breath *

Oliver felt a chill creep up his spine. Slow at first, but then sharp and fast. Hadn't *The Damned* asked him a similar question inside the Forest Temple? The memory came back to him easily, contrasting sharply against the warm, cozy, book-laden office he and Watkin now occupied.

> *"And what do you consider the opposite of evil? Will you serve as an arbiter for good? As a man of principle? Fools look to morality. True politics require we remain agnostic of self-inflicted burdens."*

Oliver returned his focus to Watkin in the present, giving the man an appraising look. "I'll have you know," he said, forcibly calm, "Tupper asked me a *very* similar question."

"I'm sure he did," Watkin posited. "But answer the question."

Oliver almost tsked his tongue again but buffed his nails against his pants instead—as nonchalantly as possible. He wished Watkin would give him an explanation instead of a question, but after the man's little speech on "benign neglect," there was little chance of that happening.

"What defines right versus wrong?" Oliver repeated out loud. His first thought went back to Santiago's catholic upbringing. "Is it your religion?" That didn't sound quite right, so he added, "your background?"

Watkin leaned back in his chair, grinning from ear to ear. "Oh, I never meant for you to think there would be a definitive answer to the question."

Oliver intentionally loosened his cheeks, eyes, and lips into a disgusted frown.

"For what it's worth," Watkin continued unperturbed, "I think you're exactly right.

"We as human beings pass on our cultural, spiritual, ethical, moral, and philosophical norms to our next-of-kin, teaching every scrap of it as absolute, paradigmatic truth. In essence, it's our own cultural and ideological heritage that defines what is good or right versus what is evil or wrong."

Oliver felt like he followed some of Watkin's words. But the overall messaging made his head spin. "You're saying we know what's good and evil based on our ancestors?"

"That's one way to put it," Watkin breathed. He leaned forward, his chair creaking in the process. When he spoke again, his brow had furrowed. "Said differently, our moral codes are defined, and even limited, by our localized heritage. Does that seem shallow to you?"

"Umm," Oliver hedged, "not if we... know we're right..."

Watkin raised a finger and tilted his head inquisitively. "Ah, but we couldn't possibly *know* we're right. If we come against another culture or ideology, both sides will insist they are just as correct as the other."

Oliver opened his mouth for a rebuttal, only none came. He scrunched up his face and thought hard. "I guess you're right, Professor. Assuming my morals as more 'right' than somebody else's *is*, umm, 'shallow'?"

Watkin slapped his hand on the table. "Excellent! That is the mentality required of everybody in the world for a utopia to exist."

Oliver shook his head, keeping an eye on Watkin's hand. "But I don't know anybody like that, Professor. Most everybody thinks they're the

* Chapter 21: Nova's Breath *

right ones. Even if we forget about religion or ancestors, most everybody I know thinks they're right about... well, everything." Even as he said it, Oliver suppressed a smile. Emma would likely have rolled her eyes at Watkin—there was no way her principles were wrong in her eyes.

Watkin leaned back in his chair, looking supremely satisfied. "This would include someone's political preferences, correct?"

Oliver had never cared much for politics, so he shrugged. "I guess. But even if I you make a believer out of me, that only makes two people—out of how many billion are we at now?—wise enough for your utopia where everybody respects each other's differences."

A dry chuckle escaped Watkin's lips. "Well, I'm glad you see the problem. But I would contend we already know of a third."

"Oh yeah?" Oliver asked frowning. Was Lalandra of the same mindset as Watkin? "Who?"

Watkin's smile faded and his eyes dulled, abandoning the twinkle he'd previously held. On his shoulder, Jaiba let out a low, grave squawk.

"Isn't it obvious?"

Oliver gasped as he realized the answer to his own question.

"So, Tupper was an idealist?" Emma asked, drawing the left side of her lips back into the slightest of smirks.

NOVA 02

Oliver frowned up at her from where he sat. They were getting ready for Coatlball tryouts in the Eastern locker room beneath the bleachers. Oliver had only just caught up to them and was gearing up as quickly as possible, fumbling his boots' laces in the process. Emma and Lance had dallied intentionally to wait for him, but the rest of the Hutchites had already exited, clapping each of them on the back as they shuffled out. Abe had even stared around the locker room wistfully before sighing. "A shame we have so much talent this year," he said, his normally bright, cheery eyes downcast. "Not everybody's gonna make the team."

"An idealist, Oli?" Emma repeated after Abe had left. "The man killed thousands if not millions, yeah? And you're saying he was just a misunderstood guy who wanted to build a perfect, new world?"

Oliver rolled his eyes, frustrated that she didn't understand.

It ended up being a waste of energy, however, because Emma had bent down to fix her hair. When she flipped back up, she'd transformed her messy bun into a tight ponytail.

Next to her, Lance pulled on his old Coatlball boots, grimacing as the leather caught on his calves. The hide threatened to rip as Oliver looked at his friend pleadingly.

"Oli, you're not making a lick of sense," Lance grunted. After he managed to get both boots on with a flare of Power, he looked up and assumed something close to a diplomatic expression. "Ehh, if Tupper was an idealist, then why the rehabilitation centers? Why imprison and get rid of people like my dad?"

Chapter 21: Nova's Breath

Oliver almost threw his hands up in the air and flared Wisdom. But he stopped himself, remembering a snippet of his earlier lesson with Watkin. *"In repeatedly flaring Wisdom to stay calm, you're merely treating a symptom. Do you want to remedy the symptom or the underlying problem?"* He'd made it sound so easy. *"Target the problem by training yourself to stay calm, neutral, and diplomatic without depending on flares of Wisdom."*

Oliver took in a deep breath. It mostly worked, he thought, even if his teeth were semi-gritted when he resumed the conversation. "But that's the point! Tupper *thought* everybody could get along better if everyone just accepted that we're all from different backgrounds and…" He looked around at the ceiling, trying to find the word Watkin had used, but he couldn't remember it—a lot of big words had circulated around Watkin's office during their first one-on-one lesson and none of them had come from Oliver.

Emma and Lance exchanged glances, creasing their brows.

"Then why the murders?" Lance repeated.

Oliver clicked his tongue, re-focusing on his bootlaces and hating the timing of the Coatlball tryouts. After having just learned about Tupper's foundational views, he wanted to get right back to researching the madman's life, not squabble with his friends about whether Watkin's theory was right. If they wanted to have any chance at defeating Tupper when he escaped his purgatory, which Augustus guaranteed would happen, they needed to understand *how* the boy transformed from the idealist into the monster they'd seen in the Forest Temple.

"Look," Oliver said, switching tactics with a pleading expression on his face. "I'm not saying Tupper was a good person or anything like—,"

Emma stopped smirking. "Hang on," she interrupted, her eyes expanding. "This has you proper spooked, doesn't it?"

"Yes!" Oliver said, not even bothering to mask the desperation in his voice. "Don't you get it?!"

"You gonna tell us," Lance said gruffly, "or continue getting upset?"

Oliver took in another breath and somehow stopped himself from raising his voice. "If," he said holding his hands up invitingly, "we assume Tupper started as an idealist who wanted to fix the world,"—he gave Emma and Lance a chance to nod their heads before going on—"then that means, at some point he turned into the monster that wanted to clear the world of anybody who didn't meet his standards, yeah?"

"People like my dad," Lance agreed. "So what? He went crazy, didn't he?"

"That's one option," Oliver said. "The other option is that he didn't go crazy at all, and that everything went to plan."

Oliver paused again, allowing the message to sink in.

Emma crossed her arms while Lance thought visibly. "Then why's he in purgatory?" she asked.

"Okay!" Oliver said impatiently. "He messed up once. That's why he's in purgatory. But before that, nah, it was all planned out."

"Why does it even matter?" Lance growled. "We just gotta stop him when he escapes, right?"

* Chapter 21: Nova's Breath *

Just as Oliver was about to start yelling, he heard a breath escape Emma's lips. When he turned to face her, she looked surprised for a moment, before turning fierce. "It matters," Emma said slowly at first, "because it tells us what we're coming up against."

"Exactly," Oliver said, letting out a relieved sigh. "A raving lunatic is one thing—we can handle that. But a sensible man with a plan is even scarier, if you ask me."

Emma adjusted the magical sleeve underneath her tryouts jersey, sizing Oliver up. "I think... I agree with both of you."

"Yuss!" Lance breathed, clenching a raised fist in victory.

Oliver crossed his arms, waiting for an explanation.

Emma tilted her head so that she could look down on him with a very satisfied look on her face. "Okay, yes, *The Damned* being a psychotic genius is an issue—which by the way, makes a lot of sense given the ten-thousand articles we've already read about the jerk."

Oliver rolled his eyes and shook his head. "But..." he prodded.

Emma laughed, banging open the locker room doors, blinding them with sunlight. "Our MO is still the same, isn't it?" she asked, leading them to the front of the bleachers and then the Coatlball trench. "Lance is right. Genius or psycho, our mission is to take the guy out."

"Okay fine," Oliver agreed. "But we gotta plan for the genius, not the psycho, got it?"

Both Emma and Lance waved Oliver's concern away.

"Was that really the whole lesson," Lance asked, disappointed. "No top-secret magic training?"

NOVA 02

"I told you we spoke in Watkin's office, didn't I?" Oliver asked irritably. "Do you see us crammed in there with all those books taking on baboon monsters or pigs with sickles?"

Lance laughed. "Well ask him about it next time, will ya?"

"Watkin says it's all connected," Oliver mumbled. "But I'll believe it when I see it."

Emma stopped walking towards the Coatlball trench as the familiar sound of fluttering wings caught their ears. "What about Goodwin Forest?" she asked.

Oliver slapped a hand to his forehead. "I should have started with that!"

"Go on, then," Lance said, shoving Oliver lightly on the back.

"The Fire Drake's Cavern," Oliver rushed out. The feathered serpents would arrive soon and though he trusted Archie, he couldn't vouch for the rest. "Augustus said we'd find Cuahtemoc's artifact in there."

"We already knew that," Emma said, her tone haughty. "Good-win-For-est?"

Oliver ignored the jibe. "Watkin says he knows the Fire Drake's Cavern is *in* the forest."

Both Emma and Lance stopped peering at the approaching throng of feathered serpents to gape at Oliver.

"It's in the Forest?" Lance asked, his face going pale. "Where the disappearances are happening?"

"And Watkin is searching it every night for a hidden temple?" Emma asked.

* Chapter 21: Nova's Breath *

For a few more moments, Emma and Lance exchanged aghast stares. Eventually, however, Emma nodded, impressed.

"Are we sure Watkin doesn't have Bravery? That man is something else."

NOVA 02

Chapter 22: The Tlamacaz

I tried telling Tío that I'm a human being. That I'm allowed to be frustrated. That it's annoying to watch Watkin's opposition campaign delay our progress. That it's outrageous to see Lalandra come from nowhere and drum up resistance in the Midwest.

Tío just laughed at me. Evidently, "emotions are for the weak."

2nd of October, the second year of the 10th Age

Before Oliver could answer Emma, three feathered serpents descended from the skies in quicksilver, circular motions, looping down to land on the grass preceding the Coatlball trench.

Rasmus touched down first, settling his four-hundred pounds onto the grass with a less-than-graceful plop. Then, Merri and a new serpent Oliver didn't recognize followed, landing even more awkwardly. As a rule, feathered serpents appeared other-worldly to Oliver's eyes when in the air. On the ground, however...

"Hurry up now," Rasmus said, flittering his tongue at Emma. *"The Earth is no place for a sacred beast."*

With trepidation, Oliver sized up Archie's replacement. He almost looked away immediately.

Where Archie exuded an effervescent warmth, the newcomer radiated a sense of feral lethality and aggression that tugged on Oliver's instincts to run for shelter. Even if the beast turned out to be just as good of a

* Chapter 22: The Tlamacaz *

Coatlball companion, Oliver could already tell they wouldn't share half as good a relationship as he and Archie did.

He needed his friend back.

The newcomer crested its snout to regard Oliver with curiosity. *"Your disappointment is palpable,"* it said, interrupting Oliver's thoughts with a deep voice and an accent that had more in common with Rasmus than Archie. *"You may call me Nero."*

Nero's accent sounded wrong to Oliver's ears, which was of course ridiculous. It wasn't Nero's fault he spoke in a posh British accent—he must have been born under Augustus' watchful eye. It was a stark reminder of how much older Archie was than some of his counterparts. Archie had grown up before Cuahtemoc, so his accent carried Nahuatl and Spanish influences more than English ones.

Eventually, Oliver got over his disappointment and waved an awkward hello. "Am I making that good of a first impression?" he asked sarcastically. Then, finding that he didn't particularly care if he wounded Nero's pride or not, he approached the serpent and began scratching his neck just beneath the ear. At first Nero shirked away, or at least tried to, wiggling his enormous gold and azure blue form on the grass, but then his eyes expanded, and the corners of his mandibles lifted into a satisfied smile.

"Question for ya," Oliver asked as the serpent stretched its neck out so that Oliver scratched just the right bunch of feathers. "Do you know where Archie is?"

Nero shirked away violently, recoiling at the question with a great hiss.

NOVA 02

"*ARE YOU **INSANE**, BOY?!*" the serpent's voice screamed telepathically, forcing Oliver two steps back. "*The Tlamacaz does not deign to communicate his every move with us!*"

To Oliver's astonishment, the quetzal didn't stop there. He watched, in amazement, as Nero contracted his upper neck close to his body and swallowed with fright. He even looked around timidly to confirm nobody could have overheard them.

"Oh," Oliver said, dissatisfied. Even so, his curiosity spurred him on. That had not been a normal reaction from the young serpent. "What did you call Archie? Tlama-something?"

"*Enough of this,*" Nero hissed with his mind and tongue. "*My name is Nero, and this is all you should or need know.*"

Oliver nodded passively at Nero's reply as he lodged himself onto the serpent's back. He knew a lost cause when he saw one, so he gave Nero a couple pokes with his knees. Nero took off without question, fluttering his wings until they reached the rest of the Hutchites in between the Coatlball goalposts.

"Good to meet you, Nero. I'm Oliver."

"*I know who you are,*" Nero grumbled. "*I'm to be your replacement Guide.*"

"Mhmm," Oliver intoned. "And how long will the *Tlamawazit* need replacing."

Nero's back-feathers bristled a full inch, scratching against Oliver's leather boots. Some even punctured his tryouts jersey and scratched against his skin. Oliver yelped with pain, swatting the feathers away. "Hey! Watch what you're doing with—,"

* Chapter 22: The Tlamacaz *

But Nero cut Oliver off, turning to face him with bright, nervous eyes. They looked strange on such a fierce, feathered face. *"I beg of you, Trinova,"* he pleaded. *"Do not speak of your relationship with the Tlamacaz with me. I do not hold his station, nor any of his protections. If any quetzal were to hear these words and assume I hold the same… the same beliefs?! I have a family! They would not survive without their father!"*

"Woah!" Oliver interjected. "All I asked was if you'd seen Ar—,"

"I MUST INSIST," Nero's voice roared in Oliver's mind. *"THAT YOU DIRECT ALL INQUIRIES REGARDING THE TLAMACAZ TO OUR INTERIM LEADER!"*

"OKAY!" Oliver shouted back, garnering confused looks from Emma and Lance, nearby. Out of the corner of his eye he saw them nudge Rasmus and Merri to join him. "Who's the interim leader I should be speaking with, anyway? Maybe he can help me find Archie." For a moment Oliver berated himself for not thinking of the idea sooner. Some of the other feathered serpents might know where Archie would go to recover—or at least have a hint of an idea. It'd beat any of his own wild guesses.

"Musfati of the Emaiun."

Oliver sagged in place. "Isn't that Beto's guide?" he asked, frowning at the thought. Unless he was mistaken, Nero had just hinted his family would be in danger if he were to speak to Oliver too much about Archie. If Musfati were the new leader, then the threat was likely legitimate. Archie often enjoyed lecturing Oliver over his personal feud with Beto, but Oliver had long considered the advice hypocritical after witnessing the amount of vitriol Musfati and Archie exchanged any time they got too close to each other.

Nero shuddered beneath Oliver, forcing him to channel the static electricity between the feathers in front of him and chant, *"remasco,"* to stop himself from getting sick.

"I do not know of this Beto," Nero answered, coming to a halt.

"Well," Oliver said between a few burps, "I do know Beto, and, let me tell you, he's just as kind and warmhearted as Musfati of the Emaiun."

Nero hesitated before replying. *"I do not dabble in human sarcasm, Trinova, but this Beto must be a very great leader indeed if he holds any similarity with Musfati the Terrible."*

"Uh huh," Oliver said, no longer paying attention.

"What's going on?" Emma asked.

Oliver hadn't missed Rasmus requiring a handful of aggressive heel kicks from Emma to finally approach Oliver and Nero. Whatever Nero didn't want to talk about, neither did Rasmus.

"I'll tell you later," Oliver said, shaking his head.

Emma raised a skeptical eyebrow before prodding Rasmus to zoom away towards Lizzie instead.

With Emma gone, and Elton now hounding Lance over who'd get the central midfield position from atop his giant bald eagle, Oliver shifted his attention to the growing number of students filling the trench.

* Chapter 22: The Tlamacaz *

At its simplest, the game of Coatlball came down to one simple rule: score more points than the opponent by throwing a "pigskin" into a net. As Oliver quickly discovered during his extraman year, however, the sport became much more nuanced the moment you began playing.

Much more nuanced.

None of the players, for instance, ran on foot like in most sports Oliver had grown accustomed to. In fact, none ever touched the ground at all, only ever riding on their Guides. This meant that at any given moment, approximately twenty-four-hundred pounds of feathered serpent, great eagle, or osorius hurtled around or above the trench. It was a frightening sight to behold from the bleachers, let alone from inside the trench itself.

Extraman students could be forgiven for needing time to acclimate to the breakneck, terrifying speed of the sacred beasts alone, but the flying masses of feathers and fur were only the first layer to the game. From the students, any and all magic was allowed, even encouraged. Common practice within a match was for opposing midfielders to devise more and more creative ways to gain the upper hand on their opponents using dastardly forms of magic like summoned flocks of attacking owls or quickly formed brick walls.

The only real rules to the game were magic could only be applied indirectly—no direct attacks with a sword or elementals—and students couldn't move forward if they held the ball on a feathered serpent or eagle. Only a pass downtrench could progress play.

NOVA 02

"So," Watkin said from the center of the Coatlball trench, rubbing his hands together. "Any questions?" He sat nestled on the back of a wizened giant eagle, surrounded by a couple dozen Hutchites trying out for the Hutch team. Watkin's eagle surveyed them with one yellow-blue eye and a second greyed-out, dead eye, but Oliver wasn't fussed about the eye. What was *really* interesting was just how comfortable Watkin looked on the back of a giant eagle. The man carried himself as though he'd been born to ride sacred beasts. Oliver had known Watkin played Coatlball in a professional capacity after school, but seeing evidence of it with his own eyes was something else.

Next to Watkin, Blackwood snarled, ushering his own eagle away from the circle of Hutchites. "I just reminded them of the rules, Cato. Do we have to repeat them?"

"And yet," Watkin said, his eyes twinkling, "Mr. Kemper has a question for us. Yes, Trey?"

"What's the points distribution again, sir? By distance?"

Blackwood snarled with frustration. "You ought to demand more from your dormitory's students. If anyone in Champayan asked a question like that—,"

"Yes," Watkin said, cutting Blackwood off with an impatient wave of his hand, "I'm sure they'd have your wit with which to joust. Consider us thoroughly chastened."

Blackwood bristled from the back of his eagle. "Don't make an enemy out of me, Cato," he threatened.

* Chapter 22: The Tlamacaz *

"I shudder at the thought," Watkin replied dryly. Oliver, Emma, and Lance exchanged grins. Would Blackwood challenge Watkin if he'd seen what they'd witnessed in Snowgem? A duel between the two professors would be a fun watch as far as Oliver was concerned.

Watkin didn't waste time moving on. "Now! Mr. Kemper," he continued, clapping his hands together. Blackwood didn't stay to hear the rest, ushering his eagle to ascend without another word. Which caught Oliver by surprise. Blackwood *loved* getting in the last word. The man was so petulant that he cared about beating students in stare-downs, so why didn't he say something nasty back to Watkin? Maybe the man did know just how strong Watkin was after all...

"If you hit the board, it's one point," Watkin told Trey while Oliver kept his eyes on Blackwood. The giant man didn't stop his eagle until he circled high above the trench. He'd supervise them from there for the remainder of their tryouts just like he'd done last year. But unless Oliver was mistaken, Blackwood wouldn't be saying nearly as many nasty things as he had last year when they were extramen. Back then, Zapien supervised their tryouts as the Dorm Head. This year, however, under Watkin's watchful eye...

"And if you hit the net," Watkin went on, the picture of confidence, "that's three points. And remember the points double if you score from further than thirty yards out."

Next to his right side, Oliver felt somebody lean in close. He hadn't planned on flinching, but then Emma's voice cut in at a whisper. "He's likely just mad Watkin got you out of detention," she said tilting her head up at Blackwood knowingly.

Oliver nodded, trying to ignore just how much the sound of Emma's whispering voice made him weak in the knees.

"Are your legs in need of strengthening, Trinova?" Nero chided haughtily when Oliver tried prodding the feathered serpent's sides to usher them forward for their first drill. *"You'd struggle to motivate an old pony with these paltry kicks."*

Oliver flared Power, shooting them forward with little issue thereafter.

For their first drill, Watkin split them into groups for short-range passing drills. He demonstrated how to perform the drill himself, pinging short accurate passes to Se'Vaughn, hitting the boy's chest with every throw no matter how much his eagle twisted or turned. This time, more of the Hutchites than just Oliver gaped or nodded at Watkin's capabilities.

The tryouts continued for nearly two hours, ranging from full-field defensive drills to one-on-one penalty shoot outs. As had been the case last year, Oliver's favorite test came when crossing the length of the entire trench while dodging dozens of obstacles thrown at them by Watkin within the trench and Blackwood from up above. A sneaky attack from a murder of crows caught Valerie unawares, dragging her off her Guide and onto magically appearing cushions at bottom of the trench. Then, for a second year in a row, Trey ran straight into a wall, this time made of glass, knocking him off his steed and onto the cushions next to Valerie. Unlike the prior year, Se'Vaughn beat Lance to cross the trench quickest. He made sure to

* Chapter 22: The Tlamacaz *

flex his biceps at both Wyatt brothers when they reached him, placing second and third.

Though they wouldn't hear the tryout results until later in the day, Oliver was certain he, Emma, and Lance would make the Coatlball team. During the hour-and-a-half of drills, Emma had earned a "well done" from Watkin when scoring past both Lance and Elton, both of whom were clearly the best defenders on the team. Oliver, meanwhile, continuously impressed by somehow always staying a step ahead of everyone else. With his Wisdom, there wasn't any feint or move he couldn't see coming, which he could use to great effect despite both his passing ability and chemistry with Nero not being the best.

After a brief water break, Watkin led them on to the Dungeon Simulator for their next set of tryouts. While the rest entered, Abe pulled Oliver aside and asked if he, Emma, and Lance would be comfortable forming the bones of the second-string dungeon solving team instead of trying-out for the first-string.

"Strategically speaking," the bespeckled boy argued, "we'd guarantee more points if both our dungeon solving teams go far in the tournament later this year."

Oliver furrowed his eyebrows at the question. Not because he disliked it, but for some reason Abe had looked nervous when asking, wiping sweat from his forehead more than once.

"A-and," Abe snuck in, stammering, "it'd be good training for you three. You'll want to keep your core together won't you? For training for the real world, right?"

NOVA 02

Oliver put a hand on Abe's shoulder. "I think it's a great idea," he said smiling warmly.

"Thanks for understanding!" Abe said, his words tumbling out of his mouth. "I'll be taking Stevie's place as the team lead but otherwise the rest of the A team will be the same."

Abe made to follow the rest into the simulator, pointing back at Oliver and shaking his hand. "You won't regret this!"

Oliver kept his smile up. It didn't really matter who was on the A or B team. Abe was right, having a strong B team would get them even more points in the tournament.

A thud of wood against stone caught Oliver by surprise.

Thunk.

When he turned, he saw Watkin, both hands on his staff. How long had he been waiting there outside unseen?

"Very Wise of you," Watkin said, hefting the staff to walk past Oliver. "Trusting your older friends to do what they do best. A lesser man in your position would insist on being the lead himself."

Oliver had never been one for compliments so all he managed was an awkward pressing together of his lips as Watkin stepped past to join the rest inside.

* Chapter 22: The Tlamacaz *

By the end of the afternoon, Oliver, Emma, and Lance celebrated with the rest of the Hutchites in the Dining Hall, applauding in turn for everyone who'd made either the Coatlball, dungeon sims, or dueling teams. Having made all three, Oliver felt more relaxed than he had since starting the year.

But he couldn't fully relax. Not really.

"It'll be good for our reflexes, you know?" he told Lance at dinner, trying to find a way in his head to justify spending time on sports. Could it work as training for *The Damned?* "Ms. Joan," he added, rapping his ring on the wooden table, "I'd like steak and potatoes for dinner, please and thanks."

Lance grumbled over the trough's-worth of chicken, beans, and rice he'd ordered. "Yeah, I'd have liked to make the dueling team, too, but dungeons sims and Coatlball will be good enough for me." When he finished, he flicked his eyes forlornly towards Emma.

Oliver followed the look, understanding Lance's sad face. Emma had also made all three teams. Of the three of them, only Lance hadn't.

"I wouldn't worry about it," Oliver snuck in. "We'll get you all trained up with anything we learn. It can be something we do at the start of our Tupper Sessions or something."

Lance brightened. "Yeah," he said. "That sounds good."

Grinning, Oliver turned his attention to his steaming pile of steak and potatoes. It smelled heavenly, covered in just the right amount of butter, and when he cut into—

NOVA 02

Oliver's smile loosened on his face. Ms. Joan had included a message in his potatoes.

"You better visit – and not just during a detention!"

Shame bubbled up in Oliver's stomach as he read the message over three times. Closing his eyes, he put his hands on the edge of the table and scooched his chair back.

"Where are you going?" Lance asked, cresting his eyes in confusion.

Oliver motioned with his thumb towards Ms. Joan's hidden kitchen behind the western wall. "Gotta go apologize," he mumbled.

Lance didn't look any less confused but Oliver had already made his mind. More than just friendly Hutchites peered at him as he marched over to the sliding door between the Dining Hall and Ms. Joan's kitchen. The whispers came loudest from the Champayan table, but he ignored them.

"Ms. Joan," he hissed, arriving at the wall. "Let me in! I look like an idiot standing out here!"

With an almighty grating sound, the wall slid open a crack, just wide enough for him to enter. He slipped inside before Ms. Joan could change her mind.

As the door shut behind him, a tall, lean woman addressed him with her wrists pressed against her hips. She wore an apron over a stylish dress that matched the head cover she'd artfully placed over her short, black hair.

* Chapter 22: The Tlamacaz *

"Now *where* have you been?" Ms. Joan asked, her face as haughty as her wrists. "You've been back for a month and never once did you think to check on poor, old Ms. Joan." One of her wrists went to her upturned forehead. "Have you forgotten the little people so quickly, Mister Trinova?"

If Oliver hadn't known Ms. Joan better, he might have worried she was actually mad. He grinned at her, shrugging. "I've been a little busy," he said, pulling a chair from under the sprawling table covering the middle of the room.

"Nah uh," Ms. Joan said, brandishing an industrial spatula at him. "Did I say you could sit down?"

Oliver sat down anyway, grinning. "It's good to see you."

Ms. Joan softened immediately, lowering the raised spatula and smiling roguishly.

"And I *am* sorry," Oliver emphasized, blowing out a raspberry with his lips. "I really am busy."

Ms. Joan laughed, pulling up a chair next to him. With a snap of her fingers and a touch of her hand to the ruby necklace on her neck, the pots and pans surrounding them kept cooking without her. "And you think I'm *not* busy?" she challenged, gesturing at the bedlam ensuing around the kitchen as ovens, grills, and stoves worked to complete ongoing orders from the students.

"They seem to be doing just fine without you," Oliver countered, half-laughing at the self-sustaining kitchen.

Ms. Joan smiled some more.

NOVA 02

"You trying to gain some weight?" she asked. "I see your boy Lance is ordering enough food to feed a village. I can give you some extra helpings if you need 'em, too."

Oliver opened his mouth to agree to maybe an extra serving here or there, but Ms. Joan surprised him, standing abruptly and shooting her hands back to her hips.

"Hang on!" she said, raising her voice. "You can't charm me that easy. What are you doing landing in detention again? You should be a better influence for your friends!"

Oliver shrugged again. "You know what Blackwood's like."

"Hmmm," was all Ms. Joan agreed to.

Oliver thought a story might lie hidden behind the 'hmmm' but didn't go prodding. "How'd your summer go, then?" he asked, steering them towards a safer conversation.

Ms. Joan sat down next to him at once, placing her hands on her knees emphatically. "Well," she said, pretending to push long hair that didn't exist over her shoulder, "I had a blast, if you must know. Caught up with all my culinary school friends in France for a few weeks. Then I saw all these cool temples in Thailand—all on the Original Side of the Key, mind you—while I attended a summer institute for southeast Asian cuisine. You've got to keep your cooking up to scratch, you know? It's nice to get away from magic and just cook sometimes…"

Oliver leaned back in his chair, contently listening to Ms. Joan's summer traveling itinerary. It was nice to have someone to talk to about life, and not *The Damned* or whatever else might be stressing him out.

* Chapter 22: The Tlamacaz *

Before he even realized what he was doing, however, she did end up getting him to talk about his stresses and start to the academic year. Oliver bristled at first, but then he realized he didn't mind talking to her about it. Ms. Joan genuinely *cared* about him in a way none of the other adults seemed to. Yes, Watkin was an ally, but sometimes the man's pragmatic approach felt downright transactional. With Ms. Joan, on the other hand, they just talked for the sake of talking. And it felt *good* to get some of the things worrying him off his chest.

"You sure do like to travel," Oliver stated half an hour later, when they circled back to the highlights of her trip. Ms. Joan mirrored him, rising from her chair to give him a warm hug.

As they broke away, she laughed and pointed at a map above a desk near a short staircase. "You bet I do!" she said. "I've pinned everywhere I've ever been on that map. Go on, give it a look."

Oliver stepped over, shaking his head incredulously the closer he got. Every country in Europe was pinned, along with half of Africa, numerous spots in China, Korea, Japan, Thailand, Tibet, and places Oliver had never even considered.

As he took in the map, Oliver wondered, and not for the first time, why wizards and witches enjoyed traveling so much. *The Damned* had done it after school, and Stevie was doing so at that very moment.

"Did you care about history when you traveled?" he asked, stepping away from the map. It was too close to the staircase for his tastes—the one that gave off enough heat to… well, he didn't know what exactly the heat down the stairs was for, but it had to be a source of energy for the kitchens or maybe the dormitory below.

Ms. Joan raised an eyebrow to look at him wryly. "I cared about food and wine when I traveled. Both of those things *are* human history if you ask me."

"Hmm," Oliver said, thinking out loud. "I may need to ask you questions about different places of the world some day. Is that alright?"

Ms. Joan began pushing him outside with light shoves to his back. "You don't need to be stressed all the time, Oliver," she said as the sliding door scraped open. "Try to remember to be the boy your uncle raised,"— she poked him with her spatula as he crossed back into the Dining Hall— "the boy you really *are* whenever you start acting like a Trinova."

* Chapter 22: The Tlamacaz *

NOVA 02

Chapter 23: A Well-deserved Break

Tío's confidence keeps me going—he's sure we'll win because he's a "man of principle."

7th of October, the second year of the 10th Age

Over the course of October, Oliver began to wonder if somebody had picked up a clock and begun messing with time. One moment he'd find himself on a Monday morning blinking away the crust on his eyes, the next, stepping into a Friday night with a mountain of homework, research, and training left on his plate.

"If we don't give ourselves Friday nights off," Lance grumbled by the last Friday in October, "I'm *going* to die." They sat in the Dining Hall, and to emphasize his point, Lance leveled a forked tuna steak in Oliver's direction accusatorily. "Do you want my death on your conscious, García? Do you?!"

Oliver kept his eyes on the tuna for a moment and let out a sigh. He didn't feel like reminding Lance they had no time to waste so he rotated his head towards Emma instead. Maybe she'd have the energy to whip Lance into shape.

The only problem was Oliver's neck was so stiff he couldn't move far enough to see her. With a hand to his chin, he cracked his neck until his eyes met Emma's.

"*Belay that movement!*" Roli protested from the top of his head. "*I am full of potatoes!*"

* Chapter 23: A Well-deserved Break *

Oliver paid Roli no attention. He'd begrudgingly allowed the persistent iguana a semi-permanent spot on his head or shoulders, but he'd actually go crazy if he let the lizard govern his every move. Instead, Oliver kept his attention on Emma. Her barely-put-together bun of hair unraveled as she shook her head at him.

"Oli!" she said, shriller than he would have expected. "We just wrapped a week of thirty lessons, four Big-Five practices, seven work-outs with Elton, four Tupper Sessions, and I can't even tell you how many hours of homework!"

"See?!" Lance growled. His forked tuna steak whisked flecks of oil in every direction as he spoke. "We deserve a night off once a week *at least!*"

Roli's dewlap bobbled as he began to laugh. *"The Damned does not rest and neither should you."*

As Roli and Emma traded dagger-eyes, Oliver realized he agreed with… both of them.

"Not helpful, Roli," he said, grunting and swallowing guiltily at the same time. When he eventually nodded his head to agree with Lance—much to Roli's annoyance—Lance exhaled for a full five seconds, deflating into his chair in the process.

"But!" Oliver added, pointing an emphatic finger in the air. Lance's deflating halted.

"Yes! Wield your authority like the divine intended! Relieve yourself of your BOYISH BURDEN AND MANIFEST YOUR—,"

NOVA 02

Oliver cut off Roli before the lizard gathered up too much speed. "I'm not trying to be bossy here," he said, leaning in towards Emma and Lance, "but we do have one more thing to do… remember?"

Before going on, Oliver glanced around the room, gauging whether anyone could hear them or not. Most everybody else, including their fellow Hutchites, had eaten much earlier in the evening so it was unlikely anyone would overhear. But it never hurt to be safe.

"*Stratum silentii,*" he muttered.

Emma's eyes flashed the same moment she slammed a palm to her forehead. "I totally forgot!"

"What?" Lance asked, finally deciding to eat his tuna. He ripped a bite off with his teeth, foregoing the knife on his plate to eat the meat right off the fork.

"Abe and Brantley's update!" Emma hissed.

Lance dropped his fork. "Sure," he said. "What better way to cap off a month of hell?"

Roli stepped down onto Oliver's shoulder, eyeing the remaining piece of meat on Lance's fork like a wild dog in front of a butcher shop. *"Surely you don't mean to leave that tasty morsel behind, Master Wyatt?"*

"You only call me master when you want food," Lance sighed.

* Chapter 23: A Well-deserved Break *

A moment later, after shoveling down the rest of their food and mouthing *thank-yous* towards Ms. Joan's kitchen, they dashed outside past Tolteca's foyer towards the southern bridge and the Academic Building. Only when their footsteps padded along the wood of the bridge and then the stone of the brick pathway did they speak again.

"Now," Roli said, coughing in his dewlap altogether unnecessarily given that he communicated telepathically. *"What do we intend to achieve with this conversation with Abraham and the portly fellow whom you call Brant-man? Surely that can't be his real name. It's ridiculous."*

Oliver exchanged looks with Emma and Lance before replying. Over the course of October, they'd gotten to know Roli's personality a bit better, and to say the iguana was a micro-manager would have been an understatement.

"Um," Oliver said with no small amount of irritation in his voice, "to see if Beto was lying or not. We don't know whether the Goodwin Forest disappearances are connected to Tupper. Abe and Brantley have been looking into what's going on other there while we've researched *The Damned.*"

Roli stamped a little foot on Oliver's shoulder. *"Again, with the irritation! Stop! Stop walking this instant!"*

Oliver opened his mouth to disagree, but Roli forced him to stop by sticking his tongue in his ear. Oliver's high-pitched scream brought several seconds of laughing out of Emma and Lance.

"ROLI!" Oliver shouted. "You can't just boss us around all the time! It's—,"

NOVA 02

Roli sprung from Oliver's shoulder onto a nearby tree branch. *"Enough!"* he commanded. *"Sit! Each of you. This has been coming for a while now anyway."*

Angry at having been scolded by his pet lizard, Oliver sat first, muttering under his breath. A moment later, Emma and Lance joined him, plopping down onto the stone.

"If anybody walks by, they're going to be very confused," Lance chuckled.

"Do you remember what Augustus told you this summer?" Roli asked, glaring down at them from his tree branch.

"That Tupper's going to escape," Emma growled. "And that we gotta be ready for it. Look, man, we get it, we're low on time and—,"

"No!" Roli shouted, cutting Emma off. *"He said that you do not come out ahead in many of the strands of fate available to him."*

Oliver choked on his own spit. He'd forgotten about that particular nugget of information.

"We know!" Emma shouted right back. "And we're doing EVERYTHING we can to—,"

"How did you know that?" Oliver asked Roli quietly. He didn't remember sharing any part of their conversation with Augustus.

"I was there, wasn't I?" Roli scoffed.

Lance chuckled. "You were a skeleton in my backpack! Could you hear everything as a skeleton?"

"Don't be daft, boy!" Roli growled. *"I was with my original master! Augustus!"*

341

* Chapter 23: A Well-deserved Break *

Oliver's entire face loosened with disbelief. If it hadn't been for his months of diplomacy and reaction training, his jaw would have been on the floor, along with Emma's and Lance's.

"Why didn't you tell us, Roli?" Oliver asked, still quiet. The implications of Roli's statement were overwhelming. Roli hadn't been born from the skeleton they'd found beneath the willow tree. No, he must have died, become a skeleton, and somehow came back to life. Just how much did this little creature know?

"Wasn't it obvious?" Roli sneered. He leapt down from his perch and approached Oliver, his movement deliberately slow until he arrived at Oliver's crisscrossed feet. There he leveled a clawed leg, poking Oliver through his shirt. *"I gave up **everything** to be here for you, Master García. Yes, I am pretentious. Yes, I am bossy. But when Master Augustus looked into fate, he saw you defeating our foe only in possibilities where **I** sacrificed my life to abandon my family and my people to join you now, as a member of your troop. Whether you appreciate me or not is of little consequence, but you need me to succeed, you understand? You need my ability to plan ahead, no matter how many faults I have that accompany it!"*

Heat rose to Oliver's cheeks as he blustered at Roli. He knew he had to maintain eye contact, otherwise what he'd say next wouldn't come across well. His neck vibrated as he spoke, guiding him on. "I had no idea you were… from Augustus' time. We're grateful for your sacrifice and will do our best to listen to your wisdom."

He'd thought he'd feel better after apologizing but his cheeks only reddened further. He was pretty sure he'd said the right thing, but he had

NOVA 02

no clue what Roli sacrificed to mummify himself and join them now. Had it been his friendship with Augustus?

Roli's physical cues didn't offer up any hints. The iguana's tongue flitted in and out and his dewlap expanded but Oliver had no clue what either meant. He didn't have much experience conversing with lizards.

"As you dilapidated users of English like to say," Roli eventually grumbled, *"'don't worry about it.'"*

"Roliiii," Lance fawned, venturing a smile, "did you just crack a joke?"

Roli hopped back on Oliver's shoulder, laying his tail down on the opposite. *"Yes, and it does not settle well on my conscious."*

"That's okay," Lance said, standing up with Oliver so he could stroke Roli's small head.

"Mm, yes, delightful. Don't forget the dewlap."

Oliver eyed Emma as she stood up last, wondering if she was thinking the same thing. Roli had just used one of Santiago's tactics—a joke to tone down a very serious conversation. He'd used the tactic on Oliver and Emma last year in front of Miyada's armory when Oliver had been nervous about picking out his channel and source.

Emma winked at him as she dusted off her clothes. Then, she took off walking and motioned for him to join her. With all the muscle Lance had put on, they couldn't all fit side-by-side on the path anymore, so Oliver didn't feel rude leaving Lance to take the rear-guard. When he joined Emma up front, he appraised her confident stride. She didn't look so tired anymore.

"Hey," she whispered roguishly, "what do you call a cow with one leg?"

* Chapter 23: A Well-deserved Break *

Oliver shoved her with excitement. "I knew it! Just like Santiago, remember? Oldest trick in the book!"

She re-joined him on the path and shoved right back. When he stumbled back onto the bricks a second later, grinning from ear to ear, he laughed louder than he had all month.

"Humidity's finally going down," Lance said from behind them. "Remember this time last year? We were worried sick about the Ceremony of the Gifts. And now we're just worried about... just dying I guess!" His voice cracked as he spoke.

Oliver and Emma ignored him.

"So," Emma said, beginning to skip in her stride, "why aren't we meeting Abe and Brantley in Hutch?"

"It's like we're not even here," Lance said, grabbing Roli off Oliver's shoulder.

"Have you considered becoming an iguana?" Roli asked as he settled down on Lance's head. *"As a superior species, I find indifference from a human to be a most pleasant experience."*

Oliver only had eyes for Emma. "Nah," he told her, "I changed the secret location to Watkin's terrace. Even if we use *stratum silentii* in Hutch so nobody can hear, that won't stop Elton and Joel from *seeing* us talking in secret. If they do, they'll want in."

"I thought you said you were working on trusting people."

"I am."

Emma smacked her lips. "Real trusting of you. Two whole people you've already known for a year. *Really* branching out there, aren't you?"

NOVA 02

"Hah-hah."

Lance shrugged, again from behind them. "Eh, I wouldn't trust Elton or Joel yet either. Those guys talk about everything."

Oliver pointed at Lance and then turned back to Emma looking as smug as he felt.

Emma surprised him by shaking her head and smiling.

"What?" he asked, almost disappointed that she didn't rise to the bait. He liked it when she got fierce.

"Told you taking a break would be a good idea," she said, looking smug. "We haven't smiled like this all month."

Oliver wanted to crack a grin at that, but the reality of the truth was too depressing. "Yeah," he offered, looking down at his old sneakers as they walked. "Let's definitely make Fridays a thing."

"Yes," Roli mused, *"when The Damned barges into your dormitory on a Friday evening, simply tell him it's your night off, and I'm sure he'll apologize and request to schedule a more convenient time."*

Emma's nose wrinkled as she laughed. Then, she sidled closer as they walked up the rest of the hill.

For several minutes they walked past different pods of trees; mostly palm, palo verde, maple, hickory, and oak. Within the branches of the tropical trees, Emma pointed at toucans or monkeys fighting over nesting areas. Then, in and around the roots of the deciduous trees, Oliver drew her attention to the occasional osorius taking an evening snooze.

* Chapter 23: A Well-deserved Break *

Feeling giddy, Oliver then checked in on Lance. He expected his friend to look annoyed by being left to walk solo, but Lance looked anything but put out.

He waggled his eyebrows at Oliver and pretended to put his arm around the waist of an imaginary figure. Then, with a focused expression he typically reserved for bench press record attempts, he pointed at Oliver and then Emma with aggressive juts of his finger.

Butterflies swooped in Oliver's stomach at the mere suggestion of holding onto Emma's waist. He turned his head back around, praying Emma wouldn't see him blush.

But Emma wasn't looking at him at all. By then, they'd reached the Academic Building. Its four floors loomed above them, but Emma didn't look at those either. Instead, she peered into the bushes flanking the final bit of the pathway before the stairs.

"I think there's something in the—,"

A ghoulish hollering snapped all three of their heads a few yards closer to the Academic Building.

Instinctively, Oliver raised his hands for a fight, likely from Beto, Cristina, or James, and lifted two mounds of Earth on either side of his shoulders, ready to fire.

A few silent seconds trickled by. Then, from the thicket, out sprang a pumpkin.

"Wot! Wot!" Roli shouted. *"Destroy the enemy!"*

The pumpkin squealed in fright as it landed on the pathway.

🎃 NOVA 02 🎃

But it didn't loiter. Without a glance, it hollered some more and shot down the path back towards Hutch, bobbing up and down as it went like a bouncing ball.

Lance began to laugh. "The enemy? Roli, that's a pumpkin!"

"Yes! Feed it to me!"

An explosion of snapping twigs and crumpling leaves followed, drawing their attention back to the bushes just as a jack-o-lantern appeared. It paused for several seconds, locking its carved-out eyes and manic grin on the four of them. Next to it, a dagger floated in space where a little arm might have existed.

The jack-o-lantern cackled and twisted its knife around, ready for a fight. When it sighted the fleeing pumpkin bobbing towards the Dining Hall, it let out a mad laugh and took off after its prey, popping its lid on and off as it went, spilling the occasional seed or bit of pumpkin flesh. Further ahead, the pumpkin squealed as a second jack-o-lantern appeared, joining the hunt.

Lance wiped a tear from his eye before pushing past Oliver and Emma to take the stairs. "Pretty sure Joel offers six-to-one odds on any bet in favor of a pumpkin surviving the hunt every year."

Oliver stood on his tip toes to keep watching the retreating pumpkin in the distance. The jack-o-lanterns were catching up, making Oliver doubt that Joel's bet had decent enough odds for anyone to take it. He said as much out loud.

Emma flicked him on the head in response, bringing his attention back. "Doesn't take a Wiser to see that."

* Chapter 23: A Well-deserved Break *

Oliver waited a moment to allow the butterflies in his stomach time to settle before following her and Lance up the stairs.

Chapter 24: News from Goodwin Forest

I've seen him recommend no less than seven of his caucus-members for rehabilitation after "betraying themselves with inconsistently applied resolve."

It's enough to make me wonder what he'd do to me if I ever changed my mind about anything.

19th of October, the second year of the 10th Age

"You cleared this with Watkin, right?" Lance asked when they reached Watkin's classroom.

Oliver gulped. "Uh, was I supposed to?"

Emma let out an impatient breath while Oliver creaked open the door and stuck his head inside.

"All clear?" Lance asked from behind. "Can you do Watkin's pulse-thingy to check?"

"This is ridiculous," Emma growled.

Before he knew it, Oliver was tumbling into the classroom. Emma had forced open the door with a push, unbalancing him in the process.

"Give me a warning next time, will ya?" he said, dusting his shirt off in embarrassment more than anything else.

Emma shrugged and moved on to the terrace at the rear of the room where Abe and Brantley waited for them.

* Chapter 24: News from Goodwin Forest *

"Took you long enough," Abe clucked from a reclined position on a lounge chair.

Brantley tsked several times to emphasize Abe's point, but Oliver didn't take the bait. They both looked comfy enough on their chairs, enjoying the Friday night sunset on Watkin's terrace.

"We've been waiting for an hour now," Abe continued, "haven't we, Brant?"

"Coulda been two," Brantley grunted, wholly disinterested as he fished in his pocket for a snack-cake from Ms. Joan's Friday cookie table. "You want this update or nah? I've got things to do."

Emma lit up at that. "Oh?" she asked, taking a seat at the foot of Brantley's lounge chair. "Do share. We've been doing *nothing* but work for what feels like forever now." She made sure to shoot Oliver a pointed look as she spoke. "No time for fun these days."

"Forget about it," Brantley said between bites of his cake. "Update or nah? I'm leaving if nah."

Emma's grin deepened.

So did Abe's. "He's going on a date!" the bespeckled boy shouted. He was forced to shoot out of his chair to slip away from Brantley's crushing grip.

"Listen here you little—," Brantley growled.

Lance blocked off Brantley off with his warhammer before the much larger boy could reduce Abe to paste. Lance traded a mischievous expression with Emma as Brantley bounced off his weapon. "With who, then, Brant-man?"

NOVA 02

"Whom," Oliver muttered under his breath, undecided on whether or not it was a good thing that nobody heard him amidst all the fuss.

"Eh hem," Roli coughed, still atop Lance's head. *"I heard you."*

"Yeah, but you don't exactly count."

Roli contracted his dewlap haughtily. *"Don't count?!"*

Chaos unfolded as Roli stamped a clawed foot into Lance's hair and Abe shouted, "Makayla Grant! The Tancol captain!"

"Oooooo," Emma chorused.

"Ouch," Lance whined.

Brantley tried flaring Power to shove Lance aside, but Lance countered with a flare of his own, relishing the fact that he could now hold off his old RA.

Since Emma and Lance had things covered, Oliver beckoned Roli over. The iguana leapt from Lance's head to Oliver's shoulder in one swift motion.

"Watch out!" Oliver jeered as Roli landed. "Your claws hurt! What would Augustus say?"

Roli leered at him. *"He'd advise me to dig my claws deeper."*

Oliver swatted at Roli with one hand and tossed the lizard a sweet potato chunk with the other.

Roli dodged the swipe with little fuss and lashed out with his tongue to snatch the sweet potato from the air. *"My, my, you are easy to manipulate,"* he said between squelching bites. Then, he rolled his dewlap into a chuckle. *"Dance my puppet! Dance whenever I deem it **prudent**!"*

* Chapter 24: News from Goodwin Forest *

The word hung in the air for a second while Oliver chuckled ruefully. Then, he felt his neck tickle again. *"What is going on with these vibrations?"* He had no clue what his Wisdom was trying to tell him every time his neck buzzed, and it was starting to get *very* annoying.

With a growl, he slapped at the back of his neck to drive the sensation away. Then, seeing that Lance and Brantley were still wrestling, he ventured a question.

"Roli?" he asked while the sensation in his neck faded, "do you know if certain words have *power* in magic?"

Roli clicked in his throat again to laugh—Oliver was still getting used to the sound so he couldn't be sure if it was a laugh at all. *"Master Augustus often engaged Cuahtemoc and Madeline in debate over the subject. I must confess they always found an excuse to do something else when he did—the conversation bored them to tears given that it never bore fruit."*

Oliver debated Roli's answer for a moment before tucking the question away for his next lesson with Watkin. Maybe it had something to do with his theories on *The Damned?* No, that didn't feel right. But he knew it was important.

By then, Lance and Brantley's flares of Power began shaking the veranda. Emma's and Abe's cheers didn't help.

"Alright, guys," Oliver said, tightening his jaw. "Time for the update."

Brantley looked up, sweating, but also smiling. Then he looked back down at Lance who he'd come close to pinning. "Just how much muscle did you pick up over the summer, anyway?"

NOVA 02

With a hand to his knee, Lance pulled himself up, looking supremely satisfied.

"It's not just physical strength," Abe announced, popping up over Lance's right shoulder. "I think your Power is growing!"

Brantley shifted an uneasy glance at Oliver. "Maybe hanging around with the Trinova is putting you on the juice."

Emma's eyes widened excitedly. "Oh!" she exclaimed, turning left and right for some prey. Her eyes settled on Abe. She looked him up and down for a moment as if debating something.

Then, she pushed him.

"Ouch!" Abe shouted, ricocheting off her and onto the cushions of his lounge chair.

"Would you look at that?" Emma said, marveling at her still-outstretched arms. "We *are* getting stronger!"

Abe rubbed at his chest and glared at Emma. "Next time test it out on somebody else!"

"Eh hem," Roli announced from atop Oliver's head. *"We are owed an update!"*

"Thank you," Brantley grunted. From his seat, he crossed his arms. "Let's do this quick."

"Because of your date," Emma repeated. "You have to finish this quickly… so you can go get ready for your date… with Makala… on a date."

Brantley tsked. "Chill out. It's just a date."

Emma snuck Oliver a look, raising an eyebrow.

* Chapter 24: News from Goodwin Forest *

Oliver felt the entire world narrow in on him as her gaze settled on him.

"Hmm," Roli's voice echoed in Oliver's head, so that only he could hear. *"I think your friend is in need of a date."*

Oliver flared his Wisdom so acutely that a pillar of blue light burst from him, shooting up into the night sky like a beacon. Winds buffeted off his frame for a full three seconds until the beacon settled back into his spirit.

Everyone leaned back in their chairs until the gusts of air came to a halt. Abe and Brantley stared at him, aghast. Emma and Lance just looked smug.

"Sorry," Oliver said, coughing in his throat. Though he was glad nobody was commenting on Emma's not-so-subtle hint, he didn't like the look on Abe's or Brantley's faces. "I, um, appreciate that you've got a date coming up, so let's get straight to it, okay? What have you learned about Goodwin Forest?"

Lance raised an eyebrow while Oliver rubbed the back of his head like Santiago might, feeling sheepish. He didn't like how he'd sounded like the strict version of Watkin. That man wasn't very enjoyable to be around. Then again, he needed results.

"W-well," Abe stammered, "where do you want us to start?"

Brantley shifted in his chair, placing a hand to his chin. He didn't look at Oliver directly when he spoke, keeping his attention on Abe. "Start with the mayor." Abe nodded, but when he spoke, he also avoided Oliver's eye, focusing on Emma instead.

"The mayor went on the news last week," he said, his expression turning grim. "They've had twenty-three kidnappings to date—he's calling them kidnappings—and the most recent to disappear were an old couple."

NOVA 02

"Diego and Melissa Ogden," Brantley confirmed.

"Ogden?" Emma asked as Lance drew in a breath.

Abe swallowed. "Yep, Stephen's grandparents. You remember Stephen from our hall last year, right?"

"His grandparents ran the town's general store," Brantley said, his voice quiet. Even he had a faraway look in his eyes as the implications of their conversation sunk in.

Emma nodded, mirroring Abe's solemn grimace. "What else?"

Brantley shifted in his seat again. "They're evacuating the town."

Oliver raised his eyebrows purposefully. He needed to look a little less Trinova-y than his heightened state of Wisdom would allow. "Evacuating?" he repeated, feigning shock like a normal person might. "Do they even know what from yet?"

"Yeah right," Abe scoffed, finally looking Oliver in the eyes again. "You're crazy if you think the Mayor would talk about that in a press release."

Oliver furrowed his eyebrows. "Then why is the Mayor calling them kidnappings? To me that sounds like he knows a bit about how people are disappearing."

Abe opened and closed his mouth several times.

"Don't worry about it," Oliver interjected. If the Mayor wasn't revealing everything to the public, there was little chance Abe and Brantley would unearth the secret from news articles. "What about the people themselves?" Oliver went on. "Any patterns?"

Abe shook his head and looked to Brantley.

* Chapter 24: News from Goodwin Forest *

The larger boy let out a long exhale. "Not really? Mostly adults from what we can tell. The only kid was a troublemaker apparently. Always pulling pranks, like—,"

"Throwing eggs at people's houses," Abe cut in.

"And then the adults don't really have a pattern to them," Brantley went on. "At least one that we can see."

Abe crossed his arms and nodded his head.

"Hmm," Oliver thought out loud. "Were the adults getting into trouble?"

Abe laughed. "Like egging houses?"

"No," Oliver went on, "like were any of them criminals or anything like that?"

Abe and Brantley thought in silence for a moment.

Eventually Brantley opened his mouth. Curiously, however, he closed it before saying anything.

"What?" Lance asked.

"Well," Brantley blustered, "I don't want to say anything offensive or stuff like that, but now that you mention it, a handful of the folks who disappeared were the free-spirited type."

Oliver furrowed his eyebrows. Emma seemed to understand, however, because she began to laugh. "What's that supposed to mean?" she chortled.

"You know," Brantley said, shifting his eyes uneasily. "People who like living in vans and going off the grid. I'm not saying there's anything wrong with it—I'm not saying that at all—but isn't going off the grid technically illegal?"

NOVA 02

Abe snapped his fingers. "And then those old people! Remember what the article said?"

Brantley raised his eyebrows. "Uhh…"

"Apparently," Abe continued, too impatient for Brantley to remember, "they were great—loved by everybody! The writer of the article wondered why anybody would kidnap a couple who'd only ever been guilty of smuggling banned vegetables into the country!"

Both Emma and Lance snuck Oliver wide-eyed looks.

"What was that?" Abe asked, pointing at the three of them in turn. "Come on. Spill the beans." He even pointed at Roli.

"They're the people you pretend to care about," Oliver intoned, recalling Beto's taunt for all of them to hear. "*Sinovas. Bums, vagrants, thieves, underachievers. I even heard one was just a kid who wasn't doing well at the local elementary school.*"

Abe placed a hand to his mouth as he gasped.

Brantley looked just as uncomfortable. "Oli, you really think this is *The Damned*, then?"

Oliver didn't answer. Instead, he approached the railing to buy himself some time to think. As the last of the sun set, he thought back on what Watkin had told him during his one-on-one lesson. Would *The Damned* really consider something as small as a free-spirited lifestyle, or an old couple's illegal produce, worthy of death? How had the boy who'd started off wanting to create a utopia turn to imprisonment and murder?

Oliver gulped in his throat as a nasty thought settled in his head. *'That's how he could create his utopia. By killing or locking away anyone who didn't fit into his vision."*

* Chapter 24: News from Goodwin Forest *

Oliver didn't turn around to share his thoughts. He hadn't even finished processing them himself, so how could he? Instead, he kept his eyes on the western portion of the lagoons where the sun set into the horizon.

"Brantley?" Emma asked, getting everyone's attention off Oliver's back. "How come Beto never got punished last year for saying 'sinova'? How does he keep getting away with it if it's a slur?"

Abe and Brantley exchanged embarrassed looks. "I," Abe stammered, "I—,"

"We told Zapien about it last year the first couple times," Brantley said, shrugging. "We gave up after nobody ever followed up on it."

"She'd have to go through the *Dean of Discipline*," Oliver growled, wringing his hands on the railing. He could feel their stares return to his back, and even Roli's eyes from his shoulder.

Footsteps and shuffles sounded, and eventually all of them joined him on the terrace's railing, looking out onto the red-and-orange-laden grounds. "Oli," Abe asked, "what's going on?"

As Oliver watched the last of the sun set past a pack of chupacabras that prowled the western edges of the lagoons, he realized the time had come to entrust Abe and Brantley with a bit of the **Truth**. There'd be no going back. Either of his friends could betray his trust. But his Wisdom hummed at the idea of committing to them anyway.

"Last time," he said, feeling the tickle in his neck spread across his shoulders and chest, "*The Damned* gathered up all the types of people Beto mentioned—the desperate and homeless, anybody who was too free-spirited, thieves, criminals, underachievers, troublemakers; anybody who didn't fit his vision of perfected society—and he put them in rehabilitation centers."

Nobody said a word. So, Oliver kept going.

"He didn't do it as a tyrant, either. He did it as one of the most popular politicians our country has ever seen. Supported by most everybody. And that's why… the adults don't talk about it. That's why… Beto doesn't get punished for saying *sinova*. So many of them bought in to what *The Damned* wanted—a perfect world, free of conflict—that they agreed with the imprisonment and even turned a blind eye to the murders."

Oliver paused for another moment, thinking back on something the ghost of Madeline had said.

"You must demand good for all, not just the greater."

It was then and there, with his hands on the railing, surrounded by his friends, that Oliver promised himself he'd hold onto that standard. After a quiet moment, he spoke again.

"Even if Blackwood wasn't our Dean of Discipline, I doubt the faculty would punish Beto. Half of them might agree with him and the other half might be too afraid to punish him in case *The Damned* came back."

He sighed, barely feeling Lance's hand of support on his shoulder, and then Emma's. "We're going to have to fight more than just *The Damned*," he said. "It goes deeper than that. His messaging brings out the worst in us."

A sharp *caw-caw* rang in the air behind them.

They all turned, ready to obliterate the disruptor with magic.

* Chapter 24: News from Goodwin Forest *

Watkin stood behind them with Jaiba on his shoulder and his hands resting on the jeweled pommel of his staff. Oliver didn't know what emotion he saw in the man's eyes, but if he had to guess, it came close to pride.

Chapter 25: Skeletons and Jack-O-Lanterns

Come to think of it, I don't think I've seen any of the caucus-members since Tío shipped them off to rehabilitation. I wonder where they go afterwards? He probably just has them sit at a desk or something. He doesn't mind a petty punishment here and there.

24th of October, the second year of the 10th Age

With the Big Five Coatlball and Dungeon-Simulation teams formed, the campus' attention shifted towards fall and, more importantly, the Day of the Dead. The allure of undead festivities proved too much for the skeletons residing in the Swampy Woods to resist. By the first of November, they emerged to hide across the grounds in great numbers, poking their heads through deciduous bush or jungle foliage to prank students, professors, and Guides indiscriminately.

"At least they're cheerful," Oliver heard Joel say to Elton outside of Hutch. One of the skeletons had given Elton such a scare that he'd dropped Old Blueboo's crate on his way out to feed the snail.

"You're not even scary!" Elton bellowed at the guilty skeleton that darted away, cackling with glee.

Whenever the skeletons pranked anyone—student, professor, or sacred beast—they made sure to unhinge their jaws and let out ghoulish laughs. With time into the season, however, even the most cowardly student grew

* Chapter 25: Skeletons and Jack-O-Lanterns *

accustomed to the jump scares, forcing the skeletons to heighten the quality of their pranks.

Wanting to avoid a repeat of the food fight that had broken out last year, Ms. Joan enlisted Tolteca to keep the skeletons out of the Dining Hall.

"BACK, YOU TWISTED SPIRITS!" Tolteca shouted the next afternoon. "HAD YOU COME IN JULY, I WOULD HAVE WORKED *WITH* YOU! BUT NO! YOU CATER TO THIS HALLOW'S EVE AND DAY OF THE DEAD HYBRID HOLIDAY! A BASTARDIZED EXCUSE OF MY PEOPLE'S FESTIVAL! I WILL SMITE YOU! HAH-HAH! YES! COMBAT ME, DENIZENS OF THE UNDERWORLD!"

When a battalion of skeletons stormed the Dining Hall with crude wooden shields and stone swords, Tolteca swept down on them like a boulder in a tornado. Oliver made a mental note to never mess with Tolteca after witnessing the quick exchange. Within seconds, the skeletons were reduced to piles of bones that rolled all the way back to the Swampy Woods. Even then they cackled.

The jack-o-lanterns, meanwhile, had grown in numbers over the weekend, confirming Emma's hunch over the poor pumpkin they'd seen on their way to Abe and Brantley's update. During the pack's early days of the season, the jack-o-lanterns hunted strategically, hiding behind thickets or trees before ambushing innocent pumpkin-couples who'd stepped out from their patches for an evening bob across the grounds. Only later in the season, when fewer and fewer pumpkins remained, did the pack transcend into its final form; that of a belligerent, whooping and hollering posse that reminded Oliver of the villains in old Western films he'd watched with

NOVA 02

Santiago. "Here," Santiago had said when Oliver was ten, handing him a box of John Wayne movies. "This is how we become Americans."

Given the sheer amount of work on his plate, however, Oliver barely had time to notice the psychotic skeletons or plundering pumpkin posse whenever he saw them. Though he, Emma, and Lance did end up taking their Friday evening "off" to play cards with Lizzie, Valerie, Trey, and Se'Vaughn, by Sunday, it was business-as-normal again.

Holed up in Hutch, they knocked out a four-hour Tupper Session, watching every bit of recorded footage they could find from the boy's time at school. Maddeningly, most of the footage revealed Tupper as nothing less than the coolest, most intelligent, all-rounded student any of them had ever witnessed.

One interview, however, had nested itself into Oliver's brain. And he was racking his head to figure out why.

It had gone like all the others, showcasing Tupper's talents—this time, his grasp of history—and yet there was something about the way Tupper had presented himself in this particular memory.

Even after they'd called a halt to head to their dungeon-sim practice, Oliver still found Tupper's youthful, normal, and completely unscary face floating around his brain, making little sense when compared to the man who'd tried to kill them twice now.

It wasn't until they arrived outside the dungeon-sim room that Oliver understood *what* about the boy nagged at his mind.

Before they stepped inside, Oliver grabbed Emma and Lance by the wrists and hauled them towards a particularly large branch of ivy hanging

* Chapter 25: Skeletons and Jack-O-Lanterns *

from the roof of the building. When he spoke, he was forced to raise his voice because, not twenty yards away, the jack-o-lantern pack descended upon three more pumpkins. He didn't bother with *stratum silentii* given they only had pumpkins to worry about.

"What?" Emma asked. She grimaced at the gurgles and screams from the nearby pumpkins when Oliver replied.

"If you ask me," he said, barely able to keep his voice calm as he put his thoughts together, "I think Tupper looked like a guilty kid at the back of a candy shop during the whole second half of that interview with the annoying girl."

It had taken him nearly thirty minutes to realize what his mind had subconsciously identified. Tupper's young face had *betrayed* the older man. Even though *The Damned* hadn't explicitly said anything out of the ordinary, Oliver inferred just as much from the boy's sharp eyes, subtle smile, and tense posture.

Just thinking about it made Oliver's heart pump faster. Finally, after all the time they'd spent chasing smoke, he had a clue. A *real* clue.

The sound of shoes scraping against stone echoed towards them from within the sim room, and voices followed soon thereafter. Oliver wrinkled his nose at the interruption, flicking his eyes around for a quieter place to talk. With a nudge of his head, he motioned for Emma and Lance to follow him past the corner of the building, behind large clumps of overgrowth.

When they peered back at the entrance, semi-hidden behind even thicker strands of ivy than at the front of the building, a handful of extramen exited, including Sara, Drew, and Ethan. Strangely enough, at least to Oliver's eyes,

NOVA 02

Drew, not Sara, commanded the extraman conversation. Oliver stared for a full three seconds, wondering why Sara wasn't the one doing the talking—that girl's beauty and presence was otherworldly. Given his hiding place, he didn't particularly care if his face looked bewildered by what he was seeing. Nobody could see him anyway.

"If we increase our efficiency in platforming," Drew's voice carried, "my model shows we can shave three to four minutes off our time—depending on how many platforming rooms are generated, of course. We should also consider the efficacy of—,"

Oliver shook his head. These extramen weren't nearly as important as his new theory on Tupper. When he turned back to face Emma and Lance, they looked at him, eyebrows drawn up in open confusion.

"*The Damned.* Guilty kid. Candy shop," Oliver repeated. "Thoughts?"

Emma continued furrowing her eyebrows unhelpfully.

Lance, however, began to grin. "You've never swiped candy before, have you?" he asked Emma scrunching up his face in delight.

Emma's eyes drew sharper than knives. "You mean, *stolen?* Yes, I've never *stolen* anything."

Oliver couldn't believe his ears. "Forget about the candy analogy!" he growled. "That's not the important part!"

Grumbling, Emma slapped the back of her neck, clearly still irritated.

Oliver ignored it. "All I meant was... I think that Tupper—Lance, what did Stevie used to say all the time?"

"That the patriarchy never sleeps?"

"No, no. The other one!"

* Chapter 25: Skeletons and Jack-O-Lanterns *

"Spilled the beans!"

Oliver snapped his fingers. "That's it! I think Tupper spilled the beans!"

Emma crossed her arms, challenging Oliver without having to say a word.

"Think about it," Oliver went on, his excitement getting the better of his diplomacy training. "That newspaper lady—,"

"Jane P. Smith, of *The Star-Spangled Sentinel*," Emma interrupted, miming the words of the interviewer with disdain.

Oliver shrugged. "Sure. Whatever. She asked him, 'what do you like to do when you aren't writing fancy essays on political theory?'"

"She never asked him that!" Lance stated incredulously.

Oliver leaned closer still. "Not exactly. But something close to that, okay? What matters was how Tupper responded. Did you guys see his eyes?"

Emma pushed her lips together, thinking hard. Then, she let her head clunk into the wall she was leaning on. A bit of ivy wrinkled away from her touch—if it could have, Oliver was sure it would have hissed. "Oli," Emma said, her tone making sure he knew she wasn't convinced, "that boy's eyes looked like eyes to me. You wanna tell us what *you* noticed? We're just normal people, remember? Not Trinovas."

Oliver was so excited he didn't even mind the jibe. "His eyes *twinkled*."

Lance and Emma exchanged quizzical looks before Lance chortled again. "How are we supposed to notice eyes twinkling, man? What does that even look like?"

NOVA 02

Roli popped out of Lance's backpack. *"Master García, I must agree with these baboons."* He held onto Lance's notebook with one of his clawed feet, waving it at them. Lance took the cue and grabbed the mirror. *"Are you certain you saw twinkling?"* Roli added. *"Perhaps you were simply falling for the boy's devilish manifesto?"*

"Bah!" Oliver said, physically waving away their doubts. He felt too confident about what he'd seen. "They twinkled, okay? And you know what he said after his eyes starting twinkling?"

"That he liked history?" Emma suggested, stifling a yawn. "And Trinova theories? Big whoop. That's not news, is it? We already know the Trinova is real." She gestured at him with her hands as if she were revealing him to an audience. Nearby, the jack-o-lanterns followed her motion, eventually turning, one by one, to lock their hollowed-out eyes onto Oliver. A couple of the pack twisted their knives around, raising their pasted-on eyebrows questioningly.

"Jack… o… lantern?" they asked in horrible, scratchy voices.

Oliver leered at the pumpkins warily for a moment. Then, he ignored them and resumed his pitch. "Tupper was *obsessed* with history, alright? First, he got excited. and then he backed down. It sounded like somebody saying too much and regretting it…" His voice trailed off. He knew his hunch was close to revealing something—he just didn't know what. He admitted as much out loud.

Lance's laughs died down while Emma offered up a sardonic reply. "Maybe he was embarrassed about going on the record sounding like a nerd."

* Chapter 25: Skeletons and Jack-O-Lanterns *

"No, that can't be it," Roli answered thoughtfully.

"She was being sarcastic," Lance offered, flicking Emma on the head.

"Ah," Roli mused. *"Sarcasm. The least efficient way to communicate. Does our time mean so little to you?"*

Emma popped off the wall she'd been leaning on to glare at Roli with outrage. "You spent half of yesterday on the Hutch terrace bathing in the sun!"

"I have no regrets. Can you say the same?"

Oliver grabbed the notebook from Lance's hand and commanded it to re-project the same interview they'd watched earlier. In less than a second, a three-dimensional recording shot up on the notebook's surface.

"Wow, Genghis Khan, huh?" the miniature newspaper correspondent asked a young version of Solomon Tupper.

"Exactly!" the teenage Tupper replied. For the briefest of moments, his eyes sparked to life, lighting up his otherwise slightly sunken eyes. Oliver gestured at the change manically to Emma's and Lance's unconvinced faces. "Genghis Khan, for instance," Tupper continued, his voice feverish. "Does he strike you as somebody who didn't have access to magic? I'd love to study where he lived someday."

"That's neat!" the interviewer replied cheerily. Oliver cringed as the words crossed the projected woman's lips. Sure enough, Tupper began hedging his replies.

"It's just fun research, you know! Helps me with my coursework!"

Lance put away the notebook as the woman signed off. "This was Jane P. Smith, of The Star-Spa—,"

NOVA 02

"See!" Oliver said as the projection and Lance's notebook disappeared back into Lance's backpack.

Lance shrugged his shoulders, half answering Oliver and half re-arranging the shoulder straps of his backpack.

"Ehhh," Emma answered, "there's no way to know with that Jane P. Smith of *The Star-Spangled Sentinel* making him feel like a nerd."

"You really don't like that woman, do you?" Lance asked as he stuffed his notebook past carefully wrapped sacks of extra food.

"Why'd she have to say her name so many times?" Emma huffed.

"Another root vegetable, Master Wyatt?" Roli begged, his eyes focused firmly on the backpack.

"Guys!" Oliver said, not even bothering to cough politely. "Focus! I think we just saw Tupper when..." It all began to click in Oliver's head. And the conclusion made his mouth dry up. "He was just as rough as we are with his people skills—don't you see? Lalandra told us to work on our people skills—,"

"Diplomacy, actually," Emma cut in, rolling her eyes, and resuming her lean against the wall.

"Whatever! She told us to get better at it because if we don't, we show our cards. Just like Tupper did in this interview!"

"And why does it matter?" Emma retorted, beginning to play with the vine that curled away from her.

A noise like whirling water sounded next to them.

* Chapter 25: Skeletons and Jack-O-Lanterns *

Oliver wasn't sure who jumped higher as a person appeared from thin air, right between him and Emma. All he knew, was his jaw fell to his chest so fast it hurt.

Headmaster Elodie Lalandra stood next to them.

"Because, Ms. Griffith," Lalandra said, her tone casual and her eyes merry from behind purple-framed glasses, "you now know something about your foe they would never have wanted known!"

None of them replied, too shocked to do anything other than bluster out "Headmaster!" or "Doctor Lalandra! What a surprise!"

For her part, Lalandra, surveyed them like a jovial auntie. Her expression contrasted against the formality of her typical charcoal-gray suite and white blouse combo. Oliver still had no clue what her channel was—her necklace? One of her many rings? Sunlight reflected off a rather large one set with a diamond in the middle.

Emma recovered best, eventually pinching her nose and shaking her head. Lance's antics, on the other hand, made Oliver's dropped jaw look tame by comparison. He had jumped a full three feet back, holding onto his backpack like a lemur defending its food from a hyena. Roli, meanwhile, regarded Lalandra with suspicion, his eyes reduced to narrow, untrusting slits of green and white.

"It's not polite to eavesdrop, Headmaster," Emma said, her tone icy.

Roli nodded, but otherwise kept his thoughts to himself.

Lalandra's smile only grew. "Consider this a quick lesson from me to you. I didn't teach you *stratum silentii* for you to hold secret conversations in public. Indulge me by using the spell whenever you speak of whomever it is that I cannot remember."

Lance gasped. Oliver kicked him. If Watkin hadn't trusted Lalandra with Tupper's name yet, he'd have a good reason.

"Didn't realize you could use light refraction, Headmaster," Oliver mumbled apologetically, hoping to move past Lance's lack of 'diplomacy.' "We thought the coast was clear."

Elodie regarded Oliver for several full seconds, her expression unchanging. The look, simple as it was, cut Oliver down like a scythe. The words that followed didn't help either.

"Do you really think nobody else could learn to refract light? Was it not *I* who left you the words in the Temple Beneath the Willow. And I know you've read my published essay on the subject. Where is your humility, Oliver?"

Oliver kept his eyes up, resisting the temptation look down at his shoes. "You're right," he said, annoyed with himself. "It was stupid of us. We won't do it again."

Emma crossed her arms and leered at Lalandra. "All this sneaking and fake talk is driving me crazy, Headmaster. What do you *want?*"

Oliver felt his heart lighten inside his chest. Emma would always have his back.

Lalandra's eyes lingered on Oliver as she answered. "Secrecy and diplomacy, though repugnant as they may seem, are required of Oliver, and you two, by extension. To—,"

Emma huffed audibly, cutting Lalandra off.

* Chapter 25: Skeletons and Jack-O-Lanterns *

The silence that followed made Oliver more uncomfortable than the time he'd stared down Xihuacota in the lagoons from an ice raft in the freezing cold. There was loyalty… and then there was stupidity. Emma was edging towards the latter, and Oliver had no clue how Lalandra might react.

For her part, Lalandra didn't look mad at all. She stared at Emma with open curiosity, as if she were reading the nutrition label on a box of unhealthy cereal.

Then the woman's demeanor shifted.

Suddenly, the space around them felt constrictive, as though less oxygen was available in the air. Worse yet, in Lalandra's eyes, the cold, fierce expression of a dictator took over. Lance squeaked when Lalandra stepped closer to Emma.

"Dear girl," she said, dangerously quiet, "your pride will be the doom of us all. When you three engage with *The Damned,* he won't need more than *one* slip-up to twist your words into enough reason to incarcerate you with the full approval of the people. Do you understand? When I ask you to focus on your diplomacy, I don't ask out of pretention or any other misguided fool's sense of propriety; I ask because I have engaged with the mind of your enemy and know of the only way to successfully combat him. You can't beat him in stand-alone conflict. You'll need a multi-pronged approach, along with picture-perfect diplomacy. Do I make myself clear?"

Emma didn't move until after Lalandra finished her scolding. In his head, Oliver pleaded for her to nod her head or, better yet, apologize.

But this was Emma. He'd have better luck asking Blackwood to join him on a friendly stroll across the grounds.

NOVA 02

Emma clicked her tongue and somehow managed to fold her arms deeper together around her core. "You can say what you want, but it's not right to be lying all the time! You can't just tell the Trinova—who's stronger than you—*by the way,* to—,"

Whatever Emma thought Lalandra couldn't do, none of them could hear. With a lazy flick of her index finger, Lalandra slammed Emma's lips shut. When Emma raised her hands to protest, Lalandra flicked a second time, holding Emma down in place.

At that, Oliver's mood began to mirror Emma's. He turned to Lalandra, frowning, and even surprised himself by reaching for the magic in his ring. "You can stop that now," he said, keeping his voice calm in spite of the anger he felt. "I thought you were on our side."

Lalandra's expression shifted again. Back to a smile.

"Very well delivered," she said. "I can feel your anger and yet you reply as if we were discussing the weather. Forgive me for shackling your friend. I have a busy day ahead. It's time for your first lesson. That is why I've come."

"Now?" Oliver asked, still angry at the way Lalandra had treated Emma.

She answered him by just looking at him and blinking.

"Okay," he said, drawing the word out. "I'll take that as a yes. What about my dungeon-sim practice?"

Lalandra waved a hand towards the building. "It's done. I've just provisioned you three infinite access to the simulator. You may use it whenever you wish, at its fullest capabilities. Improve yourself as the Trinova at your own pace.

373

* Chapter 25: Skeletons and Jack-O-Lanterns *

"Now come. You waste our time."

"Wait," Oliver said, unsure of what he wanted to say. He couldn't just let Lalandra treat his friends like pests. And even though he desperately wanted to apologize or say 'never mind,' he cleared his throat, deciding to throw his Trinova weight around for once. "First," he said sternly, "you release Emma."

Then, unable to help himself, he tacked on a "please."

Lalandra flicked a finger. "As you wish," she said.

Emma stumbled in place as her pent-up energy released at the same time as the spell. Lance caught her to make sure she wouldn't fall.

"In the future," Oliver added, his ears blushing, "don't make a habit out of immobilizing my friends."

Lalandra cocked her head at him. "I'd never shackle anyone who didn't waste your time, Oliver."

With a hand to her forehead, Emma cut Oliver off. "Just go," she grunted. "Lance and I can let Abe know what's going on. We'll just practice another time now that we have access."

Lalandra nodded towards Emma, her lips twisting into a satisfied grin. "Good girl," she said. Then, turning towards Oliver, she motioned for him to join her on a walk back down the hill.

Before Oliver got too far away, Roli sprang from Lance's back, landing on Oliver's shoulder. There, he settled down like a cat.

He still hadn't said a word since Lalandra appeared.

NOVA 02

Chapter 26: The Nightmare of Linlithgow

Desmoulins asked me to define Tío's principles over dinner last night. I have to admit, I had no idea what to say. I eventually settled with I just believe he'll succeed no matter what he comes up against—because he's fair. He holds everyone to the same high standards. And no one more than himself.

27th of October, the second year of the 10th Age

"*Stratum silentii,*" Lalandra muttered. She'd uttered the spell as soon as they crossed the threshold into her apartment. All the way at the top floor of Founders Temple.

Oliver raised his eyebrows. "Even in your own home?" he asked.

"The eyebrows," Lalandra said, her lips taught, and maybe disappointed. He didn't know her well enough yet. "Diplomacy, remember?"

Oliver kept his eyebrows up. How had she seen his face? She hadn't looked at him once when she walked past the foyer into her living room, had she? He closed the door feeling confused and, if he were being honest, intimidated. He was glad Roli had come with him.

"And yes," Lalandra's voice continued as he shut the door, "always allow yourself privacy when talking about something important. You remember my husband, Dave? You might have met at last year's eggnog soiree?"

A man Oliver vaguely remembered stepped into the living room the same moment Oliver entered from the foyer. He'd come from what appeared to be a kitchen, where a seven-foot-tall statue of a chicken stood.

* Chapter 26: The Nightmare of Linlithgow *

Oliver remembered the chicken well enough—it had grabbed his attention last year, too; only then, he'd been in the Lalandra apartment without an invitation, on his way to the Forest Temple with Emma and Lance.

Dave regarded Oliver with a handsome face from behind two curtains of brilliant white hair. The man's high cheekbones could cut glass.

"Mr. Lalandra," Oliver grunted, sticking out a hand.

"Oliver!" the man said, taking the handshake. "Call me Dave, eh?" He spoke with a warmth that took Oliver off guard—it rivaled Professor Zapien's.

"The man of the hour, right?" Dave went on, grinning. "Elodie tells me you've had quite the fifteen months." His hand lingered on Oliver's like a favorite uncle's might, and Oliver couldn't help but be swept up by the charm of it. The man even took a half moment to press his second hand over their handshake, squeezing at the same time the wrinkles around his eyes and smile re-doubled. "It's very good to meet you. You remind me quite a bit of myself, you know?"

From a green couch, where Lalandra had sat down, the headmaster let out a crystal laugh. "Is that right?" she asked her husband.

Oliver's mouth dried up for a second time that afternoon. He was very much out of his element with these two. Could he trust Dave's warmth? Who exactly was Dr. Lalandra? What was her past? Could—better yet, *should*—he call her Elodie?

"Oh, don't mind her," Dave said, leaning in slightly. "She's been a genius since she was born. Did she rough you up on your way here with some nasty big words?"

NOVA 02

Oliver couldn't stop himself from smiling back at Dave. The man treated him with a level of paternal affection he'd never felt before. "Umm," he said shyly. "Not me exactly. But she did say we were wasting her time."

Dave leaned in closer, shooting an annoyed glance at his wife, before grunting, "you should hear how many times I get scolded for wasting time." He winked at Oliver before stepping away. As he did, he popped a chocolate-covered almond overhead, catching it with his mouth.

"Speaking of which," Lalandra said, pointing towards a tufted leather chair across from where she sat. "Let's not waste any more time."

Cautiously, Oliver stepped further into the living room, putting a hand on the chair. Lalandra sat opposite him on a couch with her back to a thirty-foot-wide veranda offering a clear view of the campus grounds. Late afternoon sun shone through the opening, making it hard to see Lalandra clearly, if at all.

Once Oliver settled into the chair, Roli vacated his shoulder to lounge on a nearby side table.

"Nice iguana you got there," Dave said re-appearing with a small dish full of more almonds. He handed them to Oliver without a word.

Oliver accepted the dish with a "thank you" but didn't take one of the treats just yet.

"I thought we'd be practicing magic during these lessons," Oliver said pointedly. He didn't want to be in Lalandra's apartment any longer than he had to.

"We'll get there," Lalandra mused, her face still semi-obscured by the glare from the setting sun. Oliver didn't know how to read her tone. When

377

* Chapter 26: The Nightmare of Linlithgow *

she spoke again, she leaned forward, revealing her face and giving Oliver an opportunity to read her emotions.

Curiosity. He only saw curiosity on her face. At least that's what her slightly bowed brow and soft eyes would indicate on most other people.

"How have your lessons with Watkin gone?"

Warning bells tolled in Oliver's mind. "I mean this with all due respect, Headmaster, but if Professor Watkin hasn't talked to you about our lessons yet… then I won't either."

Lalandra leaned back, retreating to the rear of the sofa where the sun's glare hid her face. "Oh," she said, sounding cheery and admonished at the same time. "My apologies. I meant my question literally. How have the lessons *gone?* Are you enjoying them? You don't need tell me anything you're not comfortable sharing."

Oliver swallowed. That had been smooth. Lalandra could ask a question and control how each reply played out. If Oliver had answered properly, and revealed Watkin's teachings, she would have gotten what she wanted. When he hadn't, she could play the question off as more innocent.

The realization didn't help Oliver any. It only made him more keenly aware of just how unmatched he was.

A little foot placed itself on Oliver's thigh. It was Roli's. Oliver stared down at the iguana and was tempted to scratch his friend under the chin— that touch helped calm his nerves.

"They're going well, thanks," Oliver said quickly. He didn't want to sound curt, but he didn't want to give Lalandra any ammo to work with either.

NOVA 02

Lalandra smiled large enough for Oliver to see, even despite the glare. "Excellent," she said. "He's a fantastic Professor. Likely the best we have at school. Do you know much about him?"

"Sure," Oliver said, still quickly. "Didn't he go pro at Coatlball before teaching here?"

"You tell me."

The conversation broke for a moment as Oliver considered the question further. Come to think of it, just how much did he know about Watkin? Clearly, the man had been working against Tupper before joining Tenochprima Academy as a professor. But just what exactly had Watkin been doing to fight against Tupper all those years go?

"Umm," Oliver said, feeling his ears turn red as the silence lengthened.

"Oh, don't worry about the question, dear," Lalandra said, leaning forward again. Her face looked calm enough, but Oliver had no idea what to make of it. Was she done asking about Watkin?

"Cato is the last man of principle remaining in this country," Lalandra explained. "He abides by his own internal code of morality and never compromises, even when difficult. He is the only man I've ever known to pull it off."

A glass of water appeared in Lalandra's hand as she spoke. Oliver was proud he didn't even flinch at its surprise appearance. She swirled the water around for a second, tinkling the ice against the glass, before taking a sip and carrying on.

"Then again," she said with a dramatic pause and a pointed raise of her eyebrows, "he's only able to pull it off because his allotment of Wisdom is

* Chapter 26: The Nightmare of Linlithgow *

unmatched. I don't think we've seen anybody with such a disposition in— how many years do you think, sweetie?" She'd added the last question when Dave returned to the room with his own dish of almonds.

Dave shrugged. "Dunno. Four-hundred years?" He settled down on the couch next to his wife, pecking her on the lips along the way. "Those aren't poisonous, you know?" he added, pointing at Oliver's dish of almonds.

Oliver grabbed a couple of the treats from his tray and began crunching.

"Nevertheless," Lalandra went on, "you should know Cato Watkin went *toe-to-toe* with *The Damned*. Has he told you as much?"

The room felt a lot hotter to Oliver than it had when he first entered. He wanted to tug on the collar of his shirt to let out some steam.

"Umm," he said, stalling. He needed time for his brain to catch up to Lalandra's, but based on what Dave said, she was a genius. So, was there even any point?

"We've talked about it, yeah," he finally committed.

Lalandra went back to the shadows. Dave kept munching on his almonds.

"Do you know about the Sanctum Disaster?" Lalandra's voice asked.

Munch. Munch. Munch.

"Uhh," Oliver hesitated.

"No?" Lalandra asked, sweetly enough. "Has Watkin not trusted you with the knowledge yet?"

That question annoyed Oliver. Of course Watkin trusted him. They were working together. "I know about the Sage's Sanctum," he grunted. "And about *The Damned's* experiment there."

NOVA 02

"Good," Lalandra said, leaning forward again. This time she looked excited. But that couldn't be right, could it? Was she excited to move on? He'd expected her every expression to reveal nothing about her intentions. But here she was, smiling, looking at him like an excited little kid.

Again, Roli's foot touched his leg.

Oliver kept his mouth shut as Lalandra went on. "There'll be less to explain to you, then. But you still need more than one source of information, don't you agree? Blindly trusting one person can be a recipe for disaster."

"I thought you said Professor Watkin was a man of principle," Oliver challenged, feeling a feistiness come over him. "Doesn't that mean he should be trusted?"

"Ah," Lalandra answered, raising a finger. "Trusting a man for his principles would depend on his principles, wouldn't it?"

A chill swept over Oliver as he processed Lalandra's words. It was the same chill he'd felt in Watkin's office back in September and this time it crept all the way us his spine. *The Damned* had asked a similar question when Oliver fought him off inside the Forest Temple. Then, Watkin had discussed it with him, too. Hadn't Watkin argued that nobody could be right or wrong? Because everyone has their own, personal definition of good and evil? *"If we come against another culture or ideology, both sides will insist they are just as correct as the other."*

Over a month later, Oliver finally understood Watkin's lesson. It all came down to principles.

What were his principles?

* Chapter 26: The Nightmare of Linlithgow *

Whose did he trust?

Watkin's or Lalandra's?

He didn't need to think about his answer for very long.

"My hunch is usually right about people," Oliver answered, feeling a bit reckless while he raised and dropped his shoulders. "I trust Professor Watkin."

Lalandra's tight smile grew wider, and her eyes softened. "Oh, to be so young and confident."

Anger and frustration boiled up inside Oliver's stomach. How had Lalandra remained so cheery? Hadn't he just insulted her?

Buying himself a few seconds to think, Oliver drummed his fingers against the side of his chair. While he traded appraising stares with Lalandra, he realized Emma was right about Lalandra. The headmaster's slimy, dishonest way of problem-solving was downright unhelpful. Here she was trying to get him to question Watkin's teachings without ever explicitly telling him to do so. Her scheming muddied their relationship, making him wonder if she could even be trusted. If she'd just be honest, he suspected she could be their ally in an instant.

Feeling compelled to say something, Oliver pressed on. "When I have a hunch about somebody," he said, clearing his throat, "it's *never* wrong. I know you're a genius, Headmaster, but I'm the Trinova. If you want to be my friend, you're going to have to start being honest with me."

Lalandra's crystal laugh returned as she leaned back in her chair to chuckle like a politician at a fancy dinner party. "Do you remember what it was like to be so young and full of energy?" she asked her husband.

NOVA 02

Dave popped another almond into his mouth and pointed at Oliver with an outstretched arm. "Your energy is PALPABLE, Oliver García! Keep this up, and it'll take you far in life!"

As Dave filled his and Oliver's treat dishes, Oliver exhaled in frustration. The Lalandras would die before they gave up their mind games. He'd have to find a way to convince them.

"Now," Lalandra said, her expression turning serious. "Let's be your second source of information for a moment more, shall we?"

"The Sanctum Disaster, sonny," Dave said, taking over. "It was an experiment gone wrong. At the tipping point of *The Damned's* influence, he decided to open a line of communication with the Founders of this very school. Do you follow?"

Still frustrated by the Lalandras' decision to scheme, Oliver nodded along idly, chewing on the treats in his dish. This wasn't anything Watkin hadn't already told him.

"*The Damned's* intent?" Lalandra asked, carrying on the conversation. "He publicized it without shame—he wished to bring the Founders back from the dead so that they may bless his political manifesto."

Oliver's chewing stopped. That was new information. Why would *The Damned* think the Founders would be on his side?

* Chapter 26: The Nightmare of Linlithgow *

Lalandra's lips pursed into a victorious smile. "He claimed the Founders' blessing was merely a formality required to convince any remaining doubters to commit themselves to his cause."

"Like Watkin," Dave snuck in, his lips pressed tight.

Oliver kept chewing, unwilling to interrupt. In his heart, he knew he wanted to hear another person describe *The Damned* at the peak of his powers. And learning more about Watkin's past at the same time wouldn't hurt either.

"Cato Watkin's principles had attracted enough attention by then, you see? And *The Damned* knew he couldn't just create a martyr out of Cato by killing him. Either way, the experiment backfired as a terrible monster was drawn to the attempt to communicate with the dead. Not only that, but during the events, *The Damned's* true identity became scrubbed. Whether that's tied to the pesadriya or another otherworldly power is anyone's guess—,"

This time Oliver did interrupt. "Hang on," he said. "Otherworldly?"

Elodie and Dave took a moment to share a look. Then, Elodie gestured to her husband with an open-palmed hand.

Dave leaned forward from his seat on the couch. "How much do you know about the legend of the pesadriya, son?" he asked Oliver.

"Umm," Oliver hesitated. For several seconds the Lalandras patiently waited for his answer, but Oliver could only open and close his mouth. Sweat gathered on his temple as he realized he'd neglected researching the monster what with all the time spent looking up Tupper instead. Just as Oliver resigned himself to saying, "a terrible monster," Dave raised a hand.

"It was a bit of a trick question," the man said, a kind smile on his face. "There isn't much to research outside of legend and myth."

Elodie nodded, a far sterner expression on her face. "The pesadriya," she said matter-of-factly, "serves the afterlife—according to legend at least. This is why Dave said *otherworldly* earlier."

"But!" Dave interjected with a raised finger. "Nobody's actually confirmed seeing one in this Age—let alone had a chance to study them."

Oliver gulped, realizing what the Lalandras were hinting at. "Nobody, except Professor Watkin." Hadn't Watkin told him, Emma, and Lance that he'd seen the pesadriya in the Sage's Sanctum when he showed up to the ceremony late?

Elodie's serious expression turned into a satisfied one, her tight lips cresting into the faintest of victorious smiles.

Oliver couldn't hold her stare, shifting back to Dave instead. Was she suggesting Watkin was lying about the pesadriya?

"That said," Dave went on, "based on texts from the Middle Ages, if pesadriyas were real, then the newborn versions would be like those Watkin described at the Sanctum Disaster."

Elodie leaned forward in her cushion, placing her hands on her crossed knees. "Meaning," she said softly, "they kill without bias. Indiscriminate death."

The immobilizing screeching from Oliver's old visions flooded his brain as the headmaster spoke. Was the pesadriya, the monster that hunted Tupper, really a servant of the afterlife? What would Santiago think?

* Chapter 26: The Nightmare of Linlithgow *

"Superstition in ages past," Elodie continued, "indicated the adolescent pesadriya only had one purpose. To offer as many souls to the afterlife as possible."

Oliver looked on in horror as Dave took over again.

"And though it's tempting," the man said, "to dismiss that theory as localized fearmongering from simpler times, it becomes far more believable when combined with descriptions of the *adult* pesadriya.

"You see, a final stage pesadriya doesn't just run around killing innocents. By that point, its grown sentient enough to act as intelligently as a human."

"What do you mean by sentient?" Oliver asked, his voice hollow.

"Ah," Elodie said, taking over with a tap of her finger against her nose. "A good question. In the Middle Age tapestries that document the beasts… well, let's just say the mature pesadriya is a far more frightening prospect."

Oliver felt his mouth go dry. He wasn't even in the Sage's Sanctum with the pesadriya, and yet the mere idea of it immobilized him on the Lalandras' leather chair. For a brief moment, he even felt sympathy for Solomon Tupper—how had the man survived this monster for over fourteen years?

"Instead of running rampant," Dave added, leaning forward in his chair alongside his wife, "these adult pesadriyas go about identifying targets and then…" Dave reached out into the air in front of him and mimed snatching at something. "They drag them away through a void to the underworld."

Desperate to do something with his hands, Oliver grabbed another almond and popped it into his mouth. Ever since they'd begun talking about the pesadriya, a sense of dread had begun to build up in his chest.

Yes, Watkin had described the monster as evil, but was it far, far worse than that? From what the Lalandras described, the pesadriya sounded more like an agent of a separate underworld rather than an evil creature from this one.

Between nervous bites, Oliver thought hard. "What if," he said, "the myths are just describing a monster dragging somebody through a normal door? Like taking them to the Other Side of the Key or something?"

"Perhaps," Elodie answered, a wry smile on her face. "But the tapestries all documented the same phenomenon."

"Which is?" Oliver asked, reaching for another almond.

"Well, this is just a myth of course, but… eventually the pesadriya comes back out of the same portal."

"For more victims?" Oliver asked, raising the almond to his mouth.

"No," Dave said, looking grim. "Let us show you."

"It's worse," Elodie added as Dave fetched a dusty book from a nearby bookshelf. "You have to understand," she said when Dave handed Oliver the book, "the pesadriya doesn't come back alone."

"What do you mean?" Oliver asked. He dropped the almond back in the dish, feeling his dread rise up from his chest and into his throat.

"See for yourself," Dave answered. He didn't look like an uncle anymore; more like a haggard, old man.

Without fully realizing what he was doing, Oliver found himself looking at a copy of a middle-ages tapestry. The inscription at the top read, "The Nightmare of Linlithgow, 1012 A.D." but Oliver didn't read over it long.

* Chapter 26: The Nightmare of Linlithgow *

Instead, his eyes focused on the artwork. On the monster that haunted Solomon Tupper.

The Nightmare of Linlithgow had ravaged what appeared to be hundreds of villagers in the year 1012. Where Linlithgow was, Oliver didn't have a clue, but for a second time in the span of five minutes, he heard the screeching, sniffing, and clicking from his old visions return to his head. This time the sounds melded with the artwork in front of him, forcing a flare of Bravery from Madeline's necklace so that he wouldn't get sick with fear.

On the tapestry, the Nightmare of Linlithgow glowered past tempest red eyes set within an angular head that could not be mistaken for a human's. It's skin was that of a dark purple, having more in common with obsidian glass than natural skin, and its lanky arms and legs were knotted with bulging muscles that grew well wide of its thin joints

Some of the crowd facing the monster held their hands against bleeding ears and Oliver didn't need long to connect the injuries to the pesadriya's narrow and jagged jaw. The monster's mouth was unhinged as it let out a terrible scream Oliver could hear in his head.

Oliver swallowed as he stared at the tapestry. The monster aligned perfectly with the descriptions Watkin had given him at the start of the year, not to mention his own visions. Did that mean the fairytale side of the legend was real, too? Was the pesadriya really a servant of the underworld?

With his apprehension growing, Oliver turned his attention to the other two images in the tapestry. In the first, the monster dragged a screaming victim away from the villagers. In the second, it returned from the same portal, with…

Oliver needed a full ten seconds to recover from the horrible implications of what he was looking at before he could even think to reply. When he finally did, it was with a soft voice that he asked, "they turn their targets into more monsters?"

"We said 'otherworldly' intentionally, Oliver," Lalandra answered. "I know you're confident in whom you place your trust, but has Watkin stepped you through his Virtue Theory yet? He believes all of this to be connected. You can decide for yourself if you wish to employ the same principles or not, but be sure of your decision when the time comes. There are more ways than one to combat the evils in this world. But if you pick the wrong path—the wrong principles—you'll lose every time."

Then, as though she'd simply finished recounting what she'd had for breakfast, Lalandra stood up. "Now, enough of that depressing talk, eh?" she said.

Still horrified by the pesadriya, Oliver could only gape. Then, he looked back down at the image of the tapestry still in his hands. Was the monster something else he'd have to fight? Or would it only ever be Tupper's problem?

"Let's work on your light refraction," Lalandra said, taking the book depicting the tapestry from his hands. "I can see you every time you use my spell, which means *The Damned* will, too. So, let's try…"

* Chapter 26: The Nightmare of Linlithgow *

When Oliver left over an hour later, he furrowed his brow the moment the apartment door shut behind him.

"Roli," he shot over telepathically, *"if it really is a pesadriya haunting Goodwin Forest—what are we supposed to do?"*

Roli shook his head solemnly from his perch as they bobbed down the stairs to the Dining Hall below. *"My first reaction was to seek counsel from the only man I know who could hold a candle to a conversation about virtues or the underworld."*

Oliver swallowed in his throat just as they reached the Dining Hall. *"Who?"* he asked. He knew he sounded desperate, but with Roli it didn't matter. *"Watkin?"*

"Hmm. Though I'm sure you're right to trust the man, no, I thought of Master Augustus."

The noise of dozens of loud conversations over dinner deafened Oliver's ears as he responded. *"But Augustus is dead, Roli. He's dead. We can't talk to him."*

"What of the sacred beasts? Whom do you trust, among them? We require the counsel of somebody older and wiser than humans."

Oliver stopped in his tracks—halfway to where he'd seen the Hutchites sitting. A croissant fell from Emma's mouth as she made eye-contact with him. Did he look that bad? A nudge later, Lance stared at him too, his mouth gaping.

NOVA 02

"*Archie,*" Oliver answered, gutted by the reminder of his friend's absence.

"*I need you.*"

He'd kept the last thought to himself.

* Chapter 26: The Nightmare of Linlithgow *

NOVA 02

Interludes VII – VIII

Rachel Choi broke through a thicket of bushes, choking back panicked sobs as she ran faster than she could ever remember having run in her life.

Two days ago, she and her boyfriend had joined six of their closest friends for a relaxing weekend trip in the Smoky Mountains. What they'd found instead had been a nightmare.

Crying, Rachel wiped away a growing smattering of blood and sweat off her face to get a better look at her phone's screen. She'd picked up a lot of cuts in her mad dash away from the camp site. Not that she could feel them. Shock overpowered her senses. Shock at what she'd seen lumbering towards them in the night.

She let out another crazed sob as her tear-logged eyes latched onto a single, merciful bar of cellphone service just visible on her screen.

"C'mon, c'mon, c'mon," she begged, waiting for her father to pick up. As the line continued to ring, she pressed her slick, bloody hand hard against her forehead and closed her eyes, almost sick with fear.

What if she hadn't gotten far enough away?

What if... the *monster* had followed her?

A sound interrupted her thoughts, freezing everything but her trembling breath in place.

It wasn't the sound of her phone ringing.

* Interludes VII – VIII *

Or the tone of her father's comforting voice.

It was a noise that made her skin crawl. A noise she'd first heard thirty minutes ago. Just before the violent deaths of her friends.

It was the sound of a ragged, ancient, and insatiable breath.

Rachel's sobbing returned as the noise filled her ears for a second time that night.

Then, the same nightmarish creature she'd seen at the campsite poked its head into the clearing, rustling through the leaves.

"Hello?" her father's voice rang from the other side of the line, tired and confused.

Rachel didn't even have time to let out a whimper.

Within the serving-staff's quarters of the Warren estate, Inez Maldonado closed the door to her bedroom and turned the padlock behind her.

With a grunt, she looked around her room. A small bed, an even smaller dresser, and a desk waited for her. Satisfied she was alone, she grunted again before shuffling over to the desk as fast as her little, old legs could take her.

Inez was tired.

She felt it in her bones as she sat down in her wicker chair. But acknowledging her age wasn't going to make the aches and pains go away. No, like she'd done for the past seventy-eight years, she'd have to push on.

NOVA 02

She clicked her tongue at herself. What was she doing being tempted by self-pity? Now wasn't the time for a child's behavior.

Ignoring her sore feet, Inez looked around the room again—just to be safe—and put her hand in her pocket where she felt rough parchment.

"Good," she thought, as relief coursed through her dilapidated veins. *"If I'd dropped that somewhere in the house…"*

Earlier that evening, when turning down Mr. and Mrs. Warren's bedroom, Inez had *accidentally* forced open a mysterious-looking hidden drawer in Mr. Warren's desk. She'd noticed the hidden drawer's outline before, of course—she had been serving the family for two generations now, after all—but it had never mattered before. Not really.

But that night Mr. and Mrs. Warren had fought over something. Something, Inez saw stuffed away into the drawer after her masters retired from the study for drinks on the veranda.

Well. It was only natural she investigate after they'd gone. If she wanted to take care of the family, she needed to know all their affairs. Even the nasty ones.

With a peek at her door's padlock to make sure it was still locked, Inez pulled out the envelope she'd taken from the desk.

Prepare for my return.

~~ ~~

* Interludes VII – VIII *

Inez frowned at the short letter, creasing her already wrinkled face into a dozen more lines than usual. *Who's return?* she thought. And why had they signed it with gibberish?

Then the answer came to her, and she took in a breath.

NOVA 02

Chapter 27: The Day of the Dead

I've never seen Tío this angry about anything. We've got the centers and recon systems rolled out across most of the East Coast, Texas, and Oklahoma. But now the Midwest is officially standing with Watkin out of Virginia.

1st of November, the second year of the 10th Age

On the first of November, Día de los Muertos formally arrived, providing Oliver, Emma, and Lance with a well-deserved break. Even if they had wanted to continue looking up ways to prepare for Solomon Tupper's unannounced return, or worrying about the Lalandra's intentions, there was just too much unfolding at any given moment. November had come. And it was just *too* important of a month to not become distracted.

"Do you think we'll see another Trinova this year?" Oliver heard Trey ask Se'Vaughn as they walked towards the Dining Hall for lunch before the Ceremony.

Se'Vaughn had looked at Trey as though the boy had asked whether an osorius might consider a meatless diet, but more students on campus than not had entertained the question in recent days, leading to many an unwanted stare in Oliver's direction.

The older students' looks he could handle—he was used to their attention. But the stares coming from the pitiful extramen were entirely discomforting. The new students had no idea what to expect from the test that came with the Ceremony, and Oliver could sympathize with that. He

* Chapter 27: The Day of the Dead *

still remembered how he'd frozen up, having required Emma to snap him into focus before the test even began.

"Buck up," he heard Emma mutter earlier in the weekend after a particularly depressing crew of extramen squealed questions after Oliver.

"Will they really send us home if we fail?" they wailed.

Oliver ignored most everybody under the guise of self-preservation.

He had to, because the Ceremony of the Gifts wasn't the only exciting part of the early November season. Later that week, the Magical Five Tournament would also begin, kicking off with Hutch versus Champayan.

Even the sacred beasts began to grow restless ahead of the game. Up in the skies, feathered serpents congregated into frenzied dogpiles, roaring and shooting streams of fire much to the annoyance of the giant eagles who usually occupied the higher skies alone. Then, on the ground, the osori could be seen engaging in frightening wrestling matches.

Even if the sacred beasts hadn't gone stir-crazy, the most distracting of all the November changes were the frockcoats that began to pop up on the older students and faculty.

As Oliver, Emma, and Lance headed to lunch, every single hardmore and up donned their frockcoat. It was tradition for them to be worn during special events, and none came more special than the Ceremony of the Gifts.

Though Oliver hadn't realized it last year until after he'd completed his exams, each extraman received their own frockcoat after completing their first year. His had come with Founders Hall's Magical Five title memorialized in gold-lettered stitching on the front… along with… well something else that had made him stuff his coat deep into his trunk.

NOVA 02

But, it was a requirement to wear it to the Ceremony, so, earlier that morning, he'd taken it out of the recesses of his belongings, and put it on. But only begrudgingly.

"Wear it with pride!" Emma jeered at him as they walked into the Dining Hall ahead of the Ceremony. An ocean of faces already occupied the room for the pre-ceremony lunch. The sight made him wish they'd found a seat earlier.

"I'm just gonna take it off," he said, turning back around. He'd already slipped one arm out when Lance grabbed him none too gently.

Emma laughed, latching onto his other arm. "Nope," she said while Lance shoved Oliver's coat back on. Then, they both dragged him to where the other Hutchites were sitting.

Oliver did his best not to register the number of faces that fixated on him as they made their way over.

But it was useless. Almost everyone in the room turned to look at him.

Exactly one year ago, he'd been revealed as the first confirmed Trinova in human history, and much to his horror, his frockcoat memorialized it, drawing all eyes to him like moths to a flame.

While everybody else had their *one*, normal Gift etched onto the back of their coats, his lavishly displayed all three. It was the Trinova's symbol. *His* symbol. A memorialization of his Power, his Bravery, and his Wisdom, along with all the responsibility they put on his narrow shoulders.

* Chapter 27: The Day of the Dead *

"I wish we only had to worry about the Ceremony," Lance said, his mood sullen as he shoveled down steak, eggs benedict, hashbrowns, and sauteed mushrooms.

"Don't you ever get full?" Emma asked, staring aghast at the sheer volume of food disappearing down Lance's gullet.

A grinding noise announced Elton joining the conversation. He slid his chair forward several times until he was practically sharing a bench with Oliver. "That's rich, Lance-a-lot. Last year you three needed to change your pants before making the hike up the hill for the Ceremony."

"Yeah," Lance said, pausing over his mountain of food, "but we were dumb as posts, weren't we?"

"Depends on the post," Abe snickered from across the table.

"It's all a bit mean though, isn't it?" Oliver asked, wincing at the sight of Sara, Drew, and Ethan furiously going over notes only four tables away.

Emma followed his gaze looking thoroughly unimpressed. "Ehh, it builds character."

Oliver glanced back at her as she said it. She looked away before their eyes met.

"*She knows I'm not ogling at Sara,*" Oliver thought. "*Is she just jealous? Why?*"

NOVA 02

Oliver shook his head. As far as he was concerned, Emma was breathtaking in her own right.

Brantley's chair groaned rebelliously from where he sat next to Abe, garnering not just Oliver's attention. "Alright, García. You gonna let us know what you want or nah?"

Oliver nodded. After Lalandra's lesson the previous evening, Oliver, Emma, and Lance had debated whether the time had come to bring more than just Abe and Brantley up to speed.

"Yeah," Oliver told Elton, clearing his mind. "I need Archie back and I need him now."

Emma raised a hand. "Hang on," she said, looking around the room. Her stare lingered on Beto, Cristina, and James for a moment. Then, she intoned, *"stratum silentii."*

As the world around them siphoned noise away, Oliver wondered if he'd ever get used to the sensation.

"Good looks, Red," Elton said, pushing together his lips in an impressed grin.

"Red?" Oliver asked, trying to play the question off coolly. When had they gotten onto a nickname basis?

"You see," Joel said, speaking to Oliver as though he were lecturing a toddler. "When somebody has red hair, a common affectionate nickname for them—,"

Oliver raised his hands for peace and interrupted. "I get it." Inwardly, however, he berated himself for not calling Emma 'Red' first. It suited her in more ways than one.

* Chapter 27: The Day of the Dead *

"Call me Red again," Emma said, her voice icy, "and I'll cut your pretty blonde hair off."

With an exaggerated twist of his wrist, Elton clutched at his grown-out hair. "Not my lettuce!" he cried. "I spent so long neglecting it!"

"Steadyyy," Lance said, tapping his warhammer on the table like an auctioneer. "Everybody button-up and listen to Oli."

Oliver placed a thankful hand on Lance's shoulder as he stood up. "Yall heard me," he said, strong enough so that his voice would carry. "I need Archie back. And I need him back yesterday. How do we find him?"

Every single one of the older students' mischievous smiles dropped. They even began to exchange bewildered looks.

"How are we supposed to find a lost, flying sacred beast?" Abe asked tentatively.

Oliver shrugged. "I dunno. I just need you to do it."

None of them replied. Elton even began running his hands through his "neglected" hair. "We don't even know where to start on something like that."

Joel tried half-smiling and putting on a jokester's face. "You want us to ask some geese if they've seen any four-hundred-pound snakes on their way down from Canada?"

Oliver didn't reply while Emma—*"bless her"*—stared Joel down until he wilted in his chair. "Would you rather be prepping for a one-on-one duel with *The Damned?*" she asked.

Joel flourished his fingers and wrinkled his nose. "Nah, think you three have that covered."

"Anything else?" Lizzie asked, trying her hardest not to smile at Emma's take-down.

"Yeah," Oliver said. "We'll still need reports on Goodwin Forest, too."

Abe opened his mouth to comment but barely got out a syllable before Lance's voice hissed an interruption. "Bald and Brash coming!".

Without a word, Emma dropped her silencing charm. A half-second later, Dean Blackwood's heavy boots came to a halt, just behind Abe.

"AND that's," Elton boomed loudly, "why you always condition your hair."

"Ohhhh," they all chorused, nodding their heads sagely as Elton ran his hands through his "lettuce."

Blackwood, meanwhile, rolled his jaw. "Unless I'm wrong," his boulder-toned voice growled, cutting off their voices, "you and your friends appear to be holding a private conversation, Mr. García."

Emma somehow managed to cross her arms more than usual, practically hugging herself as she glared. "Are there any rules against keeping quiet?" she asked. Oliver wasn't sure if her eyes or tone were fiercer.

"There are never enough rules for you three," Blackwood shot back, holding back a smile.

Oliver smelled trouble. Anything that made Blackwood want to smile couldn't be good. Especially when the smile looked contained.

Right on cue, Blackwood's head re-locked onto Oliver. "Normally," he said, "I hear your voices carry around the *entire* Dining Hall." He let the words hang in the air for a moment while they held their breaths. "But today I hear nothing. Do you withhold information from your Dean?"

* Chapter 27: The Day of the Dead *

Now Oliver smelled *danger*. Was the dean posturing? If not, maybe Lalandra was right. They should be using *stratum silentii* more often.

Blackwood's grin kept growing as he swiveled back to Emma. He took a step nearer, latching his enormous, gnarled hands onto the back of Oliver's chair to stare her down. Oliver had to move around in his chair so he could keep an eye on the man—he wouldn't be letting the man's brutish hands go unsupervised. "You wanted a rule, Ms. Griffith?" Blackwood breathed dangerously. "Insolence and insubordination are two. Especially,"—Emma rolled her eyes while Blackwood pulled his black notebook out of his frockcoat's pocket—"when directed at your Dean. Double detention then, is in order. Kitchens. Saturday at 9:30pm after dinner."

While cries of indignation spread around the table, Blackwood grew seemingly taller. Either that or his barrel chest expanded while he took in a satisfied breath. When he let it out, he tapped Oliver's chair with the notebook. "You'll be there as well, Mr. García."

Oliver stared at Blackwood, too dumbstruck for words while more mutinous cries echoed from one side of the table to the other. It was so unfair Oliver didn't know whether to feel outraged or confused. "Sir," he eventually said, his tone genuinely polite for once, "what for? I didn't say a word."

"I couldn't have said it better myself," Blackwood purred with the tone of a man thoroughly enjoying himself. "You didn't say *anything*, did you, Mr. García? No, while your little friend disrespected her superior you sat in *silence*. As a Trinova, you must hold yourself to higher standards and call your friends to match them."

With a swish of his frockcoat, Blackwood turned and left, clasping his black mirror shut and stuffing it back into his pocket in the same movement.

"He's in a good mood, isn't he?" Elton grunted. His expression had darkened considerably while watching Blackwood join the faculty table, and his hands twitched in the air as if he were about to clasp them around somebody's neck.

Oliver just sighed. "Don't worry about it," he said. "I'm honestly not even surprised anymore."

"But that's completely unfair!" Joel hissed between gritted teeth. "Someone oughta teach that bag of—,"

"I'll come with you guys," Lance said, cutting Joel off. "Ms. Joan can use me for the cleaning while you keep researching Tupper or something."

Oliver let out a dry laugh. "Not sure that's doing me a favor, but I like the way you're thinking." With a wry look at Abe and Brantley he added, "I think we just found a good a time for your next Goodwin Forest update."

Abe scrunched his lips together, confused. "During your detention?" he asked.

"Might as well!" Oliver said, pushing his chair away from their table. "C'mon," he added while standing up. "Let's go get a decent seat. I want to know what the Ceremony looks like when you're not the scared little kid being watched."

* Chapter 27: The Day of the Dead *

By lunch the next day, a few extraman names echoed around the Dining Hall as the older students re-visited the previous evening's events. Ahead of the Coatlball season opener, Sara, Drew, and Ethan—the wacky trio that had introduced themselves to Oliver, Emma, and Lance—were the three to watch.

"Sara reminded me of Lizzie during her test," Abe whispered towards Oliver after they'd stepped outside of the Dining Hall. More than a few murmurs of *"iuxtairis"* were repeated by the Hutchites as they marched in the sun towards the Coatlball trench. Their season opener would begin against Founders in less than an hour.

Oliver chanced a look behind his shoulder before saying anything back to Abe. A few yards away he saw Emma and Lizzie talking about something with animated gestures of their hands—likely maneuvers for the upcoming game.

"What makes you say that?" he asked Abe, matching the older boy's tone.

Abe let out a long breath before answering. "I dunno," he said, scratching the back of his neck. "It all just seemed so effortless, right? Her every move was so graceful. She never even broke a sweat. It's like she was born to use magic."

Thinking back on the Ceremony, Oliver couldn't exactly disagree. When they'd watched Sara take her turn at the Founders' tests, Tolteca had boomed, "TEST OF COURAGE," pitching Sara against the same hallway of death Oliver and Emma faced the prior year. Sara had only needed a few seconds to understand the nature of the challenge before practically dancing her way through the narrow hall of sliding blades, fired arrows, toxic gases, and hurtling axes. Oliver remembered himself sprinting through in a much less dignified fashion, with his head down, laughing like a madman.

"What about that Ethan kid, though?" Elton asked, his tone low as he butted into the conversation.

Abe laughed. "Now there's a sight I've never seen before. Look at you Elton—are you scared of an extraman?"

"No!" Elton shot back, all too quickly.

Lance joined the conversation next, shoving Elton off the path and through the thicket of bushes just before the Coatlball trench. "Elton's right," he said solemnly. "Ethan is the one to keep an eye on. Did you see him sigh when they teleported him up to celebrate passing—he looked bored by the whole thing! How can someone so boring be that strong?"

"You're both pretty strong though, aren't you?" Abe asked, a twinkle in his eye.

Oliver laughed while the Wyatt brothers exchanged confused looks, missing the insult. "Didn't you see the way he swung his sword?" Elton asked, pushing Lance off the path for a turn in front of Oliver and Abe.

Brantley budged them all out of his way, cresting through from behind Oliver and Abe just as they arrived at the trench. "Yup," he announced. "I'm pretty sure the rest of us used Earth elementals to get through the Test of Power. But this kid."

* Chapter 27: The Day of the Dead *

Elton imitated a slicing motion with a make-believe two-handed sword. "Cleaved that giant in two, didn't he?"

"He must have flared Power," Oliver said, thinking back. "He's tall, but he doesn't exactly look as strong as you guys. I'd have to flare Power just to pick up that sword."

Elton wrapped an arm around Oliver's shoulders. "Which brings us to a good question. What did you overhead press this week during shoulders day?"

Oliver removed Elton's arm from his neck.

"You put weights on the bar, right?" Elton asked. His face fell as Oliver jogged on ahead to where he spotted Nero and Rasmus waiting.

"WEIGHTS, LAD?" Elton bellowed after him. "HOW MUCH DID YOU LIFT?"

By the end of the Hutch team's warm-up drills, Oliver noticed more than a few of his teammates glancing nervously up at the bleachers on either side of the Coatlball trench. He understood those looks, having felt them himself before every game last year—at Tenochprima Academy, Coatlball meant *everything* to the students.

For his part, Oliver welcomed the blooming sense of excitement growing in his stomach. The more that the bleachers filled up with students eager to watch the season opener, the easier he'd find it to set aside his concerns about Tupper and the location of Cuahtemoc's hidden artifact. If only for a moment, the tantalizing prospect of competitive Coatlball outweighed everything else.

Oliver's growing smile faltered, however, when he spotted Blackwood amidst the Champayan students. The giant man loomed over the students with a sadistic grin on his face, firmly reminding Oliver of Tupper's constant influence, even from a place of imprisonment.

"Well at least he's not the ref today," Emma shouted towards Oliver from atop Rasmus. When Oliver looked to her, she pointed at Blackwood and mimed the face of an ogre with her hands on her ears.

Oliver smiled but shook his head without comment. In case Blackwood was watching, he didn't want to give the brute the honor of his attention.

Emma saluted. "Have it your way, then," she said, prodding Rasmus ahead so she could take up her position on the left wing before the match started.

Within a few moments, the noise from the crowd quickly drove Blackwood out of Oliver's mind. From the highest position of the eastern bleachers, Brantley and Joel led the Hutch festivities. They wore feathers, paints, and furs to honor the sacred beasts in the trench and banged on drums with great mallets. The sounds of the drums reverberated across the bleachers and trench, echoing all the way to the western bleachers where Valerie and Clay Kim answered the call with synchronized beats off their own drums. Amidst the ruckus, Oliver's grin grew widest when spotting Brantley take a moment to wet his lips and blow into the same quetzal horn Elton had used to signal the start of the Lord of the Squelchers tournament.

409

* Chapter 27: The Day of the Dead *

Brantley had enough sense to hide the artifact beneath his drum shortly after cutting off the call. Oliver began to laugh altogether at the sight of Blackwood peering around suspiciously for the source of the noise.

Then, Oliver's chuckles stopped.

From the opposite side of the trench Sara waved animatedly. At him… "Good luck out there, Oliver!" she shouted cheerily.

Oliver returned the wave, but only half-heartedly given the intense stare he felt coming from Emma. Closer still, Oliver kept a wary eye on the other two extraman standouts, Drew and Ethan. Both took up the forward positions, and Oliver still didn't know what to make of them. The same moment Drew pushed his glasses up the bridge of his nose, Ethan readjusted the monstrous sword on his back.

"How much does that thing even weigh?" Oliver shouted, pointing at the sword. "Wouldn't your rather have something else for Coatlball? Like a necklace or something?"

Ethan looked at the sword with a glance over his shoulder. Then he shrugged.

"Eh-hem," Drew interrupted. Oliver visibly recoiled when he realized the shorter boy was only a few yards away. When and how had he drawn so close?

"We find," Drew began, a dorky grin spreading across his face, "Ethan's sword decreases opposing team morale by sixty-eight percent."

Unsure of how to respond, Oliver pressed his lips together before drawing out a prolonged, "uh-huh."

NOVA 02

Then, before the awkward silence that followed could balloon too far, a more familiar voice boomed over the air. Oliver's head snapped to the commentator's box at the top of western bleachers, welcoming the distraction.

"A PERFECT AFTERNOON, DON'T YOU THINK?" Tolteca hollered through his mic. "ONE TO MATCH A PERFECT OPENER, EH? AND ON A PERFECT DAY NO LESS…"

Oliver winced the longer Tolteca spoke and was even forced to place his fingers in his ear. In the commentator's box, he saw Makayla Grant, the Tancol Coatlball captain, do the same. She mirrored his pained expression as she fumbled with a few knobs that controlled the volume. A moment later, Tolteca's continuing stream of thoughts lowered to a more acceptable level.

"Sorry about that folks," Makayla said. "But welcome to the first game of the Coatlball season. This year we've got—,"

"FOUNDERS VERSUS HUTCH!" Tolteca interrupted, spinning in place as he spoke.

"Would you shut up for a moment, you bag of rocks?" Makayla jeered. "I was giving the introduction, wasn't I?"

Tolteca's laughter boomed across the pitch. "I WITNESSED THE BIRTH OF THIS SPORT IN THE SECOND CENTURY BEFORE YOUR DEITY WAS BORN IN FLESH, BUT YES, PLEASE. GO AHEAD. ASSUME CONTROL."

While the crowd laughed, Oliver took the opportunity to distance himself from Drew and Ethan. Pulling on Nero's reins, he drove them

* Chapter 27: The Day of the Dead *

toward his midfield position above Elton. From down below, the blonde boy waggled his blonde eyebrows. "Ready to go?"

Oliver shot back a thumbs up, looking around everywhere else to gather his bearings. Elton had won out against Lance for the other starting position in midfield primarily because, unlike his younger brother, he rode an osorius. Just like Abe.

With a look over his shoulder, Oliver nodded at Abe and Lizzie who took up their defense. Then, checking on Emma, he saw Se'Vaughn exchange high fives with her on his way to take up the right-wing role at the front. Last of all, Lance and Trey rounded them out, waiting as subs on the bench.

Once Nero settled fully into place, flittering his wings like a hummingbird to keep his position, Oliver shifted his gaze forward towards the center of the trench where Lalandra entered from the back of a stocky feathered serpent. She wore a purple pantsuit, white blouse combo and had even donned a frock coat for the special occasion.

"And here comes our fearless leader!" Maykayla announced over the air. "Now what's all that gold stitching on her coat for anyway, Tolteca?"

Oliver raised his brow in surprise. Sure enough, when Lalandra went to shake hands with Abe, gold lettering on the back of her coat caught in the sunlight, reflecting more a *dozen* titles or accomplishments.

"HOW COULD ANYONE FORGET HER FOUR DUELING CHAMPION TITLES?" Tolteca chided. "SHE WAS UNDEFEATED DURING HER TIME AT SCHOOL!"

NOVA 02

For a moment, Oliver wondered about Lalandra's past. Her obsession with putting on *diplomatic* fronts to keep her enemies guessing struck him as odd. If she was such a good duelist, why bother putting up a front? Couldn't she just outduel the enemy?

Then, Oliver's thoughts froze when he saw Lalandra shaking hands with the Founders captain.

"Sara's the Founders captain?" Elton asked loud enough for Oliver to hear, echoing his own stunned thoughts. "An extraman as a captain?" He started to laugh the longer they stared.

From behind, Lizzie shouted at them. "Sara's RAs wouldn't have made her captain if they didn't think she'd do a good job!"

"If you say so," Oliver countered.

A second later, he ran out of time to think on it further. Lalandra had tossed the pigskin into the air, starting the game.

* **Chapter 27: The Day of the Dead** *

Chapter 28: The EWoC Initiative

Tío's moved on from anger to pity, and I wish I could feel the same. I'm still just frustrated. Opposition against our movement doesn't make any sense. In every state where we've implemented our vision, crime rates have plummeted, and citizen satisfaction surveys are off the charts. Why anyone would resist positive change is beyond me—they're too shortsighted.

12th of November, the second year of the 10th Age

At Tenochprima Academy it was a well-known secret that the beginning of a Coatlball match had more in common with a rowdy bar fight than a sporting event—assuming, of course, the fight included several giant bears, eagles, and feathered snakes weighing anywhere from four-hundred pounds to two tons.

Oliver, who was now used to the frenzied rush for the pigskin after Lalandra's first whistle, positioned himself just outside the melee, hanging back as the sounds of hissing, snarling, screeching, and roaring took over.

"You always want the first possession," Oliver remembered his previous captain, Ronnie, saying before every match last year. "It sets the tone for the game, you understand? If the enemy thinks you're going to attack hard all game, it'll put them on the backfoot! ALWAYS put them on the backfoot!"

But Ronnie was a Brave. To him, jumping into a scrap between magical beasts capable of ripping off your head likely felt no different than deciding

* Chapter 28: The EWoC Initiative *

to walk out the door for an afternoon stroll in the park. For better or for worse, Oliver also had Wisdom guiding his decisions, and to him, the opening brawl didn't exactly scream out as *wise* to join.

Before Oliver could think on the merit of either strategy much further, Se'Vaughn emerged from the throng of roars and shouts. Like a rocket, he shot back towards the safety of the Hutch half of the trench, weaving between enemy nets, boulders, and summoned swords of light. He dodged every attack the Founders RAs could throw at him, earning a prolonged "oooo" from the crowd in the process.

Then, instead of passing the pigskin to Abe, Se'Vaughn surprised Oliver by dropping the ball straight into his hands. Time stood still for a moment as Oliver debated what to do. By his count, four different Founders players atop screeching eagles were barreling towards him. What should he do?

His reflexes took over.

Without a formal thought guiding him, Oliver twisted in his saddle to catch the falling ball. A second later, while Se'Vaughn and his feathered serpent barreled down the right wing at a blistering pace, opening themselves up for a return pass, Oliver motioned Nero into action and grinned. Beneath his legs, Nero roared with agreement, lurching left in an instant. The quicksilver, circular motions of a feathered serpent were enough to force a novice rider green with sick.

But Oliver wasn't a novice rider anymore.

A thrill of excitement surged through him a second later when a parliament of owls descended onto them from high overhead. If he and Nero hadn't kept moving, the owls would have torn them to shreds and

NOVA 02

forced him to abandon the pigskin. As it was, he and Nero stayed ahead of the pecking owls, with only a handful managing to snip at Nero's tail at all.

From within the commentators' box, Makayla Grant's voice rang out with glee over the crowd. "Now that's some proper Coatlball! An excellent use of conjuration from Maggie Marsh, the Founders RA! Those owls nearly had the Trinova on the ropes! And did García move forward illegally there?"

Jeers flooded forward from the Hutchites in the crowd. Brantley even beat on his drum a half-dozen extra times, glaring at Makayla. "If you want a second date you better start singing a different tune!"

Still moving, Oliver reminded himself to avoid the temptation to spur Nero closer to the Founders goal. Forward movement was illegal for a feathered serpent player, so he'd have to either pass the ball forward or get the pigskin into the hands of Abe or Elton, their osorius-bound teammates. Osori could move as much as they wanted in any direction.

Making up his mind, Oliver rid himself of the ball before breaking the only other real rule of the game: handling the pigskin for more than five seconds. When Nero reached a point directly above Elton, Oliver dropped the ball into the gorilla-sized boy's waiting arms.

Or at least he tried to. Somebody else swooped in to snatch the falling pigskin just before it reached Elton's outstretched fingertips.

"NOW THAT IS CLEVER PLAY FROM THE EXTRAMAN, IS IT NOT?" Tolteca's voice boomed.

* Chapter 28: The EWoC Initiative *

Next to the sundial, Makayla giggled into her mic with agreement. "Maybe the Trinova shouldn't be banned from sports after all. The Founders captain just read him like a book!"

Oliver felt so shocked by his intercepted pass, he gaped at the interceptor for a full five seconds before giving Nero any updated instructions.

"Sorry!" Sara mouthed his way as she darted between crushing boulders from a visibly irritated Elton. Shaking the pigskin over her head, she added, "didn't mean to make you look bad, Oli!"

Oliver still gaped when Drew barreled past him a second later, also shouting. "You made that drop pass twenty-four times last year, García! You really thought we wouldn't notice it in the tapes?"

"We've been over this," a third voice sighed, zooming past Oliver's other side. It was Ethan, the third member of Sara's troop. "They're not called tapes on This Side of the Key," he went on, as bored as ever. "Saying 'tapes' makes you sound like an idiot."

"OLIVER!" a final voice shouted. Oliver snapped to its owner at once and saw Abe pointing to the gap in their defenses. Blinking, he urged Nero back into motion, but before he could fill the position, Sara had already passed the ball to Ethan.

At thirty five yards out from the Hutch goal, Ethan unstrapped his four-foot sword from his back, used it to bat away a cushioned projectile of wind sent his way by Abe, and hurled the pigskin at the Hutch net.

"GOOOOOAAAAALLL!" Tolteca shouted as Oliver's jaw dropped.

NOVA 02

Next to the sundial, Makayla jumped up and down with glee. "That might be the best opening play we've seen in years! And all of it coming after the Trinova's turnover! Ladies and gentlemen, this season just blew wide open!"

Ironic cheers came Oliver's way from the Champayan section of the crowd, reddening his ears. He didn't bother looking towards them or mouthing them off—the sight of Blackwood or Beto would force him to flare Wisdom and he'd promised Watkin he wouldn't do it needlessly anymore.

A second later, Sara, Drew, and Ethan tested his resolve as they retreated to their defensive positions. Cackling with glee, Drew shouted, "I told you Ethan's sword decreases opposition morale!"

"C'mon, guys!" Abe shouted as Lizzie resumed play with a quick pass to him. "No sloppy turnovers! We're better than this."

With his ears stinging even more scarlet than before, Oliver mumbled an apology and raised an owning hand to his teammates. Then he spurred Nero to carry them to the middle of the trench.

"How on Earth," he asked Nero, *"do a bunch of extramen know to intercept a pass like that?"*

Beneath his legs, Nero rumbled up and down as he laughed. Then, smoke blew out of his mandibles, clouding Oliver's vision. *"Perhaps your skills are not as all-encompassing as you've led yourself to believe."*

Not for the first time, Oliver wished he had Archie back.

* Chapter 28: The EWoC Initiative *

By the time Lalandra blew her whistle to signal the halftime break, Oliver looked over his shoulder to double check the score.

Hutch: nineteen. Founders: twenty-six.

Oliver winced as he dismounted Nero to join his teammates in their halftime huddle. Lizzie and Abe were already there. While Lizzie addressed Lance's and Trey's manically-delivered observations from the bench, Abe paced in a small circle, gearing himself up to say a few words.

"What are these kids eating for breakfast?" Emma groaned, joining Oliver with a hop off Rasmus. Across from them, Elton roared with frustration and kicked into the ground, scooping out a boulder sized chunk of mud that he sent flying. "You'd think *we're* the extramen out there, not them!"

"Everybody huddle up!" Abe demanded with a snap of his fingers. A moment later they'd all crossed their arms over each other's shoulders to form a circle.

"I don't have a clue who these extramen think they are," Abe hissed, "but watching replays of Oliver, Emma, and Lance from last year doesn't make them better than us! That just makes them—,"

"Creepy," Emma offered.

"Obsessive?" Lance mused.

"Hero-worshipy?" Se'Vaughn suggested.

NOVA 02

"Does it matter?!" Oliver growled, taking over. "We're getting whooped by some extramen, AND,"—he jabbed a finger towards the Founders huddle across the trench—"they're confident they're going to win!"

Every head in the Hutch circle turned to join Oliver in glaring at the extramen. On the other side of the trench, they saw Sara cheer on her teammates with pointed claps of her hands and Drew scroll through page after page of pre-rehearsed plays in front of Ethan, who stared along with the unbothered disposition of a seasoned executioner.

"Abe's right!" Oliver yelled, feeling a rare temper come along. He knew he couldn't lean into rage when doing something real, like fighting *The Damned* down the line—it'd be an easy way to lose his head in more ways than one. But for a game of Coatlball? In an attempt to energize his friends? Sometimes emotions mattered. Sometimes being cold and calculated was the wrong play and being fired up was the right one. As he went on, he knew he'd made the right decision just by the sheer insanity he saw taking over Lance and Elton. They nodded their heads slowly at every word that came out of his mouth, grinning maniacally with outstretched, twitching fingers.

"We're still the better players!" Oliver shouted. "The better team! And we're not gonna lose to a bunch of new kids on the block just because they've stalked our every play and maneuver!"

When he finally stopped to gauge everyone's reactions, he was surprised to see Emma glance away. Everyone else had met his gaze with determination. So why was she blushing?

* Chapter 28: The EWoC Initiative *

"You should, uh," Lizzie interrupted, grinning with a sideways look at Emma, "get fired up more often."

It was Oliver's turn to blush.

"It's a good look on you," Lizzie finished.

Elton leaned back his head and let out a mad howl in agreement.

Abe readjusted his glasses and mirrored Lizzie's knowing grin. But then his sincerity took over again. "Oli's right," he said, slamming down a thin wrist and fist into his other hand. "Just stick to the basics. We'll switch up our plays so we're not doing the same stuff over and over again, and send these kids back to Founders wishing they'd never formed a team!"

As they retook the field, Oliver noticed more than just Elton looked ready to sprint through a brick wall. Se'Vaughn alone looked capable of jumping off Xhak, his feathered serpent, and tackling the next extraman to look at him funny. And then there was Emma's fiery glare. She stared at the extramen with a level of ferocity Oliver typically saw in feathered serpents, not humans.

As they took their positions, Abe egged them on even further, shouting, "short passes and high percentage shots only! No—Elton, I don't care if that Ethan kid is draining three-pointers from thirty yards out—we're doing this the right way. Okay. Everyone readyyy?"

When Lalandra blew her whistle to restart the game, Sara kicked things off with a short pass to one of her RAs.

"Aaaand we're off!" Makayla Grant's voice echoed across the trench. "Will Hutch make a better showing of themselves this second half or will

NOVA 02

the Founders team hold on and pull off an upset against the Trinova's team!"

Oliver leered at Makayla—that was the third time she'd mentioned him unnecessarily. Sure, she was the Tancol Coatlball captain and was likely just excited Hutch could be held back by some extramen. But Oliver didn't care much for all the public shaming. His Wisdom told him to shove the thought aside, but he was a García. Santiago had always taught him to be proud of himself. So far, he'd kept his magic limited to the abilities of everyone inside the trench. It wouldn't be wise to draw attention to just how much he'd grown since playing in front of the school last year. But was he really going to allow Makayla to question whether he was as Powerful as he should? That he was capable of losing to extramen? No, if he wanted to stand against *The Damned* he couldn't appear weak. Oliver had read enough newspaper articles by now to understand word of this game, and his performance, would spread outside of school. Public weakness would only galvanize supporters of Tupper, and he couldn't allow it.

For a moment longer, Oliver watched Maggie Marsh take Sara's pass and press forward down the trench on her osorius. As Oliver thought to himself, debating what to do, the older RA tore through waves of Earth from Emma, shots of ice from Elton, and a conjured brick wall placed in front of her by Abe.

"Maybe I should let loose a bit," Oliver finally whispered telepathically to Nero. *"Or at least get a proper workout in."*

Nero expelled flames from his mandibles. *"Do what you must, human."*

It wasn't exactly Archie's approval, but it would have to do.

* Chapter 28: The EWoC Initiative *

Takin in a breath, Oliver pulled Nero into a dive.

"Oooooo," the crowd chanted, catching his movement.

"LET US SEE WHAT THE TRINOVA HAS IN MIND AFTER AN EMBARASSING FIRST HALF," Tolteca's voice rumbled across the trench.

With wind howling in his ears, Oliver raised his ringed hand and collapsed it into a fist. As he readied his working, the memory of the last time he'd used it flooded into his brain, and he grinned.

Back then, he'd used this magic against John Tupper. His enemy's son.

"Estalla," Oliver commanded.

A hush spread out amongst the crowd as the air in the entire trench billowed towards a pin's point worth of space in front of Maggie. Banners, signs, and hats were all drawn in by the maelstrom without discrimination, gathering within a rotating drop of energy that practically screamed with danger.

Eyes wide with panic, Maggie pulled her osorius to a halt and yelled, *"defenderis."*

But before Oliver blasted the older girl outside of the trench, Oliver modified his working. The moment he pulled on Nero's reins to stop their dive, he opened his fist, commanding the condensed energy to dissipate in the same way it had aggregated. In a real fight, he would have never held back his attack, but there was no need to send this girl to the infirmary. He'd proven to himself—and everyone watching—he could pull of the working whenever he wanted.

NOVA 02

For a moment he floated in place just over the older girl, frowning down at her while she quivered at the sight of him. In that moment he knew that Maggie understood he could have blown her well outside of the trench if he'd wanted to.

Tilting his head with a nod of respect, he reached in and grabbed the pigskin from her frozen hands. "Sorry about that," he said, hesitating slightly as he realized the terror in her eyes was directed towards him. "I was just, um, practicing some advanced magic…"

Maggie let out a crazed laugh as he took the ball away from her without much resistance. He apologized again, unable to stop himself, but all the girl could do was continue to stare with shocked horror plainly evident in her wavering eyes.

Oliver gulped. *"Maybe I should have started with something more basic…"*

Nero's sides bobbed up and down beneath him as the feathered serpent rolled with laughter for a second time that early afternoon.

"Your, umm," Oliver said to the Founders RA. "I think your five seconds are up…" He shook the ball in his hand. "So, I'll just be taking this."

The girl nodded far too quickly for his liking. Was she really that scared of him? John Tupper had handled his attacks much better… Oliver swallowed nothing but dry air when he realized what he'd done. And just how quiet the crowd had gone around the trench.

John Tupper had been the most Powerful student at school since his father before him. Of course he'd been able to keep up with Oliver's magic—attacks from a Trinova.

* Chapter 28: The EWoC Initiative *

Estalla wasn't a spell for regular students, Oliver realized as whispers broke out like wildfire across the bleachers.

It was a spell for a Tupper.

It was with numb hands on Nero's reins that Oliver watched Elton take his pass and proceed to hot potato the ball all the way down the trench with Se'Vaughn and score. As the net bulged, they wheeled away, high-fiving each other and laughing, oblivious to the shift Oliver had already begun hearing in the crowd.

When Lalandra blew her whistle a few breaths for a Founders timeout, the whispers in the crowd began morphing into outright jeers. The longer the pause in the game went on, the greater the jeers sounded, making Oliver's skin crawl. One horrified look around told him everything he needed to know. It wasn't just a few Champayans jeering. Pockets of every dorm pointed their fingers.

At *him*. The Trinova.

With his hands shaking, Oliver dismounted Nero for the timeout huddle and joined his friends. When he reached them, Emma reached out a hand to grip his forearm as tight as a vice, concern in her eyes. It was enough to bring him out of his own shock. Until, at least, Abe delivered a shock of his own, pointing to the bench.

"I think it's best if you sit out the rest of the game, Oli," his captain muttered, not looking him in the eye.

Oliver had already begun to nod his head to agree—what had he been thinking using *estalla* on a normal student?—when a far nastier voice interrupted from behind.

NOVA 02

Murmuring broke out across the Hutch team as Oliver turned around to face their interrupter.

"I must commend you," a glacier deep voice barked. The sound of it forced Oliver to close his eyes and take a deep breath. "For seeing what I could not," Dean Blackwood went on. With every fall of his heavy boots, the loose stones on the floor of the trench vibrated in protestation.

"And what's that?" Elton put in, crossing his arms next to Abe.

"Not you, simpleton," Blackwood said with a dismissive chuckle. Then he gestured to Abe with a seemingly benevolent outstretched arm. "Abraham, you are *absolutely* right."

Abe placed two fingers on his nose and shook his head. "About what, sir?" he asked, humoring Blackwood.

Oliver turned from Abe to Blackwood, leering.

But Blackwood's eyes were already on him. Without shifting his gaze, the brute pulled out a rolled-up document from within his frockcoat. "For removing Oliver from the game, of course," he said, his voice far too satisfied for Oliver's liking. "Do you know what this is Mr. García?" he added, tapping the document against his open hand.

It took Oliver a great deal of effort not to roll his eyes. "A grocery list?" he offered dryly.

Blackwood's jaw rolled in frustration for a moment, but then it stopped, and the man drew up a cruel smile. "It's a petition," he announced, clearing his throat.

"A petition for what?" Emma snarled, taking a step forward to flank Oliver.

* Chapter 28: The EWoC Initiative *

"A call to equity," Blackwood said, enjoying the moment so much Oliver began to fear for his safety. "Of course, I understand I would have missed it, but not you, Abraham. The *Wisest* course of action must have been obvious to you and our Trinova here. Thankfully, however, you are not the only Wisers on campus." With that, Blackwood sneered at them contemptuously, lingering his attention on Oliver last, before unfurling the document and reading aloud.

"Oliver, as your Dean of Discipline, I *ban* you, henceforth, from all competitive events—,"

"You're joking?" Lance snarled before Blackwood finished. With a nasty frown on his face, he stepped up to flank Oliver opposite Emma while Se'Vaughn threw up his hands and laughed at the back of the group.

"And just when we thought you couldn't be any more corrupt," Se'Vaughn muttered. From his sports coat, he pulled out an amey and flicked it towards Trey, presumably having lost a bet. Trey didn't even look happy to have won the money.

Blackwood, meanwhile, had gone on speaking unperturbed, a manic, satisfied grin taking up nearly his entire face. "Under advisement of Provision 430, the Trinova's involvement in student competitions is, at best, a mockery of fair play and, at a more likely worst, a danger to our student population. Under Provision 430 the Trinova is called to remove himself from competitions so that we may maintain EWoC across all our sports."

"EWoC, sir?" Oliver asked, barely keeping his voice level given the injustice of the situation.

NOVA 02

Blackwood put a hand on each knee and leaned in closer patronizingly. Oliver came close to tsking his tongue and backing away from the bald man's head, but just managed to stop himself.

"Equity Within our Competitions," Blackwood drew out in his deep voice. "Your involvement in our competitions is a farce. Go on, now," he added, straightening so that he could motion Oliver away with waves of his fingers, "your presence here is no longer tolerable."

* Chapter 28: The EWoC Initiative *

NOVA 02

Chapter 30: Shameless Simulation

Watkin looks a shoo-in to winning his election next spring. Same for Lalandra. Eldrick's gone missing after fumbling his anti-federalist campaign and crashing out of the polls. Rumor has it, Tío hand-delivered him to center 13 himself.

23rd of November, the second year of the 10th Age

"D'you think he's…" Lance began. He stood on the other side of the door leading into the dungeon simulator.

A huffing noise followed. So did Emma's voice. "Do I think he's what?" Based on the way she'd asked the question Oliver knew she hadn't liked it.

"I dunno!" Lance squawked defensively. "D'you think he's okay in there?"

More huffing. "He's the Trinova, Lance. Of course, he's okay."

Oliver cleared his throat to let them know he could hear. But he didn't open his eyes. He didn't feel like disconnecting from his meditative state just yet.

Emma banged the door open. Instead of clattering against a wall, however, the door bounced silently off a mushroom.

"What on Earth?" she breathed as she walked inside.

"Woah," Lance agreed.

Still, Oliver kept his eyes closed. He knew he must look strange, sitting at the top of a short, moss-laden hill, cross-legged with his back to the door.

* Chapter 30: Shameless Simulation *

But it hardly mattered. At that moment, he was closer than ever to feeling Nova's direct push and pull.

Ever since Blackwood had banned him from all Magical Five competitions, he'd been dutifully practicing the neglected parts of his training. That meant many of his previously occupied hours were now spent in the simulator. Before Lalandra had given him full access to the room, he'd have wasted a lot of time practicing his magic in Hutch, surrounded by countless distractions.

But now he had full access to the simulator, and his options were limitless.

The first thing he asked the simulator to develop was "a place to train." When the room blinked green above the controls, telling him to enter past the lobby, all he could do was walk around and marvel at the different rooms presented to him with tears in his eyes. The "place to train" included a separate facility for each application of magic, and though he'd spent most of his time to date in the Destruction facility, other rooms full of natural elements like raging fire and billowing air were also available to him. He even found a weight room to make Elton green with envy towards the rear of the compound, including dozens of machines, racks, and stations to work on any muscle group he could think of.

Since that first day, over five weeks ago, he'd also found the simulator to be uncannily good at coming up with real-life dungeon scenarios he might find himself in. That morning, for instance, he'd decided to face off against a simulated version of Xihuacota in a lagoon setting. The idea had sounded good in his head, especially after having found recent success against venomous baboons, lizard monsters, and even humanoid pig-creatures taller than Blackwood. In practice, however, Oliver was now more frightened of Xihuacota than ever before.

She'd murdered him eleven times in a row, averaging nineteen seconds to either drown, behead, or strangle him. After the eleventh re-spawn, Oliver paused the simulation, disgusted with himself, and queued up a space to meditate instead.

After lowering his heart rate, and reflecting over just how reckless he, Emma, and Lance had been last year when crossing the lagoons to find the Iguana's Scroll, he entered the meditative trance Emma and Lance now saw him in.

As if from another set of ears, Oliver heard Emma's and Lance's footsteps padding across the moss-laden floor to join him at the top of his knoll. He breathed in the cool, damp air of the room, ignoring how good it felt in his lungs, and, not for the first time, he wondered if it was laced with some of the focusing elixir Santiago had taken when he first started working for Miyada. Around him, a pond surrounded the base of his hill and water gurgled over stones from out-of-sight feeder-streams. All the while, frogs croaked, and birds chirped, formally cementing the space as the most relaxing one Oliver had ever been in.

"Oli?" Emma asked. She and Lance had come to a halt at the top of his hill. Emma didn't stop there, opting to sit down with him. By the time she'd settled herself, she'd pressed her back against his, testing his focus and releasing more than one butterfly in his stomach.

433

* Chapter 30: Shameless Simulation *

It had been her idea to take advantage of their full access to the simulator.

At first, he'd balked at the idea, shouting, "I'm getting Lalandra to put me back on the team right now," as they stormed away from the Coatlball trench.

But Emma had stopped him with a not-very-gentle tug of his shoulder to shout back, "quit pouting and turn this into a win!"

Two weeks later, Oliver agreed with her completely. Part of him even wished Blackwood had banned him *sooner*.

Yes, he missed Coatlball like a farmer missed rain in a drought. And, yes, the pangs of jealousy he felt when watching Emma and Lance head off to Coatlball practice or dueling qualifiers without him hurt like knife wounds to the chest. But the fact of the matter was, Blackwood had gifted him a perfect opportunity without even realizing it. Now, more than ever before, Oliver finally had time to tackle *all* aspects of his training.

So, when Lance flicked him on the forehead, Oliver didn't need to open his eyes to know his friend was worried about him. No, he could *feel* it. In fact, there was surprisingly little Oliver couldn't pick up on now that he'd been practicing *Nova's Touch*.

And yet, despite his new-found ability, Oliver felt frustrated at how little he could do with it. On the one hand, he'd taken Watkin's pocket dimension theory and pushed the concept further, enabling himself to feel the world indirectly and observe more than his normal senses could. On the other hand, he wanted *more*.

NOVA 02

So far, every time he latched onto Nova's energy directly, and asked *it*, not his own energy, or the energy in the elements, or even the energy stored in his ring, to lift a rock, or disturb the pond, or close a frog's croaking mouth, Nova had ignored him. Right now, he could only use the direct energy to get a feel for his surroundings.

When is that supposed to be helpful? he thought. Tupper wasn't exactly going to give him twenty minutes to meditate before a fight, was he? Watkin hadn't thought much of the theory when Oliver first presented it to him, and maybe that was why—was there no real practical way to use the magic?

With a wistful sigh, Oliver turned his attention away from *Nova's Touch*. He'd settle for the indirect use for now. In his mind, he could see the room, even with his mind closed. Nova wiggled in the air, it churned in his body, and vibrated in living things around the room. It even touched Emma's vocal cords as she spoke out, helping Oliver put together the picture.

"Oli?" she repeated, sounding much more timid than she'd led Lance to believe when getting feisty before they entered. Would Oliver have picked up on that without *Nova's Touch*? The air in the room circled around her, behind his back, and Oliver could feel the change in her arms. They went from playing with the moss at her sides to somewhere wrapped around her core.

Sure enough, when he turned around to grin at her, there she sat, her arms crossed, and her brow etched with concern. "How are you holding up?" she asked.

"I'm not a hospital patient, you know?" he answered, bouncing up to a standing position with a push of Earth to his bottom.

* Chapter 30: Shameless Simulation *

Emma and Lance exchanged a look.

"Guys!" he insisted. "I'm honestly fine."

Lance coughed politely as Emma stood. "You... um... talking to anybody while you're in here or... just being crazy all by yourself?"

"Did you know you were muttering the whole time?" Emma tagged on, nodding like Lance.

Oliver hesitated. Maybe he needed to dial down the isolation a bit. He hadn't even realized he'd been muttering out loud. No wonder they thought he was going crazy.

He raised his hands for peace. "I'll make sure to talk to more people during the day." Then, with a grin, he added, "but you can't argue with the results! Emma, you were right!"

Emma raised a skeptical eyebrow. "About what?"

"Turning this into a win!" he insisted.

Lance furrowed his eyes. "You're going to meditate with Tupper to bring on world peace?"

Oliver opened his mouth, ready to step them through just how much he'd been improving. But then a better idea occurred to him. "No, not meditation," he said. "That's something else I'm working on. Here, let me just show you the rest."

Emma and Lance exchanged yet another look.

Oliver ignored them and cleared his throat. "Sim!" he announced. "Training facility!"

Roli's peeping voice answered. *"Training facility, coming right up! Though a please would have been nice..."*

"We loaded in Roli's voice," Oliver whispered, leaning in towards Emma and Lance so they'd hear. "The stock voice was a little…" He paused to tilt his head back and forth.

"Cliché?" Roli suggested. A pleasant woman's voice took over for a moment, speaking in a lofty English accent. *"Would you prefer I talk like this, sir?"* the voice asked. *"How may I satisfy your every need, Master García?"*

Oliver nodded at Emma's aghast face. "Yep," he said. "Weirded me out, too."

Lance peered around the mossy room, squinting his eyes. "Roli, where are you talking from?" he asked quietly, overturning a nearby stone with the butt of his hammer.

Roli's contracting dewlap echoed across the room. *"I am everywhere and nowhere, all at once. I am the inner machinations of YOUR MIND. I COMMAND YOUR EVERY TH—,"*

"He's on the controls," Oliver answered, pointing back out the exit. "They're beneath the stairs to the observation deck."

Roli grumbled mutinously in their heads while Lance smiled at Oliver.

Then, the room shifted, turning into Oliver's training facility.

"So?" Oliver asked them, rubbing his hands together. "Which room do you want to see first?" With an open palm, he motioned over his shoulder towards each of the different facilities. "Destruction, anyone?"

* Chapter 30: Shameless Simulation *

Twenty minutes later, Oliver finished the tour by conjuring a wood nymph—the subject of Zapien's latest lesson in Channeling 201. With a final, ethereal giggle, the kitten-sized guardian disappeared, popping out of existence with a dispersion of green leaves.

Whistling, Lance clasped his hands behind his head. "We'll have to write Blackwood a thank you letter at this rate!"

"Ehhhh," Oliver said, rubbing the back of his neck. He was trying to stop himself from growing red in the face. Between Emma's stunned face and Lance's excited one, the room suddenly felt as hot as Miyada's armory. "I still can't win a lot of my duels," he hedged. "You should see me when I face off against Xihuacota."

Emma echoed Lance's whistle. "You mean you can duel in here, too?" She stood on her tip toes trying to see if they'd missed a room during the tour.

"If you call being violently drowned and sadistically strangled a duel," Roli pipped, *"then yes!"*

"Thank you, Roli," Oliver said dejectedly. Then, agreeing with the iguana, he added, "I'd recommend starting with a lizard or snake monster."

"So, I can use it sometime?" Emma asked. Her voice had pitched higher, and Oliver got the impression she was trying to come across as carefree. Either she was trying too hard, or *Nova's Touch* made it clear her posture was tenser than a wooden board.

He shot her a smug grin to let her know he was on to her.

"Ugh," she growled. "Fine! I want to practice against Beto! Is that too much to ask?"

NOVA 02

Oliver's smile grew wider. "You thinking about the dueling playoffs next semester already?"

"They're not that far away," she countered in irritated fashion.

Lance raised a hand, adopting a pained look that reverberated across his entire body. "We don't have to talk about the tournaments if you don't want to!"

Both Oliver and Emma rolled their eyes.

"He's not a little kid!" Emma blurted out. "You don't need to coddle him!"

Oliver nodded his head, agreeing with Emma. "I'd love to hear about it."

When Lance's face compounded into pity, Oliver sighed and added, "honest! I've been stuck here all day every day. All I'm caught up on is our homework list and my training schedule. How are things looking?"

"He's lying," Roli's voice snuck in. *"He's asked me at least a dozen times this week to pull up the Coatlball schedule. In fact, here are the standings and matches I showed him this morning."*

A mirror popped up over them, jutting against several creaking tree branches as it bloomed into existence. It was the same mirror that had displayed the tests and results from the Ceremony of the Gifts. "Yes," Oliver sighed again. "Thank you, Roli."

"You're quite welcome, Master García."

It was Emma's turn to smile. "Okay, so you're caught up. Lance's three-pointer got us the win on Preston. That means we're up on points overall."

* Chapter 30: Shameless Simulation *

She pointed at the board. "But! Champayan has the easiest run-in through February by far."

"They play Founders twice," Lance said, taking over with a grimace. "And they're…"

"Yeah," Emma said, tightening her lips. "They're awful. But look at who's the favorite for the dueling tournament."

Roli's dewlap chuckled in their heads as a red circle highlighted the number one ranked person on the duelers list.

Beto Warren.

Several lines below, Emma took eighth.

"Still," Lance said, trying to sound polite. "You're not tenth…"

Emma growled until Lance backed away.

Oliver, meanwhile, leered at the list. Beto had come back to school different this year. A lot of other students, young and old, had begun calling him the next John Tupper, and John had been the best duelist at school since Headmaster Lalandra had been a student in the late 80s. If Beto was causing a stir by being touted as something even close to that level, he was cause for concern. Especially if he supported *The Damned*. He'd become a powerful member of the Tupper family whenever their leader escaped.

"I can get you trained up," Oliver said, feeling his chest boil in anger at the thought of Beto's family. "Let's get you in here on Thursday nights. You can duel me to get a better feel for tournament conditions."

Emma let out a hollow laugh. "What good is that going to do? I might as well duel Xihuacota."

"Emma the Brave worried about a friendly duel?" Oliver teased.

NOVA 02

Emma mouthed *"hah-hah"* at him.

Then she shoved him off the hill. By the time Oliver climbed back up grinning from ear to ear, Lance faked a retching noise.

"Yikes," he said.

"Oh?" Emma asked. "You've got something to say, Lance-a-lot?"

Lance sighed and grumbled something under his breath. Then, he turned to leave, still muttering.

"What's that?" Emma shouted as Lance slammed the door. "We couldn't hear you?"

But Oliver had heard Lance's grumbles. With Nova's indirect touch now under his command, every single one of his senses was more refined. He'd clearly heard Lance say the words *flirting*, *disgusting*, and *shameless* before leaving. And suddenly, Oliver couldn't help but get the feeling he was falling into a trap.

If they'd rehearsed this, then that meant... Oliver risked a look at Emma.

She stared right at him, only a few feet away, smiling innocently enough. Oliver's entire stomach flipped at the sight, and suddenly the anger he'd felt towards the Tupper and Warren families evaporated. Emma's green eyes never wavered while his thoughts raced in his head. They locked onto his own, daring him to say something.

She'd changed quite a bit since last year... he remembered thinking the same thing when she showed up in Santiago's kitchen four months ago, and it didn't look like the process had stopped between now and then. Her face was sharper around her eyes, nose, and jaw, all in a way that took his breath

* Chapter 30: Shameless Simulation *

away; especially when she gave him the free opportunity to just take her in. Her posture now resembled Lizzie's, perfectly poised and confident, and her hair... even when she twirled it into a bun behind her head, like she had today, it looked effortlessly sleek and soft. He had no idea why Emma was jealous of Sara. Yes, some boys might say Emma's jawline was a bit too defined, or her nose a bit too long, but as far he was concerned, she was the most admirable, beautiful girl on campus.

Oliver knew what he had to do. What she likely wanted him to do. Lance had even left to give them some privacy...

"Well," he blurted out, his voice awkwardly high, "we better get back to Hutch, yeah? We've got exams next week and *lots* of studying to do!"

Emma blinked a few times, her entire body radiating complete confusion.

Without quite knowing what he was saying, Oliver added, "I'll go grab Roli if you want to meet outside in a minute?" Then, without hesitating, he turned and followed Lance's echo out the door, cringing to himself more than he ever had in his life.

"What was that, García?" he thought to himself. *"At least tell her the truth!"* Annoyingly, his neck vibrated in agreement with the thought. He slapped it so hard it sent a concerning jolt all the way down his back.

To his horror, Roli's voice spoke in his head, riddled with mirth. *"You handled that well—assuming you wanted to ignore her. That was your goal, right?"*

In the safety of the console room beneath the stairs, Oliver grabbed fistfuls of his hair. "ROLI, WHAT DO I DO?!"

NOVA 02

Roli somehow managed to shrug his little shoulders before he put a clawed foot on Oliver's shoulder. The little foot comforted him more than he dared admit, but he couldn't hide that from Roli because he and the iguana shared a mental bond at this point. *"You can start,"* Roli answered, chuckling, *"by walking that poor girl back to Hutch."*

Oliver gaped at the iguana. "I can't—walk her down the hill? After that?! I was supposed to kiss her, Roli! KISS HER!"

Roli began to laugh so hard he fell onto his side and raised a foot for mercy. *"Augustus!"* he eventually managed, gasping for air. *"Did you see this when you told me to serve the Trinova? Was my purpose to provide the savior of our times love advice?"*

Tsking, Oliver left Roli behind, moving his legs to join Emma just outside the simulator entryway. Roli could make his own way back to Hutch if he was going to be that unhelpful. With his ears burning red, Oliver made straight for Emma who waited for him outside. Behind him, he could still hear the iguana laughing, but, in front of him... moonlight and starlight sparkled, illuminating water droplets that had condensed on the path leading back to Hutch. Normally, he would have commented on how pretty the night looked, but, despite his Bravery, he could barely look at Emma, let alone talk to her. Would she understand he wanted to make a move but couldn't? Not with *The Damned* looming over them like a specter of death. Would she hate him for it?

But when she turned to look at him as he joined her in the starlight, she didn't look angry, or even disappointed. She just smirked, managing to

* Chapter 30: Shameless Simulation *

exude a warmth that made him want to turn off the boosted senses Nova now gave him.

Her look—just her look—stopped him mid-stride before he reached her.

"C'mon," she breathed while tilting her head towards Hutch. "We've got exams to study for, yeah?"

Then, she led *him* back down the hill, never once mentioning anything about the kiss he should have given her.

When he eventually reached the safety of his room, Oliver shut the door behind him and collapsed into the chair beside his bed.

From his own chair, Lance lowered his notebook an inch so he could give Oliver an appraising look. "That bad a kisser, huh?"

Oliver threw a pillow at him.

Chapter 31: Servants of the Void

I'm to go searching in the woods again. I'm proud of myself though. I pushed back against the assignment and said I'd only do it if he gave me more information this time. Last year ended up proving useless, so he needed to have a good reason if I was going to do it again.

16th of December, the second year of the 10th Age

Oliver's least favorite part of the exam season came after the exams were over, when seemingly everybody on campus took it upon themselves to relive the exams through arguments over the correct answers. He'd hated the exercise last year, embarrassed by the sheer number of questions he'd gotten wrong.

This year felt no different.

Even in Ms. Joan's kitchen, where he thought he could dodge these conversations, Lance and Emma roared over who'd taken the better approach to Perrindorph's timed essay. When Oliver had read the prompt—

Describe the three branches of government on the Other Side of Key.

—he'd exhaled for a full five seconds before scrambling together the best he could remember. He knew, like the United States on the Original Side of the Key, there were executive, legislative, and judicial branches of government on Tenochprima's Side of the Key. What that meant, he didn't have a clue, but he at least he'd remembered that much.

* Chapter 31: Servants of the Void *

Given his responsibility to save the world from Tupper, he'd found it hard to care about his exams when he took them, and even harder to care about them now, after they were over.

So, while Emma and Lance continued raising their voices over who'd been more right, he banged his head against one Ms. Joan's marble countertops.

They'd taken to eating lunches in her kitchen instead of the Dining Hall in recent weeks, using *sorbelux* to get there. Emma thought hiding in the kitchen to eat a meal was "cowardly behavior," but Oliver couldn't care less. Anything to get away from Blackwood's taunting, Drew's near-constant apologies for having gotten him kicked off sports teams, and the general ogling from the entire extraman class. If avoiding useless interactions made him a coward, then he'd gladly run straight back to the Forest Temple and put Madeline's necklace back where he found it.

"Perrindorph specifically told us," Lance shouted, "the Senate signed the MBI into existence in the *nine*teen hundreds—NOT THE EIGHTEEN HUN—,"

Emma cut him off with a glint in her eye. "YOUR'E THINKING OF THE FBI, YOU MORON! LITERALLY LAST WEEK HE SAID THE MBI CAME FIRST! IN 1892! ARE YOU AS DUMB—,"

Before Emma could get too far, Ms. Joan's voice rose loudest. "NO SHOUTING IN MY KITCHEN!"

Oliver lifted his head from where he banged it and rubbed the welt forming on his brow, muttering "thank you."

NOVA 02

Ms. Joan had raised more than her voice when she shouted, shaking plates and clattering knives all around her. It reminded Oliver of the time when Brantley flared Power to grow in stature and darken the room to scold him and Lance last year.

"Except if it's me doing the yelling," Ms. Joan added with a flutter of her eyelids.

Emma let out a huff and crossed her arms, *"hmmph!"* Then she took the stool next to Oliver and ran nervous hands through her hair. "Well, I'm sure we all did fine. Enough for Bs anyway."

Oliver pushed his lips together and tilted his head from side to side, debating whether that'd be true. He'd be stunned if he got a single B.

Ironically enough, the only exam he'd felt like he deserved full marks in was Blackwood's shielding exam. Whether intentionally or subconsciously, he'd refined his shielding capabilities during his month in the simulator. Now, he could fend off even a direct attack from Xihuacota. During their practical exam, he'd gone on and blocked every attack from the dummy course Blackwood set up, and even a direct attack from Blackwood himself, earning many plaudits from Zapien in the process.

But this was Blackwood's class they were talking about. The evil man would probably give him a D for bad "form" or something ridiculous.

"I can't believe I didn't read up on chupacabras," Lance groaned, taking the third and last stool at the white marble counter. "I spent all last night studying the wrong stuff for it."

"You're supposed to study it all," Emma chided. "You're talking about the chupacabra best friend question?"

* Chapter 31: Servants of the Void *

Lance buried his head into his hands. "It wasn't, 'man,' was it? Man's best friend?"

Lance's misery was enough to make Oliver laugh and join the conversation. "That would be a *dog*. C'mon, man, chupacabras are supposed to be buds with griffins, even I remembered that."

The door to Ms. Joan's kitchen slid open, bringing in an explosion of noise from the Dining Hall. Ms. Joan turned from where she supervised the chopping of a few dozen potatoes to address their interrupter with a knife in hand. When she recognized who'd entered, however, she withdrew the blade and smiled sheepishly.

"There you are," Professor Zapien said, huffing. As the door closed behind her, she moved towards Oliver, ignoring Ms. Joan's knife. But then she saw the growing welt on his head and stopped in her tracks. She flourished her fingers, as if deciding whether to comment, before shaking her head and continuing forward, her silver curls bobbing as she went. "Oliver, Professor Watkin asked to see you."

Oliver stood up so fast he shot two feet into the air.

Watkin had cancelled their November lesson after the most recent Goodwin Forest disappearance. He'd begun to think December would go the same way given Christmas Break was around the corner. But if Watkin wanted to meet now… that meant more news.

"Where is he?"

NOVA 02

As a Brave, Emma couldn't flare Power to run at the speeds Oliver and Lance were capable of going. Even then, they only had to slow down for her once as they sped up the ridge towards Watkin's office. Oliver dreaded the news they might receive, and he knew Lance, given his father's potential history, was likely feeling more than just dread.

Every time they heard of another Goodwin Forest disappearance, Lance's face took on a complicated combination of anger, frustration, and anguish that didn't belong on someone with such a naturally goofy disposition. He wore that same expression now, no doubt fearing the same news Oliver expected Watkin to share. By the time they reached the Academic Building, he led the charge up the stairs, not Oliver.

Oliver worried for his friend as he watched him take five steps at a time. Though he thought of himself as fast and intimidating after watching replays of his fights in the simulator, Lance was something else entirely. When the boy flared Power to run at these speeds, with his eyes and jaw drawn like they were now, he had more in common with a rampaging bull than a human being.

Seconds later, they barged into Watkin's office, stumbling over one another in the process.

Watkin, lean and athletic, turned to face them with a face that made it crystal clear which version of the man they were getting.

The intense one. He didn't even pretend to waste time with pleasantries. "It's time for another lesson," he announced.

449

* Chapter 31: Servants of the Void *

"What happened?" Oliver managed while heaving to catch his breath. Then he got a proper look at Watkin.

The man looked exhausted. Dark circles shadowed his eyes in a way Oliver had never seen before, and his hair had been pulled together into a disheveled bun instead of his usually pristine ponytail. More surprising yet, he seemed to be pacing around his office. Oliver stared at him, stunned. Watkin had a purpose for *everything* he did, but unless Oliver was mistaken, the man simply paced to burn off nervous energy.

"Before we begin," Watkin said, finally taking a seat at his desk, "please provide me with an update on your training."

Oliver opened his mouth to disagree, but then remembered which Watkin he was dealing with. The intense Watkin wouldn't take back-talk well, and the man had already asked Oliver to trust his methods more than once. So, when Watkin gestured to the red leather chairs in front of his desk, Oliver closed his mouth and plopped down. Emma sat in the other without hesitating because Lance had taken up Watkin's pacing, closing and opening his fingers into fists as he went.

"Report," Watkin demanded. Oliver felt a jolt on his shoulder as Roli leapt off him to join Jaiba in a windowsill. They began to chatter in animal tongues as Oliver reported.

Watkin nodded more than a few times as Oliver spoke, only interrupting to get further clarification on the *Nova's Touch* technique. "You can feel the world around you at any given moment?" the man asked, openly wearing incredulity on his face.

NOVA 02

"Yep," Oliver confirmed. He found it hard to keep a sliver of pride from entering his voice as he described his success in further detail. "Like right now, your heart is beating fast, and I'm pretty sure Jaiba just turned his head to look at me."

Watkin's eyes flashed for the briefest of moments, but Oliver couldn't glean enough from the change to know what the man had felt.

But *Nova's Touch* could. Watkin's entire body had relaxed when Oliver answered the question.

"That relieves you, sir?" Oliver asked.

This time Watkin grinned so much Oliver was able to ignore the dark circles under the man's eyes. "Yes, I daresay it does. But I am sure you will **trust** me to expound upon my relief at a later date? We have more urgent matters to address."

At Watkin's words, Oliver's upper neck vibrated so fiercely it felt as though a swarm of beetles had landed on his skin. He managed to stop himself from yelping, but he also didn't need a mirror to know he stared at Watkin with his jaw agape and his eyes aghast. Watkin's smile somehow looked even more satisfied than before.

Oliver didn't know what to say. The word **trust** had hung in the air, warping time to a brief halt that coincided with an aggregation of energy in the room Oliver couldn't recognize. The moment was gone—Watkin even stared at him, impassive and impatient to move on—but Oliver couldn't help but associate the feeling with how he'd felt in Lalandra's apartment.

How many times now had he felt his gut encourage him to trust others? Last year he'd hated himself for not trusting Stevie sooner after learning

* Chapter 31: Servants of the Void *

she could have told him where to find the painting of the Forest Temple whenever he'd wanted to. All he'd needed to do was trust her with the knowledge of the Iguana's Scroll, and he would have found the Forest Temple that much sooner. And all this year he'd felt disgusted with Lalandra and Watkin for playing their politics and games instead of being truthful with one another. Was it more than just a gut feeling guiding him on? Was something else, more powerful, and more tangible, at play?

Oliver felt a desperate urge to ask Watkin if he'd intended to make the word **trust** hang in the air—he had to know the answer—but then *Nova's Touch* alerted him to something else.

So slow that it was almost imperceptible, Watkin shook his head.

"Okay then," Oliver replied, trusting man's judgment. They could hash this out in a later lesson. "What's the news?" As the words crossed his lips, his neck hummed in satisfaction, and Oliver wondered if the feeling came from self-satisfaction or the new branch of magic he suspected.

Watkin's smile dropped.

Before he answered, his haggard intensity returned. "After many petitions from members of Federal Hall, Headmaster Lalandra led an investigative party into Goodwin Forest this past weekend."

Oliver and Emma exchanged concerned looks. If Lalandra had been asked to lead a party into Goodwin Forest, that meant the town was in trouble. What was going on that required the greatest duelist of the age?

Behind them, Lance stopped pacing to look up for the first time since entering the room. He placed a hand on his chin. "The feds couldn't handle it themselves?"

NOVA 02

Not for the first time, Oliver wished he'd grown up on This side of the key. Who were the feds? What was Federal Hall? He made a mental note to pay better attention to Perrindorph's political science, or poli-sci, class.

Watkin shook his head. "No, Federal Hall representatives went the weekend before, and nobody's heard from them since."

Lance gasped, taking a needed seat on the arm of Oliver's chair. "The feds?" he repeated. "They got taken, too?"

Emma threw her hands up into the air. "What's going on over there, Professor? We've got Brantley and Abe giving us reports every month, but all we've got so far is that a *boogeyman* of some sort is kidnapping people!"

As politely as possible, Oliver raised a hand to interrupt. "Hang on, Professor. What about Lalandra?"

"*Headmaster* Lalandra," Watkin answered. "I'm afraid the news only gets worse. She and her entire investigative party have not responded to over a dozen requests to report."

Nobody spoke for several seconds as understanding dawned across the room. Oliver almost didn't register the sick feeling in his stomach, such was his shock. Elodie Lalandra, kidnapped? Sure, he didn't see eye-to-eye with the woman's approach on *diplomacy* or whatever she called it, but this was the greatest duelist in the world they were talking about. Other than Tupper…

When Watkin resumed speaking, even he sounded grim. "I've searched those woods every other night for the past five months, but I cannot unlock the area's secrets or even begin to fathom where the missing victims are taken." He let out a long sigh. "As you say, Emma, a boogeyman is afoot."

Chapter 31: Servants of the Void

Caw-caw!

Jaiba hopped over to Watkin from the windowsill, nuzzling into the man's shoulder. Absentmindedly, Watkin began stroking the bird's feathers and beak.

"I begin to worry," he went on, flicking his eyes from Jaiba to Oliver, "our foe may be behind the disappearances."

Oliver gulped.

Watkin flourished his fingers and nodded again. "Which brings forth a host of unsavory theories to mind."

"Wait!" Emma exclaimed. "You told us this summer that Tupper's stuck in some tomb?"

"Yes, without a doubt he's sealed within the Sage's Sanctum," Watkin confirmed.

"Is that anywhere near Goodwin Forest?" Oliver asked. When he asked the question, he glanced over his shoulder at Lance.

Lance just shrugged. "You're asking me? How am I supposed to know? Goodwin's in Tennessee, right?"

Watkin sighed a second time. Before he answered, he looked around the room until his eyes locked in on his staff. Seeing that it rested out of reach against the windowsill, he blustered his lips, opened a drawer, and pulled out a ring. After he slipped the metal onto his left hand, he closed his fist. His cloak fluttered as a breeze shot down from above, straightening out the fabric of his cloak and somehow straightening his hair back into its normal ponytail.

NOVA 02

"Ah," he muttered, "that's better." Still not done, he magicked a goblet into existence with a lazy flick of his fingers. Before Oliver could think to ask, "what's in that?", the man had already chugged down the purple contents.

A moment later, Watkin's haggardness vanished and the man's eyes even began to twinkle. He smacked his lips. "Like a full night's sleep in a cup!" he said, smiling fondly at the goblet.

"To business." Without much warning, Watkin waved a hand again, this time sending the contents of his desk flying. Instead of crashing into the walls of the small office, the contents met cushioned bubbles of air, before being guided to rest carefully—and thoughtfully—onto the surrounding shelves.

"Is Tupper sealed in the Sage's Sanctum?" he asked out loud. "Yes! But,"—he pulled out a map from somewhere near his chest and slammed it onto his cleared desk—"seals can *always* be broken. We cannot eliminate Tupper's escape from the realm of possibility. Though I find it unlikely, our dear friend may already be on the prowl."

Oliver stared at Watkin, dumbfounded. How was Watkin being so cheery about this? "B-but you said I should focus on training and school! That we had time until he escaped! Now you're saying he could already be out?!"

"It's a *possibility*, not a guarantee," Watkin said, winking.

"Now," he went on, swiping dust off his map. "I won't pretend to know everything there is to know about every branch of magic, but there's a

Chapter 31: Servants of the Void

particular breed of magic we only teach at the Academy as an elective course during your senior year."

Oliver, Emma, and Lance exchanged bewildered looks. "Accounting, professor?" Oliver asked impatiently.

"Corruption," Watkin declared. "Most students never even hear about it, but Headmaster Lalandra herself teaches the elective. You might have heard Abraham speak of the subject?"

Oliver thought hard, barely remembering a conversation Lalandra and Abe had shared in the Dining Hall. Hadn't Lalandra been researching something abroad over the summer? Back then Oliver had worried she was looking for more artifacts, like Augustus' ring and Madeline's necklace, but had there been more to that conversation than he realized?

Watkin kept going, his eyes crawling over the outstretched map. "Corruption has historically been referred to as dark magic; which is childish, of course. Darkness is a matter of perspective—you'll remember our earlier conversation regarding good and evil, Oliver—but corruption is something else entirely. It opens up many doors that other branches of magic cannot."

He gestured at Oliver without looking up, nearly knocking Oliver back into his chair after he'd stood up to get a better look at the map. "The spell you adopted from John Tupper, in fact, is a mix of destruction and corruption. *Estalla* doesn't just move air around at explosive speeds. In moving air and wind around at speeds they'd not normally reach, you corrupt the world a little bit to achieve it. All elementals dabble with the concept.

NOVA 02

"But the corruption component I'm worried about is the monster we discussed after our visit with Augustus."

"The pesadriya," Oliver breathed in a hollow voice. He gulped, only barely comforted by Emma and Lance sidling next to him to look over the map together. Oliver had a hard time seeing the map, let alone anything else at the moment. The memory of the tapestry images Dave had shown him in Lalandra's apartment burned fresh in his mind. It had been a depiction of the pesadriya in its final form, returning from—hell?—wherever it had taken the innocent villager.

"Yes," Watkin confirmed, dropping the twinkle in his eye. "Do you understand?"

Oliver thought he did. But he almost couldn't bear to say it out loud.

"You think Goodwin Forest is being haunted by a pesadriya?" Lance asked in a whisper.

Watkin angled his head back and forth, debating an answer. "Well," he drew out, "my theory is actually more specific than that, but to call it farfetched would be an understatement."

"Professor!" Emma shot. "When are you going to realize your theories are correct like 99% of the time?! Quit wasting our time and spill the beans!"

Watkin hesitated. "If you must know, something Oliver told me at Jacque's Place back in August caught my attention."

"What?" Oliver asked. Had he somehow predicted a pesadriya haunting a random town he didn't know about?

* Chapter 31: Servants of the Void *

"The monster haunting Tupper in your dream. You described it differently than witnesses at the Sage's Sanctum disaster over fourteen years ago."

"Oh no," Lance breathed. Oliver looked him over but didn't understand why his friend had gone so pale.

Watkin gestured at Lance with an outstretched hand, almost pityingly. Still, Oliver didn't understand. "What are you saying?"

"The monster Tupper first faced was brainless, violent, and reckless. Witnesses confirmed this. But what you described from your dream—it was more than that wasn't it?"

Horror struck Oliver like a cold bucket of water to the face. "The pesadriya reached its final form?" He thought he finally understood.

"Exactly," Watkin confirmed. "Which means it no longer charges recklessly to kill, but consciously seeks to corrupt any soul it comes across."

"So what?" Emma said, throwing up her hands again. "It's got Tupper's soul to chase for a life time!"

Watkin shook his head, half-opening his mouth with what looked like an apology forming on his lips. Then, he looked to Oliver.

"You think Tupper could have offered the smarter form of the monster a deal?" he asked, feeling sick to his stomach. "Trade some other souls for his own?"

Watkin's intensity returned as he nodded his head.

"So," Lance squeaked, "you're saying the evilest psychopath to ever exist has possibly teamed up with a purely corrupted spirit that will drag anyone it comes across to hell?"

NOVA 02

"And," Oliver piled on, "a batch of fresh souls has been disappearing in a town near a hidden temple we think Tupper may have visited in the past?"

"Ok, Professor," Emma nods. "Are we going there now?"

"We can't," said Watkin. "The area can't be found."

Goosebumps erupt across Oliver's arms. "Hang on! Say that again, Professor!"

Watkin and Jaiba cocked their heads at an angle. "The area can't be found?" he repeated.

Oliver opened his pocket dimension, tearing a momentary void in the world. Watkin raised his eyebrows at the display appreciatively. Without delay, Oliver yanked the Iguana's Scroll off a shelf and zipped the space shut again. Then, he read out loud:

Begin with the Forgotten Wood, for there, your Gift has stood, the entrance lies within our grounds, good luck – it cannot be found.

Lance snapped his fingers. "We just need to find the right painting!"

Emma and Watkin looked skeptical, but Oliver *knew* he was right, and his neck vibrated to back him up. "Any painting for a fire temple hidden in a teacher's common room or apartment?" he asked.

Cracking a smile, Watkin went to pick up his staff. When he doubled back to the desk, he joined the three of them on their side and placed a hand on Oliver's shoulder. "**Trust** your instinct in this regard. I've never seen any painting of a fire temple at this school, but I won't be foolish

Chapter 31: Servants of the Void

enough to doubt the instincts of a Trinova." Again the word had vibrated in the air. "Find it, mobilize any friends you have to search for it."

"You're not going to help?" Emma asked, crestfallen.

Watkin eyed her. "You three chasing this thread will allow me to chase three others. I must depart."

"Hang on?" Oliver countered. "No more secrets right?"

Watkin tightened his sash belt and beckoned for Jaiba to hop onto his shoulder. The bird obliged with a *caw-caw*. "This won't be a secret in due time, but you have enough on your plates for now. I must prepare us for Tupper's escape while you three attempt to delay it."

"How much time do we have?" Oliver asked, half-distracted. His eyes had finally settled onto Watkin's map.

"That depends," Watkin hedged, pausing with a hand on the door. "Who was the better poker player? Tupper? Or the pesadriya?" Then, he left, leaving Oliver, Emma, and Lance to blink at each other owlishly.

Eventually, Oliver returned his attention to the map on the table. He hadn't been able to concentrate on the contents when they spoke before, but now that Watkin had left, he finally understood what he was looking at.

It was a map of a mountain range that straddled the border between North Carolina and Tennessee.

Emma tapped on the label at the top. "The Great Smoky Mountains, eh? Is this where Goodwin Forest is?"

It was Lance's turn to tap on the map. His finger did the work, bringing Oliver's attention to a dot labeled Goodwin Forest. The drawn-in houses and town center looked up at Oliver innocently enough, sitting right on the border of the two states. Just how many innocent people had the pesadriya dragged away so far?

As he stared, Oliver's stomach felt more and more hollow by the second. This was his fault. If he were just a few years older and more trained up, he could visit the town himself and defeat the pesadriya—he was sure of it. Even now he felt tempted to try it.

Emma began tracing a dotted line. "Is he serious?" she breathed with a stunned expression.

Oliver blinked and took a better look at the line. At first he'd taken it to be one of a couple hundred hiking trails. Only now did he realize Watkin had drawn in the dotted line.

Oliver gaped as more and more lines grabbed his attention. Every single square inch of the map was covered with crisscrossing dotted lines. And they weren't hiking trails… Based on the legend on the right-hand side of the map, Watkin had searched the mountain range one-hundred-and-fifty-four times since the start of the semester.

Lance let out a long whistle.

"Well," Emma laughed, tracing her finger down the dates listed in the legend. "At least he took Thanksgiving off."

* **Chapter 31: Servants of the Void** *

Chapter 32: Project SMG

I'm all packed up. Even though he didn't tell me exactly what I'm looking for, he did hint at a theory he's been holding onto since he was a teenager.

17th of December, the second year of the 10th Age

Before the rest of the Hutchites left for Christmas break, Oliver, Emma, and Lance took the time to update them on the new plan. Oliver did the announcing, stepping onto an open chair in the Hutch common room so everyone could see him. He grimaced as the crowd quieted down and more and more faces locked on to his own. How would they take being given an assignment only hours after wrapping the most gruesome exam season in recent memory?

"We need to find another painting," he announced, still grimacing.

To his surprise, however, nobody jeered or even groaned. In fact, most of the faces in the room nodded back at him determinedly. The ones that didn't looked deep-in-thought. Like Abe's.

"Is it like the forest painting from last year?" Abe asked, raising his hand. The fabric of his puffer coat swished as he moved. Most everyone in the room wore something similar, ready, as they were, to brave the snowstorm outside on their way to the platform above the clouds and then home.

Emma shook her head. "Nah, pretty much the opposite." She held out a hand and began counting one finger at a time. "We're looking for lava, red-looking buildings, fire-drakes—that kinda stuff."

* Chapter 32: Project SMG *

"Fire-drakes?" Se'Vaughn repeated. He tilted his head to punctuate his confusion.

"A type of dragon," Lance answered.

"Oh," Se'Vaughn said, blanching more than a Brave should. "Didn't realize dragons... well, existed."

Lance shook his head. "Don't worry, they're all dead—we're just looking for a place called the Fire-Drake's Cavern."

"But there will definitely be some big-scaries in there," Emma said, relishing the thought with a dreamy expression.

Oliver cleared his throat from atop his chair. "Thanks everyone. I'll start looking over the break, but when y'all get back it'll be all hands on deck." And because he didn't want anybody to think he was being "bossy," he added, "only if you have time for it, of course."

This time the crowd *did* cluck their tongues. Some even growled.

Elton's face radiated pure disgust. "You think we don't know that what you're doing is more important than a couple weeks off? I'll stay behind to help you search."

"Alright, alright," Emma interrupted, raising her hands for quiet. "Anyone can stay behind with us if they want to, but don't piss off your parents doing it, alright?" Oliver's heart skipped a beat.

Us? Was she staying behind over the break, too? They hadn't talked about it yet—he only knew her family was going to Greece. He'd assumed she was going, too.

Emma sighed as everyone stared at her. "I'm sure half of you are in charge of pies or stuffing or something,"

NOVA 02

Oliver looked at her curiously. Why would the thought of pies and stuffing make her sound so sad?

Parts of the room nodded, departing with cheery waves and promises to join the search the moment they got back. Several dozen exchanges of "Merry Christmas" and "Happy Holidays" later, only Oliver, Emma, and Lance remained from the hardmore class. Trey had tried his best to stay, too, until Se'Vaughn pointed out, "aren't you cooking the turkey for your folks this year?"

By the time Lance stopped laughing, Trey was leading the pack out the door, shouting, "see y'all in January!"

Once the dust settled, Oliver took stock of who remained. Even though a majority of the hardmores had left, most juniors and seniors had lingered, chatting amongst themselves.

Now that Oliver thought about it… didn't he see mostly juniors and seniors stay behind last year, too?

"No Christmas for you guys?" he asked.

Every single face turned away, blushing. Except one.

"Are you kidding?" Elton asked, grinning from ear to ear. "No classes, exams, or adults for two weeks? It's the most wonderful time of the year!"

Joel slapped his hand on a couch's armrest, a wild glint in his eye. "Think of all the inappropriate things we can get up to!"

"I, for one," Elton declared, "will be splitting my time between searching for the Trinova's painting *and*,"—he cleared his throat, pulling out an enormous piece of parchment—"OPERATION EGGNOG!"

* Chapter 32: Project SMG *

As the older students descended onto Elton and the parchment, shouting loudly and pointing aggressively at different parts of the schematics on the paper like bidders at an auction, Emma leaned in to whisper.

"Operation eggnog?"

Lance rolled his eyes. "Stevie started it her hardmore year. Every Christmas Eve they try and get their hands on the faculty eggnog."

"WHOMST WISHES TO SERVE AS THE DISTRACTION?!" Elton bellowed.

Brantley of all people stood, breathing in until his chest swelled enough for him to resemble a small whale. "IT SHALL BE I!" he bellowed.

Oliver couldn't help but smile at the insanity of it all. If Brantley, normally gruff and stoic, was giving into the antics, it meant there was some fun ahead.

While Elton rammed a red and white hat onto Brantley's head and bowed, Lance shook his head.

"It never works."

Oliver's excitement for Operation Eggnog died down to a barely registerable smolder by Christmas Eve. But only by necessity. He kept it in the back of his mind as something he could re-kindle into a well-deserved and enjoyable reward after searching for the Fire-Drake's Cavern painting.

NOVA 02

He just wished they'd found it already.

Since the end of exams, he, Emma, and Lance had scoured everywhere they could think to look. From the shores of the lagoons to even a small shed on top of the landing strip that a friendly ice golem led them to, they found nothing more exciting than purple carriage parts.

"Nothing," Emma snored out loud, frightening Oliver out of his meditative trance. They'd posted up in the simulator, adding the meditation knoll and a cozy researching nook to the simulated training facility so they wouldn't have to reload the space every time they switched from dueling to researching or meditating.

Distracted, Oliver broke off his connection with Nova, and checked on Emma. He'd been working on extending the range of *Nova's Touch*, and though he couldn't see everything around him as well as he might with his own eyes, the exercise improved his focus and ability to tap into the technique without much delay. Satisfied with his progress, he snagged an apple from a fruit bowl in the foyer just outside the meditation chamber, munching happily, until he reached the research nook a few rooms down.

"You realize that's not a real apple, right?" Roli's voice asked in his head.

Oliver ignored the iguana.

Emma snored loudly, her head and arms bundled together into a pile of limbs and red hair. Only a corner of the book she'd been reading was visible, but he knew what it was. *"Solomon Tupper; The Man Before the Politician."*

It was the only book they could find in the Research Center that even attempted to cover Tupper's time before his political career. So far they'd

* Chapter 32: Project SMG *

found plenty on the man's time at school, and even more about his heralded career. But trying to find something, *anything,* about the man's travels had been going about as well as finding the painting of the Fire-Drake's Cavern.

"Maybe," Roli's voice suggested, *"I should simulate a less comfortable chair?"*

It was a testament to Oliver's dread and anxiety that he considered the request. They hadn't seen Watkin since he'd left, and if Santiago hadn't messaged saying he and Miyada were going to meet Watkin on the landing strip that afternoon, Oliver would have worried Watkin had been kidnapped, too.

After a few more munches of his apple, he sent Roli a "nah" in his head. Emma could use the break. Even if she said she'd rather be here with him than her family in Greece, that couldn't be one-hundred-percent true. Everyone needed a break sometime, and she'd shown him photos of the villa her parents had booked—she couldn't hate her family *that* much. Still, they'd both had some fun training over the break. And it wasn't just for his benefit either.

Emma's training over the last week had taken on a fervor she'd never shown before. When they dueled each other or simulated enemies in the simulator, she made it clear she didn't intend to lose. She *really* wanted to beat Beto in the Dueling Tournament, and Oliver respected the drive she showed in the process. Though Roli couldn't simulate Beto specifically, he could pit them up against a generic senior-year-caliber opponent. Emma had gotten whooped the first few times until Oliver paused the simulation and told her to focus on the enemy's movements *before* they struck.

NOVA 02

"Take a look at Jimbo," he said, gesturing at the featureless shadow opponent on the other side of the simulated arena.

"I thought we agreed on Jimothy."

"Whatever. See how he's pulling a leg back right now?" He touched the shadow's hip. "Usually, that means they're going to push their arm forward next to launch something at you. Don't worry about the projectile, you can dodge it with your flexibility, no problem. Instead, try and trip them up. Use an elemental like earth to disrupt their stance and weaken their shot. Or conjure a companion like a woodland nymph to mess with their footing."

The way Emma had looked at him, breathing heavily to catch her breath with the faintest of smug smiles on her face, left him weak in the knees and blushing red in his cheeks.

Lance and Elton, meanwhile, had gone home the day before to talk to their parents before the Christmas Eve Cocktail Hour. Oliver had recommended it, and the brothers had not taken it well. They said they'd come back in time for the Cocktail Hour, but Oliver wasn't so sure.

In his head, he relived the conversation before they left, grimacing.

> *"Shouldn't you be using this time to talk to your dad about his imprisonment?" he asked.*
>
> *Lance and Elton exchanged looks at the question. But only briefly before turning to Oliver to glare like twin cobras. "Look, man," Elton said, "it's not exactly easy to bring up. What are we supposed to do.*

* Chapter 32: Project SMG *

'Hey, dad, did you get put into a rehabilitation center back in the day for being weak? Okay then, Merry Christmas!'"

Oliver stared back, shocked to his core. It didn't make any sense.

"But we need to know! He could give us information on how the centers worked!"

"Oli," Lance grunted, "we know you're right, but sometimes it'd be nice to have you as a friend, not the bossy Trinova."

"Wow," Roli's voice echoed in his head, *"I can even play your memories for you in here."*

Back in the simulation room, Oliver grumbled. "I wasn't that robotic about it." Roli had taken liberties with the replay, making Oliver look like a monster incapable of understanding Lance's and Elton's dilemma.

"I captured the gist of it perfectly, thank you very much."

Oliver sighed, returning his attention to Emma. What a great friend he was—he'd angered one by micro-managing the timing of a difficult conversation and punished the other by making her turn down a glitzy trip to Europe.

Just as his shoulders began to droop with self-pity, a grandfather clock popped into existence next to Emma's chair, showing the time.

"What-ho?" Roli's voice asked. *"A device that tells time? Let us hope it combats self-loathing, too!"*

"I know, I know," Oliver intoned for Roli's benefit. "We've gotta head up to the landing strip."

"And you think you're good at micromanaging," Roli chuckled.

NOVA 02

Oliver sulked for a moment yet. "You're just trying to make me feel better."

"Is it working?"

"Yes," Oliver admitted.

Stepping forward, he crouched next to Emma, still hesitating to wake her. Even when sitting there disheveled, her hair gleamed like a warm fire, free of tangles and knots. For the second time that month he found himself in a position where he could just stare at her. She looked content and cozy as she slept, snoring endearingly. The prolonged free look made his heart race, reminding him of their near kiss in this same room.

The grandfather clock chimed loudly.

Emma shot up as though a rifle had been shot, flailing her arms around to fight off would-be-attackers. Panicking, Oliver played it off as if he'd just nudged her awake and not been staring at her.

"Nice," Roli said privately. *"Very convincing."*

"Whatimeisit?" Emma asked, settling her arms.

Oliver picked up the table she'd knocked over, which was, he realized as he nervously put it back in place, as much of a waste of time as eating that apple had been.

"Um," Oliver grunted, not looking her in the eyes, "sorry for waking you up. Just checking to see if you wanted to see Santiago, too?"

She yawned and stretched before she answered. "Of course I want to see Santiago." Then, waving a lazy hand, she added, "lead the way. I won't be awake until we get up there."

* Chapter 32: Project SMG *

Wind whipped at their faces on the airstrip, cold and harsh, making Oliver wish he'd asked Watkin for whatever spell the man had used to keep them all warm outside the Ruins of Snowgem. He'd tried using some fire elementals, but that had only helped burn off a part of his puffer coat.

"At least its not hailing," Emma said, shrugging, while Oliver patted his coat down furiously.

Then he looked around them. Snowing or not, he was freezing. Still, the existing blanket of white powder that covered the whole plateau made for a pretty setting. It was also quieter than it should be. He always marveled at how snow seemed to absorb every loud noise the world could throw at it.

A crunching noise snapped his attention back to the stairs leading down the ridge.

Emma chuckled. "Chill out. It's just an ice golem."

While waiting for the others to arrive, they watched the golem, and then three others. Oliver had wondered why the creatures wandered so far up away from the lake, but the answer revealed itself in moments. One by one, the golems waddled to the edge of the hill at a stubby run and rolled all the way back down at a frightening pace. Oliver imagined them squealing with delight the whole way.

Before long, a door appeared out of thin air only a dozen yards away, shining green at the edges.

Emma nudged Oliver in the ribs repeatedly. "You excited to see Santi?"

NOVA 02

Oliver swatted her arm away, allowing a smile. "Of course I'm excited to see Santi."

A moment later, Watkin stepped out of the doorway. He nodded towards them before checking a watch in his coat's front pocket. Without looking up, he casually flicked his staff in the direction of the door behind him.

The door exploded into splinters.

"Good, you're here," he said, looking up into the sky as if nothing out of the ordinary occurred. "Ah and here come Miyada and Santiago."

Following Watkin's gaze, Oliver and Emma looked up. Oliver had expected to see an eagle-drawn carriage descending, but he could only see two far-away dots. *They must have a different way to get down,* he thought.

The dots drew closer.

"Professor," Oliver asked, "how's the Goodwin Forest search going?"

Watkin shook his head, but otherwise kept his attention on the falling meteors. "About as well as your painting search, I'd imagine." Then, Watkin did turn his attention away from the meteors. But not to focus on Oliver.

"Roli," the man said, "did your master ever tell you where to find the Fire Drake's Cavern?"

Roli regarded the question haughtily. *"I would have shared this knowledge had I held it."*

Watkin winked at Oliver, looking less tired for half-a-second. "Worth a shot." Then, the dark bags took over again.

* Chapter 32: Project SMG *

The meteors landed with back to back thuds that shook the earth. Though Oliver hadn't been able to tell what they were when far away, he had little doubts now.

They were coffins.

The wider of the two slammed open and out stumbled Santiago, heaving with his hands on his knees. Then, from the narrower one, came Miyada, as tall and eccentric-looking as Oliver remembered. He was strong, too, but in a wiry sort of way. On his head, he wore the same yellow-green helmet he always donned, this time with none of the attached scopes, lenses, or lasers in use.

"Remasco," Watkin intoned. Santiago lifted a hand to thank Watkin before accepting Oliver's hug.

"Good to see you, Jefecito," Oliver heard from within his uncle's embrace. When they separated, Oliver allowed himself the smallest flare of Wisdom to stop his eyes from watering.

"Who's, uh," Santiago began, a wary eye on Oliver's shoulder.

Roli stuck his tongue into Oliver's ear. *"I am Roli,"* he announced as Oliver yelped, *"the brains and engine of this contingency."*

"He's an iguana," Emma translated as Oliver swatted at Roli. "Helping us out against *The Damned.*" Roli sidestepped the swat with little issue, landing on Oliver's other shoulder.

Miyada regarded Roli with fascination. "An iguana? Is it the one from the scroll?"

"Good to see you, too, Mr. Miyada," Emma said, miming a handshake with the air.

NOVA 02

Miyada waved a gauntleted hand. "Forget it, girl. I've never been one for pleasantries."

"You're not so spooky outside your shop, are you?" she countered.

"You're quite right, good sir," Roli purred after inflating his dewlap to answer the question. *"I am the iguana from the scroll. I served Lord Augustus in the past and now,"*—

"If you'll excuse us," Watkin said, giving them a stiff bow. He pulled himself and Miyada away from the group while Roli continued talking himself up, shifting his speech to Santiago instead.

—I serve the Trinova in the present! I move continents from the shadows! NO LARGER THAN A LOAF OF BREAD, I COMMAND THE WILL OF THE HEAVENS! I—,"

"He's a great help to us," Oliver admitted.

Santiago nodded, but now that Miyada had stepped away, Oliver caught a glint of something else in his uncle's eyes. And it wasn't the man's old steel.

While trying to keep as low a profile as possible, Santiago darted to his coffin and back, checking frequently over his shoulder to make sure Miyada didn't see. It wasn't subtle, but Miyada and Watkin appeared too engrossed in their own conversation to notice. They spoke in hushed, but animated, tones, and if Santiago hadn't returned from his coffin with a bulging, glowing knapsack, Oliver knew he'd likely have already been using *Nova's Touch* to snoop on the other conversation.

As it was, the possibilities of Santiago's knapsack proved too distracting.

* Chapter 32: Project SMG *

"It is good to meet you, Ro-ro," Santiago said distractedly. He stuck out a hand to concentrate on fishing through the bag with his opposite on.

"Ro-ro?" Roli repeated, indignation flattening his every scale. *"Roli is already my nickname!"*

Santiago waved his free hand to shush the iguana. Roli sputtered, but Santiago ignored him as Emma laughed. Oliver took note—maybe Roli's bossiness didn't have to be accommodated all the time.

"Get a look at this bad boy," Santiago said, pulling out a four-foot long package from the knapsack. "Apúrate!"[6] he breathed. "Open it before Miyada notices."

With a cushioned puff of wind, Oliver popped open the lid of the package.

"No way!" Emma breathed.

Roli balanced past Oliver's shoulder to peer down. *"What is this abomination?"*

Oliver laughed out loud. His uncle had brought a rifle. Unlike any Oliver had ever seen. Polished dark wood formed the stock while a lighter than normal gray colored the barrel. Santiago immediately drew their attention to the heel with a tap of his finger. "We're using an extra big vein of jadeite to store magical energy in the grip cap."

Emma let out an, "oooo aaaa."

Encouraged, Santiago traced his finger past the trigger to the chamber. He barely moved his lips when he continued, forcing them all to lean in.

---

[6] Apúrate is an informal way to ask someone to "hurry up" in Spanish.

NOVA 02

"We've even got *magnolia sinica* inserts," he whispered. "They channel the source energy, but that's a secret, alright? On the outside it looks just like regular treated oak for the channel."

"Magnolia sinica *and* jadeite?" Emma hissed.

Roli laughed in his dewlap. Emma looked up at him while Santiago looked down. *"Judging by your pitifully surprised tone,"* Roli said with a sneer, *"I take it this plant is now considered rare? Our grounds hosted many when I lived last."*

"Rare?" Emma repeated. "Santi, tell me if I'm wrong, but isn't magnolia sinica one thousand ameys per *ounce*? Pretty sure that's what Desmoulins told us in *Fauna of the Magically Inclined* last month."

Oliver's stomach went hollow, well-trained from a childhood of financial insecurity. He almost sealed the box and chucked the whole knapsack back into Santi's coffin with one Wisdom-enhanced movement. He settled for slamming the lid back on. *"What,"* he asked through gritted teeth, "are you doing with something this expensive out in public? What if somebody steals it?"

Santiago's eyes sharpened, even going steely, reminding Oliver of the man he'd grown up with, and not the man Santiago had become.

Oliver backtracked immediately. "I'm sorry!" he snuck in, hanging his head low. "I'm getting used to calling the shots I guess. I don't need to boss you around, too." When he finished, he looked up tentatively while rubbing the back of his neck. He didn't care if he showed his emotions with Santiago—he wasn't going to play games with family.

"This again?" Roli complained. *"Decease with the self-pity! You are the Trinova! You will command armies!"*

477

* Chapter 32: Project SMG *

Santiago laughed with a puff of his chest. "The lizard,"—he raised his hands to apologize as Roli grew haughty again—"Ro-ro, sorry."—

"That's not my name!"

—"I've got to adjust to this, too," Santiago went on, rubbing his own neck. "You're not just the chamaco[7] sleeping in my spare bedroom any more are you?"

Oliver nearly teared up again, but Santiago's machismo had already sensed the danger and moved on.

"But it doesn't matter. This is called project SMG, okay? I had to show it to you!" The steel in his eye gave way to manic excitement that reflected off the barrel as he snapped the chamber open. "We put in big caliber bullets loaded with source energy, too."

Emma scratched at the side of her head. "Thought you said the back of the gun has jadeite in it? Why two sources of magic?"

Santiago's chest puffed out again. "It was my idea! Even I can use the gun now. We've only just got started but think about it, I could go on your adventures with you! Or be your bodyguard!"

But Oliver's mind had moved way past the gun. The possibilities of the theory behind the rifle were *endless*. Anybody could use magic if they picked up something like this rifle. The channels of the magnolia sinica directed prescribed spell-work using the existing stores in the back of the gun. They could do the same with armor if they wanted to, or transportation, or literally anything.

---

[7] Basically translates to "kid." More often than not used affectionately.

NOVA 02

Oliver's eyes suddenly took on the same mania as Santiago's. He placed both his hands on his uncle's shoulders. "Project SMG?" he repeated.

Santiago nodded.

"This is revolutionary," Oliver breathed, shaking Santiago like a rag doll. "You'll also need armor to ward off enemy attacks on you while you fire it."

The fire in Santiago's eyes died. He looked surprised when he spoke.

"You're starting to talk like Watkin." As Oliver gulped away his guilt, Santiago looked over his shoulder—Watkin and Miyada still spoke, bent over in hushed tones. When Santiago turned back, he smiled and ruffled Oliver's hair. "Probably comes with the Wisdom, right? Don't worry jefecito, you can talk however you want."

"What are they talking about over there anyway?" Emma asked, peering past Santiago.

Santiago motioned for them all to draw in close around him. "It's something about rocks."

"Rocks?" Emma repeated flatly.

Oliver shared a look with her and agreed. "Why are you talking about rocks?"

"I don't know much!" Santiago hissed. "I just heard them talk about it once at the forge. Cray rocks, or something like that."

Emma looked over at Watkin again, mutiny painted on her face. "Thought he said no more secrets…"

"Probably a 'back-up' plan," Oliver countered. "Give me a second, I can tell you what they're saying."

* Chapter 32: Project SMG *

Oliver slowed his breathing and reached out to *Nova's Touch*. Within a second, Watkin's voice carried across strands of Nova's influence straight into Oliver's ears.

He felt Watkin stiffen as he spoke. "No, I've been focused on finding the people missing near Goodwin. A poor girl named Rachel, along with her friends, if I'm not mistaken."

"Well," Miyada grumbled, "I'm still bound to you so don't be afraid to enlist me for further help."

"I appreciate it, but to be honest the work with Santiago may bear fruit. Unexpected sources of magic are often the best ones."

Miyada nodded. "And what about the Craydl—"

Watkin cut Miyada off. Literally, with a hand in a chopping motion. "Oliver," he said loud enough for everyone to hear. "It's rude to eavesdrop."

After Santiago and Miyada rocketed up into the sky within their coffins, Oliver and Emma joined Watkin on a brisk walk back down the ridge.

"Will we see you at the cocktail hour?" Emma asked.

"Sadly not," Watkin said grimly. "I've been neglecting my actual day job while investigating *The Damned*. I must prepare for the second semester."

"Aw, that's a shame," Emma offered, sounding cheery, like Sara the new extraman.

NOVA 02

Oliver's ears perked up. Emma never spoke like this. In fact, the only other time he could remember her sounding similar was when she'd worked out a secret from Professor Zapien last year. Otherwise, Emma took pride in making fun of people who sounded this bubbly.

"Well," Emma went on, just one step short of twirling her hair. "How about a quick free lesson, then?"

"Oh?" Watkin asked, pausing at the fork in the path between the Academic Building and the rest of the grounds further below. "Not enough on your plates already? I can always give you more."

Emma grinned in a would-be-innocent kind of way. "I'll get straight to it then. How'd you keep us all warm at the Ruins of Snowgem? You doing something now for yourself? That traveler's coat isn't near thick enough to keep you warm."

Watkin laughed out loud, showing off his handsome teeth for the first time in ages. Oliver found the energy infectious and smiled along without fully realizing it.

"It's similar to *iuxtairis*," Watkin instructed. "You use the warmth in the objects around you to keep yourself warm. You'll notice I leave icy Earth beneath my feet when using it now."

"The spell, professor?" Emma asked impatiently.

"*Iuxtalor*," Watkin said, bowing. "Use it well."

As Watkin walked away, Oliver tried the spell, reaching out for the residual warmth in the ground several yards beneath them.

* Chapter 32: Project SMG *

Warmth trickled over his whole body immediately. He breathed a sigh of relief and chucked his half-burned, blood-stained coat into his pocket dimension at once.

As the space zipped close again, Emma waggled her eyebrows at him.

"What?" Oliver asked. "You want to research these 'cray rocks' right away, too?"

Emma laughed, her tone almost hysterical. "I gotta be honest, Oli, I'm focusing on the cocktail hour for the rest of the day. We've been working nonstop."

"But," Oliver said, praying she wouldn't think he was being bossy, "we know Tupper is using people's souls to escape? How can we take a break?"

Emma waved the concern away with both her hands. "Eh, *The Damned* could bust out tomorrow or years from now. Let's just try and be kids tonight, yeah? Maybe sneak some of that nog."

Oliver's jaw fell.

"Kidding!" she said, smiling in that same would-be-innocent way. "Unless…"

Oliver gave in to the smile. "Yes, to the party." Then, as Emma beamed at him, he snuck in, "but 'no' to Operation Eggnog."

"It's a date!" Emma agreed.

Oliver nodded, turning to walk down the hill but then froze mid-step when he realized what she'd said.

"Um," he stammered, "uh-what now?"

Emma dashed away, skipping, before his question finished crossing his lips. "See you at eight!"

NOVA 02

"*Eh-hem,*" Roli's voice said in Oliver's head. "*If you're going to stand there, gaping all night, would you at least please share your iuxtalor spell with me?*"

Oliver barely registered the iguana's voice. He could only stare at Emma's fading figure. "A date?" he repeated, feeling a dread that somehow felt not too dissimilar from whenever he thought about *The Damned*.

"*My scales, Master García. They begin to freeze.*"

* **Chapter 32: Project SMG** *

NOVA 02

Chapter 33: The Cocktail Hour

Saying goodbye to Johnnie was tough but hey, this is for the good of the many, right? I have to think about more than just myself.

23rd of December, the second year of the 10th Age

"Are you kidding me, García?" Elton's garbled voice rang. "Take the damn girl to the Christmas Eve party."

Oliver didn't reply for a full five seconds. When he did, he shook his head, unable to look at the holographs displayed on his notebook mirror. "I still think it's a bad idea."

Sounds of exasperation followed from more than just Elton.

"Can you believe this guy?" Lance's voice complained.

"Unbelievable," Elton agreed.

"He can't help it," a third voice chimed. Stevie's holograph entered the projection, twirling in a dramatic dance. "He's in *love.*"

"He does this over *everything,*" Lance added. "Love or not."

Oliver smiled in spite of himself. "Well that's not entirely fair."

"No, he really does," Roli interjected from his shoulder. *"I'm in his mind at all times. He's obsessed with control. Every decision is calculated and meticulous to an inefficient fault. With greater conviction he'd rise to heights not seen since the great leaders of the American Revolu—,"*

"Thank you, Roli," Oliver, Lance, and Elton all said at once.

Roli ruffled his dewlap proudly but settled down.

* Chapter 33: The Cocktail Hour *

"Ouch, little dude," Stevie said, looking down at what Oliver assumed was a projected version of himself and Roli.

"Okay, fine," Oliver said, trying to keep an ear-to-ear smile off his face. "I'll take her."

"Finally," Elton muttered.

Lance rose from his seat in his family's living room to lift his arms in triumph.

"I think it's sweet," Stevie said. She wrapped her arms around the back of an open chair, resting her chin to look dreamily at Oliver's projection on their coffee table.

Taking a risk, Oliver steered the conversation toward what he thought was the more important topic. "How'd it go with your parents?"

None of the Wyatts looked at each other. Lance even began scratching the back of his head, a habit he'd indirectly picked up from Santiago through Oliver.

Stevie eventually waved a hand, her dreamy expression long gone. "You worry about Emma tonight, alright? Elton and Lance will catch you up when they get back."

Just when Oliver thought Stevie would disconnect the call, she raised a hand with a pointed finger. "Before we let you go give that girl the night of her life,"—

Oliver blushed as Elton and Lance crooned, "eyyyy."

—"you should know I'm going to work in *The Damned's* secret travels into my blog." When she finished, she dropped her hands to her sides and looked at him as if she'd just given him a million ameys.

NOVA 02

"Um," Oliver said, trying to sound thankful and not confused, "that's great!"

"Stevie," Elton chided, as though he were lecturing a misbehaving toddler, "you gotta explain things to people otherwise they won't have a clue what you're talking about."

Stevie waved Elton away, and then twirled back around to face Oliver's projection. "He gets it," she said pointing at Oliver and winking. "Wisdom can be such a burden."

Elton and Lance groaned.

"You guys are struggling to figure out what *The Damned* was up to before rising to power, aren't ya? I'll figure it out for you. Just do me a favor and tell me where to look. Cuz I'm flying blind to start."

An awkward "thank you" later, Oliver disconnected from the call.

Only then, without the Wyatts' voices in the room, did the reality of his situation dawn on him. He was going on a date. With Emma.

"I'm still here," Roli said, caressing his neck with an outstretched leg.

Oliver nearly jumped at the sound and touch.

"I'm gonna leave you in here for the night," he said after he'd recovered. Gingerly, he lifted Roli off his shoulder and placed the iguana on his bed without looking him in the eye.

Roli opened his mouth and pointed to it. *"A root vegetable, if you please. Payment for my needless isolation."*

* Chapter 33: The Cocktail Hour *

More than one table broke into whispers when Oliver walked into the Dining Hall an hour later; not that he could spare them a thought.

Ten minutes prior, Emma had taken over his entire brain when she stepped outside Hutch wearing an emerald dress and a nice pair of shoes.

The mere sight of her had sent Oliver's brain into a spiraling panic. Should he have worn a suit or something? He didn't own a suit, but she'd put on more than the usual blazer and slacks uniform combination—should he have done the same?

He'd been so taken aback by Emma's appearance that he forgot to tell her how pretty she looked.

But that didn't slow her down. This was Emma. After grabbing his arm, she practically dragged him to the Dining Hall.

"*Okay,*" Oliver told himself as they drew closer and closer to the junior and senior Hutchites at their usual table. *"It's just a date. That's all. Not facing off against Xihuacota. Or The Damned. Just Emma… should we really be holding onto each other like this in public?"*

When he saw Joel, Brantley, and Makayla—who appeared to be Brantley's own date—grinning like Cheshire cats, the color in Oliver's face drained away. How was he supposed to have a normal conversation with everybody watching? It was hard enough knowing how to act like a normal person on a date, but a public date?

Gulping, Oliver tilted his head to sneak a sideways glance at Emma. Her shoes clicked on the stone floors as they got closer and closer to the Hutchites and Makayla, but why were her lips pressed together so tight?

NOVA 02

Was she angry? Nervous? She'd snuck in the word "date" on their way back down from the airstrip that late afternoon, and then she'd run off before he could even think to say, "hey, don't you think dating might be a bad idea?"

For a moment, Oliver let several questions hang in his head for Roli to answer as his panic grew.

But then he remembered he'd left Roli behind in Hutch with a small feast of sweet potatoes and strawberries. *Who am I supposed to ask for help, now?*

"Nice," Joel crooned a moment later when Oliver pulled Emma's chair out for her.

"The consummate gentleman," Makayla agreed.

As Oliver debated whether he was happy to see Makayla or not—her commentary at his last Coatlball game hadn't helped him any—Lizzie conjured a floating hand to lightly slap Joel and Makayla on the backs of their heads.

"Behave, y'all," she said sternly as the hand of light turned into a stern, pointing finger.

"Geez," Joel whined, rubbing the back of his head.

Sticking out her tongue, Makayla responded by driving a conjured dagger through the floating hand. Both dissipated within seconds, letting out faint screams.

Lizzie didn't seem to mind at all, however, as she'd already moved on to fuss over Emma's dress. Oliver, meanwhile, shot Lizzie a thankful tilt of his head as he made his way around the table for his seat opposite Emma.

* Chapter 33: The Cocktail Hour *

Between the length of the table, and the continued looks from Abe, Brantley, Joel, Ma—literally everybody in the room—the walk soon stretched into an eternity in Oliver's semi-frozen mind.

He missed a step when his eyes reached the faculty table. Usually when he gawked at the faculty table like a child would a zoo exhibit, it was because of somebody's presence; like Dean Blackwood's. This time, however, Oliver gawked because of someone's *absence*.

"*So,*" he told himself, momentarily staring at the Headmaster's empty chair. "*Lalandra's still missing. The greatest duelist of her generation, gone without a trace…*"

When he sat down a few seconds later with thoughts of pesadriyas in his head, Oliver found it easier to look at Emma. Clearing his throat, he shot her a pointed look and nodded his head towards the faculty table. The news of Lalandra's disappearance hadn't broken out yet. Publicly, at least. But he still wanted to talk about it. When he realized he preferred chatting over the return of good-ole, murderous Solomon Tupper and the pesadriya that haunted him than a batch of small talk, Oliver blinked in shock.

"*What is wrong with me?*"

Emma followed his pointed expression and creased her brow. When she turned to face him again, she shrugged and reached a hand across the table to squeeze his own. Then, she muttered, "*stratum silentii,*" and Oliver felt a blanket of silence envelope them.

"HEY! YOU CAN'T—" Joel's voice tried cutting in. Before he could finish, Emma's spell nestled into full effect.

NOVA 02

"That better?" she asked, wrinkling her nose. Outside their private bubble of conversation, Joel raised his hands in frustration.

Oliver let out a long sigh and leaned back into his chair. "You have no idea," he said. Without having to worry about anyone listening anymore, he allowed an ever-widening grin.

Then, he laughed. "Do you ever feel," he began, tilting forward excitedly to take a shot in the dark—maybe Emma felt the same way as him? "Like it's easier to just stress about Tupper stuff, or schoolwork, or training, or literally anything else other than..."

He pressed his lips together awkwardly as she kept her attention on him, her eyes fierce. "Well..." he stammered, suddenly realizing what he was about to say.

"Us?"

For a breath or two, Emma only stared at him, her green eyes cutting him down like a scythe. Then, she snorted with laughter.

Oliver relished the sound and snorted right back, finding her chortling to be the perfect antidote to his nerves. As they carried on, talking over some of their recent classes, the Magical Five Tournament standings, and Hutch's odds of winning without the Trinova on their teams, Oliver felt the pressure of the date melt off his shoulders.

Better yet, he noticed Emma's tight expression growing more and more relaxed as the night wore on. By the time they reached dessert, still under the privacy of *stratum silentii,* her face took on its rarest form. One of a calming kindness.

* Chapter 33: The Cocktail Hour *

Oliver attributed the change to the amount of times he got her long, button nose to crinkle with laughter over the evening. He loved making her face look like that. It was a sight he, or anybody else, rarely got to see given how fiercely she carried herself under normal circumstances.

Sooner than he would have liked, however, a tug on Emma's shoulder brought their private conversation to a halt.

"What?" Emma asked Brantley, her green eyes fierce again.

Brantley let out a deep laugh and pointed towards the faculty table. Oliver joined in the laughter a second later, forgetting his disappointment when he saw Joel executing Operation Eggnog—poorly, at that. The moment Ms. Joan's eggnog cauldron wheeled out of the kitchen, with her right behind it, Joel approached with a forget-me-not smile plastered across his face.

"What a moron," Abe breathed back at the Hutch table. "He was supposed to wait until after she started talking to the faculty!"

Ms. Joan entertained Joel for all of two seconds with a sour expression on her face before sending a back-up cauldron his way. It chased him with a brandished ladle into the kitchen and back, getting a laugh from everybody in the room in the process. Eventually it reached him and began forcing "student-appropriate" eggnog down his throat.

By the time everyone settled down again, Emma surprised Oliver by standing up.

"You turning in?" he asked, feeling a combination of relief and disappointment bloom in his chest. He knew she'd had a good time but how was he supposed to end a date? With a kiss? The thought of initiating one in public forced him to tap into the Bravery exuding from Madeline's necklace. It vibrated on his chest, growing hot enough to make him wince.

Emma gave him one of her typical half-smiles. "Not quite," she said, holding out a hand. "Take me on a walk in the snow first."

Oliver wasn't sure how much his heart rate picked up as he walked her outside into the December snow, but when she muttered *"iuxtalor"* out in the cold and grinned up at him, he felt his throat dry up, too.

Emma had planned the whole night out without him even realizing it. Down to every detail… including making sure she weaseled Watkin's *iuxtalor* spell out of their professor ahead of this very walk.

"So much for being a Wiser," Oliver thought to himself as Emma led him towards the lagoon shores.

* Chapter 33: The Cocktail Hour *

Chapter 34: Counsel Worth Little

Tío's theory is that there are artifacts out there in the world—hidden after being used in ages past. He's looking for them—or something else—that can help him become a better leader.

24th of December, the second year of the 10th Age

"Remember last year?" Emma asked when they reached the shore of the lagoons.

Oliver let out a nervous chuckle, still worried about having to kiss her. Then he actually heard what she said, and a different type of anxiety took over his chest.

"Xihuacota," he breathed, scanning the dark, murky waters for any hint of a fluttering cloak or white glow. Where was that evil specter, anyway? This time of year, sections of the water were frozen over, including most every water lily and cattail, and Oliver had little issues remembering the terrifying journey last year through the same ice and water to find the Iguana's Scroll.

Emma laughed so hard she had to break away. "Yes, Xihuacota!" she eventually managed. "How many times have you lost to her in the simulator now?"

"Who told you about that!" Oliver asked, furrowing his eyebrows. "Lance?"

Emma laughed some more. "You did, Oli!"

* Chapter 34: Counsel Worth Little *

Oliver crossed his arms, looking over the lagoons again. "You try getting drowned, stabbed, or clawed by her! Simulation or not, it *isn't* fun!"

Emma returned to his side, recovering from her fit of giggles. "How many times, then?" she asked, lowering her voice as she looked up. "You García boys really don't like your ghosts, do you?"

Oliver sniffed stiffly, not returning her gaze. "Forty-seven times."

Emma smiled, jostling his arm, wanting something from him.

But before Oliver could grow enough of a spine to lock eyes with her, a rustling from within a nearby patch of frozen cattails and lilies grabbed their attention.

Expecting Xihuacota, Oliver took a step away from the shore and yelped.

Instead of the haunting specter, however, out came a pack of flightless birds Oliver hadn't seen since last year.

"Awwww," Emma hummed. "It's the little Christmas bird guys!"

Feeling his heart rate come back down, Oliver breathed out a sigh of relief. It was just a handful of pinguinos.

Red and blue, the pinguinos charmed everyone they ever came across when they traveled to campus for the Holidays. Oliver hadn't seen any yet during the year and had begun to worry he might miss them.

Four feet tall, the pinguinos waddled towards them, squawking as they dragged along burlap sacks larger than an osorius. Oliver and Emma took care to squawk back at the pinguinos, a custom demanded by the strange birds.

NOVA 02

"Thank you," Oliver said reverently as the nearest bird offered him a box of half-eaten chocolates in thanks for his squawk. Last year Oliver had received a walking stick, so he'd been hoping for something better than junk, but you never knew with the eccentric birds.

Emma looked up, this time clearly out of her element. "What do I do?" she asked, trying her hardest not to laugh. In her hands, just past the long sleeves of her emerald dress, she held onto over a dozen cotton balls that the remaining pinguinos had stuffed into her grip.

But the birds were already waddling away, dragging their sacks up the hill towards Founders Hall where the lights of the Christmas Eve Cocktail Party still shone.

Oliver waved goodbye with his free hand as the birds disappeared up the hill, squawking intermittently.

"Thank you!" Emma shouted after them, emulating Oliver's wave.

Then, she leaned back into him.

Feeling his heart pick up again, Oliver steeled himself. Now was the time to kiss her.

Making up his mind, he traced his hand down her forearm until he held her hand in his own. Then, he gave her a light pull so they were face-to-face.

Emma smiled at the tug, and he wasn't about to miss the fire in her eyes.

But then the sound of thudding paws interrupted.

"Now what?" Emma muttered, as Oliver turned his head to lock eyes with the second distraction.

* Chapter 34: Counsel Worth Little *

He flinched at once, backing away and pulling Emma with him. "Not birds!" he shouted. "Not birds!"

"Isn't that a chupacabra?" Emma asked, squinting her eyes. *"Tuxtairis!"* she murmured.

Oliver followed suit and knew the answer within a second of his eyes adjusting. There was no mistaking the green, leathery skin, footlong quills, or long, horrible face of a chupacabra.

"That's definitely a chupacabra, alright," Emma whispered into his ear. The sound of her voice so close to him made Oliver go numb for a second, but then, when she adjusted her magical sleeve under her dress for potential combat, his senses returned to him.

He took a step closer, holding out as friendly a hand he could muster. "But what does it wan—,"

The Chupacabra let out a blood-curling howl.

Oliver retracted his hand at once. The noise sounded more like a scream than a howl, really, but based on the way the chupacabra shaped up to issue the screech with its head tilted up to the midnight sky, Oliver considered it closer to a howl than anything else.

Concerned that the beast was calling for its brethren to join it, Oliver conjured a wall of light between them.

When he looked through the semi-transparent wall, thanking Zapien for her lessons on conjured light, Oliver realized the beast had already darted away.

As it fled, however, the chupacabra gave Oliver an unmistakable lingering stare.

NOVA 02

A breath later, it was gone.

Oliver creased his brow as he thought. "I've never seen a Chupacabra look at me that way before."

Next to him, Emma let out a sigh that would make Ethan the extraman proud.

Oliver winced as he turned to face her again. He tried grabbing onto her hands again, but her once dreamy eyes only looked disappointed.

"Let's pretend" Oliver rushed out, a sense of panic ballooning in his stomach. "That I said I've never seen *you* look at me that way before!"

Emma forced a smile but stepped away. "It's fine," she cut in, looking away. "Moment's gone."

Oliver's entire frame wilted as the words came out of her mouth. He'd messed it up. All because of a handful of pinguinos and a chupacabra.

Before he could provide a counteroffer, Emma's smile turned more sincere. "Look," she said, re-grabbing his hands and shaking them sternly. "I know how *I* feel about you. You're kind and thoughtful even when you have all that Power."

Then she smirked. "And I know how *you* feel about me, too."

"You do?" Oliver asked, feeling a growing sense of excitement combat the panic in his stomach.

Emma shrugged. "Elton told Lizzie."

Oliver tried leaning in close, but Emma let go and put out a hand. "But," she said, sighing. "I know you've got to focus on Tupper, chupacabras, and everything else for a while yet. I get it."

499

* Chapter 34: Counsel Worth Little *

Oliver took her hand again and nodded slowly. "You're—," he began, taking in a deep breath. "Loyal, fierce, kind—to be honest,"—he paused to release a nervous laugh—"I can't find a word to capture all of you."

"But," Emma said, giving him another shake and a sad half-smile.

Oliver wanted to smile back, but he couldn't. All he could do was frown. "Look," he said, turning his eyes away from hers. "Us starting something might be a bad idea. I don't want—,"

A third interruption came, cutting Oliver off yet again. This time, it originated from a whooshing noise overhead.

Out of patience, Emma snarled up into the night sky. "OKAY!" she shouted. "THIS HAD BETTER BE XIHUACOTA OR *THE DAMNED HIMSELF!*"

Oliver's mouth dried up as a presence began to tug on his conscious. It felt familiar, pulling at a knot of hurt in his heart. It wasn't Roli's mind. No, this could only be…

"Is that a feathered serpent?" Emma said, lowering her voice considerably.

Oliver nodded without giving her his full attention. He thought he knew who approached, but he didn't recognize the descending creature's movements. The familiar circular pathing looked stunted, as though the flier were… injured.

NOVA 02

With a great, unceremonious thud, a feathered serpent landed between them, sending a great splash of water and mist into the air as it landed on the perimeter of the lakeshore.

Emma yelped at the sight of the beast, and Oliver couldn't blame her. Whoever had interrupted their night-time stroll was covered in blood from tail to beak.

"Archie?" Oliver inquired, tentatively approaching the creature. It didn't levitate in front of them like Oliver expected. Instead, the newcomer lay, collapsed, heaving in great, shuddering breaths.

Finally, after several concerning seconds, the beast answered.

"It is I," Archie confirmed.

Relief flooded through Oliver, overwhelming him. Before he knew what he was doing, he rushed forward to close the gap and throw his arms around his friend. He didn't care about the bloody mess, or how disconcertingly hot the blood felt against his skin. He didn't even care that his eyes began to water, or that the same pod of flightless Christmas birds from earlier waddled nearer to get a better look at the commotion.

"I thought I'd lost you," he managed to say past a growing lump in his throat. At long last, he had his friend back.

Archie responded by wrapping his torso around him and giving him a light squeeze. *"I missed you, little one,"* he said, conveying warmth and love in spite of spiderweb strands of blood masking his eyes.

Oliver jerked his head back at the sight of the eyes.

* Chapter 34: Counsel Worth Little *

"Why are you covered in blood?" Emma asked in an urgent voice. When Oliver looked up, she backed away. "Oli," she said, politely looking away. "Your clothes are burning off."

"*Remasco,*" Oliver commanded, stepping away from Archie as the mess on Archie—and himself, for that matter—began to siphon away, dispersing into essence. By the time the working finished, Oliver only had half his frock coat left, and Archie answered Emma's question.

"*I defended my title as the Tlamacaz,*" he said stiffly.

Oliver raised his eyebrows. "Nero called you… whatever that word is… at the start of the semester."

With a roar, Archie whipped the end of his tail towards a rock at the edge of the lagoon. The rock was reduced to dust. *"Did he now?"* Archie growled with a growing snarl on his mandibles. *"That was wise of him."*

From their mental connection, Oliver felt more than just a growl. Anger and frustration raged inside Archie's mind like an unkempt wave of lava overflowing from a volcano. Only then did Oliver give Archie's injuries a better look.

He gasped before he could stop himself. It was almost easier to spot gaps where there *weren't* bitemarks, gashes, or missing clumps of feathers.

"What did you defend yourself from?" Emma asked, her face aghast. "A dragon?"

Laughter rolled in Archie's enormous torso, but Oliver wished his friend hadn't moved at all. His wounds didn't react well to the movement. Few of them had closed fully, and those that had just re-opened added to the flow of blood gushing over Archie.

NOVA 02

"*No, not a dragon,*" Archie managed after a great shudder. Then, chuckling again, he added, "*but I wouldn't be surprised if one of his ancestors mated with one.*"

Oliver and Emma exchanged confused looks.

Archie exhaled fire and annoyance. "*Given his comportment,*" he explained.

Oliver had no idea what Archie was getting at.

"*It was Musfati!*" Archie shouted into their heads, roaring at the same time. The sound sent the same flightless birds scuttling away in fright. "*When I returned this evening,*" Archie continued, "*that impertinent snake staged a coup, labeling my absence an evidence of a mental imbalance—as a demonstrable reason to deem me unfit to lead our den.*"

"No way," Oliver breathed. "Like a mutiny?"

Emma nodded, as though feathered serpent rebellions were every-day occurrences. Then, she shrugged and gestured at all the blood. "So, d'you kill him or what?"

Oliver choked back a shocked laugh. While he stared at her with his eyebrows raised, she gave him a light push. "I said what I said."

Archie's mandibles pulled up into an undeniable grin. "*I've missed you, too, Emma. Rest assured your colleague Beto will be riding a replacement for the rest of the year and maybe even the rest of his tenure at school.*"

Emma grinned back, but Oliver didn't.

As a contracted Guide, Archie shared a mental bond with Oliver. So Oliver didn't need to look into Archie's frantic eyes or use *Nova's Touch* to guess at what the serpent was feeling—all he had to do was check their mental connection.

* Chapter 34: Counsel Worth Little *

Archie's conscious throbbed through their bond like a heartbeat—the serpent didn't just hurt physically, but mentally as well. From his mind, Oliver felt a twisted sadness he'd never remembered Archie sharing before. Whatever the pain was, it cut deep, and though Oliver couldn't quite place it, the feeling reminded him of whenever he thought back on times growing up. Times when Santiago hadn't understood him. Times when his uncle had been angry. And all the lonely nights spent wondering whether he was to blame for their miserable household.

"Archie," Oliver said tentatively. "Are you doing okay?"

"These wounds will heal without issue," Archie answered, his tone and tail stiffening.

Oliver stared him down… which, took every ounce of his Bravery. Friend or not, Archie was still a four-hundred-pound sacred beast that could rip him from limb from limb.

"I must admit," Archie said, sagging, *"I find it difficult to reconcile my relationship with the boy that became the man you must now hunt. Though I've come out stronger after these months of self-reflection, I can't help but loathe myself for bringing my own people so close to the same curse that afflicts humans."*

Emma turned her head towards Oliver. He knew she was just as confused as he was without looking back. Why did feathered serpents always have to speak in riddles?

Emma cleared her throat. "Look, Archie. Oliver's too polite to say this, but that doesn't make any sense to us."

Oliver did turn to look at her this time, his face aghast.

NOVA 02

Archie let out a long growl but answered, nonetheless. *"All you need know is I've recovered and can now resume serving you as a Guide in full. If you must ask, we can revisit my memories of the Solomon Tupper that I knew. Though my relationship with him ended after he left school, I can tell you everything about the boy from his time at school."*

Excitement spiked in Oliver's chest, pushing away his curiosity about the human curse Archie mentioned. But then Archie carried on, and cut Oliver off before he could ask any of the thousand questions at the top of his mind.

"However," Archie said, his tone shifting, *"my personal woes are not why I joined you this evening."*

"What is it then?" Oliver asked, narrowing his eyes. "You sure you don't need a hospital visit? At least let me try to heal you." He raised his ring hand and muttered *"vulna recuperet"* before Archie even had a chance to decline.

As the serpent's wounds stitched together, Archie grunted and hopped closer to them. Then, to Oliver's surprise, Archie glared at him.

"You two becoming closer than friends is recklessness bordering on stupidity. I felt your emotions from the Swampy Woods. That is why I am here. I left as soon as I could, after tossing aside Musfati's ruined form, mind you, but I fear I may already be too late."

Oliver's ears blushed so hard that looking at Emma for support wasn't even an option. Emma, on the other hand, placed her hands on her hips and glared back furiously.

"We do not want to give Solomon Tupper ways to hurt you, Oliver," Archie went on.

* Chapter 34: Counsel Worth Little *

Oliver's eyes widened, and he tried telling Archie to stop talking with a private relay, but Archie pushed the warning aside and kept going. *"In fact, Santiago will have to be guarded, too, whenever Tupper escapes. What were you two thinking? Emma will be more at risk of kidnap and torture should you get too close."*

Emma let out a fake laugh and threw her hands up into the air, furious. "What a load of garbage!" She turned to Oliver, pointing a finger at him. "Is that what this is about? You think I'll be some kind of damsel in distress? A *tool* to be used against you?"

By the time she finished, her finger shook and her eyes watered as she glared at him fiercely.

Oliver answered more slowly and deliberately than he could ever remember having ever answered anything in his life. "Archie's words!" he insisted, taking a step forward. "Not mine! I'd like to see *anyone* try and capture you alive."

Emma's fury simmered down, but only slightly. He took it as a good sign and kept going, moving closer still with exaggeratedly slow steps.

"I'm just worried about how much training I have to get through," he said, tapping his fingers against his chest. "Between classes, Watkin's lessons, searching for a lost painting, the practices in the simulation room! I wouldn't be a very good boyfriend! I'd have to focus on me for a very long time. And that wouldn't be fair."

Time stood still as he waited for her to digest what he'd said. For several moments she looked angry, and then for even longer, she turned stony, her expression unreadable.

NOVA 02

Eventually, however, the lightest of smirks crept back onto her lips. Then, she walked right up to him and drew herself close. "You're right," she breathed, staring up at him. "We can put this on hold if we have to."

"Why'd she have to get so close?" he thought. If anything, that made it harder to put his feelings on hold. Her freckles looked prettier than ever in the moonlight, and he knew he could stare into her green eyes for hours. At least if Archie hadn't been there.

Then, without warning, Emma nestled her wrists behind his neck, pulled his head forward, and kissed him.

For a moment, Oliver was too stunned to enjoy the kiss. But only for a moment.

For several moments he breathed her in, reveling in the light smell of her coconut and lilac perfume that had taunted him all year. More than once they broke apart into temporary laughter, but instead of backing away, either he or she made sure to pull the other back in for a second longer. As the moment drew on, every worry slipped away from Oliver's exhausted mind, making him wonder why he'd ever debated not pursuing more than just a relationship in the first place.

"Sorry," Emma finally whispered. She didn't look sorry at all, which only widened the goofy grin on Oliver's face. "Had to make sure you're worth the wait."

"Did I pass?" Oliver murmured back.

"What do you think?" she asked, grinning mischievously.

* Chapter 34: Counsel Worth Little *

Archie huffed, breathing fire into the night around them. *"Seeing as my counsel is worth little, I take my leave for tonight. I must heal my wounds. Oliver, it is good to see you again—I apologize for my delay. I—,"*

"No apology necessary," Oliver said, raising a hand. He still kept his eyes on Emma—how could he look at anything else? "I can't imagine dealing with the memories that came back to you."

"Yes," Archie agreed. *"We will need to discuss them. When next I see you in the Dining Hall, we will set up a schedule."*

A whooshing sound indicated Archie left.

Emma still smiled. "Just one more kiss?"

"Here," Oliver said, finally breaking away, "you can hold my hand instead."

Emma pouted but took the hand all the same. "Scandalous."

NOVA 02

Chapter 35: The Case of Mr. Wyatt

I won't ever admit this to Tío, but being back on the road, away from the politics, is energizing. It's a nice change of pace and gives me plenty of time to think of effective policymaking. Watkin and Lalandra have me thinking—isn't that funny. What are better ways we can convince the rest of the populace that holding the American public up to standard is necessary to improve?

6th of January, the third year of the 10th Age

Lance and Elton didn't return until the evening before the second semester began.

"Psst," Se'Vaughn hissed at Oliver's door.

Behind him Trey motioned wildly over his shoulder, a frantic look on his face. "C'mon!" he urged. "Elton and Lance just got back!"

Oliver shot up immediately. "Where?"

In the late-evening light of the Dining Hall, Oliver found he wasn't the only Hutchite who'd gathered to support the Wyatt brothers. Around their usual mahogany table, their expressions were bleak, and no amount of sympathetic pats on the back from Abe or Brantley appeared to be cheering anyone up.

"Well," Elton said gloomily to the small crowd, "Lance's hunch was right."

* Chapter 35: The Case of Mr. Wyatt *

Lizzie, who sat next to Elton, took in a sharp breath. "So, you're saying your dad… " her voice trailed off, unable to finish the question as she put a hand to her mouth.

Elton couldn't look anyone in the eyes as he nodded his head; he did so slowly, a far cry from his usual overexuberance. Next to Lizzie, Emma shook the older girl's shoulder consolingly, her own expression a mix of fury and disgust. Elsewhere at the table, Se'Vaughn, Trey, Joel, and Valerie sat with either their jaws drawn in horror or their heads focused on the table with unblinking eyes.

From the front of the table, closest to Ms. Joan's kitchen, Oliver kept an eye on each of them using *Nova's Touch*. He knew some of them might find it odd, but he needed the practice… and, if he were being honest, looking at Lance in the face right now was tough. For the time being, he kept his back to them. Only a few other students were in the Dining Hall—mostly Tancols or Foundlings as far as he could tell. To be safe, he muttered *"stratum silentii"* anyway, flexing his ring hand a couple times to get a privacy shield up.

When the now familiar suffocating sensation finished crawling over the world, he challenged himself to keep the magic going indirectly, only paying attention to the working in his ring when he felt it slip from his concentration. The spell faltered for a second, causing those at the table to wince, but then it stuck. He cracked a grin at his success, his back still to his friends as he faced Ms. Joan's kitchen, wondering who would be more impressed, Lalandra or Watkin.

NOVA 02

"Dad as good as told us he'd been taken to one of *The Damned's* rehabilitation centers," Lance confirmed in a croak. "But only for a couple months. Which was towards the end of *The Damned's* movement just before—,"

His voice broke, and he shook away tears in his eyes.

Elton took over with a heat in his voice, stretching the muscles in his arms as he spoke. "That's the only reason why dad even *survived*. The Atlanta center got liberated before they'd finished processing everybody."

Oliver's eyes snapped open at that, sharp and furious. "It must have been just before the Sanctum Disaster, then," he said, finishing Lance's earlier thought.

Several blank faces blinked in Oliver's direction. "The what?" Brantley asked. He followed up with cluck of his tongue. "Man, you holding onto *more* secrets?"

Abe threw his hands in the air, his eyebrows drawn together crossly. "We've been over this!"

Emma took to massaging her forehead. "It's when *The Damned* fell from Power."

"Towards the end of his movement," Lance croaked. "We've read up on it... a lot. He was a senator in Connecticut—could only convince states outside the Northeast to roll out rehabilitation centers after the public wanted it."

Elton let out a full exhale as several faces at the tables swapped winces or grimaces. "Mom was in denial about the whole thing," he said, twisting his hands over an apple.

* Chapter 35: The Case of Mr. Wyatt *

"When Stevie got her to finally admit it," Lance droned on, "she just broke down crying. 'If *The Damned* comes back,' she said, 'and if anybody knows he was in there last time, he'll get thrown right back in.'"

Nobody spoke for several moments, digesting the news in their own ways. For most, it meant holding onto their horrified expressions. For others, like Abe and Lizzie, it was easier to burn off nervous energy by drumming their fingers on the table.

Eventually Oliver cleared his throat. "I guess," he said, bitterly, "now we know why none of the adults ever want to talk about it."

Every head in the room turned to look at him, and though uncertainty bogged him down, he was beginning to get used to it. And he knew he was right. The truth of it was clear to him now.

"If you're a supporter of *rehabilitation*," he explained, failing to keep a sneer out of his voice, "you don't want to say anything because if *The Damned* never comes back, you'll be labeled as evil."

Emma nodded her head, understanding dawning on her face. "And if you're against him," she said, firm and confident, "you don't want to say anything either, because if he does come back... well..." She made a swishing noise and swiped a thumb across his throat.

All of them either nodded or gulped.

Then Lance let out a nervous laugh. "All y'all still sure about helping us get prepped up for *The Damned,* then?"

The table erupted into nervous laughter, and, watching them, Oliver felt his anxiety syphon out of him like water from an unplugged drain. *Nova's*

NOVA 02

Touch kept him appraised of just how tense they'd all been, along with how grateful they now clearly felt to have a reason to laugh and smile.

But then a lone figure appeared at the edge of *Nova's Touch*, and Oliver flinched. The magic drew his attention to the foyer entrance where Tolteca rested in his alcove for the night.

Oliver's eyes narrowed when he saw who'd entered.

Beto stepped inside, dressed in a new, sharp traveler's cloak that would pass as uniform-appropriate, even if it did stretch the frock-coat rule. Oliver was tempted to flare Power and rush the boy, but he settled for a flare of Wisdom instead, shooting a pillar of blue-lit energy from floor to ceiling in a half-breath.

A second later, the rest of the Hutchites followed Oliver's stare, scrambling out of their seats. Already, Oliver realized, he was seeing a benefit to *Nova's Touch*—he'd been the first to spot the enemy.

To Oliver's surprise, however, Beto didn't so much as glance their way. Keeping his chin high, the curly-haired boy went straight for a far table where he joined… Cristina and James. Oliver staggered at the sight of Beto's cronies. How had he missed them during his earlier scans of the room? Cristina looked away nervously at his glare, a glimmer of a satisfied grin disappearing on her face.

As soon as Beto sat down, Cristina and James huddled their heads close and began to whisper furiously.

"Must have had a nasty Christmas," Brantley grunted.

A cruel smile spread across Joel's face. "Course he did. We all know who his family is."

* Chapter 35: The Case of Mr. Wyatt *

"Family always comes first, dunnit?" Brantley asked, winking.

The whole table laughed again.

But Oliver didn't. "Cristina's got a way to block *Nova's Touch,*" he said to Roli on a private relay. "Tell Emma and Lance, will you?"

"At once," Roli agreed, sharing Oliver's concern. *"And well done. A Trinova should give out orders. You're not a little boy any longer—it's about time you act like it."*

Oliver ignored Roli. Instead, he watched Beto, Cristina, and James a little longer. For once, Beto didn't look full of confidence. Whether Brantley had picked up on it or not, something really was gnawing at Beto. He looked tired all over his face where it usually gleamed like he'd just stepped out of a spa, and he didn't look comfortable in the slightest as he answered Cristina's and James's ever flowing questions.

After Roli finished relaying the message he turned back around. "Alright, y'all," he said. "I'm off to research."

The table groaned in unison. Oliver made to answer the complaint but then stopped when he realized the table itself had joined in with his friends. Suppressing a grin, he tapped on the wood with his ring finger and pulsed a thought that felt like *"are you eavesdropping, Ms. Joan?"*

Emma and Lance stood, too, shooting uneasy glances towards Beto and Cristina before nodding at Oliver.

"Wait," Abe said, raising a hand. Oliver stopped. If Abe had worked up the courage to stop him leaving, it could only be important.

"What is it?" he asked, giving Abe his full attention. "Is it a Goodwin Forest update?"

NOVA 02

"Nope," Lizzie said, taking over.

When Joel flashed his teeth into a wide grin and nudged Elton in the ribs, Oliver's curiosity only grew.

"Did you find the painting?!" Oliver asked, stepping close. Before he knew what he was doing, his hands were on the edge of the table, all thoughts of Beto forgotten. If they'd found the painting already...

"Rumor has it," Lizzie said, pushing Oliver a step back and smirking towards Emma, "that you two were something of an item at the Christmas Cocktail Hour."

Oliver's entire mind halted.

"Care to comment?" Abe asked, becoming a representative of smugness itself.

Eventually, after ignoring crooning sounds of approval from Se'Vaughn and Trey, Oliver's eyes flicked onto Lance's.

The blonde boy wilted.

"I should have made you cross your heart," Oliver muttered.

Lance at least had enough self-respect to mouth, "sorry."

"That's nobody's business," Emma huffed, crossing her arms while Oliver continued staring daggers into his friend.

"I've always thought of myself as a nobody," Joel chimed. "How about you, Elton?"

Elton buffed his nails for a half-moment against his puffer coat. "Been a nobody since birth, really." Looking up from his nails, he added, "Lance about laid an egg when you texted him a few days ago about a 'date,' Oli. The jig is up."

* Chapter 35: The Case of Mr. Wyatt *

"Spill the beans, you two," Brantley commanded, lacing his hands together behind his head.

"Come on y'all," Abe agreed, quiet and earnest. "We could all use some good news right now."

Oliver risked a glance at Emma. She seemed to be taking the attention better, so he opted to let her speak on his behalf. He was just being polite, that's all. Not at all concerned about his friends would take it...

"Do I smell lies in here?" Roli challenged. Oliver ignored him, blocking out his thoughts as best he could.

Emma sighed. "Well, there isn't any news. We decided 'dating,'"—she smacked Lance lightly on the back of the head when she said it—"wouldn't be a good idea until Oli's strung *The Damned's* innards across—,"

"We're focusing on preparing for *The Damned,*" Oliver interrupted.

The table collectively booed at him. And this time Oliver definitely heard one of the decorative candles on the handles hiss at him, too.

"Well, that's a royal bummer," Lizzie moaned. "What am I supposed to do with that gossip?"

Emma waggled her eyebrows. "We did kiss, though," she snuck in.

Oliver's entire face went redder than Emma's hair while Elton, Joel, Se'Vaughn, Trey, Brantley, and even Abe went wild with excitement, shaking their chairs, attempting to flip the bolted down the table, and hurling leftover food at one another.

"Yeah?" Joel asked Emma through the din. "How was it? Always wanted to know what kissing a Trinova would be like." Then with a more serious expression he added, "not you, specifically, Oli—I'm talking about you in a past life, you know what I'm saying? A hottie with a big ole—,"

"Personality," Elton agreed, nodding sagely.

"Honestly?" Emma went on, closing her eyes and grinning. "It was pretty great. Right Oli?"

Oliver turned to leave. "I'm going to the Research Center," he announced.

Studying and practicing around Emma became a challenge over the next few weeks.

"Yes," Roli muttered sardonically as Oliver thought on his way to the Coatlball bleachers. *"I can't imagine why concentrating on the return of The Damned would be important with something so noble as love in the air."* When he finished, he stamped a small foot into Oliver's hair. *"That was sarcasm, you silly boy! You should listen to your Guide!"*

"I get it, okay!" Oliver said, semi-shouting. A nearby pod of extramen jumped at the sound of his voice so he flared Power to speed himself up on his jog through the thicket between the main campus temples and the Coatlball trench.

"I love sorbelux," he breathed as he zipped past most of the student body, invisible to the eye.

* Chapter 35: The Case of Mr. Wyatt *

Without Lalandra around, Oliver hadn't had a chance for another lesson on light refraction—but he'd taken her advice from their lesson and refined sorbelux further to where he could now erase his footprints and muffle the sounds he made along the way.

"If only you could muffle your uncontrolled outbursts, too," Roli chided.

A deeper voice joined their private conversation. *"Mind your tone, foundling,"* Archie growled.

"Command me forcibly, serpent," Roli jeered back. *"I may heed your advice if you will it so. From the shadows consider yourself disregarded."*

"Behave you, two," Oliver interjected as Archie's thoughts raged. Almost laughing, he wondered how on Earth he'd gotten to the point where he bossed around sacred beasts several centuries older than him as if they were naughty children.

"Pay me no attention," Roli said apologetically, *"my breakfast featured far too little starch."*

"You said you wanted to try the bugs!" Oliver complained. He'd carefully ordered raw grasshoppers to Roli's exact specifications over breakfast, much to the horror of Elton and Brantley who'd sat next to him. Oliver had just been surprised to see Ms. Joan pull together a plate of bugs that fast.

"Yes, yes," Roli said, waving an invisible paw impatiently, *"I made a mistake. Sweet potatoes would have been far better."*

"Maybe a mix of the two?" Archie offered up.

A silence followed. *"I appreciate that,"* Roli said stiffly. *"Thank you, Archibald."*

NOVA 02

Oliver smiled all the way down to the bleachers. After Archie had recovered from his wounds in mid-January, the serpent had begun joining them during their sessions in the simulator with Emma and Lance.

In the simulations, it hadn't taken long for Archie's laid-back approach to teaching and Roli's hands-on micro-managing to clash like tectonic plates during an earthquake. After several shouting matches, Lance of all people suggested they, "shut up, focus, or get out."

So, Archie's peace-offering in the form of meal advice was well-received by more than just Roli. It was a step in the right direction.

"You sure this is a good idea?" Oliver asked as he took Lalandra's seat in the faculty section of the bleachers. He shifted in his seat invisible but uncomfortable, with an eye and *Nova's Touch* on Blackwood two rows down. Poor Zapien, who sat behind Blackwood, had to stand on her chair to see the game.

Archie grunted through their mental bond as he landed on the oversized floating magical mirror that broadcasted the game and score far above the crowd.

"That means don't worry yourself," Roli translated. *"It's an inefficient use of time, oxygen, and your mental faculties."*

Resigned to stay quiet, Oliver settled down into Lalandra's seat, ready to watch the final game of the regular season. A pang of jealousy shot across his body like one of his flares of Power as he watched Emma and Lance take the field on Rasmus and Merri. This was the biggest game of the regular season, Hutch versus Champayan, and he wouldn't be able to help his dorm

* Chapter 35: The Case of Mr. Wyatt *

during a second of it. Suddenly, his advances in magic, and all he'd learned about Tupper felt like a cheap participation trophy.

NOVA 02

Chapter 36: Of Kings, Pharaohs, and Warlords

I take it back. Travelling invisibly is the worst. I don't understand why I couldn't have brought an assistant or anything. At least I don't have to deal with the Whigs anymore. Tio can deal with Watkin.

22nd of January, the third year of the 10th Age

Inside the simulator, Oliver placed a hand to his chin while watching Emma and Lance duel.

"Is it me," he directed towards Roli, thinking out loud through their private connection, *"or has all my training in the simulator made me... well, better?"*

"Don't get me wrong," he added as Emma cartwheeled away from a blast of jettisoned water Lance had whipped towards her with the butt of his warhammer. *"Emma and Lance are top notch. But I feel like I'd beat them pretty quickly, right? Maybe it's all my extra simulating against monsters like Xihuacota?"*

Roli didn't respond for a full five seconds. When the pause continued, Oliver looked up at the ceiling of the simulator and frowned.

"Yes" the iguana's voice eventually replied, dullened with thick sarcasm. *"That must be it! Either that OR your being an instrument of the heavens comes with several distinct advantages!"*

Oliver winced at his own stupidity. Then he shook his head, thinking back on his last *Tupper Session*. Now that he had the simulator, he could research Tupper from the comfort of a squishy, leather chair in the "library" Roli had provisioned in the back corner of the facility. Just recently, he'd

* Chapter 36: Of Kings, Pharaohs, and Warlords *

watched a recording of the young Solomon Tupper soloing an entire dungeon by himself, just like Watkin had inside Snowgem. Oliver's jaw had tightened the longer he watched the film. Though he'd made a considerable amount of progress with Nova's Touch and indirectly sustaining magic while dueling simulated wolf-monsters, snake-creatures, or Xihuacota, he still couldn't defeat any of the enemies in as quick fashion as either Tupper or Watkin.

"I'm still not where I need to be," Oliver whispered out loud, feeling dejected.

"You'll be ready when the time comes," Roli tried saying cheerily.

Oliver waved a hand—he knew Roli would see it from where he supervised in the simulator's control room—and returned his attention to Emma and Lance.

Even if he could beat Emma and Lance in nine out of ten duels, his friends' progress impressed him more than his own did. Emma could now cycle between a handful of different moves in the span of a minute, making Oliver feel concerned over her body's ability to recover from the impact of so many workings in quick succession. Elemental magic was one thing—it didn't take a toll on the body given the energy being used came from the elements themselves. But the blades of light she summoned? And the blasts of concentrated destruction aura? She was delivering those with her own energy. Her entire body likely felt like it was on fire after any given duel.

But anytime Oliver decided she was pushing herself to hard, he stopped himself before speaking up. Emma was her own person. She didn't need

NOVA 02

him to tell her to control herself. She'd learn that lesson on her own, if she ever had to.

And then there was Lance.

Oliver didn't know whether it was the continued work at the gym, the Coatlball practices, or the mock duals in the simulator, but Lance's Power was getting *strong*.

So much so, that Oliver wondered if Abe's theory was right. Was his influence as a Trinova accelerating his friends' own abilities?

A retching noise interrupted Oliver's thoughts. *"If you'd like to explore the finer points of narcissism,"* Roli chided, *"allow me to recommend a mirror? At least then I won't have to hear this tripe."*

Oliver raised a hand in apology the same time Roli manifested a small mirror in front of Oliver's face. "You're right," he said, his cheeks flushing as Roli played a recording of the last time Xihuacota had dragged Oliver's body across sharp rocks. "They're working just as hard as I am."

"You bet they are," a voice interrupted.

Oliver didn't turn to address the newcomer. He'd felt him entering with Nova's Touch.

"I will admit your mastery of Nova's Touch is worthy of my praise," Roli said stiffly.

"How's it going, Abe?" Oliver asked as the mirror disappeared.

Abe sidled up next to Oliver to watch alongside him. "Good," he said, with his eyes on Emma and Lance. "How are they holding up?"

Oliver let out a long exhale. "Better now, I guess."

* Chapter 36: Of Kings, Pharaohs, and Warlords *

Only a couple days prior, Champayan had flattened Hutch in one of the biggest Coatlball matches of the season. None of the Hutchites had taken it well. Especially after Beto flaunted his win by bathing in the limelight with many prolonged bows to the cheering crowd after the game.

"At least," Abe took over, tilting his head from side to side as he debated something, "those jerks lost to Tancol twice already. Tancol's gonna be the first seed for the tournament this spring. If we can beat them, we'll snag third seed."

Oliver nodded. Then, he did turn to face Abe.

Looking the older boy in the eyes, he asked, "and Blackwood? Is he still looking happy?"

Abe frowned.

Ever since banning Oliver from sports, Blackwood's power trip had only catapulted a level further. With Lalandra still missing after her trip to Goodwin Forest, Blackwood had assumed the position of interim Headmaster. With a dangerous glint in his eye, he could now often be seen stomping across the grounds handing out detentions as though they were party favors.

"That's why I'm here," Abe grumbled, keeping his attention on his shoes. "I've got detention this afternoon for 'getting too close to the lagoons' when I was snooping around, looking for that damn painting."

"But don't worry!" he snuck in before Oliver could respond. "Elton's going to take over my shift!"

Oliver couldn't help but laugh at how miserable Abe looked.

"Cheer up," he said, patting his friend on the back. "Blackwood gave me detention last year for not saying 'sir.'"

Abe brightened. "Thanks for understanding," he said, sounding less miserable than before.

Then he departed, leaving Oliver to turn his head back towards the battle unfolding in front of him.

"Poor guy," Lance shouted as he finished conjuring a stone golem twice Blackwood's height.

Emma curled her lip, agreeing with him. "I'd love to see Blackwood taken down a peg," she grunted while blocking a chunk of hurled Earth from the golem. "D'you think he's happy because Lalandra's gone, or does he know something we don't?"

Oliver raised his eyebrows at the question while the battle continued. He hadn't thought of Blackwood's good mood that way before. Was Bald and Brash secretly happy about something unrelated to Lalandra's disappearance? If so, was it related to *The Damned?*

Not for the first time that day, the text of the Iguana's Scroll flashed in front of Oliver's eyes.

Speed is of the essence...

What did Blackwood know that they didn't?

Before he could think on it much further, the duel came to a close.

* Chapter 36: Of Kings, Pharaohs, and Warlords *

With an elaborate twist of her sleeved arm, Emma took control of Lance's conjured stone golem. When Lance floundered, she rushed forward with a glint in her eye.

At least Oliver thought she did.

Only after Lance raised his hands in defeat and the simulation washed away in a sea of swirling green magic, did Oliver realize Emma had pulsed a wave of her—now signature—destructive wind aura, towards Lance via the form of a menacing, red silhouette that mirrored her appearance.

Oliver clapped, slow, loud, and impressed.

Emma bowed. When she straightened, she couldn't keep a trickster's grin off her lips. "Can't tell you all my secrets, can I?"

Lance growled from the other side of the arena. "This is a waste of time."

"Boo-hoo," Emma shot back, rubbing at fake tears in her eyes. "I'm a big boy and I just got whooped by a little girl."

Lance visibly calmed himself with a deep breath before he even entertained Emma's taunt. When he did, he smacked his lips at her, unimpressed. "After a lifetime of dealing with Stevie, you're just a cheap imitation."

Emma snarled at him.

Lance responded by sticking out his tongue contemptuously.

"Yesss, squabble, peasants!" Roli needled inside their heads.

Oliver scowled and sent a pulse of his own blue wind across the room. Though Roli washed the magic away with the energy of the Simulator, Oliver didn't mind. He just wanted everyone's attention.

NOVA 02

"You're both right," he said, doing his best impression of Santiago when serious. Now that he'd bulked up a few pounds with Elton's training, it didn't feel too disingenuous to imitate his uncle—in some ways, it felt right.

"Lance," he said, "you shouldn't be losing that easily. Chin up and trust your Power to break through most anything coming at you."

Lance straightened, and a spark of energy rekindled in his eyes.

Then, Oliver pivoted to Emma. Her eyes, green and fierce, made him hesitate. At seeing him stumble, she pulled on a self-satisfied smile. Oliver recovered after a second. It didn't matter if they wanted to date, Emma needed to improve, too, if they wanted to keep up with Oliver and not be fodder for Tupper once he escaped.

"What are you going to do when you come across a Wiser?" Oliver asked, pressing his lips together.

Emma's grin fell and she shifted in place. "Go at 'em quick as possible," I guess. "Otherwise, they'll outthink me overtime."

"Hmm," Oliver contemplated. "Maybe. But I'd say dial it back a bit—any Wiser worth their salt is going to see your quick plays coming from a mile away."

"Hmmph!" Emma bellyached. "You saying I'm a blunt instrument?"

Oliver shook his head, ignoring the bait. Emma was being feisty because she knew he liked it when she was feisty. "I'm saying you should trust yourself to practice slower moves. Not everything needs to be quick and on-the-attack."

Emma tapped a finger to her chin. "I'll consider it…"

* Chapter 36: Of Kings, Pharaohs, and Warlords *

"She won't," Archie countered with a yawn from a corner in the room. *"You ask a snake to hunt prey like a wolf."*

"I'm not a *snake!*" Emma shot back angrily.

"That was a compliment," Archie replied, flittering his tongue to accentuate his point.

"Oh, right," Emma said, kicking at the floor, her cheeks tinged with embarrassment.

"Consider it against Cristina, okay?" Oliver asked.

Emma deflated. Cristina Morris's name had become a gossiper's staple over the last several weeks. Whether they were baked in truth or not, rumors had spread, saying Cristina was going toe-to-toe with none other than Beto in Champayan's practice duels ahead of the dueling group stage in March. Everybody knew Beto would be taking the first seed for Champayan, all but guaranteeing his path to the final in the knock-out stages. Now that Cristina was emerging as an equal, Champayan's odds at having a perfect record in the group stage and then placing first and second in the playoffs were higher than anybody in Hutch cared to admit.

"Fine," Emma said, giving in. "Let's go again, Lance."

Oliver nodded appreciatively. "Take your time making decisions!" he yelled as they began.

She replied with a rude hand gesture, so Oliver stepped away from the duel and walked towards Archie.

NOVA 02

Roli had been kind enough to simulate a nest from the quetzal hallowed grounds at Archie's request. Made from enormous slabs of bark from willow trees, the nest was as large as Oliver and Lance's room in Hutch. Flames licked up from the edges of it, so Oliver stopped a few feet away. Knowing Roli, he'd feel the bite of those flames in the simulator, real or not.

"Smart boy," Roli said. A floating picture of the iguana popped in front of Oliver's eyes, winking at him. *"Can't have you developing bad habits."*

Oliver sighed. When he made to sit down, a leather chair appeared. Oliver didn't know what magical barrier he actually sat on, but it was comfy.

"Let's pick up where we left off," he said to Archie.

Archie's inner eyelids clicked open. *"Very well. Solomon's travels, was it?"*

Oliver nodded. "We've learned enough about the boy at school. He had some red flags,"—

"Some?!" Lance's voice bellowed from the arena. An explosion followed. Then, a mousy yelp from Lance as Emma took advantage of the distraction.

—"but we still can't figure out," Oliver went on, ignoring them, "what Tupper was doing between summers. Looks like he may have gone overseas between his junior and senior year, but then he just disappeared for a couple years after graduating?"

"Hmm," Archie thought. *"It's far simpler to identify 'red flags' with the benefit of hindsight."*

* Chapter 36: Of Kings, Pharaohs, and Warlords *

Oliver conceded the point. "That's true, but what about the summer and the traveling?"

Archie slunk to a better position in his nest before speaking. *"That's better.... Hmmm, well, the boy was certainly taken with history while at school. Any conversations I recall about his travels were inspired by his studies, weren't they? I vaguely remember much of his time was spent in the Research Lab. Sometimes he'd ask me about his research—he seemed to care a great deal about the Trinova, the cycles of the planets, and any myths he could dig up from your human history."*

Oliver nodded. "Myths..." he repeated. "What other myths was he researching?"

"Let's see," Archie said patiently. Before going on, he closed both the inner and outer levels of his eyelids to think. *"Legends of several figures amongst men if I'm remembering correctly."*

"Like who?" Oliver asked, straightening in his chair.

"Think, serpent, think!" Roli demanded in their heads.

Archie huffed a cloud of smoke. *"It's difficult to remember exactly as the names aren't of my people."*

"Well, try!" Oliver said, standing. Finally, Archie had something helpful to say about Tupper. So far, all they'd gotten out of him was the same single message—Tupper hadn't exactly been flagged as dangerous at school. In fact, more often than not, he and Archie had spoken about the possibility of creating a utopia amongst all sacred beasts, including humans.

With *Nova's Touch,* Oliver saw Emma and Lance abandoning their duel behind him to see what the commotion was about.

NOVA 02

Archie fully roused himself from his nest, picking up on Oliver's growing concern. *"Let's see, there was a warlord, a few kings, and maybe a queen, or was it a Caesar of Rome? There were several, but I can't remember their names—an impossible request. Impossible, I tell you."*

Sweat began to percolate on Oliver's forehead. What had Tupper been up to? What myths had he been so obsessed with and what drove the obsession? They already knew *The Damned* had been obsessed about the Trinova legend... and Tupper hadn't been wrong about that one.

"These kings he studied," Oliver said, his voice frantic as his thoughts cascaded over themselves. "He must have researched where they were from, yeah?"

Archie hesitated. *"Well, yes, that came with the research..."*

Of Emma and Lance, Emma got to Oliver first.

"So he visited a bunch of graveyards?" she asked, biting her lip.

Lance, meanwhile, kept his mouth shut, moving his eyes from Archie to Oliver and then back.

The door to the training facility burst open, and in scuttled Roli. Eventually, he came to a halt at the edge of the nest where he stuck his tongue in and out. *"Did he travel to any of these graveyards?"*

"Yes, of course," Archie said dismissively, *"during school-sponsored trips over the summer breaks as far as I'm aware."*

Oliver didn't like the sound of that, and one look at Emma told him she felt the same.

* Chapter 36: Of Kings, Pharaohs, and Warlords *

Archie huffed disdainfully. *"I'm not sure this is a conversation worth having. He paid homage to these figures. It is only natural—we feathered serpents do the same with our ancestors."*

"No," Oliver countered. "He must have wanted something."

"Only question is," Lance breathed, "did he find what he was looking for?"

Roli's tongue licked the corners of his mouth a second time. *"Was anything different about the boy when he came back from his trips?"*

Oliver knew exactly what Roli was getting at. What if Tupper *hadn't* been researching powerful figures in human history? What if the boy had been isolating graves worth robbing?

Archie, on the other hand, had taken the question differently. *"Of course not!"* the serpent griped, taking off into the air with several bats of his long, thin wings. *"The boy was the same every year! He never came back all-Powerful or all-conquering with a lust in his eye for evildoing. That's what you don't understand. He was just a boy to all of us! One who only ever argued for utopia in his essays! A boy who…"*

A light clicked on in Oliver's head as Archie kept going. *"Archie doesn't want to feel guilty about missing the signs,"* he slipped to Roli. *"He's embarrassed he didn't see Tupper's evil coming."*

"Archie?" Emma cut in. She gave Oliver a pointed look as she spoke. "Did Tupper ever switch up his source or channel when you were his Guide?"

Roli nodded in approval, looking to Archie for the answer.

NOVA 02

Archie's feathery face scrunched up in confusion. *"Well, I suppose he did come back every summer with a new source and channel. Why do you ask?"*

Oliver's chin fell slack and, next to him, he heard gasps escape from Emma's and Lance's lungs.

"Updated sources and channels?" Oliver repeated for confirmation. Then, he raised his left hand and allowed the light in the room to catch Augustus' ring. "Kinda like my new ring." He followed up by pulling down his collared shirt to show Madeline's necklace. "And my necklace?"

"Well," Archie exclaimed, almost backing away from their collective stares, *"not exactly. But I do seem to recall after his junior year he returned with a staff, similar to the one Professor Watkin uses. But it hardly seems noteworthy. When he returned from his more extensive travels after graduation, I never saw him with a staff again."*

Oliver stood to leave. "We need to ask Watkin if sources and channels can be modified. Sounds like Tupper had some luck with his grave-robbing."

"Please do have a seat," Watkin insisted after they barreled into his office a quarter hour later.

Oliver obliged, taking one of the couches on the veranda behind Watkin's classroom. Pollen puffed into the air like clouds of yellow dust as Emma and Lance followed suit.

* Chapter 36: Of Kings, Pharaohs, and Warlords *

Watkin swiveled his staff, and the pollen disappeared before anyone sneezed. "How goes the practicing?" he asked Oliver. "Can you sustain indirect magic yet?"

With a flick of his wrist, Oliver raised a narrow pillar of fire into the sky, keeping it there with only a sliver of thought. "Yes," he answered. "Access to the simulator has been a big help for practicing pretty much everything."

"Good," Watkin grunted. "Why am I here, then? Archie said it was urgent."

Emma laughed. "Straight to it, sir? No polite small talk?"

Watkin tilted his head. *"Speed is of the essence,* unfortunately," he said, recanting the Iguana's Scroll.

Oliver let his fire pillar working collapse. "Okay," he answered. "What was *The Damned* doing with all his time abroad?"

"We know he came back with a staff like yours one year," Lance snuck in while raising a pointed finger. "Does he have artifacts like Oli or not?"

Emma nodded her head and tagged on even more. "If the Founders thought of Tupper as a 'False Prophet' or whatever, is that because he gave himself all three Gifts using artifacts?"

"Should I be planning to duel a Trinova or a Powerhead?" Oliver finished.

Sighing, Watkin took a seat in an open chair next to Oliver. When he started rubbing his head with hands, Jaiba swooped down out of nowhere to land on the man's shoulder and nuzzle into his ear.

NOVA 02

"Yes," Watkin finally said, "Solomon had been obsessed with becoming a Trinova. I overlapped with him for two years at Tenochprima, remember? Even then the concept had fascinated him."

Emma cried out in indignation. "If you knew all along, why didn't you tell us?"

Oliver thought he understood—it had to do with Watkin's principles. "You wanted us to learn about Tupper ourselves, right? So that we could form our own guesses?"

Watkin beamed at him.

Oliver could tell it was a genuine reaction, too, given just how many muscles in the man's body had twitched.

"I would swear on the Seat of Truth," Watkin said, standing back up and clasping his hands behind his lower back, "that Solomon came back to school his senior year with the Gift of Bravery already secured."

Oliver wasn't sure who deflated more between himself, Emma, or Lance.

"But!" Watkin went on, taking his own turn to raise a finger. "I'd also contend Tupper *never* found an artifact that provided him Wisdom."

Oliver's pent-up breath escaped him. "I'd feel a *lot* better about battling *The Damned* if we knew he didn't have all three Gifts. How are you so sure he never found an old tablecloth or something that made him Wise?"

"Hmmm," Emma drew out, crossing her arms. "I'm not sure I buy that he didn't get Wisdom, Professor. Didn't he trick everybody into thinking rehabilitation centers were a good idea after he went into politics? Wouldn't that take a lot of Wisdom to plan out?"

* Chapter 36: Of Kings, Pharaohs, and Warlords *

Watkin didn't answer immediately, and though the man's face appeared unbothered by the question, through *Nova's Touch,* Oliver felt Watkin stop breathing for a full second.

Which was strange. Why would such a simple question make Watkin uncomfortable? They just wanted to know why he thought Tupper didn't have Wisdom.

"Because he fell," Watkin finally said, sounding hollow.

"What do you mean he *fell?*" Lance repeated.

Watkin began to pace before continuing. "I only mean the Sanctum Disaster happened," he answered bitterly. "Someone with Wisdom would not have attempted an experiment that drew pesadriyas to it like bees to honey."

"So, should we be worrying about our chances, then?" Emma asked for confirmation while fidgeting with her hair. "If... well, if he's still got Bravery and his insane Power, will we stand a chance?"

Watkin stopped pacing and smiled down at them. "As long as he doesn't get his hands on Wisdom, we should stand more than a chance. I'd imagine Augustus foresaw far more strands of success in our fate when Tupper never got Wisdom."

"Could he still?" Oliver asked, terrified of the answer.

Watkin resumed pacing. "I believe Solomon found a lance that once belonged to Lysander, a Spartan who led his people to a great victory against the Athenians."

"And it had Bravery in it?" Lance asked, fumbling his hammer out of his hands and dropping it. He picked it back up, embarrassed, but kept going. "I thought the Founders' artifacts only existed because of Augustus?"

Watkin stopped pacing to raise a finger for a second time. "Ah, but we don't know that—do we? We only know the Founders *left* these artifacts behind for Oliver to find, not that they created them for him to use."

"I," Oliver stammered, "never thought of it like that."

Watkin nodded and lowered his hand. "The Founders likely used these same artifacts during their times, allowing themselves to fully channel their Gifts despite the Age of Darkness during which they lived. Which begs the question, what are the artifacts, exactly? Where did they come from? Are they the only ones in the world?"

Lance went green in the face. "So, you're saying Tupper could just as easily find another artifact with Wisdom in it after he escapes? What's stopping him from going out and finding a special rock or something?"

Watkin paused mid-stride and stared at Lance, flourishing his fingers. "These artifacts are incredibly rare, Mr. Wyatt. We don't know if there is another artifact that could bless the user with Wisdom other than the ring on Oliver's finger."

Everyone looked at Oliver's hand. "All this time," Oliver breathed, raising the ring until it caught the overhead quartz light, "I thought if I had all three artifacts, we'd be levelling the playing field against Tupper's advanced Power. That's what Augustus said—that's why he left this ring behind."

* Chapter 36: Of Kings, Pharaohs, and Warlords *

Watkin tilted his head pityingly for a second time. Then, he slowly took a seat next to Oliver. "Only you can write your future, Oliver. For all his Wisdom, Augustus only saw strands of fate, not absolute decrees."

Oliver looked at Watkin but didn't cheer up any. Would all his training be enough? But then Watkin's eyes twinkled for the first time in months, and Oliver did find himself cheering up.

"It may comfort you to know," Watkin said, relishing the words, "I *always* have a backup plan."

Emma laughed. "You think you can plan better than Augustus? A man who could *see* the future?"

Oliver kept looking into Watkin's eyes—there was no lie there. It made him think back to the man's hushed conversation with Miyada on the airstrip.

"This backup plan doesn't happen to include Miyada, does it?"

Watkin's twinkle extended into his smile, and the man waggled his eyebrows. "Don't you think you have enough on your plate for now? If we're fortunate enough, we'll never need consider this backup at all."

"For a man of principle," Emma said, crossing her arms, "you sure do keep a lot of secrets."

Watkin's grin only grew. "That may be the highest compliment anyone's ever paid me, Ms. Griffith."

Not for the first time, Oliver wondered what else Watkin might be hiding up his sleeve. And yet, he found he no longer cared. His neck buzzed warmly, urging him to **trust** the man, and that was good enough for him.

NOVA 02

"Now," Watkin said, standing. He took a moment to tighten his old silk belt before going on—the routine of it sharpened his eyes, making him look less haggard than before. "I am running out of ways to search for something that cannot be found within Goodwin Forest. As a result, that painting becomes more and more important to us by the hour. Wherever the riddle lies, Oliver is likely the only one that is meant to solve it."

"Wouldn't that also apply to your search in Goodwin Forest?" Roli asked. *"Perhaps only Master Oliver can find it?"*

Watkin shook his head. "I believe corruptive magic hides the temple. Whatever it is, it is no work of the Founders. I would guess *The Damned* sealed the Fire Drake's Cavern after searching it in his youth. Why? I cannot imagine, but if I can't break through the corruption protecting it, our only hope is to find an original pathway there—such as one provided via a painting."

"We've got nothing, Professor," Oliver admitted. "We've looked everywhere."

"You *must* keep trying," Watkin insisted. He hefted his staff as he prepared to leave. "The corruptive forces at play in Goodwin Forest go against the natural order of the world. Solomon's remote involvement can't be good news for any of us."

Oliver gulped.

"Least of all, you," Watkin finished, pointing his staff at Oliver's chest. "Find the painting, and we complete Augustus' orders."

* Chapter 36: Of Kings, Pharaohs, and Warlords *

NOVA 02

Interludes IX – X

At the top of the landing strip, Peter Baker jimmied open his carriage door and stepped down onto noisy gravel.

"Hold on, Mr. Baker!" his too-cheery tour guide chirped, trying to catch up.

Peter waved a hand at the girl and kept going anyway. He wanted to *see* it again. To *feel* it. These were his old stomping grounds, and he wasn't about to let some young girl ruin the moment.

With his brown dress shoes crunching on the gravel beneath him, Peter beat the girl to the stairs. This had been what he missed most.

"What was it that you used to teach, sir?" the smiling girl asked when she shuffled up next to him.

Peter didn't answer. He was too engrossed in the sight beneath him—the view of the entire ridge where Tenochprima had been built. Before he could help it, tears burst forth from his tired, old eyes. Why had he waited so long to visit? All just because of the legacy of some evil boy?

"Tenochprima Academy," Peter intoned, basking in the view of his favorite place on Earth. "How long has it been?"

"Thirty years, right?" the girl asked, ever insistent on speaking to him.

Peter grumbled, wiping the tears from his eyes.

* Interludes IX – X *

"Listen," he groused. When he realized he didn't remember her name, he paused with his mouth wide open. "What's your name again?"

"Sara Reyes!" the girl chirped, entirely unbothered.

Peter leered at Sara. Why was the girl smiling so much? Was this really the best tour guide the Interim Headmaster could offer?

Frowning, Peter met Sara's eyes. "Listen, Miss Reyes," he said, taking the first steps down the long stairs leading to the lagoons far below. "Do feel free to run off, alright? I know these grounds like the back of my hand and will not require a guide for my visit."

"Aww!" Sara sang, grabbing his arm. "I love your enthusiasm, Mr. Baker."

Then, before Peter knew what was happening, the girl began guiding him down the stairs towards the Academic Building.

"Now," Sara said picking up again before he could balk. "Why don't you tell me about all your favorite memories, mkay? Pick any you like! I'm an open ear."

With a sigh, Peter gave up on trying to get rid of the girl.

"I used to teach Political Science on the fourth floor," Peter warbled when they reached the foot of the Academic Building.

"Ooo," Sara peeped encouragingly. "Professor Perrindorph teaches all of our Poli Sci courses now."

Peter's eyebrows raised as memories of a young, mousy boy flitter in and around his head. Feeling a rush of excitement, Peter began pointing to his chest emphatically. "Fred Perrindorph? I taught the boy back in the day!

NOVA 02

Between you and me,"—he leaned in and lowered his voice—"he wasn't exactly a good student."

Sara let out a kind person's laugh, lifting his spirits.

"Yes," Peter went on, feeling encouraged. "That Fred couldn't hold a candle to my... best students."

Peter's mood fell the moment he thought about his best students. About *him*.

The Damned had been the reason why Peter Baker hadn't revisited campus in thirty years. And thinking about the evil man as a boy brought back a whole suite of different memories to Peter's mind—chief among them, an ill-given interview.

"In my thirty years of teaching," he recalled telling someone from the press the day he retired without notice. *"I've only been dumbstruck twice. First, when Elodie Lalandra dropped 'The Siren Call of Totalitarianism' on my desk, and then again earlier this morning, when ~~ ~~ dismantled Elodie's magnum opus from the ground-up in only his second political science class."*

What he'd said next, still made his stomach twist with embarrassment.

"I am unfit to teach this quality of student."

A hand jostled Peter back to the present.

* Interludes IX – X *

"Mr. Baker?" the girl named Sara asked, her cheery voice suddenly etched with concern. "Are you alright?"

Peter blinked for several seconds and when he recovered he was forced to clear his throat. "Yes, yes," he spat out quickly. "I... I was just remembering the day I retired."

The girl's eyes softened. "We don't have to talk about that memory if you don't want to," she said, patting him on the hand encouragingly.

Peter couldn't help but smile. Maybe this Sara girl wasn't so bad after all. Patting her hand back, Peter felt encouraged to take his first step up the stairs to the second floor of the Academic Building.

He hadn't even finished lifting his shoe when a sudden, high pitched, and ethereal hum froze him in place.

"What the devil is that?" he blurted towards Sara, backing away from the stairs even as the noise crescendoed into an ear-splitting roar.

"Oh, that?" Sara asked, chirpy again while he trembled with fear. "That's just the Trinova flaring Wisdom somewhere nearby. Oliver must be cranky about something."

Peter backed away even further from the building. "The Trinova is real?" he asked, his voice turning entirely hollow. For a long, awful moment, he watched a pillar of blue light erupt somewhere above them. It had outshined the sun.

"That," he asked through spittle while pointing shakily towards the now-receding pillar, "is the result of somebody flaring Wisdom?!"

"Yep!" Sara answered.

NOVA 02

Peter's face fell. The girl had answered him as though the blue light were an everyday occurrence.

"The Trinova, specifically," Sara continued, unflustered. "Oliver García—you've heard of him, right?"

Peter shook his head. If the Trinova were really real, and the papers hadn't been whipping up their normal gibberish, then what did that mean about the boy he'd taught all those years ago? The boy who'd made him retire on the spot. The boy who'd gone on to become *The Damned*.

"Would you like to meet Oliver?" Sara asked Peter, looking unsure of herself. "I wouldn't say Oli and I are *close* friends… but I'm working on it! Hey! Where are you going?"

Peter was already walking back up the hill. "I am unfit to teach this quality of student!" he shouted back at her.

Within the confines of his office inside classroom 310, Broderick Blackwood clasped his mammoth hands together. Expectantly, he waited behind his desk, his back straight as iron.

"Report," he ordered, never keeping his eyes off his prey.

Across the desk, Dionysos Desmoulins stammered out some more gibberish, just as before.

"I-I've already told you," the heart-faced man mewed. "I was in my study—,"

* Interludes IX – X *

"Don't call it a study," Blackwood chided, cutting the smaller man off. "It's an *office*. Do you study in your office?"

Desmoulins stared for a moment, his eyes wavering with some form of pitiable emotion reserved for lesser men.

Blackwood rolled his eyes. "No matter. Do carry on."

"Like I said," Desmoulins said, his emotions having changed to something with a little more backbone. Blackwood didn't care what the new emotion was—all that mattered was he was now getting results. "My gateway vibrated just now when I was in my office… and I'm pretty sure I—,"

"Gateway?" Blackwood interrupted. "What is a gateway? Dionysos, you know I don't care for being left out of a conversation."

Desmoulins' angular chin scrunched up beneath his thin nose and even thinner lips. "You're literally in this conversation, Broderick."

Blackwood waved a hand and snarled. "Gateway—what is it?"

"Remember," Desmoulins snapped back haughtily, "how I saved us from the nightmare in the Sage's Sanctum?"

Blackwood unclasped his hands and leaned back in his chair. "You're talking about the door you created to get us out of there?"

"Yes!" Desmoulins hissed, growing impatient. "I've heard a voice from it just now!"

Blackwood's jaw dropped. He recovered quickly, but the damage had been done. Desmoulins sneered at him from across the desk now.

"Well?" Blackwood growled. "What did you hear?"

NOVA 02

Desmoulins' certainty faded at the question. Swallowing, he stood and circled his hand overhead.

"Listen for yourself," he offered timidly.

Inside the office, a glowing frame of a doorway appeared. It didn't shine as ardently as an intact doorway would, but even now, fourteen years later, crackling outlines of magenta still shined.

As soon as he saw the doorframe, Blackwood pushed his chair as far away from it as possible.

"YOU IDIOT!" Blackwood roared. "WHAT IF THE MONSTER USES IT?"

Desmoulins held up a hand to shush him.

Blackwood was so stunned, he froze. Desmoulins? Shushing his betters?

But then, before Blackwood could exact a fitting punishment, a voice, distant and broken, shouted through the broken portal.

*"It would be **prudent** to prepare for my arrival."*

* Interludes IX – X *

NOVA 02

Chapter 37: The Original Sacred Beast

I just need to find a place called the Soothsayer's Temple before all this alone time drives me crazy. And the only hint I have is from an old letter he found saying it's in the Appalachians. Great. Really narrows it down.

14th of March, the third year of the 10th Age

By mid-March, Oliver wanted to scream every time he thought of the Fire Drake's Cavern or its missing painting.

"Maybe you should scream," Roli suggested.

Oliver honestly considered it for a moment, which was a testament to just how frustrated he felt. In the end, however, he concluded shouting in the middle of a crowd watching the Dungeon Simulation tournament would bring attention he'd rather avoid.

"Yes, very wise of you," Roli needled.

Oliver ignored the iguana to groan along with the rest of the Hutchites in the observation deck. Down below, Lance had just taken a fireball to the face.

Hutch's A team appeared to be battling—Oliver was forced to squint at the enemy for a better look—a robed wizard of some sort. It kept teleporting around the room and only stopped when ready to summon a great fireball with a stubby wand. It did so again, cackling through a beak that poked out of billowing dark robes as a second fireball connected with Lance's back.

* Chapter 37: The Original Sacred Beast *

"Ouch," a remarkably deep voice said from nearby. Mirrored by Roli on his shoulder, Oliver swiveled his neck to meet the voice's owner.

It was Drew, the extraman.

"Ew," Roli said, recoiling away from the boy. *"When did he get here?"*

"Aren't you supposed to be down there?" Oliver asked, gesturing back down to the dungeon. To Roli, he added, *"he is on Founders' team, right?"*

The crowd roared as Lance took another fireball, this time to his midriff, and exploded into shining white light.

Drew chuckled and pointed behind himself without looking as Lance appeared in the viewing dome, having been eliminated. "I died in the first room," the boy said, shrugging. "Mind if I watch with you?"

"Surrrre," Oliver said, turning back around to view the room. A second later Lance joined, out of breath.

"You should have suicide charged the magwiz," Drew suggested.

Lance, who'd opened his mouth to say something to Oliver, gave Drew a bewildered look. Then, blinking, he decided to ignore the boy entirely and jostle up next to Oliver's right instead, shoving Se'Vaughn and Trey further down the handrail.

"How we doing?" Lance asked.

Oliver pointed at the scoreboard floating above the scenes unfolding below. Only four out of the ten teams remained. Blackwood had forced himself into the dungeon committee for this year's tournament, and instead of the usual mix of puzzles, obstacles, and enemies, there were only monsters in the dungeon. Room after room of them.

NOVA 02

"If we'd known," Drew said, reading Oliver's thoughts, "we'd have stacked our team with Powerheads."

"Yeahhh," Lance agreed. "What's Blackwood trying to pull anyway?"

Oliver shrugged. "At least Champayan didn't get tipped off." He pointed at the board a second time. Champayan's two teams had already been eliminated. "They all left when they realized they weren't placing top three."

Drew chuckled dryly. "Idiots."

"Excellent," Lance agreed, clapping his hands together.

Oliver turned to Drew, a question forming on his lips. "Why did you say Lance should have charged the… hooded bird guy."

"Magwiz?" Drew confirmed. "Because the fires were going to kill Lance off in forty seconds anyway. Mm-maybe thirty, even." The boy readjusted his glasses before continuing with a shrug. "Shoulda suicide charged, taken the next fireball, and crushed that thing with the hammer."

Lance looked down at the hammer on his belt. He patted it fondly. "Yeah, maybe you're right. Easy to say from up here though."

Drew titled his chin down, conceding the point. "Heh, I wouldn't have done it either. But I'm not a Powerhead. We can't have it all,"—he gestured at Oliver with his thumb—"like Oliver here, eh?"

Oliver and Lance exchanged appreciative nods of the head.

Drew's odd expression soured for a second. "You guys really should be consulting me, Sara, and Ethan. We can help you out where you need it."

Lance started to laugh, but Oliver found himself taking the request seriously.

* Chapter 37: The Original Sacred Beast *

"If you're the brains," Oliver began, looking at the Founders A team for the first time during the tournament, "what does that make Sara and Ethan?"

Drew gave off another one of his dry chuckles. "Isn't it obvious? Ethan's almost as good as one of the Wyatt brothers—he swings his broadsword like a brute."

On cue, Ethan roared in the room below, swinging a two-handed sword that Oliver was sure muscles on the Original Side of the Key couldn't handle. A wave of Earth followed the swing, shredding the armor of a giant wolf-humanoid that Oliver recognized from the prior year.

"And then Sara is just a genius," Drew continued. "I don't think there's anything she can't do."

Oliver watched Sara jump up and down with glee, high-fiving a reluctant and sighing Ethan as they moved into the next room. Their approach was slower than all the other teams, but they were still alive, and that was more than six other squads could say. Including Hutch's B team.

Despite there also being a junior-year RA jogging beside her, Sara appeared to be the leader of the Founders A team. When they reached the next room, the same one Lance had died in, she directed all incoming fire from the magwiz toward herself, blocking the flames with a breath-taking smile on her face while the rest of her team took stock of the enemy's patterns and positions. It took them a while, but they eventually defeated the magwiz without much issue when Ethan swung his sword again.

"Is he umm dating anyone?" Lizzie asked from behind, her attention fixed on Ethan.

NOVA 02

Oliver jumped at the noise. Then he noticed the entire Hutch A team had joined them in the observation deck.

"Oh no," he breathed.

"Sorry," Emma said, keeping her head down as she shuffled forward. Abe and Brantley flanked her, squabbling furiously over who'd been more at fault for the team getting mauled by what sounded like a pack of jaguars in the final room.

"I told you to get the BIG one!" Abe jeered.

Brantley made to push the thinner boy but thought better of it, stepping away instead with fingers on the bridge of his nose. "Elton," he growled, "you deal with him."

Emma collapsed against the railing on Oliver's left, shoving Drew aside as if he were unwanted produce in a grocery store. When she pulled herself up, she let out a puff of her lips. "Guess we need you more than we realized inside dungeons," she said to Oliver.

Oliver put a hand on her shoulder, giving it a light shake. He knew what she felt—she wanted to prove she didn't need him around to get through a dungeon like the Forest Temple or Fire Drake's Cavern.

A dry, mono-syllabic chuckle interrupted Oliver's thoughts as Drew leaned forward over the railing to look at all three of them. "No, you don't," he said. After Emma slowly turned to him with her nostrils flared, they all swiveled their heads to follow Drew's outstretched, pudgy arm to where it pointed.

In the room below, Sara dodged one jaguar after the other, flittering around the room with graceful somersaults, rolls, and dodges that made the

* Chapter 37: The Original Sacred Beast *

crowd cheer. Somehow, she'd managed to get the jaguars to focus on her, and while she evaded them, her teammates took them out. This time the RA took out the final enemy with a shining beam of conjured light.

Again, Drew chuckled. "You really should hang out with us sometime. We're not as good as you guys are, but we might be smarter."

"I like this boy!" Roli said earnestly, switching from Oliver's right shoulder to his left.

"Or at least more strategic," Drew quickly added on, backing away from Emma's thinning nose, slitted eyes, and actively pinching hands. "We can work together!"

"Get," Emma hissed between pressed-together teeth, "out."

Drew scuttled away. "Think about it!" he yelled over his shoulder before disappearing into the crowd of cheering Founders and Tancol students. Sara and Ethan teleported into the room a second later, having just secured second place. Sara grinned and waved at Emma cheerily as she saw them. Ethan just puffed his bangs out of his eyes.

After the Dungeon Simulation Tournament, Oliver and the rest of the Hutchites trudged down the hill for an early dinner.

Fifteen minutes later, when Makayla Grant stormed over from the Tancol table to bang her hand in front of Brantley, Oliver frowned.

NOVA 02

He'd initially tried ignoring her, but when she persisted and even went so far as to wave her arms in front of him, he turned his head to her.

"Yes, Makayla?" he asked, trying his hardest not to sound stiff. All around them, he allowed his *stratum silentii* working to collapse.

As always, it felt like a blanket being ripped off his skin. He wasn't the only one to wince at the ensuing noise that assaulted his ears—going from a relatively quiet conversation to a room bouncing with the ruckus of a hundred teenagers after a major tournament always strained the senses. Not four tables away, the entirety of Founders Hall sang Sara Reyes' name.

At the Hutch table, meanwhile, Emma, Lance, and the rest of the Hutchites looked toward Makayla—and then Brantley.

Brantley pulled at his collar, looking decidedly uncomfortable about his girlfriend's interruption. Oliver had been confirming everyone's after dinner search party routes—they'd all been hanging on to his every word ahead of another attempt to find the Fire Drake's Cavern painting.

They were just about to finish their planning, too, when Makayla began her shouting.

Not that she cared. Snarling, she slammed her notebook display on the table in front of Brantley and flipped her long braid of jet-black hair over her shoulder before finally crossing her arms.

"Have you seen the updated standings yet?" she hissed.

Oliver flicked his eyes over the notebook on the table but didn't bother reading the Magical Five Standings. He already knew what the scores were—and so did the extramen celebrating not too far away. By then they

* Chapter 37: The Original Sacred Beast *

were fawning over Ethan who, unlike Sara, ignored them entirely so that he could eat his dinner, which appeared to be four poached cod filets.

"Are you unhappy with Tancol's positioning?" Oliver offered Makayla as patiently as he could muster. "If that's all, we're a bit busy at the moment."

Makayla let out an indignant huff at the words and looked around at the older Hutchites, crossing her arms. "You're in fifth place *and* you let Founders win the Dungeon Sim Tournament—that's y'all's bread and butter, isn't it? For shame!" She paused to stare at Abe pointedly. Then, she turned back to Oliver. "And telling me you're *'busy.'* Aren't you getting too big for your britches?"

When Makayla finished, Emma let out an even louder huff than the Tancol captain had.

But before anybody else could join Emma in getting incensed, Oliver raised a hand for peace. He didn't even have to flare Wisdom.

"Yes, it is for shame," he acknowledged to Makayla, breaking out a light smile. The admission confused the girl, but he didn't stop there. "And you're also right that I'm probably throwing my weight around more than a hardmore should." He crinkled his grin even further before continuing. "But we've got stuff to do, so if you don't mind…"

With a shooing gesture from his fingers, he motioned for Makayla to leave.

On his shoulder, Roli squeaked with unrepressed jubilation. *"At long last, you assume the mantle of your title! YES! Command this girl in accordance with the stock of her peasantry! INSIST THAT SHE KNEEL BEFO—,"*

NOVA 02

Oliver stuffed a chunk of sweet potato into Roli's mouth.

Across the table, half of a laugh was frozen on Makayla's face. For a moment she stared from Oliver, to Roli, the other Hutchites, and then back again.

Eventually, she settled down next to Brantley, completely flustered. "Well alright then," she retorted. "What ch'all up to anyway?" she tried adding on in a would-be-dignified manner.

The table broke out into laughter, and more than a few looked to Oliver admiringly.

But the moment didn't last long.

"I'd also like to know what you children are up to," thundered a separate voice.

Oliver turned without flinching to face their second interruption of the night.

Dean Blackwood.

The evil man loomed directly behind Oliver's chair, standing tall and menacing. Even so, Oliver addressed the giant with the same smile he'd given Makayla. Blackwood couldn't surprise him anymore. Using *Nova's Touch,* he'd sensed the man marching over from the faculty table over thirty seconds prior.

"Well, Mr. García," Blackwood barked with a satisfied smile on his face. From the depths of his frock coat, he pulled out his annoying, small, black-framed mirror. Then he carried on speaking, more smugly than Oliver could ever remember—why was the man in such a good mood these days?

* Chapter 37: The Original Sacred Beast *

"Another detention for obscuring your betters from your play-acting, don't you think?" Blackwood suggested.

Everyone at the Hutch table groaned, throwing up their hands in rebellion.

Emma shot first, glaring with open disgust. "Remind me, *sir*—how is talking against the rules?"

"This again?" Lance agreed, exchanging seething looks with Brantley across a bowl of mashed potatoes.

"Sir," Lizzie began, last of all. Oliver had to double-take to make sure she was actually the one speaking up to Blackwood. Normally, she played things safe around the faculty. "We were just going over our exam schedules… you understand… lots to… prepare for…"

Lizzie's voice trailed off. With her eyes and brow drawn down in confusion, she turned her head to stare at a growing commotion sounding off from the direction of Tolteca's foyer towards the exit.

Oliver drew his attention to the noise, too, spreading *Nova's Touch* towards the foyer and beyond.

"What's going on?" Emma asked, tugging on Oliver's sleeve.

Oliver stood on his tip toes to get a better look—*Nova's Touch* hadn't reached the foyer yet.

Even Blackwood had turned to glower at whoever decided to interrupt his handing out of detentions.

To Oliver's disbelief, Professor Desmoulins was the source of the noise. When he charged into the Dining Hall, however, he didn't come alone. A small crowd of jabbering students had followed him, along with the oldest giant eagle Oliver had ever seen.

"Broderick!" Desmoulins shouted. "You must come right away!"

Oliver stared at Desmoulins in disbelief. What on Earth had made the wiry man stumble into the Dining Hall with an awestruck look on his normally aloof face?

"What," Blackwood began, accentuating each word with pointed looks at the growing crowd around them. "Are-you-doing-Dionysos?" By then, a circle, three deep in every direction, had formed to ogle at the source of the noise.

"Everyone!" Desmoulins shouted, seemingly delirious. He spun around in a spiral to look around the room at large, ignoring Blackwood. Then he pointed at the ancient eagle that had walked in with him on its hind legs. "Niamh the Great has just informed me that a *griffin* is flying over our grounds at this very moment!"

A silent few seconds trickled by as the room digested Desmoulins' words. Vaguely, Oliver remembered Desmoulins' lessons on griffins. What was a rare sacred beast doing at Tenochprima?

Then pandemonium ensued.

"I don't believe it," Roli said, speaking with a level of reverence Oliver didn't know the iguana was capable of. *"If this is true, we must head outside* **at once."**

"What the devil do you mean by a griffin?" Blackwood snarled, grabbing Desmoulins by the shoulders.

* Chapter 37: The Original Sacred Beast *

"No way!" Abe shouted, mirroring Desmoulins oddly dreamy expression. Without another word, he leapt from his chair and sprinted towards Tolteca's foyer with Lizzie and several older students just behind him. Without a word, Lance and Elton then followed, too.

Oliver hurried after them next, pulling on Emma's arm so she'd be with him. "I dunno what's going on," he said in her ear as they jockeyed between dozens of other students to get outside first. "But this must be something big if the kids who grew up on This Side of the Key are so interested."

"No kidding," Emma whispered back, staring around in amazement as students of every dorm pushed and shoved their way outside.

When they all clambered on the lawn past the statues guarding the way back inside, they found Abe pointing towards the top of Founders Temple, jumping up and down with unrestrained, boyish glee. Desmoulins of all people was next to him, hopping just as exuberantly.

"There hasn't been a sighting in the Americas in living memory!" Desmoulins shouted above all the noise.

Oliver stared at the man curiously before venturing a look up to where they stared. He knew Desmoulins was their Flora and Fauna teacher, so the man likely *did* care about things like rare sacred beasts. But still. Oliver had never expected a supporter of *The Damned* to be this giddy about anything. As far as he was concerned, jumping up and down like an excited kid was too human of a reaction for somebody who supported mass incarceration and murder.

"Nobody can predict their movement!" Desmoulins went on, oblivious to Oliver's attention. In between sentences, he put a hand over his mouth to stifle disbelieving laughter. "To see one in the flesh is just..." He laughed again, nonplussed.

The crowd gasped a second later when the griffin dove to land on top of Founders.

"What's it doing?" Abe asked Desmoulins, going shrill.

Shoving aside several students, Blackwood joined Abe and Desmoulins to look up at the beast. "Looks like the thing is taking a damn nap."

Oliver squinted trying to see what the griffin looked like. It had long wings and a beak of some sort, but it was far larger than a giant eagle. Almost like a runt osorius with wings.

"Do not approach her!" a familiar voice warned them all telepathically. Then, Archie descended from the skies to join the ancient giant eagle Desmoulins had called Niamh.

Niamh screeched in agreement, shushing the crowd. *"Lest she decide to leave,"* he said between flaps of his great wings.

"We will approach her ourselves," Archie continued. Like everyone else, he stared up at the griffin. When Oliver checked their private mental connection, all he could feel was a sense of stunned disbelief mixed with... was that anxiety?

"Should she have a purpose for her visit, we will communicate it to the faculty," Archie finished.

By then, the rest of the teachers had shown up.

"Count your lucky stars, kids," Zapien said loud enough for everyone to hear.

* Chapter 37: The Original Sacred Beast *

"What's it doing here professor?" Sara Reyes asked Zapien. For once she didn't look cheery as she stared skyward along with everybody else.

Zapien could only laugh in the same childish way Desmoulins had. "Who knows?" she replied. "Any thoughts Archie? Niamh? When was the last time either of you saw one?"

"Well, I can't remember too precisely," Archie tried saying.

"Deceit is beneath a Tlamacaz!" Niamh scolded. And, for a moment, Oliver worried the eagle might attack Archie—such was the rage in the bird's eyes. *"You,"* Niamh went on, looking directly at Archie, *"coordinated this griffin's last encounter with humankind, did you not? **You** facilitated her conversation with Augustus on his deathbed."*

Oliver stopped looking at the griffin to turn and gape at Archie. Next to him, Emma and Lance gasped, too.

"Wouldn't you have liked to be privy to that conversation?" a final voice insisted. Amidst all the ruckus, Oliver had let *Nova's Touch* slip away. So, when he turned to find Watkin staring right at him, he jumped with shock. From fewer than four yards away, Watkin waggled his eyebrows at a frightening pace. "They're said," he went on, pointing up at the griffin, "to only bring wisdom to those who *deserve* it."

Then he pointed at Oliver.

NOVA 02

Chapter 38: Truth and Injustice

It's been over a month in these cold, God-forsaken mountains, and I haven't heard a peep from the detection tool. I may double back to check out the temple in Tennessee and see if there are any hints before I head too far up past West Virginia and into Pennsylvania.

2nd of April, the third year of the 10th Age

"Any word from the griffin?" Oliver asked in a hushed tone.

"OHHH!" the crowd roared before Watkin could answer. They sat in the ninth row of the dueling pit's bleachers, watching the final duel of the group stage. Three versus three. Hutch VS Champayan. After tonight, each dorm would select their two soloists for the playoffs.

Watkin pressed his eyes shut, squeezing hard as though he were silencing the noise of the crowd in front of them.

Oliver turned to watch the match. Watkin would answer when he felt like it.

On the ornate marble strip, Beto landed in a puff of smoke, having just twisted in mid-air to dodge a destruction technique launched by Emma. It was the same one she'd projected onto Lance during their practices in the dueling simulator, and she was *furious* Beto had dodged it.

Oliver was, too. Emma had fired the technique off perfectly, even waiting for Beto to be in the air to do it. But Beto had seen it coming and

* Chapter 38: Truth and Injustice *

twisted with a wrench of Power Oliver couldn't help but admire. Up until Beto started simpering in satisfaction.

With a powerful blast of sword essence from his scimitar, Beto took charge of the duel. His technique hummed in the air, strong and resolute like the actual weapon that remained in his hand as it streaked towards Lance, Emma's remaining teammate.

Oliver put his head in his hands. Lance was being distracted by Cristina with a murder of pecking crows, so Lance wouldn't see the sword essence technique coming. And Oliver didn't like Lance's chances of shrugging off a direct attack from Beto.

Last year Beto made it all the way to the final as Founders' second seed. He'd done that as an extraman, an accomplishment that had earned him a trophy and a publicity piece over the summer. Eventually, of course, he'd lost to his crazy cousin John in the final, but this year he looked as good as his cousin, two years ahead of schedule. Oliver shook his head as he watched the boy twist, turn, and command his Power at a level nobody else in their year could. Except for maybe Oliver.

"OOOOO!" the crowd exclaimed as Lance flew out of the dueling strip, landing on all fours onto a bed of spawning pillows.

"At least he took out James," Oliver offered to Watkin, ignoring the pang of shame he felt for his friend. Everyone knew it'd be Abe and Emma taking the two Hutch seeds for the playoffs, leaving none for Lance.

Watkin blinked several times before addressing Oliver. "Lance could take on anyone and anything if he believed in himself."

"*Thank* you!" Oliver said raising an emphatic hand. "I told him the same thing."

Watkin took out his pocket watch from his frock coat. Then, frowning, he snapped the two golden clasps shut and turned to Oliver with raised eyebrows. "To answer your earlier question, we haven't heard a word from our new friend, the griffin. The quetzal, osori, and aetus have each approached with their own delegations and offerings. Radio silence."

"Aetus?" Oliver asked.

Watkin blinked at him. Just blinked. "Are you truly incapable of contextually determining which sacred beast calls itself the Aetus?"

"Okaaaay," Oliver drew out, his cheeks flushing. "The giant eagles, then."

Watkin still looked disappointed but didn't say anything else. Instead, he put his watch away, but this time in his pocket dimension, not his coat.

"What?" he asked at Oliver's look. "I've got to practice, too!"

Oliver lifted his hands in frustration. "So the griffin's just gonna ignore us all forever?"

Watkin considered the remark but then shook his head. "I'd agree with you, but by Jaiba's estimates, we agree with Blackwood's coarse conclusion."

"Which is?" Oliver asked.

"The griffin simply appears to be sleeping."

"Sleeping?"

* Chapter 38: Truth and Injustice *

Watkin nodded. "She harkens from the days of the Egyptian pyramids, if not further. To someone so ancient, taking a nap must hardly be considered a waste of time."

Oliver shifted in his seat. "Do *we* have time to wait? If Niamh wasn't lying, and the griffin spoke with Augustus all those years ago, we need to know what they talked about."

"I remember," Watkin admitted, leaning back in his seat with his hands on the pommel of his staff. "Anything Augustus might have shared with the griffin will be worth hearing—of that, there is no doubt."

Oliver waited for the 'but' he knew was coming by taking his own turn at blinking.

Watkin conceded with a grin and a tilt of admission. *"But,"* he said, "we already know the task ahead of us, regardless of what knowledge the griffin possesses. And besides, for all we know, she's merely settled down for a brief respite on her way to Argentina."

"You don't really believe that," Oliver said, grinning in turn. He knew he was right. *Nova's Touch* made him keenly aware of how casually Watkin had delivered the throwaway comment.

"Never mind the griffin," Watkin said, keeping his eyes on the duel. "What about your missing painting?"

Oliver let out a breath. "We could use some direction there," he answered, quieter than before. Then, a desperate thought came to him, and he laughed, pointing back at Founders Temple. "Hey, maybe I should just climb up and ask the griffin if she knows where it is."

NOVA 02

Watkin's shoulders bobbed up and down as he chuckled, and, for a moment, they watched the rest of the duel unfold. Only Emma remained on the Hutch team, and she was on the defensive as a constant stream of attacks came from Beto and Cristina.

The sight darkened Oliver's mood significantly.

Watkin nodded. "Not to further dampen your spirits, but your instincts regarding timing are spot on. You should know seven more individuals have disappeared from the broader Goodwin Forest area."

"What?" Oliver hissed. "Seven?!" He looked at Watkin, his eyes widening every second. "We haven't heard a thing since Lalandra... Lance was even starting to hope *The Damned* had nothing to do with it."

Watkin set his jaw. "You've not heard anything because these seven victims were from the Original Side of the Key."

Oliver was too stunned for words. His mind reeled at the idea. When Dave and Elodie had first shown him an image of a pesadriya, he'd assumed the legend about the monsters turning captured souls into other pesadriyas was just that: a legend. The image from the medieval tapestry came back to his head now, unbidden and unwelcome, like a seared brand on his brain. One pesadriya went through a portal, and two came back. Oliver could hear the sniffing, clicking and screeching in his mind, even in the middle of a roaring crowd.

"Is that even possible?" he finally breathed back towards Watkin. He looked around to make sure nobody watched them, feeling stupid the second he did—*Nova's Touch* was the better way to check his surroundings

Chapter 38: Truth and Injustice

now. "Do you think the monster in Goodwin Forest is a pesadriya traveling between dimensions?"

"It must be," Watkin answered grimly, his smile forgotten.

Oliver gulped. "Then that means it's victims will turn into…"

The crowd ooed one last time, announcing the end of the duel as Emma collapsed just outside the strip.

Watkin stood, returning Oliver's attention to their conversation. "You must find that painting," he said. "Search every room yourself if you must—mobilize everyone you **trust**."

Oliver caught himself before dropping his jaw. That was the second time Watkin had gotten the word **trust** to hang in the air long after it'd been spoken. Unless he was mistaken, a deeper form of magic was at play, and this time he wasn't going to let it sneak past him.

"Professor," he began, "a couple times now, first in your office a few months back, and just now, you've said something unusual where your words have almost, I dunno, stuck around? It's like they're still in the air."

Watkin suppressed a grin. "Have they?" he asked, brushing away invisible objects from the air. "Must be the humidity." He winked as he walked away.

Oliver growled. "Professor, no more secrets remember?" He didn't care if he raised his voice. They'd been under a modified form of *stratum silentii* since the moment they'd sat down.

Watkin waved over his shoulder without looking back. "I've already teased you about the subject—benign neglect, remember? It'll be much more fun if you figure it out for yourself, don't you think?"

NOVA 02

Oliver shook his head. He knew Watkin well enough by now. If the man wasn't ready to share, Oliver'd have better luck getting Ms. Joan to reveal her secret eggnog recipe.

And besides, Emma needed his support at the moment. She wouldn't take the loss well.

Down at the strip he saw her exchanging murderous handshakes and 'good match's with Beto, Cristina, and James. Not wanting to make a scene with Beto, Oliver hung back, waiting a few moments before joining Lance to pat Emma on the back.

And then he saw Sara approach Emma, and he stopped halfway down the stairs.

"**Trust**…" he repeated, slow and stupid.

"Oli, if you don't get your skinny ass out of the way," Brantley said from behind.

But Oliver barely heard Brantley. An idea had just occurred to him. One that the Wisdom on the back of his neck *begged* him to act on.

"Sara!" Oliver shouted through the crowd.

Sara answered with a wave, cheery and breath-taking as ever. But she also cocked her head in confusion. "Oliver! What's going on?"

* Chapter 38: Truth and Injustice *

Up from the elevated dueling strip Emma hopped down, shooting a light puff of dust up into the air as she landed. "Yeah," she said, her tone icy. "What *is* going on, Oliver?"

At Sara's side, Drew also turned to face Oliver's voice. Slowly.

He'd been giving Lance pointers on his stone golem technique—"uh huh," Lance muttered over and over again—but when he heard Oliver's voice, the boy had stopped mid-sentence, the backs of his ears prickling.

"At last," Drew breathed, grinning at Oliver as though he were a piece of prized meat.

Oliver furrowed his eyebrows, caught off guard. Between Emma's towering mood and Drew's strangely satisfied grin, he no longer felt in control.

Shaking his head, he pressed forward anyway. Watkin's news was too concerning. "Look," he said leaning towards Sara and Drew, "we need y'all's help."

Drew chuckled. "Oh, we *know*. Have you seen these two duel?"

Had Emma been less mad, she likely would have slapped Drew. As it was, she appeared too angry to do anything but close her eyes, tighten her jaws, and flare her nostrils as she took in a deep breath.

From the floor where he'd been sitting with his head in his hands, Lance looked up, a dangerous sharpness in his eyes. "Oliver, what the heck are you talking about? I don't need dueling advice from a bunch of—,"

"Not dueling advice," Oliver rushed in. "No, we need help finding something."

Emma breathed out an audible "ohhh" as Oliver leaned closer still.

NOVA 02

Lance just scratched his head. "Huh?"

A sigh from Lance's vacated spot on the side of the dueling strip drew Oliver's attention to the third member of Sara's wacky crew. Ethan gathered himself and stood from a sitting position. Between the ambling, departing crowd, and the Champayan delegation that had swarmed Beto and Cristina, Oliver hadn't seen Ethan sitting next to Lance.

When the boy sighed again, Oliver winced—what if he'd been an enemy?

"What are we looking for?" Ethan asked, his eyes dull.

"Have you seen a painting of a red temple anywhere on campus?"

Lance's jaw slackened when he finally caught on.

Oliver nodded at all of them in turn, firm and resolute. The time had come to **trust** those he knew deserved it.

"You sure looked ticked back there," Lance taunted Emma when they entered Hutch's foyer.

Oliver paused on the stairs to look back down at Emma's reaction.

She looked dangerous as she glared daggers at Lance. But, then again, she didn't look up at Oliver any.

Smelling blood, Lance pulled on a smile that reminded Oliver of Stevie at her most mischievous.

* Chapter 38: Truth and Injustice *

"Uh huh," Lance said. "Just mad about the duel, was it? Nothing to do with Oliver getting up and close to Sara?"

Oliver looked down at them with a lopsided grin. On the one hand, letting the conversation play out would be fun—Emma *had* been jealous back at the strip. And how often did she give them such a golden opportunity to tease her over her principles. She hadn't talked to them for weeks back in the fall after they'd "let her down" over their fawning. Had it been jealousy all along, and not just about *doing the right thing*?

But Watkin's Goodwin Forest news burned too fiercely in Oliver's consciousness.

"Look, guys," he said, dropping his half-baked smile, "Watkin just told me—,"

"Oi!" a voice shouted from the top of the stairs.

They all looked up to see Brantley screech to a halt on the landing at the above them. "Y'all better get upstairs," he drawled in an annoyed voice. "Blackwood's just published the dueling playoff seeds and *none* of us are happy about it."

A blur of green shot to a halt at Brantley's feet.

"I smell drama," Roli announced. He held his chin out proudly as he surveyed them for several seconds with his dewlap fully extended. Then, with a twitch, he launched himself onto Oliver's shoulder.

Oliver flared Power to enforce his skin as the iguana landed, avoiding cuts or scrapes. Privately, he relayed Watkin's news about the seven new Goodwin Forest disappearances.

"Tell Emma and Lance, too, please."

NOVA 02

"Command me, coward."

Oliver rolled his eyes. "I'm getting better at it—remember Makayla?"

"Yes, and I must prepare you to lead like a deity. To date, you have more in common with an unsupervised chimpanzee."

Oliver turned his head so Roli could see him roll his eyes all the way into the back of his head, and then he took the stairs right behind Brantley.

At the top of the stairs in the Hutch common room, a knot of students surrounded one of the larger magical mirrors. Every single person in the crowd, from Valerie to Elton, either shouted or gesticulated at a short list on the screen.

When Oliver, Emma, and Lance entered after Brantley, the ruckus stopped.

Then Elton pushed Abe out of the crowd, too angry for words himself.

Abe winced at the push. But his momentarily pained expression was nothing compared to the grimace that followed when he locked eyes with Emma.

"What?" Oliver asked.

"Welllll," Abe said sheepishly, "the good news is Blackwood's given us second seed!"

Emma's eyes widened as she rushed Abe, her anger forgotten. "That's great news!" she shouted, jumping up and down. "I thought he'd give Cristina second seed!"

"Hmm," Roli said for everyone to hear. *"That man relishes petty maneuvers."*

Lance leered in suspicious agreement. "What's the catch?"

Chapter 38: Truth and Injustice

Abe coughed, taking a step back from Emma. "Well, Blackwood, you see, he uh—,"

"HE'S PLACED YOU SEVENTH, EMMA!" Elton roared.

Oliver winced as understanding dawned on him.

"So that means…" Emma said, processing the news.

"No," Lance jeered, dashing up to the mirror. "He wouldn't."

Lizzie stepped out of the crowd to sidle up next to Abe. "Yep," she said. "Blackwood's got Hutch 1 facing Hutch 2 in round one. Pretty much guarantees we lose the playoffs."

"Not just the dueling playoffs either," Joel said dejectedly from next to Elton—he consoled his friend with pats on the back. "The whole tournament, really."

The room went silent as everyone stared at either Emma or Abe.

Eventually, Abe let out a humorless laugh. "We'll just have to go all out, Em," he said. "Let's give 'em a show and make anyone scared at the prospect of facing whichever one of us wins."

"If Lalandra were still here," Se'Vaughn grumbled, "Blackwood wouldn't have seeded us against ourselves—it's corrupt."

Emma shook her head, too angry again for a full sentence. Oliver only heard snippets of her thoughts, like "unjust" and "evil." The rest didn't make it past her clamped jaw.

With a start, Oliver realized Abe was staring at him now.

"Now listen here, Oli," he said, narrowing his eyes. "No training up Emma with top secret Trinova magic, you hear? I know you've been having Watkin lessons, but those are for you *only!*"

NOVA 02

Thunk.

Every head in the room snapped towards the stairs.

Watkin stood there, both hands on the pommel of his staff.

Abe staggered back. "Unless, of course," he stammered, "you meant for all of us to learn from Oliver?"

Watkin smiled affectionately at Abe, twinkling his eyes. "Eventually," he said, stepping into the room with several clunks of his staff, "my wish is for Oliver's lessons to trickle down onto all of you. Or at least those of you who would remain loyal to him."

"Or those I'd **trust**," Oliver countered, feeling confident about his choice. He didn't know why he knew he was right—all he knew was he couldn't be wrong. Not when his wisdom was buzzing this much on his neck.

Watkin's smile grew as the word hung in the air, just as it had in the man's office before Christmas. Only then, it had been Watkin to perform the cryptic bit of magic. Now, it was Oliver doing the advanced working. The only problem was, he had no idea how he was doing it. Even so, he'd done something only Watkin could do, and he'd be willing to bet Augustus' ring or Madeline's necklace that he was figuring something out ahead of Watkin's secret schedule.

"Indeed," Watkin agreed. His face twitched as he tried keeping his excitement constrained.

To Oliver's annoyance, Elton gave the man a way out.

* Chapter 38: Truth and Injustice *

"Hang on," Elton said, glaring at Watkin. "You can't just attack our loyalty like that. Of course we're going to stick by Oliver—no matter what happens."

Watkin didn't look moved. "Oh to be so young and optimistic about the follies of human nature," he admonished. "But I digress. Oliver, Emma, Lance. Could you come with me, please?"

He hefted his staff, motioning for Oliver, Emma, and Lance to follow him. Oliver didn't hesitate, nodding and stepping past the man down the stairs without question. If Watkin wanted to talk again so soon after just having had a conversation, it could only be important.

He stopped halfway down the stairs when he heard Watkin address the Hutchites remaining in the room.

"Loyalty comes cheap when the stakes are low," Watkin said in a solemn voice. "When *The Damned* returns, and you hear your family's screams, will you swear fealty to Oliver the same way you do now?"

Silent, determined faces followed. But Watkin hadn't finished.

"If you can manage it," he went on, tightening his silk belt, "you'll have already outperformed your parents."

NOVA 02

Chapter 39: Providence Foretold

Tío said he checked out the Tennessee temple long ago, but maybe there's a map laying around in its foyer or something that can show me where to find the Sage's Sanctum.

7th of April, the third year of the 10th Age

"Another lesson, professor?" Lance asked half-way up the ridge.

Watkin shook his head. "Not quite." He hadn't spoken much since leading them outside, but none of them had tried too hard to break the silence.

"Professor," Emma said, "what'd you mean by outperforming our parents back there? Did you know some of our parents or something when you were at school?"

Watkin angled his head left and right a few times, debating a reply. "I didn't know any of them directly, no," he finally said. "But let us quicken the pace. More important news awaits us up ahead." Without revealing anything, he sped up to take the lead at the front of their party, beckoning for them to match his pace.

Emma and Roli began whispering to each other heatedly, with Roli going so far to spring onto her shoulder from Oliver's. Oliver didn't mind. His own thoughts were all over the place and he needed time to think.

* Chapter 39: Providence Foretold *

He still hadn't had the chance to debrief with Emma and Lance on the new Goodwin Forest kidnappings. The news itched at him, urging him to scream or at least start searching for the painting of the Fire Drake's Cavern.

He took a deep breath and exhaled, calming himself. Worrying about the news was a waste of time—Watkin wanted to talk about something, and they'd have to wait and see what it was in the man's office. Maybe Watkin was finally ready to teach him the pulsing technique? It was the last thing on his list after having improved *Nova's Touch* so much. Maybe he'd finally—

A tug on his shirt drew his attention to Lance.

"What?"

Lance didn't answer directly. Instead, he pointed to something in the distance behind them.

Oliver followed the finger to the top of Founders' Temple. Though the feathered serpent statue leered across the grounds, Oliver noticed what was missing at once.

The griffin was gone.

"So much for that," he sighed.

Lance sounded glum as he agreed. "Man, I really thought we'd get some good news from her." Then, he glanced ahead to Watkin. "Let's hope maybe Watkin's got some *good* news for us instead."

With every step up the ridge, and every stair up the brick-laden Academic Building, Oliver's mood fell more and more. What if they couldn't find The Fire Drake's Cavern in time? What if *The Damned* busted out of the Sage's Sanctum before they recovered Cuahtemoc's artifact? He felt a flicker of irritation as Watkin allowed him to pass into his classroom first. He didn't know why, but he wanted to remove Augustus' ring and hurl it away out of frustration—at least Madeline's necklace boosted his Courage. So far his Wisdom had felt unchanged. He was sure it was because Wisdom was his strongest Gift, but that didn't make it any less annoying. He'd need every advantage he could get to have a chance against Solomon Tupper, and now, even the griffin had abandoned him. What else would abandon him before the end? Based on Watkin's little speech back at Hutch, his friends might jump ship the second things got tough. But that didn't—

Oliver's entire mind froze when he looked up to survey Watkin's classroom.

There, at the back of the veranda, stood the griffin. She was staring right at him.

The griffin's mind flooded Oliver's, scrambling his sense of self until he had enough wherewithal to flare Wisdom and recompose himself. Even then, the warm presence of her mind wrung his brain, crashing against his conscious with waves of an emotion he couldn't understand.

If he compared the feeling to something that he, a human, could feel, he'd call it love.

Or peace.

* Chapter 39: Providence Foretold *

Something like those two, but stronger. Much stronger. Strong enough to where he was convinced he could reach out with *Nova's Touch* and hold onto it.

Not that he would. Despite his Wisdom, he cowered under the griffin's mind. Who was he to a presence like that? Could a human keep up?

No. But a Trinova might. So, Oliver stepped forward.

The griffin regarded him with amber eyes past a beak of iridescent gold. Oliver stiffened as she took him into her sight, avoiding eye-contact with her face, where her toffee feathers grew shorter than the rest of her body. Instead, he focused on the wings furled onto her back. Without measuring, he knew they'd span as far as a giant eagle's. And the rest of her? Her fierce claws, lion's torso, and knotted muscles made it plain she could go toe-to-toe with any osorius.

When she eventually spoke, Oliver's commitment to speak with her wavered as his sense of self threatened to fade. Flaring Bravery, he locked his jaw and met the creature's gaze anyway.

"Approach me, arbiter," the griffin sang.

Unsure of what he'd been called, Oliver shuffled all the way forward until he'd joined her in the terrace. Then, not wanting to insult her, he took a knee and bowed.

"My name is Oliver García."

"Always the same," the griffin replied, cocking her head to its side. *"How many times must I meet you before you remember the touch of my soul?"*

NOVA 02

Oliver's breath escaped him, along with all of Lalandra's diplomacy training. "I-I'm sorry," he stammered, "but have we met before? I *definitely* would have remembered."

The griffin let out a tinkle of unadulterated laughter that brought a tear to Oliver's eyes—could humans ever laugh like that? Had they, at one point in the distant past?

"I've known you every millennia since man first discovered magic in Mesopotamia."

Oliver's heart quickened. So, he had understood correctly.

Evidently, so had Archie. Not four yards away, Archie's mandibles clicked open, stunned and out of order.

"Every second we speak to this being is priceless, you understand?" Roli hissed in Oliver's head. *"Her legacy extends past your entire species."*

"I will admit, however," the griffin went on, prowling in Archie's direction, *"this is my first time meeting you as a hatchling."*

Archie collapsed under the griffin's direct attention, resting his entire upper half on the tile floor of Watkin's terrace.

"What may I call you?" Oliver asked, still on his knee.

The griffin pounced so quickly that they were eye to eye, inches apart, before he could even blink.

He shuddered under her scrutiny.

"Would you presume to understand my name?" she asked, backing off and settling onto her hind legs.

Oliver gulped in relief at the distance she'd created. "Probably not," he offered.

"I am here to deliver a message."

* Chapter 39: Providence Foretold *

"From Augustus?"

Again, the griffin let out a pure laugh. *"Yes."*

While Oliver's insides scrambled, thinking of the potential secret message that would come, the griffin stared him down. What would Augustus have figured out later in his life that he felt needed to be shared outside of the meeting they already had in Snowgem?

"Would you like to hear it?" the griffin asked, curving her beak into a smile.

"Of course!"

"Reach for influence from the source and will it so."

Oliver opened his mouth to ask, "come again?" but *Nova's Touch* alerted him to somebody else's reaction. Behind him, further into the classroom, Watkin hissed something under his breath that sounded like "of course."

"At least that meant something to somebody," Roli grumbled. *"Ask her for more."*

"Is that it?" Oliver asked as politely as he could. "What does it mean?"

"It is impossible for me to know," the griffin answered, sounding playful again.

"Keep at it!" Roli demanded.

Oliver blanched. "I would, uh, welcome your wisdom in this, umm, regard."

The griffin smiled again, this time settling down on all fours, even perching her beak on her stacked front paws. *"From the beginning,"* she said, *"man sought corruption. Your race has been stripped of its sacrality for a long, long time. How could I understand the meaning of your forefathers? The comings and goings of humans are unto me as your own are unto the push and pull of the moon. Neither can make sense of the other's station."*

NOVA 02

Roli patted Oliver on the shoulder consolingly. *"I am outmatched. This bag of feathers speaks in riddles only Augustus would understand. You're on your own."*

Oliver gulped as the griffin stared him down. He felt desperate, no clue as to what to say. Up until Madeline's necklace hummed on his neck.

A spark of Bravery took hold of him. "I'm unsure of what this Wisdom offers me," he said, feeling rejuvenated. "What else can you tell me?"

The griffin cocked her head as if she were explaining something painfully obvious. *"Only humans and dragons succumbed to the corruptive influence of magic. Four other sacred beasts never fell from grace. Do you not understand? I wouldn't presume to know the intent of the message I delivered because it was shared by man for man to hear. I do not know corruption as you do."*

Oliver risked a look at Archie. Was he understanding any of this?

But Archie was still bowing, and, if Oliver wasn't mistaken, trembling?

"I will consider the message," Oliver said, feeling disappointed. Then he remembered his manners and tilted his head into another bow. "Thank you for delivering it."

"You hunger for more clarity," the griffin stated.

Oliver took the invitation without shame, scratching the back of his neck like Santiago would. "I just wanted a little more wisdom for the present, that's all. That message from Augustus will give me plenty to think about… but if it's not too much to ask, could you give me some advice for a current problem I've got?"

"Every moment I spend with you is a danger to me. Speak if you must but do so quickly."

* Chapter 39: Providence Foretold *

"Okay... I need help finding a painting. It leads to a temple that Augustus, Madeline, and Cuahtemoc built. They left a gift for me there... it's supposed to help me fight *The Damned*."

The griffin blinked at him.

"He's, umm, a bad guy. Went full evil more than a decade ago? You know about him? A decade, that's, umm, ten years for us..."

The griffin fluffed her wings playfully. *"I agreed to deliver this message despite its negative influence on my essence because the corruption you wield is pure in intent. Do you understand, Trinova?"*

Oliver nodded, but more out of habit than understanding.

"The same cannot be said about your foe. Or even your allies. The only protection available to mankind is a maintained balance of intent, which is a burden you alone can bear once a millennia. You serve as the sole harbinger of pure intent—your existence is what keeps your race from its demise. Should you fail to maintain that balance, I fear the age of man will face the same disastrous end as the dragons."

Oliver gulped again, looking around the rest of the room for help.

But then the griffin's joyous tone returned, re-drawing Oliver's attention before anyone could even give him a thumbs up. *"This very evening you demonstrated the purity of your intent. You spoke of* **Truth** *did you not? Already you become an arbiter of virtue.* **Trust** *in your allies as your race once did, and as only you can, unencumbered by the shackles of your species' self-inflicted corruption. Only then will you find your painting."*

Oliver's jaw fell. The griffin was only talking to him because he'd made the word **Truth** hang in the air. His neck cracked as he swiveled to look at Watkin again.

NOVA 02

The history professor avoided his eyes, staring fixatedly at the griffin. Eye-contact or not, Oliver took a moment to size the man up. Had he known what he was toying with when he'd gotten **Truth** to hang in the air? Had he been planning for Oliver to use the same cryptic magic as him all along? Had the man even predicted this conversation with the griffin? If so, Watkin's Wisdom would be operating at a level that exceeded Lalandra's, even Augustus'.

Finally, Watkin met his eyes. And there… Oliver saw what looked like nerves. The sight of them calmed Oliver's own within seconds. No, Watkin didn't know what was going on either.

A scratching noise brought Oliver's attention back to the griffin.

When he saw what she was doing, his heart fell. From the tile floor, she'd launched herself onto the wrought-iron railing at the rear.

"Farewell, arbiter," she sang, as peaceful as ever.

Oliver chased after her. "Hang on!" he shouted. "You mentioned me in the past? Have I ever failed before?"

A tear came to his eye again as she laughed for a third time. *"Of course,"* she said, looking at him with a pitying expression.

"Then why are you afraid for us now more than ever? If I make a habit of failing every thousand years, why's now such a big deal?"

"Because a forerunner of negative intent now walks the Earth alongside your positive influence. The last time man faced this challenge, your current predicament was the result, necessitating your balance. Were it to occur a second time, the result is of no doubt to any beast who can still claim the title of Sacred. Your corruption is at hand."

* Chapter 39: Providence Foretold *

Time stopped as the griffin fluffed her wings again, preparing to take off. Oliver couldn't believe what he'd heard—the stakes were so much higher than he even realized. If he failed now, it wouldn't just be a generation of humans to suffer, but all of humankind. Forever.

The pressure crippled him.

Then another voice joined the conversation. It was Watkin's, and the man sounded just as concerned as Oliver felt.

"Solomon Tupper can't be the first corruptive influence to face a Trinova!" the man yelled. "Oliver is right to ask—what drives your concern?"

The last Oliver heard from the griffin was her laughing voice as she launched off the railing into the night sky. *"The pursuit of corruption does not threaten you nearly as much as the corruption itself. Should The Damned convince the public to embrace corruptive intent on a global scale, his influence will outmatch that of the Trinova's.* **Trust** *your Wisdom, Oliver García. You will need it before the end."*

NOVA 02

Chapter 40: Draconic Demise

Doubling back to Tennessee was definitely a mistake. Mountains I can handle. But cliffs? There's nothing but a vertical climb at the top of this mountain!

8th of April, the third year of the 10th Age

Before the griffin made it twenty yards, Watkin shot past Oliver back into the classroom with a burst of enforced speed. The movement alone fluttered the sheepskin covers of the books littered amongst the shelving. Oliver followed the man inside, entering just as Watkin squeaked to a halt at the edge of his viewing pedestal. Normally, the man used the floating platform to display famous historical battles or cities, but now he used it to do something Oliver didn't even know was possible.

Placing his hands on the device, Watkin took a deep breath, and flooded energy inside it. A rush of green liquid leaked out of his skin, trickling towards the pedestal, and before long the entire device shone and began displaying an uncanny site—at least to Oliver's eyes. It was Watkin's memory of Oliver conversing with the griffin, giving Oliver an uncanny look at what his side-profile looked like.

When Oliver stepped close to the projection, Watkin barely registered him a glance, focusing instead on the replaying conversation.

"We will be re-watching this conversation for the rest of our lives," Roli muttered in everyone's heads.

* Chapter 40: Draconic Demise *

"What just happened?" Emma asked, loud and mirthful. She stepped up to the other side of the viewing pedestal and snapped her fingers unapologetically. "Did anybody understand a lick of that."

Watkin hesitated but then obliged anyway. "Having a conversation with a griffin is as concerning as I anticipated it would be. We may as well have been ants conversing with cats about the intricacies of grooming fur coats. An ant's purpose in scope differs so much from that of the cat's—how could it ever understand the need to groom fur?"

Lance opened his mouth to contribute, but then closed it, shaking his head instead and collapsing into a chair next to Emma.

"So, we get *nothing* out of that?" Emma asked, waving her hands in the air. "What the heck is an arbiter? Or a forerunner?"

Oliver's anxiety hadn't been helped by the conversation, so he found himself nodding along.

"Reach to the source and will it so," the griffin's voice repeated on the replay. Watkin paused it, snapping his fingers.

"Roli is correct—we'll likely be dissecting what she said for the rest of our lives. You,"—he pointed at Oliver— "serving as a harbinger of pure intent is particularly interesting."

"And what about Tupper?" Oliver interjected. "She called him something similar, right?"

Clearing his throat, Lance nodded. "A 'forerunner' of corrupt intent."

Oliver, and then Emma, turned to look at him, impressed.

Lance put his head into his hands and began rubbing. "I just have a good memory. None of that meant diddly-squat to me."

NOVA 02

"I don't know what it means, either," Watkin admitted, half-laughing. "Tupper was self-made, so he couldn't exactly be a forerunner, could he?"

"And a forerunner of what, exactly?" Roli asked.

"Corruption," Watkin breathed. With an ominous gulp of his throat, he resumed the replay.

Emma tsked. "Is somebody gonna tell me what a forerunner is?"

"A harbinger," Watkin answered.

Emma kicked at a nearby table. "Go fish."

Watkin gestured at Oliver. "It means Tupper preceded the coming of Oliver—the griffin was indicating the two are linked together more than we realized."

Emma furrowed her eyebrows, confusion taking over her annoyance. But when she spoke again, she looked at Oliver, not Watkin. "Is that what was she saying about having met you before?"

"Maybe past lives of the Trinova?" Lance asked.

Oliver could only shrug. "Like I have a clue? I've never felt anybody else's thoughts in my head."

"Eh-hem," Roli interrupted.

"Maybe you could though?" Lance theorized, looking up excitedly.

Oliver shook his head. "The only bit of advice I got out of that is what Augustus asked her to tell me, right? She—the replay—just said it again. *'Reach for influence from the source and will it so.'"*

"I disagree," Watkin retorted, pausing the replay again. "Her advice on leaning into your pure intent, and **trust**, may be more prudent for our immediate focus."

* Chapter 40: Draconic Demise *

He shifted the replay to half of the board and pulled up a three-dimensional map of the campus grounds on the other half instead. Pointing at the Swampy Fortress to the west of the lagoons, he added, "if we spread the search out a bit, trusting your friends to help, we may find the painting… sooner…"

Watkin's pointing hand fell, along with his face.

"What?" Oliver asked, scared of how tired Watkin looked on the other side of the pedestal through the projection.

Watkin began to pace before he answered. "It was her words on the spread of corruption."

Chills took over Oliver at the reminder. If he understood the griffin correctly, then he needed to take out *The Damned* to save humankind forever, not just the present.

Watkin's staff clunked as the man walked around the floating board in circles. "It makes me worry about Tupper's escape. Could we have been missing the point all along? We thought Tupper's influence was limited to his capabilities as a human—but what if it goes deeper than that? Why mention the downfall of the dragons?"

He stopped pacing and looked up at Oliver. "We have to get you Cuahtemoc's artifact as soon as possible. Do you understand?"

Emma laughed out loud, drawing everybody's attention.

"What is it?" Watkin asked. "Are you grasping something I haven't?!" He stepped away from Oliver and closer to her, a panicked glint in his eye.

Emma smirked and crossed her arms. "Nope. It's just fun to see you as out of the loop as us for once."

NOVA 02

Watkin frowned, backing away. "Not for me."

"I'm not sure how I can trust anybody more than I already have," Oliver interrupted. "We've already got half of Hutch looking, and I just brought those three extramen onboard."

Emma's eyes bulged as Oliver spoke, but he ignored them.

"**Trust**," Watkin repeated, pondering the word as it hung in the air. He said it again a few more times before snapping his fingers for a second time.

"Augustus trusted *you* to find the Iguana's Scroll, Oliver, but erased the location of it from living memory. So, we can assume *he* couldn't trust anybody else. Perhaps that is our issue. Perhaps we need to think like Augustus and not like a Trinova."

"What are you even saying, man?" Lance asked, rubbing his forehead again. Then, he gulped, realizing what he'd said. "I mean, sir!"

"Yeah," Emma agreed. "You saying we're wrong to trust everyone at Hutch?"

Oliver shook his head and gestured at the night sky where the griffin had disappeared. "That can't be right. She *just* told me to trust everyone!"

"Yes!" Watkin said, approaching Oliver with a crazed look in his eye. "That is exactly right!" A wistful grin took over his face, and he even put a hand to his mouth. "We can trust you and you can trust us, Oliver, because you're the Trinova—you wield **Trust** with a pure intent none of us could ever hope to muster because you are greater than all of us!"

Oliver dismissed Watkin's words immediately with a grimace and a wave of his hand. "No, I'm not."

* Chapter 40: Draconic Demise *

"Oh yes, you are!" Watkin challenged. "Would you like to argue with the griffin about it?"

"I recommend we do not take that approach," Roli said earnestly. *"I gather she would not take to disagreement well."*

Emma gave Roli a nonplussed look before picking up the conversation. "So…" she drew out, thinking out loud, "Augustus wasn't pure enough? So, he knew he couldn't trust anyone?"

"Exactly!" Watkin shouted. He reeled away from Oliver with his hands in the air, shaking them as he stared up at the ceiling. "We've been tackling our problem the wrong way! Augustus elected not to trust anyone, so he hid the Iguana's Scroll. He must have done the same for the painting of the Fire Drake's Cavern!"

Lance scratched his head. "How does this help us find the painting? We already knew it's hidden…"

Watkin waggled his eyebrows snapping his gaze back down and onto them. "Because nobody *but* Oliver would ever remember seeing the painting even if they did ever stumble on it. Just like the Iguana's Scroll and the Temple Beneath the Willow, it's been erased from memory!"

Oliver, Emma, and Lance gasped at the same time.

"Precisely!" Watkin agreed. "Go! Ask your friends to search around the grounds, but not for a painting! We need to find anywhere anyone comes back from feeling like they just had a weird dream, or a moment of de-ja-vu!"

Emma and Lance stood up, ready to run the entire length of the grounds at once. But Oliver raised a hand to stop them.

"What about the rest of the griffin's message?" he asked. "What about *reaching for the source and willing it so?* What about the pure intent and the corruption she talked about?"

Roli nodded up and down from Oliver's shoulder, eager to discuss.

Watkin deliberated, moving his lips without uttering a sound for a few seconds before coming back down to Earth with a pensive expression. "Good and evil? Harbingers and forerunners? To be honest with you, finding the Fire Drake's Cavern strikes me as much more important. I worry we'll spend the rest of our lives trying to understand her meaning behind reaching for the source and willing anything whatsoever. What is the source? What are you trying to will?"

He placed a finger to his lips and tapped. "No, we can think on it later. That and her perspective on magic and its corruptive influence. I feel we have the measure of Augustus now, but as for the rest of it, we'd likely require the rest of our lives to begin scratching at the surface."

A snort of fire brought everyone's attention to Archie, but the flash disappeared just as quickly as it arrived.

Oliver peered at the shadows where his Guide lay hidden in the dark. Now that he thought about it, Archie hadn't said a word since the griffin left. But why? Normally he'd be the one telling Archie to stop rehashing important information over and over again.

* Chapter 40: Draconic Demise *

With a pained expression on his face, Watkin looked over Archie's silent, dark corner. Then, he flicked his wrist to turn on a quartz panel of soft yellow light that brought the veranda into view.

"Our most sincere apologies for not consulting you sooner, Archie. Did you have any insight to share? We should have sought your counsel first."

Archie huffed fire again, and from their mental bond, Oliver expected to feel anger, or at least frustration. With all the talk of sacred beasts, Watkin was right to cringe—they should have asked Archie for his opinion first.

But when Oliver's mind touched Archie's, the emotion radiating from the sacred beast surprised him. Was Archie afraid of something? Or just as concerned about Tupper as they were?

"It's really not that complicated," the feathered serpent retorted, his deep voice loftier than normal. *"As a sacred beast—one who has admittedly seen far fewer summers than the griffin—her meaning is not as lost on me as it is you. Each remaining sacred beast maintains its sacrality for having never sought out magic's corruptive influence. To date, only two of the original six species have fallen."*

Archie's words forced the memory of the griffin's presence back into Oliver's mind. He thought back on it, remembering how *heavy* her mind had felt. Only it hadn't concerned him—if anything, he'd found it comforting. Was that the effect of the griffin's sacredness? Whatever that meant?

"So, us humans," Oliver said tentatively, "we used to be, but aren't sacred anymore?" He looked to Watkin for confirmation, but Watkin kept his eyes down, his brow furrowed as he took a seat on the edge of the pedestal, thinking hard.

"And dragons?" Emma tried prodding out of Archie.

NOVA 02

Lance choked on his spit. "Wait—dragons are real? I thought they were just myths! Like a bedtime story to scare kids!"

Emma raised her hands and started to laugh. "Now you better behave, Lance, or else a dragon MIGHT SWOOP DOWN AND EAT YA!"

Archie grunted. *"You humans may have used the legend to instill discipline in your children, but we sacred beasts view the tale of the dragons as a lesson in self-preservation for our adults. Up until the ninth age, dragons maintained their title as sacred. But they fell quicker and farther than man when your race seduced them towards corruption at the start of the first millennium."*

"The middle ages?" Roli asked. *"Augustus mentioned this time period quite frequently. But it predates all of us—how do you know of the dragons' downfall?"*

Archie scoffed, letting out more fire. *"I said it was a lesson for us feathered serpents, did I not? My sire lived during their downfall, and according to his wisdom, the dragons succumbed to corruption within a single generation of man's sharing it with them, destroying themselves completely. From what I gather, the last dragon died centuries before my birth, here in the Americas, having attempted to flee the corruption spreading from its brothers and sisters in the area you call Europe."*

The room lay silent for several moments.

Then, in a voice so quiet that it made the hairs on Oliver's arms stand on edge, Watkin broke the silence. "If what you say is true, then we have just confirmed humanity's very existence depends on maintaining a balance between pure intent and corruptive intent within our magic. That dragons failed where we have not. Only because of the existence of Oliver."

* Chapter 40: Draconic Demise *

Oliver's cheeks reddened as Emma's face, and then Lance's, turned to stare at him. Were they sizing him up? Did they think he could stop *The Damned* from turning the collective tide towards corruptive intent instead?

Mercifully, Watkin kept going, standing and looking fierce. "Why isn't this documented?" he leveled towards Archie. "Why haven't you warned man before?"

Archie floundered under Watkin's glare, even despite his four-hundred pounds of knotted muscles. *"Because to join the conversation… to attempt to understand your struggle… what if the same sickness spreads to my own species?!"*

"But you trust us now?!" Watkin shouted at Archie. "WHERE WERE YOU FIFTEEN YEARS AGO WHEN *I* NEEDED YOU?"

Under Watkin's shouts Archie recovered his dignity. He charged into the classroom, breathing fire, so Oliver stepped between them, his hands up in either direction.

"Knock it off," he said firmly.

"Oliver is more than a man," Archie snuck between growls and a slither of his tongue. *"And I trust him with the knowledge now."*

Watkin flared Wisdom, blinding the room with a burst of green starlight. The sight of it stunned Oliver—he'd never seen Watkin do it before. What was the man so emotional about?

Watkin closed his eyes and raised his own hands for peace. "Forgive me, Archie. I lost my control."

"I understand how you must feel," Archie answered stiffly.

Grabbing his staff from where he left it leaning against the floating board, Watkin turned to Oliver.

NOVA 02

"I'll have to think on your influence behind mankind's ability to wield corruption. Do not dwell on it for now—your focus *must* be on the painting. Do you understand?"

Oliver nodded, feeling a gnawing concern grow in his stomach as he looked at Watkin. There was no smile on the corner of his professor's mouth, or even a hidden twinkle in his eye.

With a gulp, Oliver realized what Watkin's expression meant. Their professor didn't control their future anymore. Now, they were fully subject to the whims of fate. The same ones Augustus had peered into and seen Oliver win in only a few times out of thousands.

"I can't think of anywhere on the grounds," Watkin went on, adjusting his traveler's cloak, "where my memory went hazy, except for the lagoons, and that's because of the protections around the Golden Willow and the Iguana's Scroll." Taking a step close to Oliver, Watkin put a hand on his shoulder. "But your friends *might* feel something in a random hallway or a random bush and then you can investigate it yourself. **Trust** in them. You are right to do so where I cannot."

With a nod to Archie, Roli, Emma, and Lance, Watkin turned to leave. "I'm off to Goodwin Forest for the night. Mobilize your friends. If corruption is the real enemy, we may be running out of time quicker than we realized."

"What makes you say that, sir?" Lance asked quietly.

Watkin paused at the circular stair at the rear of the veranda. There, he turned his head back to them, his jaw tight. "Because the keystone of

* Chapter 40: Draconic Demise *

Tupper's movement is that intent and actions do not matter. Only the end result."

Goosebumps consumed Oliver's arm as realization dawned on him. "Politics have no relations to morals," he said out loud, recounting Tupper's words from their duel last year. "The end always arrives."

Watkin grimaced at the confirmation. "If the spread of corrupted intent is to be our downfall, we cannot risk having Tupper re-galvanize his supporters. Augustus was right, Oliver. You may have to strike down Tupper the moment he escapes, and you'll need Cuahtemoc's artifact for that, otherwise Augustus wouldn't have hidden it for you to find."

NOVA 02

Chapter 41: Hazy Hot Fumes

I doubt he'd ever say it out loud, but I think he's looking for Wisdom. To get the rest of the Midwest in line, he needs more than just Power. Ironic, isn't it? Wasn't Power supposed to be the best of the three? With his underlying thesis now compromised, no wonder he has me skulking around for a quiet solution.

27th of April, the third year of the 10th Age

"Nothing," Ethan sighed, taking a seat in the Dining Hall.

Lance raised a skeptical eyebrow. "Nothing?"

Oliver let his head fall onto the dining table.

Thunk.

He'd hoped for a better update before he was stuck wasting an entire evening cleaning dishes with Ms. Joan. For the past few weeks, they'd squeezed every available second to run across the grounds, no doubt looking insane, as they tried finding places where they felt *forgetful*.

Roli and Lance had taken on the responsibility to coordinate the search parties while Oliver focused on preparing Emma for her extended run in the dueling tournament. She'd managed to upset Abe in the first round—much to Abe's embarrassment—and then barely squeaked by Makayla Grant in the semi-final.

Makayla had winked at Lance after losing her match against Emma, before turning to Oliver with her hands on her hips and a smile on her face. "You owe me big time, García!" Oliver could only agree, thanking her for

* Chapter 41: Hazy Hot Fumes *

knocking out Cristina in her first round. Though he'd never admit it to Emma, he knew Cristina could beat Emma nine times out of ten. Not that Emma wasn't good—she was just much better matched up against a fellow Brave or even a Powerhead.

Now, however, Emma had to get ready for the final where Oliver's theory was going to be fully put to the test. The other finalist, as predicted, was Beto. He and Emma would be squaring off the last Saturday of April, only a week away, and Emma had asked Oliver to help her prepare.

"It'll be good training for our eventual duel with *The Damned!*" she'd argued.

Though Oliver immediately thought of a half-dozen counterarguments, he let them all die on his lips, giving in to the request without much of a fight.

At the end of the day, he enjoyed spending the early spring evenings training with her, so why would he put a stop to it? As long as he spent enough time searching for the Fire Drake's Cavern painting every day, he could train with her in the evenings without feeling too guilty.

And he did enjoy their duels. Quite a bit. They were the closest things to dates they could share together, so he relished every minute of them.

Even when a crowd came to watch, exercising with Emma felt intimate in a way he couldn't put into words. He liked challenging her, making her work hard—hard enough to break a sweat—and it energized him to be pushed to his own limits as well. Even with his boosted Bravery as a Trinova, oftentimes Emma still found ways to out-do his own Bravery with quick, gutsy maneuvers that he knew his Wisdom would never have sanctioned mid-duel. During one practice session, she managed to weave her way past several floating blades he'd channeled to protect himself, ending the duel with one of his own blades at his throat and her face a millimeter away from his own so that he wouldn't miss her satisfied grin. Sara had jumped and cheered, hugging Lizzie, who couldn't help but return the enthusiasm, forgetting to be stoic and graceful.

But tonight, Oliver grumbled with his head down, because Blackwood's detention would be taking up the better part of his entire evening. He thudded his head again.

Thunk.

Completely devoid of emotion, Ethan looked Lance in the eyes to answer the earlier question. "Are you really going to make me say it again? We didn't find anything."

"Or did you feel forgetful anywhere, HMM?" Roli asked, leering from his perch on Lance's shoulder. *"Lance, would you pass me a root vegetable?"*

Ethan's forehead joined Oliver's on the table.

"Okay! Okay!" Lance shot back, holding his hands up.

While Roli began squelching on a sweet potato chunk, Oliver lifted his head and wrinkled his nose at Ethan. The boy could likely take a roar from an osorius to the face without flinching, and Oliver didn't understand it.

"Do you care about anything, man?" he asked Ethan, too cranky to care if it sounded rude. He stared the boy down after asking, and even held the look after Ethan raised his head to stare back with half-dead eyes.

Impressed, Oliver realized he'd likely lose a stare down with Ethan— the boy was just that apathetic.

* Chapter 41: Hazy Hot Fumes *

At least Sara made sense. She was cuter than anyone, really, and she likely hated the attention that came with her looks. She'd probably been put in a box by other people the moment she stopped looking like a kid.

And Drew, meanwhile, was just flat-out, delightfully nerdy. He probably thought of all this as a fun research project or something.

But Ethan, who still hadn't blinked, was an unknown quantity. Oliver needed a bit more to trust him.

Finally, Ethan shrugged his shoulders. "I care about saving the world," he said, dull as ever.

"Yeah, but why?" Oliver asked, thankful for the opportunity to blink. Then, with an internal retch, he realized he was acting like Blackwood, caring about winning a stare-down.

"Look," he said, recovering despite himself, "don't take this the wrong way, but you look like a wall could fall on you and you wouldn't care."

Ethan pressed his lips together as if to say, "eh," before actually answering. "Just because I'm miserable doesn't mean the rest of the world has to be." Then, after a salute that would inspire desertion, he strapped his claymore to his back and jogged straight outside Tolteca's foyer for his late-night assignment.

"He'll be searching the Champayan bathrooms," Roli hissed, following Oliver's gaze.

Oliver almost laughed. Ethan would be perfect for searching Champayan's nooks and crannies. Nobody would stop him given the look in his eyes, and even if they did, Ethan would likely just ignore them.

"Where's Sara?" Oliver asked, thinking over the list.

"Training with Emma," Lance answered without looking up from a schedule on his notebook.

Oliver pushed together his lips and nodded, appreciating Lance's diligence and attention to detail. He and Roli had put together a series of routes that would have each Hutchite, along with Sara, Ethan, and Drew, step past every square-yard of the grounds before May was up. If there was anywhere that would make anyone feel forgetful, sleepy, or even remotely tired, they'd find it.

"Let's see," Lance muttered to Roli. "We've got Abe and Brantley sneaking into the Swampy Fortress, Drew and Trey combing the Academic Building, but what about Se'—,"

"Do you remember nothing, you incompetent swine?!" Roli growled. *"Se'Vaughn and Valerie are searching—,"*

"Incompetent swine, eh?" Lance interrupted while waving a forked sweet potato around Roli's head. "You wouldn't want this sweet potato train to… have an accident, now would you?"

Oliver looked at his wristwatch ignoring the rest. "Well, I'll leave you to it," he said, standing up to leave for Ms. Joan's hidden kitchen.

A clatter and shout from behind told him Roli had lunged for the potato.

As the sliding stone doors creaked to a halt behind him, Oliver did his best to shove aside his every fright, concern, and unhappy thought. Ms.

* Chapter 41: Hazy Hot Fumes *

Joan deserved the best version of himself he could muster—especially since he'd not done a good job checking in on her over the year.

Ms. Joan showed her appreciation by whacking him on the head with a dirty soup ladle.

"You," she said, leveling the kitchen instrument at him, "are *not* good at visiting your friends."

Oliver knew she was just teasing him, but the words stung all the same. "If I had any say," he said, stepping up to the mountain of dishes she'd left in the sink at the back of the room, "I'd be in here every week. I've just been so busy is all."

"Mhmm," Ms. Joan retorted, tapping a foot. "Like the rest of us aren't any busier?"

Oliver bit off, "as busy as I am?" before the snarky thought crossed his lips. She could be busy, too, for all he knew. She did cook for hundreds of students, after all.

As if guessing his answer, she tossed the ladle onto the dishes and smirked. "Go on," she said gesturing at the pile with a wave of her wrists. "Get *busy*. And do it quick—I've got better things to do on a Saturday night than wait around here. Believe me."

Oliver smiled as he got started with some steel wool against the ladle. "Like a date with Professor Chavarría?"

"Oh-hoh!" came Ms. Joan's shout, but Oliver knew she liked the question, so he didn't worry about any more whacks. *Nova's Touch* confirmed as much. She put on a dazzling smile instead, reminding him why Elton and Joel had once voted her as *most-dateable-faculty-member*.

NOVA 02

"Yes, Jaime Chavarría and I used to be an item," Ms. Joan went on, relishing the opportunity for gossip, especially when it featured herself. "And, *yes*, I wouldn't mind if we picked up where we left off,"—she bat her eyelids several times—"but Jaime's 'focused on his career' right now. Such a nerd, I know."

Oliver turned around to look at Ms. Joan directly for a half-moment, trying his best impression of Watkin's impatient, blinking face. "Why don't you just tell him you want to date again?"

Ms. Joan snorted. "You worry about yourself. Took you long enough to take Emma on a *walk*. Just a walk, too, from what I heard. But forget about love for a second. What's got you looking like a tired racoon? You know moisturizer comes free in the bathrooms, right? And it's *so* much better than the garbage they sell at convenience stores on our Original Side of the Key. I'm talking space cream level nectar from the heavens!"

Oliver blew out a breath of air, scrubbing at a dish that looked caked in tar. "You know, sometimes washing dishes is actually kinda nice for a change."

"That bad, huh?"

He sighed. "We can't find something the Founders left behind, and we gotta find it yesterday."

"This again!" Ms. Joan said, half-laughing. "Isn't that what you were doing all last year, too?"

Oliver chuckled at the sink. "We found the thing from last year," he admitted, **trusting** her to the answer. "Turns out it was hidden for only me to find. We think maybe the same thing is happening now. You see…"

* Chapter 41: Hazy Hot Fumes *

Oliver's voice trailed off as he felt the back of his neck explode into a hivemind of satisfaction. He'd just **trusted** Ms. Joan with some secret information. And he knew he was right to do so because he was unique, as a Trinova, and could trust people to do what was right by him given his positive intent. He was a harbinger of positive influence—or whatever it was the griffin had told him—and he kept magic, no, the world, balanced. So why was that making his neck buzz so much?

With the back of his head beginning to feel uncomfortable, Oliver stopped washing the dishes and finished the rest of his thought as his heart rate picked up. "We, um," he went on, feeling his voice tremble, "just asked everyone to search the grounds for places where they feel hazy or forgetful."

He turned around to face Ms. Joan to finish his thought. To ask his question. To **trust** her. Why hadn't he thought of it sooner? Feeling like he already knew the answer, he pushed past his goosebumps and breathed out, "Ms. Joan, is there anywhere on campus where *you* feel woozy in the head or have a hard time remembering what's going on?"

Ms. Joan gestured over her shoulder with a pointed thumb. "You mean like whenever I get too close to that little door over there?"

Oliver turned his head to follow Ms. Joan's outstretched thumb as if in a dream. She was pointing at a short flight of stairs he hadn't thought about in months, if not a year. He'd seen the stairs and the little door at the bottom sometime around the start of his extraman year, during his very first detention.

NOVA 02

The sight of the stairs and door stabbed at his consciousness accusatorily, shouting at him for having forgotten about them. Then, he remembered the conversation he and Ms. Joan had shared back then.

"Nope," the memory of Ms. Joan said after he'd asked her to use magic to clean the dishes. "Now you'll think twice before disrespecting your elders."

"I didn't disrespect anybody," Oliver remembered replying. Then, he'd stepped past the stairwell and door, and frowned as a heatwave hit him in the face.

In the present, he mirrored his expression from all those months ago as the same heatwave blasted forth. Back then, he'd assumed the little wooden door led deeper into the kitchens to a furnace or some ovens. But now...

"Ms. Joan," Oliver asked, his stomach bubbling with excitement. "What's on the other side of that door?"

Ms. Joan shrugged. "Haven't got a clue. It's so hot at the bottom of those steps that I get woozy just thinking about it. Doesn't matter how much protection I layer on, magical or otherwise, fact of the matter is, I can't get near that door."

Oliver abandoned the pots and pans behind him, stepping to the stairs in a trance.

"Hey!" one of the pots yelled as he placed a hand on the door's latch. "Do I look clean to you, Mister?"

Oliver waved the pot silent with his free hand and opened the latch.

"I can't imagine there's anything down there, Sweetie" Ms. Joan said, showing up at his shoulder. She didn't startle him; he'd seen her coming

* Chapter 41: Hazy Hot Fumes *

through *Nova's Touch*. "Otherwise…," she continued, her voice slowing down to a crawl, "I'd… know… about… it…"

Oliver turned to look at Ms. Joan just as her irises bloomed.

He gaped at her when she stumbled away from him like a zombie, returning to her table at the center of the kitchen where she collapsed into a chair. There she yawned, folded her arms, and sat her head down for a nap as if nothing strange had happened.

With electricity coursing through his entire body, Oliver turned back to the doorway and pushed it open.

Heat buffeted against him in waves, forcing him to shield his face as they blew past him and into the kitchen. When he lowered his arm, he saw the scorching air had given way to a sight he both did and didn't expect.

No ornate hallways, podiums, or foyers waited for him this time. Just a dimly lit cave. It looked to have been carved out in a hurry from the earth beneath the kitchens, with no architectural design whatsoever—maybe Augustus had dug it out himself with a shovel?

Oliver shoved the thought aside and focused on the contents of the room. Nothing waited for him other than roots from a far-above tree, an empty crate, and a painting propped against the far wall.

It was a painting of a red temple built into the side of a rocky cliff with openings that oozed out lava.

Oliver dashed to the painting without hesitating, dropping to his knees onto the soft earth in front of the red watercolors. He laughed as he stuck his hand through it. Almost immediately, he reeled it back into the safety of his cave with an *"ouch!"*

NOVA 02

It had been as hot as an oven—or worse—on the other side.

But Oliver didn't mind. He'd finally found what they'd been looking for.

Turning back to the rest of the room, he used *Nova's Touch* to quickly check the crate and roots for any hidden messages or objects. Finding none, he zipped back up the stairs, leaving Ms. Joan where she snored, to sprint out and share the good news with Lance and Roli.

But Lance and Roli had already left for the night.

Clicking his tongue in frustration, Oliver thought hard on what to do. Should he enter the painting now, right away? Or go and find his friends?

By the time he decided, his body outpaced him, flaring Power to sprint faster than most eyes could hope to follow. He reached the Dungeon Simulator within sixty seconds, leaving a wake of scorched grass behind him as he went.

When he slammed open the door to the simulator, he shouted. "I FOUND IT!" and nine heads turned to stare at him at once, accounting for most of the Hutchites along with Sara, Drew, and Ethan.

But Oliver only had eyes for Emma and Lance.

Lance stared, too shocked for reaction other than widened eyes. But Emma was a Brave. She recovered quickly, lowering her arms and undoing a technique she'd prepared mid-duel with Sara. Then, she began to smirk.

"So when are we going in?"

* Chapter 41: Hazy Hot Fumes *

"Can you walk me through it again?" Oliver asked, sweat dripping down his temple.

Watkin twitched his nose. "Perhaps we should take a break."

Oliver curled his lip at the man.

"You're right. Time is not our friend at the moment. Let us begin anew, shall we?"

The sound of Roli's vibrating dewlap filled the simulator.

"Why don't you get down here and try it, then?" Oliver jeered up at the ceiling.

The simulator blurred, and a half-dozen pig-like humanoids surrounded Oliver. They appeared identical to those from inside Snowgem, armed with sickles in their hands and curved blades affixed to their haunch-like bottom legs. Oliver took a moment to wipe the remaining sweat off his brow before closing his eyes and trying out *Nova's Breath*—Watkin's future-predicting, pulse technique.

After finding the painting of the Fire Drake's Cavern, Oliver had picked up Emma and Lance and gone straight to Watkin's classroom.

They found him there, hunched over his map of the Tennessee mountains with a twitch in his eye. At hearing the news, the man downed one of his potions, tossed the goblet over his shoulder, and muttered, "show me," before the glass caught itself in the air and bobbled over to a nearby shelf.

But when they barged back into Ms. Joan's kitchen—much to her outrage—none of them other than Oliver could get close enough to open the door leading to the cave with the painting without turning back around

NOVA 02

and falling asleep nearby. Lance even went as far as outside the kitchen and into the Dining Hall.

Eventually, they all arrived at the same uncomfortable conclusion.

"I've gotta go in there by myself," Oliver said out loud, numb at the thought. "Don't I?" Suddenly, his excitement at having found the painting felt less like a victory and more like having learned the nature of his own death.

"*Eh hem,*" Roli coughed from his shoulder. "*I remain unafflicted.*"

Oliver managed a weak smile, but only just.

Emma, meanwhile, narrowed her eyes. Then she turned her attention to Watkin and began to shout in frustration. "Why wouldn't Augustus trust us all to go in there together?! We talked to him about it only a few months ago! Did he forget about us or something?"

"You're thinking about it wrong," Lance objected, shaking his head. "It's only been months for us, but it could've been years or decades for him. Maybe he really did forget."

Watkin could only run his hands through his hair. "I convinced Augustus to help me out earlier in my life and later in his when we spoke with him at Snowgem." Watkin paused, his eyes hollowing out as a memory came to him. It took a full body shake for him to recover. "Let me tell you," he finally went on, "I can confirm he succeeded."

Emma exchanged a glance with Oliver, raising her brow questioningly.

Oliver shrugged, too concerned about his own problems to unpack Watkin's old ones.

* Chapter 41: Hazy Hot Fumes *

"But now," Watkin went on, "I learn our predecessor decided not to trust me now... I agree, Emma, it doesn't make any sense."

"Do I go in now?" Oliver asked, looking at the door apprehensively.

Watkin stood up and hefted his staff. "If you're to meet *The Damned* in combat by yourself, it must be for a reason. But before we do,"—his eyes began to look determined again—"I do believe one last lesson is in order. Emma, Lance, can you brew heat-resistance elixirs with our root vegetable expert while Oliver and I train?"

"No doubt," Lance said, swelling his chest. "We've been getting better and better with our elixirs with Chavarría all year."

Watkin nodded. "Good." Then he pulled three potatoes from nowhere—ones that looked an awful lot like the one from Jim—and tossed them to Lance. "Use these, along with chill-laced butterfly wings. I believe you'll find Professor Chavarría keeps a steady supply of them."

Emma led the charge out of the kitchens, with Roli scampering close behind. *"I must supervise this effort, directly!"* he said, his eyes gleaming at the thought of more potatoes.

Which brought Oliver back to his current predicament. No matter how many times they'd run the simulation, he hadn't yet been able to grasp Watkin's sonar technique.

They'd been at it for nearly a week.

When the pigs cut him to ribbons for the eighteenth time that night, he stormed away from the center of the room and sat down in frustration. "Maybe if we try it a different way! You said it'd be similar to *Nova's Touch*, but I just tried that, and let me tell you, it isn't the same!"

NOVA 02

His eyes began to water in frustration. Here he was, one day away from foraying into the Fire-Drake's Cavern by himself, without a back-up plan, and he couldn't get the hang of one little technique.

Watkin stooped down next to him, and Oliver felt the man's hand squeeze his shoulder. "If it were easy," Watkin said encouragingly, "then everybody would be using my technique, don't you think? Maybe even the chief pig himself, Professor Blackwood, would have already mastered it."

Oliver looked up and wiped the tears from his eyes. "I knew you hated Blackwood, too," he said, taking the chance to laugh away the built-up frustration and fear.

"That's Professor Blackwood to you. Or is it Dean Blackwood? Neither suit him, really."

Oliver chuckled some more, appreciating the levity. It was something Santiago would try, and Oliver could appreciate that.

"I just…" Oliver said, resuming the actual conversation. "I just wish I could pick it up quicker. I usually take up new magic fast, so it's just frustrating."

Curiously, Watkin's expression shifted to a far-away look.

"What?" Oliver asked.

Watkin didn't answer. Instead, he broke off and stepped away.

"What is it?" Oliver repeated, heat coming to his cheeks. Did Watkin agree with him? Was he no match for Tupper in his current state?

"It was something you said," Watkin breathed. He turned around slowly to look at Oliver again, his eyes darting back and forth as he thought over

* Chapter 41: Hazy Hot Fumes *

something. "All this time I assumed my sonar technique was the result of my connection with *my* virtue…"

"But what if," Watkin went on, looking at the ceiling, "each virtue sees its own technique?!"

Watkin snapped his fingers and returned his eyes to Oliver's. He stepped close again, this time grabbing both Oliver's shoulders and pulling him close until their eyeballs were an inch away from one another. With a squawk, Jaiba joined the inspection, cocking his head for a better look.

"Oliver?" Watkin demanded with a shake. "Ever since you began hearing the word trust or truth or any of its derivatives hang in the air, have you noticed anything different about yourself? Could you use *Nova's Touch* all along or is this a recent development?"

"Uhh," Oliver hesitated. "I don't know! I guess I'm just more confident about who I can trust and who I can't? I started using *Nova's Touch* after you told me how to create the pocket dimension!"

Watkin let Oliver go and looked at Jaiba instead. "So simple," he marveled.

Caw-caw!

"Oliver," Watkin continued, turning back around with a twinkle in his eye, "I think I've realized why you can't master *Nova's Breath* just yet." He darted up until they were close up again. Oliver tried shirking away best he could, but it was like trying to avoid attention from a hawk in an open field.

Watkin poked Oliver in the chest. "You haven't mastered the right virtue yet!"

Oliver rubbed at his chest, scowling. "But you have?"

"Let's pretend you didn't just insult me," Watkin answered, feigning hurt in his eyes as he backed away. "But yes."

"In fact," he added, sticking out his index finger and thumb, "I have *two*."

Oliver's eyes widened. Then he looked down at his own hands and marveled over the secret technique he'd unlocked, seemingly by accident. It was something even his professor didn't know how to do. Oliver looked up at Watkin as the knowledge sunk in.

Watkin waggled his eyebrows, allowing Oliver to bask in the glory of his realization.

"So," Oliver ventured, "you've got two of these words? And neither of them are **Trust**? How many are there?"

Watkin stared for several seconds. Then he drummed his fingers on his staff, looking ready to deliver a riddle. Or something else just as unhelpful.

"It depends on what you read. Or whom you consult."

Oliver's face fell. "And I bet you're not going to tell me how many *you* think there are until I've recovered some sacred artifact from an ancient Roman sewer or something?"

"I probably deserve that," Watkin answered, chuckling. "But, no, I believe there are six."

Oliver clicked his tongue in disappointment, feeling a lot like Roli. "Why not make it a perfect seven?" he asked sarcastically, throwing up his hands in frustration and settling down on crisscrossed legs. "Don't I have enough on my plate?"

* Chapter 41: Hazy Hot Fumes *

Watkin's eyes twinkled at dangerously manic levels. "Up until now, I hadn't even realized there may be different techniques depending on the word you've mastered.

"But we can give up on *Nova's Breath* for now," Watkin promised, plopping onto the ground next to Oliver. "Besides, I can tell you could do with some encouragement—I am a Wiser, after all."

Oliver shifted his legs. "I don't need a pep talk. I'll be fine."

"I insist," Watkin said, tapping the red beryl jewel on his staff with his knuckle. A tea set appeared. "Do you take sugar?"

"Umm," Oliver answered, not sure what else to say. Nobody had ever offered him tea before.

"Of course you do," Watkin muttered with a shake of his head. "Who wouldn't want tea?"

Before he knew what he was doing, Oliver sat there sipping tea with Watkin on the eve of the most dangerous mission in his life.

"Now, about tomorrow," Watkin said, gulping down the rest of his small glass. "Don't be worried."

Oliver drew in a long breath. "Gee, I should have thought of that."

"See?" Watkin asked, beaming. "Isn't it easy? No, I kid of course. I'll tell you why you shouldn't."

"Because Augustus saw me doing this in his strands of fate?" Oliver asked, his voice hollow as he poked at a loose pebble on the stone floor.

Watkin nodded as though Oliver had just discovered all six secret virtues by himself. "Precisely. It's amazing how predetermined outcomes can liberate the mind, isn't it? More tea?"

NOVA 02

"No, thank you," Oliver muttered as the man poured him some more anyway. Oliver had already realized why he had to go in by himself. If there wasn't a need, Augustus would have hidden the painting similarly to the Iguana's Scroll, whereby Emma and Lance could join him.

But something about Augustus' visions had told the man, all the way back in the sixteenth or seventeenth century, that Oliver needed to recover Cuahtemoc's artifact alone. Augustus had seen thousands, if not tens of thousands of visions of Oliver's future, and Oliver came out ahead of Tupper in only a few of them.

Which might have made entering the Fire Drake's Cavern that much easier, if not for the other dose of reality Oliver recognized.

Once he stepped foot inside, Oliver was officially entering the parts of Augustus' visions where he failed more times than he succeeded. And the thought of that brought about a sense of churning dread Oliver hadn't felt since last year. Especially when he butted up the knowledge against the griffin's story about humanity's downfall.

* **Chapter 41: Hazy Hot Fumes** *

NOVA 02

Chapter 42: The Fire Drake's Cavern

I'm not sure how I'm supposed to scale up past the clouds to reach the Fire Drake's Cavern, but I'm going to be praying I don't fall no matter how many bashies I jam into this cliff. There's supposed to be a walkway up there somewhere.

4th of May, the third year of the 10th Age

Taking a deep breath, Oliver felt *Nova's Touch* creeping up the cave behind him. First it showed him Ms. Joan standing on her tip toes, peering down the staircase she couldn't get near and fidgeting with the chain of her golden necklace. Not that much further past her, Emma and Lance sat in the noisy, boisterous Dining Hall, continuously casting nervous glances in his direction even though they couldn't see him past the hidden sliding door.

They were all worried for him. Each knew he would soon be entering the painting to the Fire Drake's Cavern. That he'd be tackling an entire temple by himself. Without any help.

"*You really don't count me as an ally, do you?*" Roli pipped cheerfully from his right shoulder.

Oliver reached out a hand to pat Roli on the head. "I do," he said, imitating the iguana's comforting touch—Roli had been there for Oliver in Lalandra's office, and he was there for him again now. "You're more of a positive attitude kinda guy, not a take-down a dungeon full of monsters sort of fella, don't you think?"

* Chapter 42: The Fire Drake's Cavern *

Roli puffed out his dewlap. *"I am rather magnificent, aren't I?"*

Oliver turned back to the painting and cracked his neck, letting go of *Nova's Touch*. The last he felt from the Dining Hall was an unmistakable nod of Watkin's head in his direction.

"Here goes nothing," Oliver whispered.

From Lance's backpack, which they were borrowing for the excursion, he took out a stoppered bottle full of an icy-blue liquid.

"We'll have twenty minutes per bottle," Roli reminded him.

Oliver squinted at the liquid suspiciously before popping off the cork. After swirling the contents around a few times, he tilted his head back and downed all but a spoonful.

"Yuck," he gagged.

Roli contracted his neck for a laugh.

Oliver cut him off mid-chuckle, pressing the bottle to the iguana's lips.

"I must meet this Jim," Roli said, smacking his lips appreciatively. *"His potatoes could have been served at Olympus."*

Oliver shook his head and stepped into the painting.

Emma's hair fluttered in the wind behind her as she stepped onto the white marble floors of the Dueling Strip. A crowd surrounded her on all sides, standing in raised bleachers to get a good look. She didn't mind giving it to them. Let them watch.

NOVA 02

The noise coming from the surrounding students, and even adults, was sheer pandemonium. The friendly faces, like those belonging to Lizzie and Valerie, shouted words of encouragement. The less friendly ones, like Cristina's and James', led the Champayan students in bellowing insults.

Still, she didn't mind. She'd tuned them all out the moment she'd arrived at the arena. Even still, she wondered if they'd be shouting words like *that* if their families were there with them?

Either way, they weren't worth her attention. Only one person mattered to her at the moment, and it certainly wasn't Cristina.

It was Beto Warren.

He stood on the other end of the strip surveying her like a haughty prince. One who'd caught a rival and was prepared to order their execution. Emma locked eyes with him all the same as she took her starting position.

Just as quickly, she turned her gaze away, disgusted.

Beto had begun rolling his large, powerful shoulders, faking a warm-up to no doubt try and intimidate her. She let out a puff of air at the sight, muttering to herself impatiently. As the last few stubborn locks on her forehead joined the remainder of the hair streaming behind her head, she rolled her eyes slowly enough so he wouldn't miss it.

She was a Brave—trying to intimidate her was a waste of time.

But then Beto shifted. He dropped his shoulder routine to fluff his long, curly hair off his shoulders with a palpably arrogant simper on his annoyingly handsome face.

Emma's rage spiked. Faking a big-man's warm-up was one thing. But to smile and fluff his hair as if preparing for a photoshoot was just downright

Chapter 42: The Fire Drake's Cavern

disrespectful before a dueling final. She had half a mind to begin the fight without Blackwood's permission—he monitored them from outside the strip with a malevolent grin connecting both sides of his bald head—but she stopped herself just in time.

She *hated* how familiar Beto's look felt. It was the same confident expression she often saw on her parents' faces. Beto knew he was going to win the Dueling Final just like her parents knew they were going to charm the pants off any donor stupid enough to come to one of their parties.

Emma broke off eye contact for a second time and clicked her tongue. She'd made a decision.

Turning, she stepped back to her corner of the strip—where Lance started waving his arms frantically. "Are you sure?!" he shouted through the din as she drew near. "I don't think it's a good idea! You'll need all your senses!"

Emma re-doubled her glare, leaving nothing more than slits of green. Oli would have understood her immediately, but he was off on a suicide mission to find Cuahtemoc's artifact by himself. The injustice of the situation wrenched her heart. She should be there with *him,* helping fight the pesadriya. Not out here dueling Beto.

Taking a deep beath, she shoved her concern for Oliver aside. He knew what he was doing. He was the Trinova, and he'd be fine. She'd have to trust him to keep himself safe just like he'd started trusting everybody else to handle their own roles.

She returned her attention to Lance. Boys had a habit of listening to her if she stayed quiet and glared long enough. Was it aggressive? Maybe. But the results spoke for themselves. Lance caved in seconds, drooping his shoulders as far as Beto had rolled his own.

Emma followed up with a gimme motion with her right hand.

"Fine," Lance grunted, tossing her a small knapsack. "But don't say I didn't warn you."

In the commentator's corner Emma heard Makayla and Joel having a conniption over something as she walked back to her starting position. She knew she was the cause of the commotion, but her eyes were back on Beto, and she was already tuning everybody out to focus on her duel again.

Just before Blackwood motioned for the fight to start, she pulled out an old pair of frayed, black headphones from the knapsack.

On the other side of the painting, Oliver stepped onto a stone walkway built into the side of a sheer cliff. Scorching hot air blasted into him as soon as he appeared, watering his eyes and smarting his cheeks despite the protection of the elixir coursing through his veins. On his shoulder, Roli kept a low profile. Neither of them wanted a blast of air to whisk them away.

Ahead, the stone walkway snaked upward, maintaining an even width of ten or so feet away from the cliffside wherever it went. A railing safeguarded the other side of the path, and, with a peak over his shoulder, Oliver saw

* Chapter 42: The Fire Drake's Cavern *

the painting of the cave beneath Ms. Joan's kitchen resting in an alcove jettisoned within the cliffside.

"This doesn't look like Goodwin Forest," Oliver said to Roli, running a hand over the cliff face to their left. The brief touch left red clay on his fingers.

"Nor are we in a cavern," Roli surmised. *"Fire Drake's Cavern? It is likely we approach the tomb of a dragon of old."*

Oliver nodded absentmindedly, peering up the side of the cliff. It loomed high above them, stretching for several hundred yards before eventually giving way to—

"Wait," Oliver breathed, "those are clouds above us." He turned to his right and squinted at the railing on the other side of the walkway. "Just how high up are we?"

Tentatively, he shuffled toward the railing. It was made of the same marble as the walkway itself. All of it had long-since been stained the same red as the cliffside.

When he peered over the railing, a gust of wind met his face like an uppercut from an osori, knocking him back several yards.

"That'd be quite the fall," Roli whispered, cowering even closer to Oliver's shoulder than before.

Oliver could only nod in agreement as he wiped dust off his shirt and pulled himself up. He glanced at the railing again before moving. It had clearly been an ornate masterpiece at one point in the distant past—before the red clay had settled over it. Every ten yards, busts of feathered serpents grimaced at them, having been built as figure pieces for the railing. Now, however, the once-pristine railing appeared decrepit at best. Where entire sections of green jade rivulets weren't missing, scratches, dents, or blotches of red riddled the handiwork, which was a real shame as far as Oliver was concerned. The decorations reminded him of Aztecan statues he'd grown up seeing in magazines. Santiago had always proudly talked about their cultural heritage, pointing out the uniqueness of the designs with emphatic slaps against the photos, and now Oliver couldn't help but agree. These busts weren't imitations of Aztec art; they were original pieces left behind by Cuahtemoc himself on a cliffside far away from his home.

Oliver looked up again, following the pathway make its way across a bend on the cliffside. This was where Cuahtemoc's gift waited for him—what would an Aztec leave behind for an Aztec descendant to find?

"*Yes,*" Roli mused, reading Oliver's mind. "*Cuahtemoc always had a flair for theatrics.*"

"Theatrics or pride?" Oliver countered, kicking at a loose bit of marble near his feet. He followed the rolling debris with his eyes until it bounced off a much larger rock that was halfway buried into the pathway. Oliver raised an eyebrow, drawing himself closer as he realized the entire walkway was littered with dozens of the rock-chunks. This one, along with some of the others were giving off steam.

Oliver turned his confused expression to Roli.

"*Your guess is as good as mi—,*"

The earth beneath them trembled as the entire mountainside shook.

Yelping, Oliver stumbled back to the safety of the alcove hosting the painting.

* Chapter 42: The Fire Drake's Cavern *

After the rumbling stopped, whistling noises followed as more chunks of rock meteored into explosions of shrapnel just outside their hiding place.

When the world finally stood still again, Roli popped his head in front of Oliver. *"I would very much like to avoid being hit by those."*

Peeking his own head out of the alcove, Oliver looked up, tracing lines of smoke from the rocks to gaps in the cloud wrapping around the cliff. "Is this an active volcano?" he asked. Suddenly the spewing lava from the Cavern's painting made more sense.

"Well," Roli bleated, *"be quick about it! I doubt the volcano will cease volcanoing just because we're here!"*

Oliver obliged, enforcing his legs with Power for a sprint up the walkway. Though he slowed for the sharper turns around the jagged mountainside, he didn't stop until they came to a cavernous entryway leading deep into the mountain.

Hot air billowed from inside like breaths from the mountain itself. Every gasp ignited sections of the air around them, sparking flames and even small explosions into life. Oliver let out a prayer of thanks for Jim's high-quality potatoes and the elixir they produced.

"Do you think this is the right way?" he asked, hesitating to enter the gloomy entrance.

Roli chuckled. *"Were you hoping for someone to hand you a steamed towel on your way in?"*

Oliver grumbled but jogged inside anyway, muttering *iuxtairis*.

"Or how about cucumber slices to drape over your eyes?"

The darkness of the mountain enveloped them.

NOVA 02

Emma twisted in midair so she wouldn't land on her cheek. Beto's most recent strike of jettisoned sword essence had speared through her defenses like a butcher's knife through flesh, sending her flying.

As she sailed back, the groans of the Hutchites in the crowd hurt her more than Beto's attack had. They were afraid. Afraid that she'd lose.

Fear wasn't about to grip *her* heart; she was a Brave after all. But dread might. Dread that she couldn't match a school bully while Oliver was on his way to fight either Tupper or a pesadriya, a literal demon of the underworld.

With a puff of wind from her sleeved arm, she leveled herself off from the twisting explosion of her failed defensive shield. When she touched down, she didn't wait for the next attack. Instead, she broke into a forward roll, praying it'd be enough to dodge whatever Beto sent after her next.

"Defenderis!" she shouted.

A blue force field formed over her just as her roll stopped. Closing her eyes, she braced herself for the ringing sound of a sword hammering against her magic.

But nothing came.

She looked up, confused. Her earlier fury returned within one short, ragged breath.

* Chapter 42: The Fire Drake's Cavern *

Beto wasn't even looking at her. He was off blowing kisses to the crowd and bowing to the Champayans. With every sarcastic prostration, he even managed to flourish his scimitar even more obnoxiously than he twisted his waist.

Just when she decided to send him skyrocketing into orbit with a strike of her own, she hesitated. He'd be expecting that. This was all a show—he was ready to deflect a hasty move and counter with a finishing blow of his own.

Beto turned to her, his arrogant expression compounding.

"Good girl," he said, winking.

Emma's heart fell. That's what Lalandra had said to her earlier in the year, too. Even Lalandra, somebody who was supposed to be on their side, a supposed genius, treated the world the same way as Beto. Was life just an excuse for the more-driven, the more-powerful, and the more-ambitious to exercise their will over the weak? Everyone wanted to use people for their own little games. Was she doomed to be a pawn in their plans? Like she had been for her parents?

For once, the fire in her soul wavered. When Beto raised his scimitar, her shoulders drooped.

Inside the mountain, Oliver grabbed an unlit torch off a bracket and ignited it with a spark of conjured fire between his fingers.

NOVA 02

Light flickered across the room, revealing—

Roli let out a squeak and scampered to the top of Oliver's head.

Just like the Forest Temple and Ruins of Snowgem, the remains of a long-dead sundial haunted the foyer of the Fire Drake's Cavern.

"*Sorry,*" Roli coughed. "*It's just strange seeing somebody you used to know looking like…*" He gestured with a clawed foot at the sundial's ruined form.

Oliver inspected the mess. "You knew them?" he asked, running a hand over the sundial's emerald eyes and frozen grimace of rubies and sapphires. The one in the Forest Temple had been charred in black soot, so it had been far easier to ignore it, tip-toeing past.

This sundial's demise, however, drew Oliver's attention like a nightmare. By the looks of it, the sundial must have been torched on sight, with time only to click open its stone eyelids before facing its attacker.

"*I knew them,*" Roli confirmed, his voice melancholic. "*This was Vistarama, Cuahtemoc's personal assistant.*"

Oliver's hand reached the edge of Vistarama's frozen grimace and stopped. The edges of the sundial were melted into the walls of its alcove between a double-side staircase leading down. Whoever had entered before them had bathed Vistarama in a fire so hot they welded the sundial to the wall. How hot had those flames been?

Oliver took Roli off his head and placed him back on his shoulder. "I'm sorry," he said, unsure of what else to say as he stepped away from Cuahtemoc's dead assistant.

Roli stiffened. "*Let's move on. Our elixirs won't last forever.*"

* Chapter 42: The Fire Drake's Cavern *

Oliver nodded, taking the stairs with his torch held high. Inwardly, he felt a sense of dread begin to strengthen its grip on his heart, constricting his resolve and breath.

It wasn't fear slowing him down, but caution. Sure, he'd trained himself up to take on any one of Emma, Lance, or simulated versions of Beto—and he very much doubted anybody at school could beat him in a duel except some of the faculty—but what could he hope to do against an attack that melted sundials into a wall? Was Vistarama's smote form evidence of *The Damned* in a bad mood whenever he delved into the cavern years ago? Or was it confirmation that a pesadriya haunted these gloomy chambers?

Oliver shuddered as memories of the monster described in Lalandra's office began haunting the darkest corners of the room.

"Oh no," Lance breathed as he watched Emma and Beto stop dueling to stare each other down.

Next to him, Sara placed a hand to her chin. "It's not like her to give up, is it?" Even when watching a friend lose a duel, she sounded cheery.

Lance couldn't believe what he was watching. This was *Emma* they were talking about. She had enough fire and stubborn will to accomplish anything she set out to do. In preparation for this duel alone she'd faced off against *Oliver* three-hundred-and-seventy-two times in the simulator. There wasn't anything Emma couldn't do.

NOVA 02

But Lance's eyes now saw a different story. Beto towered over that same stubborn, driven girl, ready to end the fight with one more swing of his scimitar.

And Emma? She looked broken, her shoulders slumped and the fire in her green eyes all but gone.

"Did Beto say something pig-headed?" Sara wondered out loud, her tone and face suddenly turning sharper than ice.

Lance put his head in his hands, unable to watch the finishing blow. "I knew putting on those headphones was a mistake."

* Chapter 42: The Fire Drake's Cavern *

NOVA 02

Chapter 43: Judgment Delayed

Found the pathway! Taking a break for the rest of the day and then I'll move forward. If Tío's notes are anything to go by, the path goes around the cliffside and will lead me straight into the Temple.

5th of May, the third year of the 10th Age

By now, Oliver knew what to expect from the first room of one of the Founders' secret dungeons. Inside the Forest Temple an eight-foot werewolf wielding a claymore had challenged them. Then, in the Ruins of Snowgem, a just-as-tall snake-monster had wriggled towards Watkin hefting a scimitar the length of Oliver's entire body.

So, when torches flickered to life bringing a cavernous room into light, Oliver was ready to bet Augustus' ring that a ten-foot flaming boar or spider was going to start waving a battle axe at him.

But when the now-familiar-sounding bell tolled, signaling the start of the fight, Oliver still hadn't seen his enemy yet. Panicking, he scanned the room with *Nova's Touch*.

Nothing.

Deciding he'd need help, he grunted and pushed out his ringed hand into a collapsed fist. The conjuring spell pulled together loose chunks of stone from the floor, spawning one of Lance's golems. With a twist of his fingers, Oliver also re-worked heat in the air to imbue ice into the sentinel.

* Chapter 43: Judgment Delayed *

The ice golem pounded together the two larger rocks at the ends of its arms, ready for a fight.

Then it tilted its head at Oliver in confusion.

"I know, I know!" Oliver hissed. "We're still looking!"

The ice golem shrugged, and Oliver wondered if he'd accidentally imbued some of Lance's personality into the summoned ally. Shoving the distraction aside, he continued flicking his eyes across the room until they settled on the far side.

There, he finally caught sight of their enemy: a hulking, red and black figure holding a halberd.

Oliver tensed his knees, ready to roll out of the way in case the enemy launched the spear at him. At the same time, the ice golem noticed the shadow, and began trudging forward without hesitation. The floor shook with its every step.

Roli poked Oliver in the neck with an outstretched claw. *"I do believe you are battling a ghost."*

"Great," Oliver breathed. He was glad the ice golem was going first.

Cautiously, he followed suit, expecting the shadow to whirl into motion and skewer him with the halberd at any moment. But then, in front of them, the ice golem stopped in place, cocking its head to the side. After a moment, it looked back to Oliver and raised an arm toward their enemy.

Oliver understood the golem's meaning—the shadow still hadn't moved.

Less cautiously than before, Oliver jogged forward and hurled the torch in his left hand at the enemy. It landed twenty yards short, but still the shadow hadn't moved. Then, Oliver noticed a pile of soot at the shadow's feet.

Oliver's jaw dropped. "Roli," he said. "I think this monster is dead, too."

The scene began to fill in Oliver's mind like an automated solution to a puzzle. He jogged the rest of the way until the pile of soot was at his boots. The shadow on the wall wasn't a shadow at all—it was the outline of an incinerated giant.

Oliver gaped at the silhouette on the wall and then back to the pile of soot again, kicking at the tip of something metallic buried within the pile. A head of a halberd fell out of the ashes.

"Whatever came in here," Roli said, sharing his thoughts with Oliver, *"slaughtered Vistarama without much of a fight, and then eviscerated a ten-foot-tall… something."*

While they gaped, the ice golem shrugged and took the halberd head, affixing it to its head for charge attacks.

Oliver recovered before Roli, gulping and scanning the room for a second time. Like they'd seen at the entrance, flames ignited every so often in the air around them, bringing dark corners into temporary flashes of light. "I guess in a place this hot, channeling fire powerful enough to melt a magical guardian is that much easier?"

He glanced back at the outline of the silhouette. He'd always thought of the wolf-giant inside Founder's Temple as a permanent sentinel that could be defeated in combat, but not killed. *The Damned,* however, had just run in here and murdered both the sundial and the guardian of the first room. Oliver looked at the soot one last time, worrying for the safety of

* Chapter 43: Judgment Delayed *

Cuahtemoc's artifact. Could this even be magic from a human? Was *The Damned* so strong he could reduce a monster the size of a brick wall to ashes? Oliver voiced his concern as he darted down the next set of stairs.

"Perhaps this wasn't the work of a man," Roli offered timidly.

When Beto raised his scimitar to deliver his final blow, Emma stiffened.

Why did the connection between this smirking boy, Lalandra, and her parents bother her so much? Was she really going to give up on a duel because cruel people took advantage of kind folks? Was she really going to mope her way to a loss simply because the world wasn't **Just**?

It felt connected to how she'd treated Oliver and Lance after they'd ogled at Sara like pigs. Even they had thought of her as too intense when she'd given them the silent treatment as punishment. So that meant this was *her* standard. Nobody could see justice and injustice like she could. Not Beto. Not Lalandra. Not Lance.

Not even Oliver.

Valerie was always warning her that she rubbed people the wrong way whenever she got too combative about others not living up to her standards, but why care about what other people thought? She hadn't ever before, so why start now? Just because Beto and Lalandra surprised her with just how awful they were? Just because Oliver couldn't see what she so easily could?

NOVA 02

The world seemed to slow down as Emma wrestled with herself. Above her, Beto's snarling face tightened as he swung his sword. Still, Emma thought hard, ignoring the duel.

It didn't matter if Beto and Lalandra were a cut of the same cloth as her parents, or that she herself rubbed people the wrong way for caring about doing what's right—this was her own decision. She knew what was **Just** and what wasn't. Maybe nobody else ever would. But she'd sooner join Tupper in his purgatory rather than give up on her principles.

A flicker of a smile touched the corner of her mouth as she made another decision. It came at the same time the song she was listening to inside her black headphones crescendoed. Then, just as Beto's scimitar reached her neck, she leaned forward and dodged the strike the same way Watkin had dodged the lizard's blow in the Ruins of Snowgem.

The crowd went silent as Beto tripped over himself.

Oliver bent down and scooped his hand through a small pile of ash. Several seconds trickled by as he let the soot fall through his outstretched fingers and thought fast and hard. Five other piles of dust blighted this most recent chamber. Each included a forgotten awl pike.

Roli stepped up and down with unease on Oliver's shoulders. *"Tupper must have been in a hurry when he charged through here."*

* Chapter 43: Judgment Delayed *

"These *things*," Oliver began—he didn't even know what the piles of ashes had been when they were alive—"were supposed to be guarding Cuahtemoc's artifact. And… and Tupper dealt with them like they were nothing."

Roli's feet shuffled again. *"A stark contrast to the approach Watkin took in the Ruins of Snowgem, don't you think?"*

Oliver thought back to Santiago's words from deep inside the Ruins of Snowgem, pondering over what Roli had left unsaid.

"You said this guy was your history teacher! Just a nerdy professor! This guy could kill us all with no problems. Did you know?"

Watkin was just as capable of reducing the beasts guarding Snowgem to ashes. But he hadn't. Because of his principles. What were *The Damned's* principles? How and why did he find slaughter and murder so easy?

Oliver glanced over the piles of soot again and gripped the torch in his left hand more firmly than before. With his jaw set, he motioned for the ice golem to follow.

After descending the next staircase, they entered an already-lit room where an enormous bust of a feathered serpent's head glowered at them. The statue had been etched mid snarl, with the sacred beast's jade tongue sticking out, warning trespassers against progressing further.

"Look at the lights overhead," Roli suggested.

NOVA 02

Oliver nodded, already eyeing the clue. Above the stone and jade bust, two beams of sunlight filtered into the room, meeting the floor in front of the serpent's head.

"We're supposed to reflect the light into the serpent's eyes," Oliver said, already thinking about using the ice golem's halberd as a shiny surface. He gestured towards the next staircase behind the bust. "It'll likely open the locked door…"

Oliver's voice trailed off. He'd assumed the next set of stairs would be locked. And he'd been halfway right. At one point steel bars had clearly barred passage. But the bars were mangled. Torn asunder so that a gap the size of an osorius had been cleared into the metal.

Oliver exchanged a glance with Roli on his shoulder. "Am I imagining claw marks?" he asked.

Roli gulped, bobbing his dewlap up and down. *"Perhaps Solomon employed an osorius to assist him?"*

"Great," Oliver sighed, stepping past the bars, taking care not to gash himself on the cut metal or get anywhere near a handful of black and red splotches of wavering magic that lingered in the air near the torn metal.

Through the gaps in his fingers Lance saw Emma dodge Beto's strike at the last second. Like everyone else in the crowd, he stood to get a better look at what happened next.

* Chapter 43: Judgment Delayed *

"How did she do that?" Sara breathed into his ear.

Lance could only shrug his shoulders and keep watching with his eyes pressed wide. As Beto staggered in place, recovering his dignity, the only person in the entire crowd to make a noise was Professor Watkin.

He stood up on the opposite side of the strip and began to applaud with slow, loud claps, a crazy glint in his eyes that Lance only ever saw the man turn on when Oliver did something clever.

"What?" Abe asked, tugging on Watkin's frock coat from the row behind.

Watkin waggled his eyebrows at nobody in particular. "Pay attention, children. Oh,"—he added with a chuckle, pointing at several different faculty members with his staff—"you may want to summon the press, too. Emma's about to make history."

"History?" Blackwood spat. "Beto has commanded every move. He is one stroke away from—,"

A pillar of green light *exploded* down from the heavens, bathing Emma in crackling energy from an unknown source.

Lance turned back to the strip the same time as everybody else, his jaw on his chest. As Emma's hair snapped back and forth in the hurricane of wind accompanying the pillar of the green light, Lance wondered if she'd even heard any of what had just happened. She still wore her headphones.

NOVA 02

Still in the dark, Oliver trudged down the long staircase that followed, holding the torch up high. As they went, gouged pockets of clay-stained marble grabbed his attention whenever they came into the flickering torchlight. More than once, Roli poked his neck to draw his attention to additional piles of ash. Every time they saw one, Oliver shuddered, wondering if he'd meet the same fate whenever Tupper or the pesadriya appeared after they touched Cuahtemoc's artifact.

Either way, he'd have to try. His fate was tied to Cuahtemoc's gift. He'd recover it to beat *The Damned* or die trying—Augustus had seen this option as the only path where they could win.

When they reached a giant set of doors that matched the ones in Snowgem, Oliver paused with his hand on the handle, chuckling to himself.

Roli hissed with concern. *"What is it? Are you going mad from the heat? Perhaps another elixir is in order?"*

Oliver shook his head. "Maybe Watkin's right. Maybe knowing your fate makes it all that much easier to seek it out."

"Hmm," Roli thought. *"You are gifted with Bravery where I am not, so I'll take your word for it."*

Oliver nodded. "Fair enough." Then he pulled the door open, wincing at how loud the rusty hinges sounded in the room that lay ahead.

It was larger than the first room past the foyer, which puzzled him. Both the Forest Temple and the Ruins of Snowgem included final rooms the size of a bed chamber. This room, however, had more in common with a royal ballroom, not that he could see much of it yet.

* Chapter 43: Judgment Delayed *

For a few seconds he stayed at the doorframe with his torch held high, squinting his eyes as he gazed into the darkness. He wasn't scared, necessarily, but he didn't like how more of the red and black twisted magic he'd seen on the shredded bars blocking the last staircase ebbed and flowed around them. The residual magic felt *wrong* in the air, like discordant music grating against his ears.

"*Are you a Trinova or not?*" Roli hissed pompously from his shoulder. "*Light the whole room.*"

Oliver ignored the jibe, but also berated himself. He needed to stop thinking like a kid. Taking in a breath, he reached out for the energy in the air around them and directed Nova to congregate the magic to a point overhead, where he ignited it into luminated flame.

A thrill rushed through Oliver's body as the energy hurried to obey him, flashing light into every corner of the room. Cuahtemoc's artifact caught his eye immediately. It was a wooden instrument of some sort, approximately the size of Lance's hammer and studded with black and red jewels. The pedestal that held the artifact drew Oliver's attention next. It looked different from the others he'd seen before, jagged and almost scaley in the light. Was it moving?

With a yelp, Oliver cut off his connection to the magic.

That hadn't been a pedestal at all.

Something large, red, and black had been holding onto Cuahtemoc's artifact. Something Oliver had only ever seen in Desmoulins' Flora and Fauna books.

Something that was supposed to be extinct.

NOVA 02

A dragon.

Sweat ran down either side of Oliver's forehead. The dragon must have measured twice the length of Reggie, Abe's osorius, and just as wide. By a stroke of fortune, the beast must have been asleep, because nothing stirred other than the sweat that had now reached Oliver's chin.

Gulping, Oliver began to tiptoe back to the door, his hand wrapped around Roli's maw to stifle any potential screams. This was not an exercise to take on by himself. He might have stood a chance against Solomon Tupper's half-summoned form, and maybe even a demonic pesadriya, but a dragon? He needed to regroup with the others.

Before he'd shuffled back more than a few feet, an intense, rumbling sound froze him midstride. Shrieking stone and crumbling marble followed, reverberating around the cavernous room's walls as something large and dense began moving in the dark, tearing into the floor beneath them as if it were water.

Silence blanketed the air next, sounding far louder against Oliver's ear than the rumbling and shrieking had. For the first time in his life, Oliver felt true fear as he waited for what might follow.

A voice broke the silence. It was deeper than Archie's, carrying a tint of insanity, like that of an enormous, rabid dog.

"I've waited a very long time for this," growled the dragon.

* **Chapter 43: Judgment Delayed** *

Chapter 44: Arbitration

This temple is a nightmare. Whatever good faith Cuahtemoc used to carry on the legacy of his people is long gone from the air. It almost smells spoiled in here. Like rot, but of magic.

Or maybe of the soul.

6th of May, the third year of the 10th Age

"My name is Vardothia," the dragon said, shaking the foundations of the entire temple with its voice alone. *"Name yourself, Arbiter. Come, face my judgment."*

Oliver stumbled forward. Better to not disrespect a dragon than risk it chasing him back up the stairs the rest of the way out.

"I'm Oliver García," he answered. Too nervous to know what else to do, he pointed at Roli on his shoulder. "And this is Roli."

Vardothia's growling grew louder. *"Are you the Trinova?"*

"Nnoo-yyess," Oliver said, drawing out the answer as anger grew in the dragon's eyes. "Why does it matter?"

"Because your station is the only reason your pestilent species can exist," the dragon spat. *"Understand the privilege of humankind to understand yourself, lest I change my mind and doom yours to the same fate as my own. Dragons were never in receipt of the same license to survival, the same mercy. We fell like common birds in a winter storm after your stupidity! Your arrogance! Your CORRUPTION!"*

* Chapter 44: Arbitration *

In a flash, Vardothia's great tail struck at Oliver's side, disintegrating the tiled floor into shrapnel. If it weren't for his quick reflexes, the ensuing bits of flying clay and stone would have left his skin in tatters.

"Defenderis," he said, dodging left, away from the still twitching tail. As he moved, Madeline's necklace vibrated on his neck, re-doubling his Bravery. "What do you want, Vardothia?" he asked, trying his best to shift into the mindset of a Trinova and not a frightened fifteen-year-old.

The dragon's black pupils waxed and waned as they moved around the room, constantly searching for something, and his tongue flit in and out before his answer came. Oliver took the pause to get a better look.

Vardothia radiated both terror *and* dilapidation. Twice Oliver's height, and as wide as an osorius, Oliver knew, deep in his soul, Vardothia could destroy him the second the conversation threatened to grow dull.

And yet, something was off about Vardothia.

Where the beast's red and black skin wasn't cracked, a sore oozed, or an open wound festered all the way down to the bone. At some spots, black scales actively flaked away, brittle and thin. But nothing came more disconcerting than Vardothia's eyes. The pupils alone radiated a mix of insanity and pain Oliver had never seen before. Centuries of wisdom, hate, and frustration beamed out of them.

As though he were reading Oliver's mind, Vardothia flicked his great irises straight onto Oliver's. *"I could kill you, you know?"* he purred in a disturbingly matter-of-fact tone. *"I don't deny I would relish the poetic opportunity to witness my corruption lay humanity to the waste they instigated."* The dragon's eyes rolled in his head as he went on and he even began to unfurl his wings, rising to his full height. *"An ironic twist, don't you think? The same curse yours afflicted unto me, afflicted back onto you. With humanity's harbinger removed, they'd succumb within a single generation."*

The manic eyes stuck onto Oliver now, and more than just the tail twitched with anticipation. On his shoulder, Oliver felt Roli's claws tense. They needed to keep Vardothia speaking for as long as possible. If they stopped talking…

"So why wait all this time to talk to me, then?" Oliver hedged. Inwardly, he thanked the heavens his voice managed to stay level. But then, his face blanched. Vardothia had opened his maw wide in reply, and Oliver felt an inordinate amount of energy accumulating in the back of the dragon's throat.

"It'd be a shame," Oliver snuck in both quickly and shrilly, "to wait however many years it's been only to change your mind now!"

Vardothia tilted his head high onto the ceiling and unleashed a maelstrom of fire. Oliver was forced to raise a hand to shield his face despite the effects of Jim's elixir. Even then, the heat felt oppressive against his clothes and skin, stripping the room of all oxygen.

Still, what Oliver saw stunned him. A dragon's fire was nothing like he'd expected. Instead of red or orange flames, Vardothia's dragon's breath twisted in a vortex around the upper half of the room in strands of blue, red, yellow, green, and purple. These were the colors of life itself.

But then the dragon's working shuddered in the air.

The colors held for a second longer until Vardothia shivered, roaring in agony, and the flames turned black and red.

647

* Chapter 44: Arbitration *

Something clicked into place in Oliver's head as he watched the dragon work its magic. After Vardothia cut off the flames with a snap of his jaw, where the fire had been, black and red ebbs of discordant energy remained in the air—the same ones Oliver and Roli had seen throughout the rest of the temple. And Oliver understood.

Magic in its natural state, like the dragon's breath, was pure and beautiful, an echo of life itself. But when tainted with corruption or negative intent, it turned spoiled. Oliver chanced a look at the dragon's sores and wounds. Were those from fights? Or was the corruption melting Vardothia's flesh away?

"Just like the Griffin warned us," Oliver breathed to Roli, still staring at the wounds.

Vardothia didn't answer, focusing all his attention on taking deep, shuddering breaths.

"A griffin visited me not too long ago," Oliver directed towards Vardothia. He took the lack of a reaction as a good sign. "She told me humans and dragons were both corrupted long ago and that the dragons were killed off by the corruption immediately. Is that what you're talking about?"

The entire room shook as Vardothia growled in reply. *"Wording is everything, Arbiter. Yes, your species and mine share the dishonorable title of having been corrupted. But we dragons didn't seek it. Yours insisted on sharing it."*

"Sharing it?" Oliver asked, his curiosity getting the better of him. He stepped closer to Vardothia, **trusting** the dragon not to strike him down with a swipe of his claws or tail. "You're saying humans are the reason why dragons went extinct? Erm, except for you of course…"

Vardothia still recovered his breath, keeping a low profile next to Cuahtemoc's wood-and-stone artifact as his enormous frame rose and fell. *"An inconvenient truth, I'm sure,"* the dragon sneered. *"Yes, your kind approached us with your pagan discoveries every thousand years, attempting to seduce us with the joys of magic. We successfully declined for millennia, but it only takes one fool to topple an empire."*

"But," Oliver interjected, "if we're the ones who shared corruption with you, why aren't we all dead, too?"

"BECAUSE OF YOU!" Vardothia roared, his irises and pupils going wild. Oliver took a few steps back as the dragon stomped around in a circle, breathing more fire and obliterating the floor wherever it went. *"BECAUSE OF YOUR STATION! DID THE GRIFFIN NOT TELL YOU? YOU ARE PRIVILEGED WHERE MY PEOPLE WERE NOT! I SHOULD HAVE BUTCHERED YOU THE MOMENT YOU STEPPED INSIDE! IT IS MY RIGHT! MINE! MY OWN, AS THE SOLE SURVIVOR! MY VENGEANCE!"*

"A-a-and how," Roli interjected, *"might have you been doing all this surviving over the years?"*

Vardothia's head snapped onto Roli in a blink, his eyes focusing again as he stared the iguana down as a cat would a cornered mouse. *"What is this abomination?"* he breathed.

"Abomination?!" Roli repeated, openly outraged.

* Chapter 44: Arbitration *

Oliver cleared his throat. "The griffin did mention I was an arbiter of pure intent or virtue or something—what does it mean? You're saying I'm the reason humanity isn't corrupted?"

"Pathetic," Vardothia spat. *"How can someone so meager keep the corruptive influence that consumes me from reaching its own people? You are a harbinger of purity—that is what makes your species unique, you undeserving fool. Every Trinova can, and will, become an arbiter of every virtue, keeping the evil of corruption at bay. The rest of us have no such luxury. It is why a griffin will speak to you in riddles. It is why the cowardly osorius, serpent, and eagle keep their mouths shut and let you humans play your own dance. Should they risk involvement, they worry they'll face the same fate as mine own kind."*

Inwardly, Oliver's heartbeat quickened. But he didn't let his surprise show on his face. "The griffin said I should **trust** others around me is that what you're saying. Is that my virtue?"

"It goes deeper than that!" Vardothia grumbled, shaking the entire room. *"It requires commitment. Complete and unadulterated!"*

Oliver felt the back of his neck vibrate as his Wisdom implored him to follow the dragon's advice. "Commitment?" he repeated. "Commitment to what?"

"To the embodiment of your virtue. You will stand as an arbiter for them all before the end, lest I kill you now. That is your station. The rest of us can only hope to master one over the course of our lives."

Oliver's neck positively vibrated now. "How do I commit?"

Vardothia sneered. *"Say the words, Arbiter. Do not waste my time with the questions of a court fool."*

NOVA 02

As if he could see the future, Oliver finally understood. He'd been getting better at trusting all year. Trusting his friends. Trusting Watkin. Trusting himself not to play the same games as Lalandra and Tupper. It all came down to trust. That's what he'd begun to embody. It was his greatest virtue.

"I am...," he began, remembering what he felt compelled to say to Beto in Chavarría's classroom at the start of the year. Only back then, he couldn't find the word he was looking for because he hadn't embodied it yet. He'd walked out feeling foolish.

But he'd been close. And now, he was there.

"I am Truth," Oliver said.

A torrential beacon of red light struck down onto Oliver from the highest point in the ceiling. As it bathed him in mercurial light, he felt it originating from an unknown source far beyond the ash-ridden rooms above them.

In the distant Western horizon, a pillar of red light as wide as the setting sun drew everyone's attention at the Dueling Strip.

"What the?" Beto breathed, staggering back from Emma even as the energy from her own beacon of green light dissipated.

When the red pillar in the distance dispersed as well, Beto turned back to Emma with a snarl. "Enough playing around" he shouted, swiping down

* Chapter 44: Arbitration *

at her with his scimitar. The world warped around the sword as it descended, so Emma knew he must have flared Power.

Beto was putting everything he had into this strike.

Emma held out her hand and caught the sword anyway.

The air *exploded* around her as though Oliver or John Tupper had just unleashed a healthy dose of an air compression spell during a Coatlball match. Battering pulses of compressed energy emanated from where the scimitar's steel met her hand, forcing everyone in the crowd to duck for shelter.

Everybody but Watkin. The History Professor still stood, applauding like a madman while his ponytail rattled in the forceable winds swelling past him.

Only then did Emma stand, still holding onto the scimitar.

With every passing second, Beto's eyes widened further and further with shock. He tried wrenching away the sword from Emma's grasp, but he would have had better luck beating an osorius in a wrestling match.

"Good, boy," Emma said. She smirked as she wrenched the sword out of his hands. **"I'm Justice."**

"Do you understand now, dotard?" Vardothia hissed, flitting his tongue like a snake. *"Your race stays protected despite its use of corrupted magic because of **you**—because of the purity of your intent. Because of the virtues you wield."*

NOVA 02

Oliver nodded, feeling *Nova's Touch* expand wider than it ever had before. This was the gift his virtue gave him. Now that he'd committed himself to it, the scope of *Nova's Touch* felt limitless, and he barely had to concentrate to see the world around him better than he ever had before.

He turned to Vardothia. The dragon looked calmer than they'd yet seen, actively curling up around Cuahtemoc's artifact like a cat settling down for a nap.

"The griffin warned me," Oliver began, a question forming in his head, "that *The Damned's* teachings would spread like a plague. If he wins, is humanity really as doomed as she said?"

Vardothia blew out an impatient puff of purple fire. *"You keep the corruption at bay. Your foe will spread it, agnostic of his intentions. If you should fail in defeating him, your race will face the executioner's relief just like my own."*

Vardothia stood to shudder and flex his great wings again, nearly touching the ceiling, but Oliver wasn't worried about an attack anymore. *Nova's Touch* told him the truth of it based on the dragon's body language. But something Vardothia had said caught Oliver's attention.

He tilted his head to catch a glimpse of Roli with his peripherals. Had the iguana found the mention of Tupper's "intentions" as interesting as he had? Just what *were* the madman's intentions?

Roli took the opportunity to point at Cuahtemoc's artifact with an outstretched claw.

Oliver's gaze snapped to the wood and stone object. Now that he could look at it without worrying about being eaten by a dragon—at least for the time being—he could almost guess at what it was.

* Chapter 44: Arbitration *

"Is that a mace?" he asked Roli privately in his head.

Roli stamped a foot down impatiently. *"Does it matter?! Grab it at once and let us depart while we still can!"*

Feeling ashamed, Oliver realized Roli wouldn't be experiencing any of the peace-of-mind *Nova's Touch* provided him. "Sorry, should have mentioned—Vardothia isn't gonna attack us for the time being."

"How the blazes can you tell?!" Roli squeaked back.

"May I take that artifact?" Oliver asked Vardothia, speaking out loud again and pointing to Cuahtemoc's artifact.

Vardothia's terrifying jaw managed to grow haughty. *"You wield the full might of Nova and yet you find the need to ask permission like a common peasant."*

"Okay…" Oliver said, stepping up to the mace, taking care not to trip over the rubble of the ruined floor surrounding the artifact. Only the pedestal and mace had been left unbothered by Vardothia's stamping. "Just be warned," Oliver said, putting a hand on the obsidian handle, "this is going to summon my mortal enemy."

The rubble at Oliver's feet began to bob up and down as Vardothia laughed, slow and steady. *"Your enemy wields Power to great effect, yes?"*

Oliver's confidence drained from him as quickly as the color did from his face. "What are you talking about?" he asked, quiet but stern.

Vardothia licked his lips, relishing whatever it was Oliver had missed. *"What need would a Powerful wizard have for an artifact granting Power? Did you really expect an enemy as capable as your own to attempt the same spell thrice?"*

Oliver couldn't believe what he was hearing. He scanned every part of the room with *Nova's Touch,* expecting, wanting, *hoping* to see Tupper's shadowy form attempting to teleport inside. "Roli?!" he shouted. "Where is Tupper?"

Roli could only stare around the room with him, his mouth also agape.

Then, Oliver's attention snapped onto something he'd missed before. Something he could only have picked up with *Nova's Touch*. Down a clawed-out corridor, inside a cave, he felt a spirit. "He's spawning down there!" Oliver shouted.

Vardothia moved quickest, cutting Oliver off from the rugged corridor with a great leap. When he landed, blocking the entrance, the entire room shook. *"You won't find anything in there but the remains of the poor souls I leveraged to maintain myself over the centuries."*

Oliver stared at Vardothia in horror. "You're the kidnapper?" he asked in a hollow voice, realizing who's spirit he'd felt down the corridor. It wasn't Tupper down there at all. It was Elodie Lalandra. Or what was left of her.

"Kill me, Trinova," Vardothia said, lowering his neck. *"I've required the souls of your people for centuries to hold me from my own damnation. I deserve worse than a painless death, but I beg you this mercy. I awaited you knowing one day I had to share the knowledge other sacred beasts would never divulge."*

Oliver's upper lip curled with every word that came out the dragon's mouth. This was a nightmare in its own right.

*"Your entire race would succumb like mine if you did not know of your role against corruption, and the balance your nemesis will disrupt. Let this be the memory of dragons. One of self-sacrifice. One of **Penance**."*

Oliver stared at the dragon, his jaw set. At the word **Penance**, some of his rotting skin had healed. "You want me to kill you?"

* Chapter 44: Arbitration *

"Let me join my ancestors in the afterlife as a son who fought against the corruption. I am ready to face my judgment. There is nothing left for me here except my ruined vessel."

Oliver cast a nervous glance down the tunnel towards where he felt Lalandra's fading spirit. There were dozens, if not hundreds, of skeletons down that tunnel. Disgusted, he looked around the more immediate room again, feeling for Tupper.

Still nothing.

Last of all, Oliver judged the sharpness of the obsidian stones jutting out of Cuahtemoc's mace. They caught torchlight and reflected his own face back at him.

They'd be plenty sharp.

Oliver swung the mace, flaring Power like he'd never done before.

NOVA 02

Chapter 45: The Cradler's Rocks

I didn't last long in that accursed temple. I'm headed up to the Piedmont next. That's the only place left to check. If the Sage's Sanctum isn't there, Tío isn't going to be happy.

7th of May, the third year of the 10th Age

When Oliver trudged back into the cave beneath Ms. Joan's kitchen with Lalandra in his arms, several voices began shouting at him from atop the stairs at once.

Too disoriented to hear them all, he ignored them until he climbed the stairs and placed Lalandra on a large table that Ms. Joan cleared with a hasty touch of her necklace and gesture of her arm.

At some point, a crowd had gathered in the kitchen, prepared for Oliver's return. Somebody appeared at his side howling with pain. It was Dave looking over the emaciated form of his wife.

A rough hand pulled Oliver away from the table closer to the stairs.

"I," Oliver said, unable to take his eyes off Lalandra's wretched state, "I did the best I could." Back at the table, Dave pulled at his hair as he screamed. It sounded so far away despite it being only a few yards away.

Fingers snapped in front of Oliver's face. They drew Oliver's attention the same moment the noise around him siphoned away, as if pulled into a stoppered bottle. Somebody had used *stratum silentii*.

"Here," Watkin ordered. "Drink this."

* Chapter 45: The Cradler's Rocks *

It was one of the man's potions. Oliver took it without question. The world around him sharpened as focusing became easy again.

"What," Watkin asked, his eyes, brow, and jaw intense, "happened?"

Oliver shook his head as if remembering a nightmare. It had been fine at the time, but now that it was over, it felt awful to relive. But he set his jaw and did so anyway.

"I killed a dragon," Oliver said matter-of-factly.

A tsking sound made Oliver realize Emma and Lance were just behind Watkin—how had he missed them?

"And I thought I had a cool night," Emma whispered to Lance.

"A dragon?!" Lance repeated.

"Is Lalandra going to be okay?" Oliver asked, looking past all three of them to focus on Chavarría muttering spell after spell under his breath as he held an ornamental dagger over Lalandra's ruined body.

Watkin turned his head, but only for a moment. "Chavarría can fix anything but death. Explain." He pulled one of the chairs away from the table in the center of the kitchen and pointed.

Oliver took it. "It was a dragon," he said, feeling his own eyes going wide. "Never a pesadriya. He said he was waiting for me. To warn me."

Oliver looked up at Watkin so he could gauge the man's eyes as he continued. "He was begging me to kill him by the end. He was too far gone. Pieces of him were just missing—like a rotting fish."

Emma and Lance stared at him, horrorstruck expressions locked on their faces.

NOVA 02

"And then what happened?" Watkin asked, beginning to pace four steps back and forth at a time. Behind him, bedlam ensued as Professors Belk and Zapien began pointing angry, shaking fists at one another.

Oliver shrugged, doing his best to ignore the chaos. "Nothing. I took the artifact,"—he unclasped Cuahtemoc's mace from a makeshift holster on his back and held it up for them to see—"but Tupper didn't show up this time."

Watkin stopped pacing. He'd stiffened like a board. Then, slowly, he turned to look at Oliver. "Did his spell not work? Did you stop him before he materialized?"

"No," Oliver confirmed, taken aback by Watkin's reaction. Was it fear? "After I grabbed the mace, no Tupper spell ever started. I was so confused. The dragon... he laughed at me. He said he'd been using the souls of his prisoners,"—Emma turned to look at Lalandra while he spoke, green in the face—"to stop his own corruption. He lived all this time because he wanted to tell me what the other sacred beasts wouldn't."

"And what was that?" Watkin asked, growing quieter still.

"That I'm an arbiter of **Truth**. That mankind requires arbiters to keep us from corrupting ourselves with our magic."

Watkin's eyes closed. "Tupper wanted you to touch that mace," he said gravely.

"Cato!" a voice snarled, temporarily rupturing the privacy of their conversation.

With a lazy flick of his wrist, Watkin collapsed his spell. The noise in the room hit Oliver like a train—Dave's quiet sobbing, Lalandra's ragged

* Chapter 45: The Cradler's Rocks *

breathing, Chavarría's soft muttering, Ms. Joan's words of encouragement as she held onto Lalandra's outstretched hand. At least the shouting between Belk and Zapien had stopped.

"Yes?" Watkin asked without turning from Oliver. "Does Elodie require my attention?"

Zapien shook her head, her silver curls bouncing either side of her head.

"No," she said, "it's…"

Belk stepped forward, cutting Zapien's mumbling off with all the subtlety of a Powerhead. She held out a strong arm, holding a notebook aloft for them all to see. "It's the senate," she said gruffly.

Watkin flinched. "What evil are they up to?"

Oliver got the impression Watkin was avoiding the notebook on purpose.

"Nothing," Zapien said. She wore concern on her brow where Belk had held something closer to anger. "It's just… well… look who turned up after the recess."

Oliver stared at the notebook in horror.

Belk took over again, reading the headline out loud. "Solomon Tupper escapes aftermath of Soothsayer's Temple experiment. Reinstated as senator of Connecticut."

Then she forced the mirror into Watkin's hands so he couldn't miss it. Begrudgingly, Watkin took the notebook and stared. The light from the broadcast reflected against his green eyes. Oliver looked there for a twinkle but found nothing but determination.

NOVA 02

Emma broke the temporary silence. "He escaped?" she asked. "How do they know his name?"

"It's as if a spell's been broken," Zapien said, her face painted with confusion. "Now that I can see him on the news," she went on, slowly, "I can suddenly remember his name and every time I met him."

She turned to Watkin, her eyes wavering with fear.

"What's going on Cato? With Lalandra out I think that makes you Head of the Whigs."

Watkin's eyes flicked towards Zapien. So fast that Oliver was sure he was the only one that saw it, Watkin's expression turned murderous. Within a half-second they turned determined again.

"What's the plan, professor?" Oliver asked. "You said we'd have to take him out, right?

Watkin ran his hands through his hair. Then, he stood up and sat down again, ringing his staff.

After standing a second time, he crouched next to where Oliver sat. "I'm sorry," he breathed, a pained look in his eyes. "He played me perfectly."

Oliver shirked back from the pathetic look, sneering. Who was this man and what had he done with Cato Watkin?

"What are you talking about?" Oliver challenged, standing up. "Tupper's escaped. So what?" He hefted Cuahtemoc's mace high for everyone to see. Even Dave's eyes followed it reverently. "I've got the third artifact," Oliver went on, projecting as much confidence as he could muster. "We can take anybody on. Even Tupper."

* Chapter 45: The Cradler's Rocks *

"We'll likely never get the opportunity," Watkin countered, standing up again. He gestured at the notebook where everyone saw Tupper shaking hands with fellow senators, a handsome smile on his face. "He's re-entrenching himself," Watkin spat. "It took me a miracle to stop him last time, and now his corruption is out in the open again, festering, and we'll go just like the dragons before us."

Oliver couldn't believe what he was hearing—from Watkin of all people.

He stepped close to Watkin, until they were eye to eye. "I don't believe that, Professor. And neither did Augustus. He put us both on this path. For all we know this was always how we were supposed to finish things. The dragon I just killed was trading the light inside humanity to keep himself alive. It wasn't Tupper spreading corruption in Goodwin Forest. It was the desperate dragon."

Lance let out a breath of air. "That means we still have time, doesn't it?"

Watkin's defeated expression gave way to a slightly more hopeful one. He stepped away to resume his pacing. "You're right, Oliver," he said, his eyes suddenly growing manic. "If Augustus saw no hope, he wouldn't have put us on this path. We must hope our faith is eventually rewarded."

"I think I preferred the cowardly Watkin," Emma said. She leaned back and crossed her arms as she watched Watkin pace around the room.

Watkin raised a pointed finger at the ceiling, thinking hard. "We'll have to rethink our approach given his move to re-entrench himself. I did not expect it of him—I thought him more likely to pursue ven… Well, it doesn't matter. Now that we know the dragon was the source of corruption and not Tupper, then maybe we have time to think of a better way to approach him than ..."

"Cold-blooded assassination?" Lance offered.

"Well," Watkin admitted, a twinkle returning to his eye, "yes."

"That never felt right to begin with, Professor," Emma said, agreeing with Lance with a cross of her forearms.

"I felt it **prudent**."

Oliver gasped. "That's what yours is, isn't it!" Oliver asked excitedly. "Prudence!"

"Yes," Watkin answered, sounding confident again. "And Emma's is **Justice**."

Oliver's jaw fell as he turned his head to ogle at Emma. "You're an arbiter, too? What did I miss?"

"I'll catch you up later," Emma retorted, putting her weight on the table and smirking. "I beat Beto tonight—it's no big deal."

"You?" Roli asked incredulously.

"Yes, yes," Watkin said, placing both hands on the pommel of his staff and grinning ear to ear. "We have three arbiters amongst our allies, and a fourth on the way, unless I am mistaken." He pointed at Lance with his staff. "But! That isn't our only silver lining."

"What could possibly be good enough news to make *The Damned's* return palatable?" Belk countered, angry tears welling in her eyes.

"He wasn't the source of the corruption!" Watkin said cheerfully.

"So?" Zapien challenged. "He's out now—he can go right back to corrupting us all like he never left off."

* Chapter 45: The Cradler's Rocks *

"It means," Watkin said, dancing through the room towards the exit, "we have the chance to take a slower approach than initially planned."

"A slower approach?" Oliver asked, leering at Watkin suspiciously.

Watkin stopped at the door and nodded vigorously.

"Ehh," Emma said, "Don't think killing Tupper is a good idea—why don't we just beat him up and throw him in jail?"

Watkin deliberated for a moment. Then he slammed his staff down against the stone door, opening the door behind him. "That's more of a plan B than a plan A.

"What's plan A, then, professor?" Oliver asked, unable to stop himself from getting excited. Watkin did always say he had a backup plan.

"If Tupper wants to play the long game," Watkin answered, waggling his eyebrows, "we can play the long game right with him. Yes, we'll just need to further arm our harbinger of pure intent, now won't we?" He pointed at Oliver with his staff as he spoke. Behind him, the door had opened up enough to bring in a hurricane of noise as the student body on the other side celebrated Emma's win.

"What's left to arm Oliver with?" Lance asked. He glanced at Oliver's ring, necklace, and now mace. "He's got the Founders artifacts, doesn't he?"

Oliver let out a sigh, feeling much less excited about Watkin's plan. If there more hidden things to find, there'd be a ton of work involved. "Just when I thought I was done."

Emma stood back up and shook out her hair, re-doing her ponytail. "Okay," she said, "shoot, professor."

NOVA 02

Everyone in the room turned to look at Watkin, including Lalandra who had weakly stirred to life.

"Has anyone ever told you three about how man first came to know magic?" Watkin asked.

All the adults in the room groaned.

"Hey now," Watkin countered, looking dangerous. "I was right about virtue theory! Be more like our Trinova here, and trust me this time!"

Even Belk shifted in place uncomfortably. Oliver wanted to hear the story behind why Watkin didn't seem to trust the others in the room, but he also knew it wouldn't be coming out that night. He'd have to weasel it out of Watkin over time.

"Trick question," Watkin said, snapping his fingers as he re-addressed Oliver, Emma, and Lance. "*I* told you in fact. Think back to your very first day of lessons last year. What do you remember about the Cradles of Civilization?"

Oliver scrunched his eyebrows together while Lance answered, raising his hand in excitement.

"Oh-oh-oh! I remember. You said civilization began in Mesopotamia, and magic was discovered soon after."

"If you're hedging your bets to not sound like a lunatic," Watkin said, brushing off some dirt from his staff, "yes, you'd say that. The dawn of civilization likely co-mingled with the dawn of man's use of magic. But what if man only ever formed civilizations *because* of magic?"

* Chapter 45: The Cradler's Rocks *

"That would make sense," Oliver said, "but what's this got to do with giving me more weapons? You saying we should be looking for a magic bracelet in modern-day Mesopotamia or something?"

Watkin raised a hand again. "Ah, but what makes the artifacts you so flippantly reference capable of granting the user another or a stronger gift?"

Oliver opened his mouth to answer but then froze.

Emma rolled her eyes. "We don't have a clue professor, do you?"

Watkin leaned forward. "They're made from pieces of *Nova*."

The adults took to shaking their heads again. Oliver, Emma, Lance, and Roli, meanwhile, dropped their jaws.

"Which means," Watkin continued, raising his finger further, "they're pieces of the source themselves and will never fail, even in ages of darkness."

Oliver felt like he was catching on to the answer of a stubborn riddle. "Which would explain," he breathed, "how the Founders used magic during the last age of darkness."

"And," Watkin drew out over the noise from the Dining Hall, "how anybody of any repute ever became reputable to begin with during an age of darkness—Lysander, Khan, Machiavelli, Cleopatra—the list is lengthy, is it not? But I digress. The more important question is then what if you found more than just shards of Nova. What if you found an entire *piece* of Nova?"

"Get out!" Lance shouted, grinning from ear-to-ear. "Hand-delivered by aliens?"

NOVA 02

"I'd never considered aliens," Watkin answered, somehow considering the answer. "I'd always been more partial to the idea of meteorites."

This time, Belk, Zapien, Dave, Lalandra, and Chavarría let out sounds of surprise.

Oliver couldn't help but grow excited by the idea. It rekindled his energy, despite the events of the afternoon. "You think there's something better than the Founders' artifacts out there?" he asked.

From the table, Emma looked him over, eyeing his necklace, ring, and mace. "What's gonna be better than a Trinova with three boosted Gifts?"

Watkin stepped back into the room as Jaiba landed on his shoulder, a piece of parchment in his beak.

Caw-caw!

"What," Watkin asked as the door drew shut behind him, silencing the noise of the students, "do you all know about the Cradler's Rocks?"

Oliver, Emma, and Lance exchanged confused looks as Watkin took the parchment from Jaiba's beak and unfurled a map onto the table next to Lalandra. "Did you really think Cortes committed genocide for some gold? It's time we started asking ourselves *why* Cuahtemoc fled Tenochtitlan in 1521."

NOVA 02

THE END

NOVA 02

The Serpent's Tongue

While I write, I often go crazy and include ridiculous scenes that have nothing to do with my world or plotline. While these scenes don't make the final cut, I include them as "bloopers" further below. Hope you enjoy.

And before you go, leave us a review on the Amazon store! It'll help other readers find books in their genre.

Do it for them... not me... certainly not me.

Link: *http://www.amazon.com/review/create-review?&asin=B0CFYWBW1V*
Instructions per my website: *https://www.ctemerson.com/contact*

THE TRINOVA SAGA CONTINUES IN

THE CRADLER'S ROCKS

NOVA 03

Bloopers

Watkin's staff flashed green, garnering Oliver's attention. Had he been doing anything but plummeting at terminal velocity, Oliver might have gasped at what came next, but he was forced to settle for an incredulous chuckle as gravity walloped his stomach around.

At Watkin's direction, a channel of funneling water *rocketed* out of the lake. It twisted in rotations of blue and green, surrounding its caster like the mouth of an Alaskan Bull Worm.

"I've seen this before!" Watkin roared over his shoulder. "We'll just need a paper clip! And some string!"

But in Oliver's soul, he felt a bit more comfortable now that he *did* know more about the enemy.

Yes, it was true a mountain of training lay before him—he still had his regular lessons and his upcoming one-on-one lessons with Watkin. But at least he now had a plan.

Last year there had been no plan. He, Emma, and Lance had done their best sneaking around and investigating the temple beneath the golden willow, but it was a huge relief knowing he could now focus on his training while Watkin researched the location of the Fire Drake's Cavern. He'd likely never admit it to Watkin, but it felt nice to just be a normal fifteen-year-old for a moment—for as long as it might last.

Watkin popped out of a man-hole cover. "We call that foreshadowing, kids! In fact, you should pay better attention to literally everything coming out of my mouth."

A note to the reader. In an earlier draft, Makayla Grant played a larger role. Alas, too many tertiary characters led to her more central role being cut. She didn't take it well.

"Someone steal your bike, García?" a voice interrupted.

Looking up, Oliver saw the words had come from Makayla, not Emma or Lance, who had both stiffened at the words. Emma's leg now felt like a board next to his.

Oliver shook his head, mainly to clear it. "No. I just remembered something I have to do, that's all."

Emma's leg relaxed but only briefly because Makayla redoubled her efforts. "No use in lying to a Wiser. Where's *your* guide? Archie, right?"

Dramatically, Oliver stood.

"You see much, Makayla, daughter of Makaylamund," he replied.

Emma stood to hold Makayla down while Lance fought off Makayla's cronies.

"Too much," Oliver went on.

Oliver approached Makayla with a sword in hand. "You are banished forthwith from the Grounds of Tenochprima and all its surrounding temples."

Makayla's eyes bloomed with pain and confusion.

"Under pain of death," Oliver confirmed.

In the distance, billowing winds tore a flag that bore the Trinova's crest from its fastening, carrying it off into the distance. Emma stood to watch, pensive and melancholic as the sound of someone practicing their violin disturbed the air.

Emma was right—they had no clue when Tupper might burst down the door and reduce them to three piles of neatly stacked dust.

Without any fanfare, the Hutch common room door flew off its hinges behind them.

Smoke billowed inside from the now open doorway. Then, in stepped Solomon Tupper.

He and Oliver locked eyes for a silent moment.

"Hello, there!" Tupper said from behind a self-satisfied grin.

Oliver felt compelled to answer with "General Tupper!" but stopped himself because it didn't make any sense.

It was his last thought before Tupper smote his ruined form across the room.

"So uncivilized," Tupper said, sneering at the mess.

"So," Oliver ventured, "you've got two of these words? And neither of them are **Trust**? How many are there?"

"Thirty-six!" Watkin answered cheerily, suddenly the size of a walrus. "Counted them me'self."

"Thirty-six!" Oliver wailed. "But last year—last year I had thirty-seven!"

Watkin frowned at Oliver. "Oliver, what the hell are you talking about?"

Oliver squealed like a piglet and bounded out of the room with several toffees in his hands. His tongue, meanwhile, had swelled to the size of a rugby bat.

"Rugby bat?" Watkin asked, staring at the narrator with a disgusted expression. "You aren't going to make me drink tea, are you?"

At the bottom of the Tenochprima lagoons, Xihuacota leaned back in her knitting chair, unhinged her jaw, and wailed loud enough to shake every shingle forming the perimeter of her decrepit house.

Across from her, on the other side of a card table brought over from Scotland by Augustus himself, three ice golems threw down their hands in frustration.

"Not this again!" the largest of the three rock-like creatures grumbled in a stony voice. "At least you got to play a major role in the *first* book! Heck, you could even get a bit of dialogue by the end if you're lucky!"

Xihuacota just wailed even louder, flattening the edges of her ruined white dress in petulant rebellion.

"H-h-he," she managed to say through sobs. "He didn't even give me an appearance when Oliver and Emma were at the lagoons! Not even a shout-out for floating around in the background. I WAS THERE AND HE IGNORED ME!"

More wailing followed. But the ice golems had had enough. Disgusted by the display, they leapt from their chairs and headed straight for the door back out into the lagoons.

"All that talk of kissing and dating and bla-bla-bla," Xihuacota droned on, long after they'd left. "Nobody wants romance!" she said, turning her horrible, ruined face to the narrator. "GIVE THEM HORROR, EMERSON! HORROR!!!!"

ABOUT THE AUTHOR

C. T. Emerson lives in North Carolina with his wife and two fluffy cats. He's the author of the *NOVA* series and enjoys eating ice cream. If you must know, his favorite flavor is salted peanut butter with chocolate flecks.

After growing up in México from 1994 through 2010, he graduated from Davidson College in 2016, earning degrees in political science, Spanish literature, and procrastination.

He believes writing is much more fun than anything else and is happy to update you on all his dealings on CTEmerson.com. Flock there – consumable goodies await. Either that, or a more up to date about the author section.